INNOCENT JOURNEY

INNOCENT JOURNEY

JAMES HARE

Matador
Unit E2 Airfield Business Park,
Harrison Road, Market Harborough,
Leicestershire. LE16 7UL
Tel: 0116 2792299
Email: books@troubador.co.uk
Web: www.troubador.co.uk/matador
Twitter: @matadorbooks

ISBN 978 1803131 719

British Library Cataloguing in Publication Data.
A catalogue record for this book is available from the British Library.

Printed and bound by CPI Group (UK) Ltd, Croydon, CR0 4YY
Typeset in 11pt Minion Pro by Troubador Publishing Ltd, Leicester, UK

Matador is an imprint of Troubador Publishing Ltd

For the girls from the County Armagh:
Kitty, Bridie, Alice, Olive, and Peggy

Day One - June 1975 - Leicester

It was time to go. Matthew had been calmly waiting for his mother. Now he was restless, impatient to get on the road. He was unable to hold back any longer.

'Christ Almighty! What are you doing now?'

'How many times? Don't say C-H-R-I-S-T like that.'

Nora held her two hands across her ears, spelling out the letters of the name. It was her way of not actually saying the blasphemous word. She made a late sweep of the hand broadly in Matthew's direction – but missing him by several feet.

'Well, are you nearly ready or what, mam?'

'I'll be ready when I'm ready.'

'You do know that we have a ferry to catch at three o'clock and it's a five hour drive.'

'Well, I'm just tidying up the kitchen and making sure that Martin and Geraldine will be able to find everything.'

'For Chri ... I mean, they do live here. I'm sure they know where the bread is kept.'

'Where's your father?'

'He's been in the car for the last ten minutes. And so has Aunty Kathleen.'

'What about the cases? Are you sure you've put them all in?'

'I'm not even bothering to answer that. Look, is there anything I can help you with?'

Nora was looking out of the kitchen window, with her back to Matthew. Almost in a trance for a few seconds. He could see the reflection of her face in the glass. She was lost for a moment in her private thoughts, worries, and doubts. She was not concerned about the ferry, or the car, or her waiting husband and sister. She did not really know what it was – it was just this feeling that kept coming over her every so often. She had been praying for what seemed like half her life for the thing which she was now on the cusp of seeing fulfilled. And with that imminence came the shock that it was actually happening for real. Her body ached with the internal struggle. She was only partly in control of herself. Something was causing her to pause, to string out the moments before she knew in her rational thoughts that she would have to get into the car. What was the problem? She should be deliriously happy, excited, lit up with a pleasure deeper than she could imagine.

'Right, then. Check the back door. I'll pay one last visit.'

Half an hour later, they had negotiated their way through the town traffic and were on the motorway heading to London.

'We're in the lap of luxury.'

This was Aunty Kathleen from the back seat of the Triumph 2000, acres of room between her and Nora. Just their handbags at the ready taking up a bit of space.

'It's a lovely motor car, Matty. Smooth as anything. Lovely seats, they must be leather.'

'Just watch your speed, son,' murmured John. He was perched in the front passenger seat watching everything on the road like a hawk. 'Don't want to blow any holes in her,' he said. But what he really meant was, 'You don't want to drive up the rear end of that car in front.'

'Ok, ok.'

Matthew generally drove fast. However, they were making good time so he could ease back a little for the sake of a bit of peace.

'Have you had the car long?' asked Kathleen, always ready with a question and some conversation.

'About six months. Picked it up at the car auctions in Colchester with my mate, Robbie. Bit of a bargain – she's a great motor, brilliant engine. A bit thirsty though.'

'Oh, don't you be bothering yourself about that. We'll be buying the petrol,' insisted Kathleen.

'I didn't mean it like that, Aunty Kathleen.'

Matthew searched for some words to explain.

'I just meant – well, it's just how we talk about motors. We're fine for petrol. Don't you even think about it.'

Kathleen was generous to a fault. She could always find someone worse off than herself to give her last penny to. She had looked after Matthew on more than one occasion. She had looked after the whole family if the truth were told. He needed to pay something back. This trip was a sort of penance and he was going to make sure that he did it right.

They had finally set off just after eight o'clock. Joan from next door and posh Lillian from across the road stood and waved them off. The long row of houses disappeared out of view as they turned left onto the main road. Joan had insisted that Nora take a little packet of goodies from her – a large bar of chocolate, a bag of mints, and a packet of digestive biscuits.

'Just a little something for the journey,' she had said as she hugged Nora. 'We'll be with you all the way. And mind and get some good photos.'

Matthew had calculated about two hours to London, an hour and a half to get across the city to the other side, and then about an hour and a half to Dover. It all depended on the traffic and how many stops they would need. Sitting in the outside lane of the M1, needle hovering on the 80 mark, the car was prowling along, eating up the dark blue tarmac. It was a beautifully clear day, sunny, with a lot of blue sky. Matthew was relaxed. Sitting behind the wheel, he felt the power of the engine and luxuriated in the comfort of the driving seat. He loved the faint smell of the leather upholstery. He delighted in the gleaming chrome of the dashboard controls and their refined simplicity. There was an underlying promise of solid and robust engineering. He felt the warmth of the wood panelling stretching the length of the fascia. As the car cruised effortlessly forward, he could not help but marvel at the beautiful lines of the bodywork flowing gracefully down the long gleaming bonnet. The sweep of the wings added balance and style to complete what seemed an exquisitely understated but supremely elegant design. Matthew did not quite articulate it like this. He simply had the impression of something that was deeply pleasing, something of beauty, and something perhaps amounting to perfection in its own way. Driving the car made him feel alive. He rarely felt more whole than when he was sitting there with his foot hard down on the throttle, one palm resting lightly on the steering wheel, his mind emptied of bad thoughts, released if only temporarily from any tension, frustration, and that occasionally troublesome conscience of his.

The escape from reality was short-lived. It was Nora who suggested the first stop of the trip. They were not far from London now and Matthew would have preferred to keep moving. However, they would have to stop some time and he was going to make an effort to meet any reasonable requests from his little bunch of travellers.

'Ok, we're well past Luton and Harpenden. There's the big Scratchwood Services in about fifteen miles. Will that do you?'

'That will be grand,' said Kathleen before Nora could answer. 'A nice cup of tea will be great.'

Nora was quiet, subdued almost. She gazed out of her window on the left hand side of the car. They were passing cars and trucks in the middle and inner lanes. The trucks with just a lone driver, and the cars containing one person on their own with just their thoughts for company. There were some cars with a passenger or two, or a full family load. All in their own little capsule, a private space that for the moment held only a tenuous connection with the rest of the world. All these people that she did not know, would never know, and had no connection with except for a glance or a smile snatched at high speed and never to be repeated. She was drifting in a swathe of random thoughts and images, nervous about the next few days. She was battling within herself to focus on the here and now, the mundane, not to get carried away with the gravity and the seriousness which, given the chance, might overwhelm her.

'Did you say fifteen miles, Matthew?' said Nora, snapping out of her daydream.

'Yeah, well it's only about seven miles now.'

'Oh, that's good. You could do with a little break and we can have a nice cup of something. John, are you ready for something?'

'Aah, never say no to a cup of tea!'

The car went silent again for a few more minutes. Matthew watched the signs and eventually moved adroitly across to the inside lane just in time to roll up the slip road and into the service area car park. He was wondering whether he should top up the petrol but thought better of it. They were still three quarters full and he would look for somewhere cheaper around Dover.

'Well, first of many,' said Matthew.

'Come on, Nora, stretch your legs,' said Kathleen who was the first out of the car. 'Where do you think the toilets are, Matty?'

He pointed across to the main building and a huge sign proclaiming the toilets. Kathleen and Nora walked across together.

Matthew lingered a moment to look at the car.

'Everything all right, son?' said his dad.

'Yeah, she's driving like a dream. I was just wondering if I should check the tyres but I think they're fine.'

They walked through the rows of cars and Matthew followed his dad into the gents. It was best to take the opportunity for a toilet stop when you had it. When they came out a couple of minutes later, Kathleen and Nora were already waiting for them. From a distance, they were watching a middle aged woman ploughing money into a noisy gaming machine.

'More money than sense,' muttered Kathleen.

'Right then, what are you having?' asked Matthew.

'John, you go with Matthew. We'll find a table. I'll have a cup of tea. And see if they've got a scone. Kathleen, what are you going to have?'

'The same for me, please.'

The two men trundled off to the counter. It was not busy and they were served quickly. Matthew tried to pay when they got to the desk but John insisted. He knew what Nora had meant, and he was not intending to fall at the first fence. There was a long way to go and he wanted to get things off to a decent start. The prices were ridiculous, of course. He tried not to think about how many cups of tea he could have had at home. You just had to grin and bear it. This would not be happening every day.

Kathleen drained her cup and lit a cigarette. She did not offer them around. John smoked a pipe in any case, and if he did have the odd cigarette, it would not be one of Kathleen's. Nora had never smoked. Kathleen did not think that Matthew smoked, but even if he did, she was not intending to encourage him.

'Well now, Matty, are we on track?'

This was Kathleen's way of asking where the hell they were and when would they get to where they were going.

'Do you want a quick reminder of the plan?' laughed Matthew.

He collected his thoughts briefly and gave them the shortened version.

'Today is Tuesday. I am aiming for us to be in Rome on Friday night. We should get to Dover around about two o'clock. We're booked on the three o'clock ferry. When we get off the ferry, we'll need to do some driving and then look for a B&B to stay overnight. Wednesday and Thursday, we'll be driving all day down France and into Italy. We'll need to stop somewhere overnight again. And then it's another day's driving to get to Rome, hopefully on Friday night.'

'That's an awful long time in the car,' said Kathleen. 'Still, if that's what it takes. As they say, all roads lead to Rome – so we shouldn't get lost!'

'Don't tempt fate now, Kathleen, will you not?' interrupted John.

'Matthew, will we definitely get there for Friday night?' asked Nora.

'Yeah, that's what I've planned. What's bothering you?'

'It's just, well … It's just that I'm hoping we can spend a bit of time on Saturday to visit some of the holy places. There'll not be time on the Sunday.'

'Do you know if we will be seeing Patrick before Sunday?' Matthew asked.

'God willing,' said Nora. 'In his last letter he said that he would be busy some of the time for the rehearsal, but there's nothing else that should get in the way.'

'What time is it on Sunday?' asked Kathleen.

'Well, it's going to be a very long session!' said Nora. 'We need to be in our seats for nine and the whole thing will last a good three hours. The seats are all reserved according to Patrick. He'll have arranged ours, so that'll be fine.'

'And did you get us booked in ok at the hotel?' This was John moving swiftly on from the thought of several hours confined in one place and, worse, with no opportunity for a puff on his pipe.

Matthew gave him the details.

'The travel agent has booked us two rooms in the hotel on Friday for four nights. Mam and Aunty Kathleen in one, me and you in the other. Bed and breakfast only. She said it's quite close to where they're having the event – walking distance. So, that is something. Oh, I've just had a thought. I wonder what the parking is like. If it's anything like London, it will be a nightmare.'

'Right, we'd better get moving. Looks like we've hardly started.'

This was John again, starting to warm up a little to this adventure. It was not an interruption to normal life that he would have chosen, but now it was here he would try to make the most of it.

August 1948

—~—

'Is that you all set, son?'

It was less a question than the mother finally resigning herself to her youngest boy leaving home. And not just leaving home but disappearing to a foreign land, or at least that is how she thought of it.

'The train leaves in an hour. I'll need to go.'

John was business-like and wanting to avoid any show of emotion. Outside, it was bright sunshine though a sharp wind was ruffling the trees. If you were not careful, a sudden gust would certainly blow your hat right off.

'You'll make sure and send me a telegram as soon as you arrive.'

Mary Hoolahan had spent the whole summer trying to put off this day in her mind. And now she faced the inevitable. Her baby, grown into a man and having to seek his fortune away from his family and home. She had seen plenty of others of her own generation follow the well-worn trail off the land. Most to England, where they dug for gold in the streets. Others to America, where they became film stars, didn't they? Everyone could dream, she supposed.

'Now, make sure you've got all the details you'll need. Those school certificates and your indentures – keep them safe. And your cousin Tommy's address. Have you it?'

'Yes, mother. I have them all safe and sound in the case. And I know the address anyway. Amn't I spending the last month memorising it?'

Blythe Road, Hillfields, Coventry. That was where he was bound.

John Hoolahan was sitting now, gazing out of the window as the train plodded through the Clare countryside taking him north from Ennis to Athenry. The steam-powered engine was pulling well but it struggled to go faster than about 35 miles an hour. There was no hurry. What would be would be. He was on his way. John relaxed a little, having survived the parting scene back at the house. He felt sorry for his mother. He felt her sadness. But could she not have made it easier for him? She hadn't. She had finally broken down and begged him not to go. Thank God that his two sisters were there to lighten the burden, to hug him and wish him well on his way. He had no choice. There was nothing really for him here in Ireland. There was a new life waiting for him over in England. He rolled the address over and over in his head. Blythe Road. Hillfields. It sounded idyllic. Cousin Tommy had summoned him over. There was a job and a room ready for him. And wages every week.

He was alone in the carriage, alone with his thoughts and dreams. He closed his eyes and dreamed. It was a dream of calmness and pleasure and anticipation. It was a feeling of hope and excitement. It was a sense of energy and belief and determination. It was a journey of tumbling memories coursing through his mind, snatches of warmth and laughter, images of faces and places, sounds of people and nature, all jumbled up and boiling in his head.

He woke as the train slowed down on the approach to Athenry. His head ached a bit from the heat of the sun that had been pouring through the window, his eyes tight as he stretched to rouse himself. As the train came to a halt, he lifted down his suitcase and opened the carriage door window. He turned the handle and got down onto an almost empty platform. He walked across to the little station office and asked where he was to get the Dublin train.

'It's not for another three hours yet. You can sit outside on one of the benches or there's a waiting room across the way. Or you can take a stroll into town along there. Turn left at the corner and you can't miss it. The Dublin train leaves at half past three.'

He said his thanks and decided to take a walk. The case was not heavy, although he did not want to be going very far with it. He had already decided that he was not for visiting a pub. Not today, at any rate. His mother would not approve, and in any case, he had no taste for beer in the present circumstances. Maybe he could get a cup of tea somewhere. He made his way along Station Road and turned left. The familiar smell of a turf fire was in the air, light and fragrant. He could see smoke coming from one or two of the squat houses that bunched together on either side of the road. Within a few minutes, he was standing at a three way crossroads. There was a butcher's shop and a grocer's opposite. A couple of older women were getting their messages. He was pondering what to do next when he heard someone speaking from behind him.

'Is that you just off the Limerick train?'

He turned round to see a woman smiling at him. She was a good bit older than his mother, but well preserved. She was dressed in a tweed skirt and jacket, the sort of clothes that might be worn only on a Sunday at home. John had the impression that she came from money, at least from somewhere a bit higher in the pecking order than him.

'It is, indeed,' he smiled back. 'I'm waiting around for the Dublin train. I'm off to make my fortune in England.'

'England, is it?' she said a little forlornly. 'All the young men are leaving us. I have two sons and they have been away for ten long years already. They're over in London. "The Big Smoke", they call it. I can't blame them, I suppose. They've great jobs. What would they be doing staying put here? But I miss them terribly.'

John was unsure how to reply. He just spoke as it came to him.

'You've got to go where the work is. And it's not like it's America. England is not so far away.'

She smiled and took his hand. 'You're right, of course. Now, I hope you won't think I'm being forward but would you take a cup of tea with me? There's a lovely little tea shop just over there and it will be my treat. What's your name?'

'I'm John. Are you sure? I would love a good cup of tea.'

'It's not every day I get the chance to have the craic with a young man such as yourself who is off on an adventure.

I'm usually stuck with the old biddies who want to know all your business. My name is Bridget, by the way. Bridget O'Connell. I'm a widow now. My husband passed away three years ago. I've the one daughter living with me. Well, she's only there some of the time. She's a nursing sister in Galway and she lives in the hospital when she's on duty. So I don't see her from one week to the next. I like to come into town every few days to do a bit of shopping. And aren't I the lucky one to meet you today? So, tell me about yourself.'

Over a large pot of tea and two scones each, John recounted his whole family history as well as he knew it. Bridget was interested in all the details. His mother and father, Mary and Paddy, and how they lived on the small farm. They weren't rich but they weren't poverty stricken either. It was a decent enough living for a family, though constant hard work. Plenty of chickens and geese, a few pigs, half a dozen cows, and the few acres to graze the animals and grow some wheat and potatoes. John explained that his oldest brother, Joseph, was already working in London. He was a qualified civil engineer. The next brother, Paul, was working the land and he would, in the natural course of things, take on the farm from his parents when the time came. He would most likely marry in due course and have his own family to support. It was expected that his sisters would marry and find a life somewhere else. For himself, John had had a decent schooling right up to age sixteen. Then he had been sent out as an apprentice at a local garage in Lahinch which handled anything mechanical from farm machinery to cars. He had served his time but he had also served his usefulness to the garage owner. There was a new apprentice. So John had written to his cousin Tommy who was over in Coventry to ask if there might be anything for him over there. Tommy had written back immediately to say that his dad, John's Uncle Owen, could get him a start on the buildings and that he could stay with them for the time being. Now here he was, at the crossroads in Athenry.

'And are you leaving behind anyone special?' enquired Bridget finally with a quiet smile. John thought for a second.

'Do you mean a girl? Of course, you do. Well,' said John, 'you have a way of getting me to talk. I suppose I can tell you. I've always been fond of a girl called Lizzie. She's the younger sister of one of my school pals. We all played together when we were younger. I see her sometimes at mass or in the town but she hardly gives me a glance these days. I can't see anything ever coming of it. She's become a bit high and mighty, wanting to go to Limerick to train as a teacher from what I hear.'

'That sounds lovely,' interrupted Bridget. 'You shouldn't give up on her. If she is as nice a young lady as you say, she won't go running after you. It's you that has to do the running. Don't you see?'

John laughed out loud at his thoughts as Bridget spoke.

'I'll say one thing for you, Bridget. I hardly know you yet you seem to know me very well. Perhaps I am running, but running in the wrong direction.'

Bridget smiled at that. She looked up at the big clock ticking away on the wall by the counter.

'There's still plenty of time for you to catch the Dublin train but maybe I'll walk with you a little and then I will leave you in peace.'

John got up to settle the bill but Bridget fought him off and insisted it was her treat. They set off up to the station. At the corner of Station Road, Bridget pointed away along to a house set back a little from the road. There was an extensive stone walled garden at the front. A little smoke was wafting up from the chimney.

'That's where I live. If you are ever passing through and you have time, come and knock on the door and give me the latest. It's been a pleasure meeting you and I wish you all God's good fortune on your journey.'

Then she touched his hand and left. John watched her for a few moments as she wandered along the lane. Then he picked up his suitcase, took a deep breath, and with renewed resolve marched down the road and onto the platform. There was another fifty minutes before the train was due. The afternoon was still sunny and warm, so he parked himself on one of the benches and idly waited for the minutes to pass. He was going to miss all this, but one day he would surely be back.

Day One - June 1975 - Calais

Matthew handed his dad the set of directions for the journey. He had spent a couple of nights the week before poring over the Philip's and AA road maps he had finally got round to buying. It had needed a special trip to Foyles in Charing Cross Road after he had struggled to find anything useful in his local WH Smith. Matthew knew he could find his way to Dover without too much consultation of maps. He was well used to driving around London and down to Dartford in Kent. It was more or less a straight road down to the coast from there. After that, it was into the unknown. His handwritten directions began at Calais. And so did a lot of old prejudices, as his history teacher had once explained. Matthew didn't feel any of those. Quite the reverse, in fact. He was looking forward to getting a taste of life on the continent. Exotic might be too grand a description, but it would undoubtedly be different and exciting in its own way.

'Remember what side of the road you need to be on, son,' said John.

'Yeah, I'm hoping my brain will adjust quickly. What I've just realised, though, is that it's going to be a bit different driving from this side of the car with all the oncoming traffic on your side.'

'Nora, Kate. Are you ok in the back there? Not left anything on the boat?'

John was doing what he could to help the journey go smoothly. He knew he was not going to be doing any of the driving. He did not feel bad about that, or emasculated in his role as father, with Matthew effectively being in control of proceedings. He just saw it as completely natural for the younger generation to begin to take the lead over their parents as time moved on. He knew that Matthew was fully capable of taking charge and loved being behind the wheel of the car. He had obviously put a lot of effort into planning the trip. All the same, John wanted to be of some use if he could. Reading maps was not his greatest skill, but he could at least follow Matthew's notes, read out the name of the next town, and help look out for the road signs.

They were already back in the Triumph on the ferry car deck as the boat docked. Matthew had the motor started as soon as the deckhand worker gave the signal. The six cylinder engine throbbed comfortingly with its low bass note, and Matthew eased the car down the ramp onto the huge area of tarmac leading up to the customs post and passport control. The column of vehicles slowly wound round to where the officials were checking documents and, in the case of customs, stopping the odd vehicle for further inspection.

'Is it the passports?' said Kathleen. 'Here, Nora, you'd better get them out of your bag.'

Nora had been miles away, thinking back to that first time she had got off the boat at Holyhead on her way to a new life in England.

'I have them here, just a minute.'

'It's ok, mam,' said Matthew, 'it's going to be at least ten minutes before we get to the passport booth.'

'Oh, well, here they are now anyway. Do you think they'll let us in?'

'Well, they'll have me to answer to if they don't,' said Kathleen.

'If there is any talking to do, leave me to do it, please,' said Matthew. He knew what officials were like, and he knew that his aunty would be more than capable of upsetting them.

A few minutes later, they were at the booth. Matthew handed the four passports out of the car window to the French official, offering a 'Bonjour' in the process. The official looked at each in turn, glancing into the car as he did so. He puzzled over the last one. Eventually, he got up and stepped over to the car, indicating for them all to get out. They obeyed the instruction and stood alongside the car. In reasonably good English, the passport officer spoke to Kathleen directly:

'You are Kathleen Gallagher, yes?'

She nodded.

'You have an Irish passport. Why are you travelling to France?'

For once, Kathleen did not seem so sure of herself. Matthew started to speak but, regaining her normal front-footedness, Kathleen piped him down and began her explanation. After a bit of repetition, the French official had a complete history of the family and was more than satisfied.

'Let's get out of here,' muttered Matthew as they piled back into the car. 'Trust you to be picked out – they can spot trouble all right, these people!'

He was only half joking when he said it. Kathleen took it in good part.

'Well, we need to keep them on their toes. He was eating out of my hand at the end there. He'll be booking his holidays to County Clare next year and eating cabbage and bacon for his dinner. I'd say he had the look of a Clare man, wouldn't you?'

'You did lay it on a bit thick, Kate,' said John.

'And why have you got a bloody Irish passport anyway?' asked Matthew. 'You've not lived there for twenty-five years.'

'If you want the truth, it was easier to renew the old Irish passport. I didn't want to bother with all those forms your mam had to fill in. So there you have it.'

No one dared to mention that Kathleen's surname had changed twice since she was Gallagher.

'Right, I need to concentrate here so can we have a bit of hush, please?'

Matthew was feeling a little bit anxious just for an instant. He needed to sort out driving on the right, and he was desperate to make sure they started out on the correct route. On top of the practicalities, there was a part of him feeling the significance of the journey that they were now really about to begin in earnest. He wanted it to be a success most of all for his mother, but really it was important for all of them.

'You've got Saint Omer and N43 written down here,' John started up.

'Ok, let's look for a signpost.'

They had been waved through customs and were heading out of the gates of the ferry terminal, up to a roundabout where the only sign said "Toutes Directions".

'I know what that means because Rob Hicks told me. He's been on holiday to France a few times. Basically, it means "all directions" and he said if you follow that you should eventually get the signpost you are looking for.'

'Who's Rob Hicks?' asked Nora, always keen to know who Matthew's friends were.

'He's actually one the bosses at work. I know him because he plays in the Sunday football team. Crap at football but a good bloke.'

'Is he married?' asked Nora. This was often the next question.

'Mam, do you mind? I'm trying to find our way out of Calais.'

They came to another roundabout. Matthew was concentrating on going round it in the correct direction. John spotted a sign. It said "Centre Ville".

'What's that "Centre Ville" mean over there, Matty?'

'That's the town centre. If there is nothing else, we just need to follow that and hope we'll pick up the right road from there.'

They trundled along the dockside roads, quickly appreciating the size of the Calais dockyard. Matthew was also starting to wonder how much he had taken on. Then a bit of civilisation appeared. The road started to look more like a town street, with a few shops starting to appear along with some housing. It all looked very foreign but also quaint, interesting, and comforting. There was life on this side of the channel after all.

Another "Toutes Directions" came up and then at the next big junction, some different places were being pointed to. John just managed to spot N43 and pointed Matthew to the correct exit. The traffic was not too bad, and he had time to adjust. It would have been nice to see a sign for the actual place, and then, as if in answer to their collective prayers, Saint Omer appeared on a board indicating it was thirty-three kilometres away. Matthew breathed a bit more easily, sat back more comfortably in his seat and picked up the pace as the road stretched out of the suburbs into the countryside. It wasn't long before he heard gentle snoring from the back seat. Both his mother and aunty were dozing, heads back and mouths half open. Already a fairly long day of travelling, that drink on the boat, and the relief of getting back on the road was enough to relax them. Matthew looked at his dad who smiled back.

'Let's see how long that lasts,' said John.

September 1948

—~—

'I don't want to marry him. I never want to be married.'

Nora was bawling and spat out the words. Then she saw her big sister's eyes and the tears rolling down her cheeks.

'I'm sorry, Kathleen. I'm so sorry. I can't help myself. And what have I got to worry about compared to you?'

Kathleen remained silent, save for the sobs that she couldn't suppress. She was still consumed with an emptiness that she thought would never leave her.

The funeral service had been two months before. Peter Lenahan, her husband of less than three years. Out in the boat from Liscannor, just doing a day's work. Never to return. Lost at sea. The weather had worsened during the day. She had not been concerned until the dark clouds descended in the early afternoon. Then she had gone out to her neighbour's for the sake of some company. At dusk, she went down to the harbour. She knocked on the doors of some of the other fishermen. No one had seen him since the morning. She was taken indoors by her sister-in-law, Nuala, and they knelt to say the rosary, again and again until they were numb with their terrified thoughts. Neither of them slept all night, sitting up in the chair and hardly uttering a sound. In the late morning the following day, the boat was found. No body. The grief was shattering. Kathleen felt her spirit cut in half. Her devotion to Peter, and his for her, made the loss impossible to bear. How could she ever go on without him? Her father and mother were summoned. They could not comfort her, but they were able to get her in the car and to take her home with them. She had merely been existing since that day, not living in any true sense.

Kathleen shook her head. She shook her tears away. She wiped her eyes and looked hard at Nora.

'What are you saying?'

'Look, I can't be troubling you with my problems. Forget I said anything.'

'I want to know. Come on! Tell me what this is all about.'

Nora breathed in deeply. She looked away from Kathleen for a moment. Then she decided.

'All right. I will tell you. I have to tell you.'

'I'm listening,' said Kathleen.

'Do you know that mother and father – well, mother mostly but he's in it as well – have been scheming to get me married off? She wants me settled and she has high hopes of marrying me into what she calls the higher echelons. Can you credit it?'

Kathleen's interest was aroused momentarily. Her own woes were temporarily overshadowed. She smiled weakly, amused at the wily ploys of her mother and the equally stubborn resistance that she knew her sister was capable of.

'They have always had their ambitions. You're their last chance.'

'Don't you start now,' cried Nora. 'They're matchmaking, that's what they're up to. She's had eyes on that doctor son of the Slaney clan for years. A "professional" man is all mother keeps on about. Status, that's what she says. Moving up in the world.'

'And wouldn't it be a match made in heaven?' Kathleen speculated with tongue firmly in cheek. 'Don't they own all that land up the coast, fingers in every pie in the county? They socialise in some very select circles.'

Kathleen spoke in a matter of fact manner but gave herself away with the wry smile that flashed across her lips. She had a rare twinkle in her eyes.

'No, it certainly would not be a match made in heaven. He's far too old, he's nearly forty if he's a day. He could be my father, God forbid. And why hasn't he a wife already? What's wrong with him? Ask yourself that. And as for the select circles? Huh! That lot may have come up in the world over the generations. They have grubbed about and made their money. They've built themselves a grand house. You know just as well as me that they are still cut from tinker cloth.'

'What has mother said to you?' asked Kathleen.

'It's all official. I have to go up to the Slaney house with her for tea there on Friday. I can't stand it. She's already well in with the missus. They want to marry him off before he becomes an embarrassment. I think they see me as just the right appendage for their darling doctor boy. Well, I can tell you now …'

Kathleen interrupted her headstrong sister.

'Ok, ok, I hear you. But don't you think you should meet him at least?'

Nora responded with a heartfelt plea.

'Kathleen, please don't take mother's side. I couldn't stand it. I'll not do it.'

A few days later, Nora was sitting quietly in her bedroom. Her head was pounding, her copy of *Vanity Fair* lying face down on the floor. She had tried to distract herself, escape into the world of Becky Sharp. But it only served to remind her of her own dilemma. And she was no Becky Sharp, out to conquer society through any means available. She just wanted peace in her mind and a simple innocent life.

Meeting the "young" Dr. Slaney had confirmed her worst thoughts. He was superficially charming with effete manners. Nora had seen him around the town and he had been into the store occasionally. She scrutinised him quietly. Tall, slim, well dressed. Very pale complexion, poor posture, gangly legs. He spoke in a high pitched refined voice, and he never stopped talking. It seemed that some of the older women spoke very highly of him. He could be a good doctor perhaps, thought Nora, but her mind was already made up that she didn't care to find out if he could be a husband, good one or bad. Around the table set for tea, he spoke of his work in the district and his sessions at the hospital in Ennis. He enjoyed recounting his time in Dublin at Trinity College. There was a lot of name-dropping. Mother lapped it all up. Mrs Slaney swooned in admiration.

Through it all, the overriding feeling that swept over Nora was repulsion. She did not get any good feelings about the "young" Dr. Slaney. Nora calculated that he had started at Trinity before she was even born. She knew perfectly well that she was hardly experienced with boys or men. She was frankly quite naïve in such matters though she trusted her senses implicitly. Young men, boys that she knew from the primary school and around the village – the likes of Martin Linnane or Joseph Connor or Anthony Pearce – were so different to this specimen. She felt a sense of normality, naturalness, an unselfconscious spontaneity with them.

She was not yet interested in any boy in particular. Well, maybe there was one that she looked at in a different kind of way. That Sean O'Callaghan who worked for the land surveyor, Colonel Slattery. Nora only knew him from a distance. He had come into the shop for cigarettes on a couple of occasions. It was just her luck that on both occasions she had been in the back room and it was her father who served him. She had listened to their chatter with a curiosity that she could hardly explain. Sean O'Callaghan, it would appear, also had the gift of the gab. Unlike the good doctor, what he talked about was interesting and funny. She had twice spied him striding out over the fields on some surveying project. He had the rugged nature of a country man and the good looks of a matinee idol. Her whole body seemed to tingle when she allowed herself to picture him. She was a young woman whose only knowledge of romance came from the books she devoured. Jane Austen, the Brontes, Thomas Hardy. Novels that spoke of both the triumph and the frequent tragedy of love. How true to life were they? Was it all an exaggeration, a distortion? Nora was longing to find out for herself. But not with Dr. Slaney.

'And the most important thing is that he makes my skin crawl. I'll tell you why he's not got a wife yet. Because no one would want to go within a mile of him. That's maybe too hateful of me, God forgive me. He seems to be well liked at the doctoring and maybe he'd be all right for someone, maybe someone his own age. I'm telling you now and I mean it with all my heart, that someone is not me.'

This was Nora exploding with the pent-up feelings that had been consuming her for the last week. She had decided to tell it to her mother straight. There was no point in keeping it in. She had made it through the ordeal of tea at the big house. And she had held her tongue for nearly two days afterwards. At mass on the Sunday she had prayed her hardest for the help of Our Lady and Saint Brigid and any other saint that would listen. As the fried breakfast plates were being lifted, she launched into her tirade, feeling emboldened by the strength of her prayers.

Mrs Gallagher was at first taken aback and then she was outraged. The insolence of the daughter was, she considered, entirely sinful. At the same time, in rejecting what seemed such a favourable marriage, Nora would be throwing away an opportunity to settle down to a very comfortable life, to better herself and the whole family. It was downright selfish.

'I'll not have you talking like that in this house. You'll see what Father has got to say about all this.'

Nora had waited intentionally until Mr Gallagher had finished his breakfast and had departed for the store. He had some stock to check for Monday. It wasn't him that she needed to break anyway. This was really her mother's plan and her mother's ambition. He would just go along with what she wanted. Nora was fired up and meant to ram home her message.

'I'll not see what Father has got to say. It's what I've got to say. I want nothing to do with the Slaneys. You can't force me. And if you try, I'll be leaving on the first train. You can't stop me. I'm old enough and that's all there is to it.'

'We'll see about that, young lady. And what will you do for money, can I remind you?'

Nora paused for a moment. This was getting harder than she had imagined. She had come so far and she was not going to stop now.

'That's it, isn't it? It's all about money with you.'

'It's well seen you've never had to go without,' retorted the mother.

'I am very grateful for everything I have been given in life,' went on Nora. 'I pray to God all the time to thank him for what he has given me. And that includes a brain and feelings. I'm not giving up on that, even if I have to starve. Why would you ever want to do anything to deny your daughter her own life?'

Mrs Gallagher's expression hardened.

'You had better change your tune or there'll be big changes here.'

And with that, she left Nora to the dishes and her conscience.

Day One – June 1975 – Douai

—ꟺ—

'It's going to get dark in the next hour. I think it's time we started looking for somewhere to stop.'

Matthew was more thinking aloud than speaking to anyone in particular. If it were just himself, he would probably have kept going. He would happily drive on into the night. However, he knew that doing so would just be putting off the moment when he would simply have to call a halt. Better to do it now than when it was dark and there might be nothing open. Anyway, he was very conscious that it was different for his mother and Kathleen. They were weary from sitting in the car for so long. They needed a break – food and drink, and a good night's rest.

Kathleen was first to speak up. She was desperate to stretch her legs and freshen up. For all the comfort of the car, they had been on the move for nearly twelve hours and she was simply not used to it.

'You must have been reading my mind, Matthew. Have

you an idea where we can get a bed for the night? We're sitting here in the back being driven around like royalty all day, and I can't believe how exhausting it is. I don't think I'll ever be joining the jet set.'

'I doubt they'd have you, anyway' chipped in John from the front. He had been nodding a little for the last hour himself, trying hard to stay awake to keep Matthew company. His gentle humour was never far away. It was as much for his own amusement as for anyone else. Kathleen took no offence. On the contrary, she loved the craic. She was well used to John's little digs, as well as giving out a few of her own.

Nora was dozing. She was half-conscious of the engine and the road noise. She felt the motion of the car as it cruised along. She was not tuned into the conversation. Images of her wedding day drifted in and out of her head, and then she was walking along the prom at Skegness. Then back at mass in Holy Cross.

For Matthew, this was the part of the trip that had never properly been thought out. It had been niggling away at him that this is where it might all fall apart. The Michelin guidebook that he had bought back in March had suggested that there were plenty of guesthouses or small hotels along the route that would provide reasonably cheap beds for the night. Rob, at work, had also said that there should be plenty of places called "chambres d'hôtes", basically bed and breakfast establishments. Matthew had been looking for signs all down the road from Calais. He had seen one or two, but nothing that gave him immense confidence. Well, it was too late now to change the plan.

'We'll be coming into a place called Douai shortly. We'll see what we can find there.' Matthew was going to stay bright and optimistic, at least on the outside.

The countryside gradually gave way to a more urban outlook and very quickly they were following "Centre Ville". Matthew drove slowly, scanning for anything that looked like a small hotel or a bed and breakfast. The streets felt uncannily familiar, redbrick terraced buildings lining long straight roads. They crossed a river and Matthew was navigating by guesswork only. The buildings became a bit bigger and grander, less residential and more commercial. Eventually, they arrived at a long open square where there were several cafes, some with tables outside. It felt pretty central, and there were quite a few people around.

'I'm going to park here and we can get out and at least stretch our legs. We'll see if we can find a little hotel.'

There were plenty of places to park. He pulled into the right in front of an office that was closed for the day – some kind of "agence". He switched off and everything felt very quiet and still for a moment. Then Kathleen said, 'Come on, then, maybe we can get a cup of tea.'

They emerged from the car with stiff legs and feeling a bit sticky and sweaty. It was a warm evening outside, but a little light breeze provided some welcome fresh air. They trailed off into the square. John stood lighting his pipe, looking around and taking in the scene. His gaze came to rest on the large ornate glass windows of a brasserie across the way. It had black and gold writing, which he could not make out. But there were some warm lights glowing inside and it looked very inviting. It was the nearest thing to a pub that he could see. He shouted over to the others who had kept on walking deeper into the square.

'Nora, Nora. Hold your horses, will you?'

He caught up with them.

'Look, let's try that place over there. Leastways we can get a drink while we figure out our next move.'

Before Nora could say anything, Kathleen intervened:

'That's the best idea I've heard today. Come on, we'll get a seat and maybe someone will tell us where we can get a bed for the night.'

"La Renommée" was not very busy. The tables nearest to the windows were mostly occupied, a few couples, one family of four, and a couple of singletons. It was a big restaurant, however, and there were lots of empty tables towards the back.

'Bonsoir, messieurs dames,' a figure in black trousers, black jacket, white shirt and bow tie greeted them.

They all looked blank. Caught on camera, their mouths would have appeared open, their foreheads wrinkled with worry lines. They were suddenly fish out of water. Matthew was stealing himself to try a couple of words from his smattering of French. To everyone's surprise, Nora stepped forward first.

'Bonsoir,' she attempted. She had read several Mills and Boons over the years, and she had acquired a few simple phrases along the way. 'Good evening, monsieur,' she was trying hard to speak slowly and clearly.

'Anglais? English?' asked the waiter. He was a mature man, in his forties. Well built, strikingly good features, full head of hair with just a few early signs of grey streaking through. He looked distinguished to the travellers, and he had a genuine welcoming touch that relaxed the quartet immediately.

'Irish, actually. But we live in England.'

'Irlandais,' he came up with. 'Excellent. Please. Suivez-moi.'

He gestured for them to follow him and he showed them to a large table near the counter. 'You wait. I come.'

He disappeared. The four sat down. The other diners seemed oblivious to the newcomers. Nora was grateful that they had not caused a scene. At least, not yet.

'It's a grand place all right,' said Kathleen. 'I hope you've been getting your head down and learning some of that French, Matty. I fear we are going to need it.'

December 1964

—∞—

'What did you say?'

No answer.

'Come on, then. I said I want to hear what you've got to say.'

'Get lost, Hooligan. Mind your own business.'

This was Clive Richards sticking up for his friend, Tony Hill. Tony had been swelling his own ego at getting full marks in the German test that they had just sat in the lesson before break. He delighted in ridiculing the likes of Matthew Hoolahan. How was it possible to get only five marks out of twenty? Must be stupid, he had ventured, deliberately loud and provocative.

There was more to it than just intellectual bullying, however. Tony Hill and Clive Richards were worlds apart from Matthew Hoolahan. Tony and Clive were signed up members of the "haves". They lived in big houses in the smart district of Southgate. They were born with a finely tuned sense of their own entitlement. They thought that they were the elite. They were unquestioning of their right to the best schooling, the best university, and the best careers. It was all part of the grand plan. It necessarily involved conforming and doing the work, but all the rewards were laid out for them very neatly. They had no understanding as to why anyone would want to be different from them. Rebels, troublemakers, time wasters and idiots. That is how they saw many of their fellow pupils. Like Matthew Hoolahan. What was the point of them being in the grammar school in the first place? Did they really belong there?

Matthew Hoolahan did not feel that he belonged. Irish, Catholic, no money, no breeding. The smell of poor housing and cooking on his cheap clothes. He knew that he was not stupid, though, and no jumped up swot was going to get away with calling him that.

'I never asked you, dick!' Matthew calmly tossed back at Clive Richards.

'So, have you got something to say or what?' he rounded again on Tony Hill.

Richards and Hill were solid all-rounders. They were in the chess club, the badminton club, the science society, and they played rugby for the school. They were part of things. They had weekends away at the coast and summer holidays abroad. Their school uniform was essentially the same as Matthew's. Black blazer, white shirt, grey trousers. Yet somehow they looked different.

When he had first gone to the grammar school, Matthew was blissfully unaware of class and social differences. All his energies were consumed in making sense of the new and strange world he had entered with little pre-knowledge or preparation. It had been a mixture of pain and pleasure. Pain in the scale and complexity of the new system he was tossed into, pleasure in the excitement and discovery of new things. It had only gradually dawned on Matthew about how different he was from a lot of his cohort. And then he had struggled to put his finger on what was different. The thing about the blazers puzzled him for ages. Surely everyone just got their uniform from the Co-op. It was only recently that the answer had blared out at him from the window of Roland and Ettridge, the gents' tailor on London Road. Not a shop window he had ever paid much attention to in the past. A smart barathea blazer was on display. Even Matthew could recognise the subtle elegance of the fabric and the cut. The average Co-op saggy, school standard, woollen mix did not compare, and nor did the price. The apparently innocuous blazer was the prompt for one of the most important lessons about life in the wider world that Matthew would ever tune into.

Used to saying what they liked and getting away with it, Richards and Hill were suddenly becoming wary of Matthew.

'Piss off, Hooligan,' said Hill, sounding braver than he actually felt. 'Do you want me to spell it out? I'm only telling you what you already know. I mean! Five out of twenty? For that test! Any idiot could have got five marks from watching a few war films!'

Clive Richards smiled. Perhaps Tony Hill had landed the required put down after all. Matthew looked at the two thirteen year olds who sounded like they were forty. It could have been their fathers talking, or the Headmaster. They were old before they were young. Matthew would deal with them. He knew what to say.

The first couple of years at the grammar school had been a very hard time for Matthew. His first school had been a small Catholic primary run mainly by nuns in one of the Irish ghettos of the city. He lived around the corner from the school and went home at dinner time. The nuns were fierce and threatening, but there was also a warmth, a cohesion, almost a cosiness in the community of the school. He was mixing with kids of his own kind, from the same streets, who played on the same local park. They didn't know that they lived in a slum, that the council had plans to bulldoze the area in the next ten years, that their families lived from weekly pay packet to weekly pay packet. There was certainly strong encouragement at school to learn but there was little or no concept of "getting a career". There were just the occasional words of encouragement from his mother and father about how it would stand him in good stead in the future. The school indoctrinated them with Christian values, as well as the catechism. They paid in pennies until they had two shillings and sixpence marked on the scorecard to save a black baby in Africa for Jesus. Weren't they really well off then? That's what the nuns told them, anyway.

The grammar school was completely different. That first day in Assembly with eight hundred other boys. The older ones looking like grown ups, deep manly voices and dark stubble on chins. The unfamiliar Protestant hymns played out vigorously on the organ. The masters swirling around in a sea of gowns of varying vintages. The place reeked of tradition and formality. All the teachers were men. They spoke with booming voices in unfamiliar accents. Classmates in the new school had names like Harrison, Spencer, and Chapman as opposed to Doyle, Callaghan and Lynch. Classmates with season tickets at the football, whose dads owned shops and ran businesses, whose mums drove them to school. It was almost intimidating, although Matthew would not have thought of it that way. He had just got on with it because that was the only way to cope.

For Matthew, the start of secondary was a period of being unnaturally quiet and withdrawn, at least in school. He managed by his wits and native intelligence. Never at the top of the class, never at the bottom. By the end of his second year, he had a better measure of the place. He had made a few friends and they actually came from across the social classes. What they had in common, if anything, was a rebellious streak. Neither Matthew nor his mates had the self awareness to think of it in this way. There was just an unconscious running against the status quo perpetuated by the school. The constrained convention, the conservatism, the conditioning. It was true that he did not really fit in with the school. He could see that. But no-one was going to say it to his face, least of all pricks like Hill and Richards.

In this, his third year, he had started to stand up to any nonsense. This approach had come with a price. He had been up in front of the Head twice during the term for fighting. He was no great fighter but he didn't hold back if there was a scuffle he couldn't get out of. His willingness to compete, rather than the actual results, was marking him out as dangerous. He had running battles with most of his teachers about missing homework. His results in weekly tests suffered as he spent less and less time on any form of preparation. He knew that he would be able to leave school at the end of the fourth year. In the meantime, he wasn't out to make trouble, but he wouldn't let himself be on the receiving end either.

Matthew felt inside like crying when he was being confronted by self-styled know-it-alls who thought that they were better than everybody else. Maybe he messed up the tests and got bad marks in class. The point was that it was not anybody else's business other than his own. He was not going to let himself be bullied, especially when there were such strong undercurrents of prejudice beneath the surface. Matthew was beginning to see it as an attack not just on him but on his whole family. His mum, who slaved away in the house, and his dad who worked long hours to bring home enough money for them to live on. He knew that he and his family were better than all of this lot. They could keep their fancy houses and their relentless ambition.

'Well, maybe we'll just have to start calling you Fritz and Adolph as you're so keen on sprechensing ze deutsch. Sieg Heil, meine Freunde! You think you're so clever. You swot up and learn a few words for a test. Very good! But you weren't so clever last week in English, were you? What was Mr Hume's opinion? I seem to remember him saying "Hill, your composition bears all the creativity of a dull amoeba." Has your amoeba brain already forgotten?'

The little crowd that had gathered around the contretemps sniggered at this. Hill reddened with anger. Richards withered with embarrassment.

'Just watch it, Hooligan,' was all he could muster.

'Watch what? The smiles drain away from your faces when you see everyone's laughing at you? You talk big but you're just a couple of fruits. Better get to the library and start your homework in case your mum's out tonight and she can't do it for you.'

Matthew could find the soft spot. He had the last word as the bell for the end of break time sounded. He wasn't triumphant. He was just glad that he was able to hit back against anyone who thought that they could put him down and get away with it. There was an amount of anger in him. But more to the point, it simply helped to confirm him in his resolve to be his own person and, when necessary, to stand up for himself.

Day One - June 1975 - La Renommée

It was a few minutes before the waiter returned. John was fidgeting. He could see the bottles of beer behind the counter. And of course the bottles of wine lying on racks covering two walls. Even better, they had a beer tap which John watched a barman use to replenish the beer glasses at one of the other tables. His thirst was mounting. The waiter returned with a bunch of menus. He handed one to each of them.

'Pour boisson?' he asked. Four puzzled faces stared back at him. He picked up a glass and mimed drinking.

'Oh, yes sir,' said John. 'Beer,' and he pointed at the beer pump on the counter.

'Oui, monsieur. Une bière a pression.'

Matty raised his hand and made two fingers together to indicate a second beer. The universal nature of sign language was now being tested.

'Mesdames?' the waiter looked meaningfully at Nora and Kathleen.

‘Tea?’ enquired Kathleen.

‘Du thé?’ the waiter checked to see if he had understood.

‘Yes, that’s right, two teas, please,’ and Kathleen did the same two fingers sign as Matthew had done.

And off he went leaving the four to ponder over the menus sitting in front of them.

Kathleen broke the silence. ‘Do you think we have to order a meal to be served a drink?’

It was just what Nora had been thinking. She wasn’t used to eating out. In fact, they were all novices apart perhaps from Matthew who at least knew his way around some of the Indian and Chinese restaurants back in London. Nora could count the proper meals she had eaten in a café or restaurant in the last two decades in single figures. She could never understand why people would pay so much for what you could do so much better at home. And who wanted to eat the muck that restaurants served anyway? At least, that’s what she told herself.

John offered his opinion. ‘Look, we will need to get our dinner somewhere. We’re sitting down now in a nice place. I think we should order something and it will set us up until the morning. I’ll sort the money out.’

That settled it. They picked up the menus that the waiter had left and started to study them. Needless to say, it was all in French. John gave up very quickly, just saying that he would eat anything. Kathleen tried to make some sense of it, but other than the odd word like “steak”, she could make neither head nor tail of it. Matthew was finding a few things he could translate like “poulet” and “boeuf” and “pois” and “pommes”. But it was Nora who came up with the best answer.

'I don't know if I am right but it looks like this thing on the last page –"table d'hôte" – is a complete meal in itself. I've no idea really what is in it, but this first thing must be soup, then there's that "poulet" – which you said is chicken. Then something else down here called "fromage", whatever that is, and fruit at the end. We could give it a try. It's 14 francs – is that dear, son?'

Matthew turned to the back page. 'Yeah, it looks like it could be something – maybe like a Chinese banquet. It seems very reasonable if that's what it is. Yeah, I reckon it might be simpler to go for this rather than try and find something we haven't much of a clue about.'

As if on cue, the drinks arrived. The waiter made an impressive show of arranging the drinks on the table. John looked disappointed in the small measure. It was about a half pint. He took a good pull. It was different from home, but he could get used to it.

'Et pour manger?' the waiter asked.

Matthew understood "manger". He picked up the menu and pointed to the last page.

'Can we order this for four? Quatre, s'il vous plait?'

'Attendez, monsieur, s'il vous plait. Je demande – I ask.'

He went off to the kitchen through the door at the side of the bar, and was back in seconds.

'Desolé, monsieur. Ça ne reste que deux poulets.'

Matthew was struggling. The waiter showed two fingers and pointed at "poulet" on the menu. Matthew got the message. "Autre chose" came into his head. It was a phrase that his last French teacher used frequently to try to coax the class into speaking a bit more of the language.

He thought of Mr Bowrer, to whom a proper nickname had never stuck. What would he make of Matthew's flimsy attempts at the language?

'Autre chose?' he asked in his best performance of a question that he could muster. The waiter considered for a second.

'Boeuf? Casserole?'

The communication was certainly monosyllabic or single words at best, yet something was getting across. Matthew readily agreed on the casserole.

'Très bien, monsieur. Deux poulets et deux casseroles,' and the waiter went off leaving Matthew to explain to the others what he thought had transpired.

Almost immediately, another two waiters appeared bearing four bowls of soup and a large basket of crusty white bread. The soup was a brownish colour and had a creamy consistency, steaming hot and giving off an appetising aroma.

'Well, here goes. I don't care what's in it. I could suddenly eat a horse.'

This was Nora, surprising herself at the excitement she felt, starting to unwind a little from the tension that had been building for weeks and which she had been suppressing as best she could. She couldn't believe it was finally happening. And here was the real proof. She was sitting in a restaurant somewhere in the middle of France, supported on all sides by her husband, her eldest son, and her dear sister. They were on their way to the greatest day of their lives.

'It's delicious,' she declared after a couple of spoonfuls.

The others were also tucking in, nodding agreement as they devoured the soup and the bread.

'That bread is straight out of the oven,' declared John. 'The only thing that would make it better would be a little butter.'

The first waiter returned with a bottle of red wine and four glasses. The table went silent. Matthew started, 'We didn't order any wine.' Then he tried a bit of French. 'Ne pas demander le vin.'

The waiter smiled. In his broken English, he explained, 'Wine is with the meal. Vin compris. Voilà.' And he poured four small glasses.

'When in Rome,' said Kathleen, giggling as she sipped from her glass.

'We're only in France,' quipped John, but he was smiling as he said it.

'Well, that's very nice of them,' said Nora. 'Must be how they do things over here.'

When the main courses arrived, they had forgotten to agree who was having chicken and who would have the beef casserole. Nora stepped in quickly to point the beef at Matthew and John, and she and Kathleen got the chicken. Both dishes looked appealing even if the portions were not very generous. Still, you couldn't expect home size meals when you were out in company. The chicken breast had a creamy mushroom sauce drizzled over it, and there were green beans alongside. The beef casserole consisted of a meaty gravy covering tender lumps of beef mixed in with a few carrots and onions. There were a couple of potatoes on these plates too. They ate heartily and quickly. They all thought it was one of the best meals they had ever had. John called a waiter over to ask for more beer. The plates were cleared, and they were all feeling more than content. Then some more plates appeared and a platter was placed on the table containing three lumps of different cheeses and some more bread in a new basket.

'I don't know if I could eat anything else,' said Nora. 'This must be the "fromage" thing that was on the menu. It looks awfully soft. And it smells a bit funny.'

John and Kathleen tried a bit of each. Matthew steered clear. He could eat cheese, but only the hard type of cheddar with which he was familiar. Red Leicester was just about the extent of his cheese palate. He definitely would not touch anything with blue mould running through it. He was not fond of creamy things in general. Some of the "fromage" looked distinctly soft and it was also giving off a powerful and noxious whiff.

Finally, the waiter brought out bowls containing a peach for each of them. When he had disappeared, Kathleen sniggered, 'What in the name of God are we supposed to do with this?'

'Eat it,' said John. 'It'll loosen the bowels.'

'I don't need anything like that, thank you very much,' she responded. 'But I suppose we had better not leave anything now that they've provided us with it.'

When they had all done their best with the peaches, Matthew managed to catch the waiter's eye. He came over, enquiringly. 'Café, monsieur?'

Matthew said, 'Non, merci.'

And then, using a phrase he had memorised from the guide book, 'Je voudrais l'addition, s'il vous plaît.'

'Is that you asking for the bill, Matty?' enquired Kathleen. 'Can you see if he knows any hotels around here?'

Before the waiter turned on his heels, Matthew began again.

'Monsieur, ici, hotel? Chambres?'

The waiter thought for a moment.

'Attendez un moment. Wait. I come.'

He went off into the kitchen.

Five minutes later, he returned. He had an older man and a teenage boy with him. The older man was wearing a shirt and tie. The boy was wearing blue jeans and a white T-shirt. He was smiling, his dark curls framing a handsome face.

'Mon père, Robert, et mon fils, Gaston' said the waiter, pointing proudly at the two newcomers. 'Vas-y, Gaston,' he said.

In slightly faltering English, and heavily accented, Gaston began:

'My father say I speak English with you. He thinks you are looking for hotel.'

Matthew took the lead.

'Yes, we need two rooms for tonight.'

Gaston turned to his father and the older man.

'Ils cherchent deux chambres pour la nuit.'

There was a lot of chatter amongst the three of them and much gesticulating. Eventually the boy turned round to pronounce the verdict.

'My grandfather has friend with house. You can stay there.'

'Is it far from here?' asked Matthew.

'Non, no,' said Gaston. 'Just two streets. Three minutes.'

'Is it a hotel?'

'Non, not hotel. Comment vous dites – how you say – guest house?'

'Is it chambres d'hôtes?' queried Matthew.

'Exact,' said Gaston.

'How much?' asked Matthew.

Gaston turned back to his father and grandfather. Another long discussion. Finally, Gaston said, '80 francs.'

'Is that per person?' asked Matthew

'I not understand,' said Gaston. 'The price – le prix – for two rooms is 80 francs.'

'Right,' said Matthew. 'We'll take them. C'est très bon.'

He was pre-empting any possible interruptions from Kathleen or his mother. He knew his dad would be thinking like him.

'Looks like we have got a right result,' he told them.

There were smiles all round, the waiter, the old man, and the boy.

Gaston said, 'We take you when you finish.' And then he and the old man wandered back through the kitchen door. The waiter had disappeared but was back in a few moments. He served everyone with a little glass of brandy, deposited the bill with John, and withdrew. John picked up the sheet but without his glasses the scrawl was too difficult to read. Matthew looked over his shoulder, down to the bottom line. It showed 62 francs. For all that food, the beer, the wine, and the brandy. It was a bargain.

'Dad, it's 62 francs. That's less than 7 quid. We'd better give a tip. We'll call it 65 francs to round it up.'

'You've got my money, son. Can you sort it out?'

'Yeah, and we'll sort out the rest of the money tonight.'

Matthew had been changing currency for weeks. He'd been following the exchange rate for ages. As soon as he was ready to get some, it had taken a dive. He'd bought some francs one day. Watched the rate go down for another week, then he'd got some more. Then his mum had given him a load of cash to change. He'd got more francs and lire, exchange still plummeting. Then Kathleen wanted some money changed. In all, he had been to the exchange bureau nine times, the final visit on the previous Friday for what he hoped was simply a top up to cope with any unexpected contingencies. He just hoped it would see them through. He had a reasonable idea how much the petrol was going to cost, but this eating and overnight stuff was an unknown. He took out his wallet, counted out seven of the 10 franc notes and placed them on the bill. The waiter returned, smiling, removed the money and returned sharply with the change and with the old man and Gaston.

'Ok,' said Gaston. 'We go now?'

'Yes, brilliant,' said Matthew.

He went to pick up the coins from the plate, thinking to leave 3 francs. Then he felt embarrassed. They had had a damn good meal. It was only a few bob. He left it all, making sure none of the others lifted it.

Bonsoirs were said all round to the waiter and the other staff who were standing around looking for something to do. They were making their way out of the door when the waiter remembered to say to Gaston to tell them to come for their breakfast in the morning. They all smiled and off they went.

October 1948

—᯾—

It was a rainy Friday afternoon at the end of October. It was gloomy outside, heavy grey cloud chasing away the daylight. The lights were on in the General Store making the inside seem, in contrast, cheerful and inviting. Hughie Gallagher was in the yard at the back of the building. There was an old outbuilding there that was used for storing supplies. He was making space for a new delivery expected any day now. And knowing Francie, the delivery man, it could be any night as well. Nora was alone in the shop. She was killing time counting how many newspapers were left. It had been a slow day, not many folk venturing out in the wet. Nora judged that they were not likely to sell any more papers at this time. She would bundle them up in a little while.

The shop was deceptively large, much bigger than you would have thought just looking at it from the street. Huddled in amongst the other establishments and dwellings of Parliament Street, it stretched back a good thirty feet. The large counter area jutted out from the right hand wall, solid wooden shelving from floor to ceiling lined the walls with a variety of wares. Hughie Gallagher had always shunned the licensed trade and, one of the other staples of the local economy, undertaking services. He stuck to his opinion that there were plenty of others who offered those particular things, and he could do better elsewhere. He prided himself on his grocery business. And he was happy to deal in hardware, animal feed, and most anything else if there was the demand. There were sacks of flour, oats and grain standing on the left hand side opposite the counter. The counter itself was busy with a large white set of scales at one end, and a red bacon slicer at the far end. The newspapers were in a rack near the front of the shop.

She heard the door of the shop being opened. When Nora looked up, Sean O'Callaghan was standing right in front of her, a broad smile across his face, water dripping off his hat onto his overcoat. The sort of hat that Americans wore in the films, more stylish than her father's anyway. Nora was off guard, almost forgetting where she was. She sometimes lost herself in a daydream when things were quiet. She could only stare for a few seconds while a thousand different thoughts went through her mind. Then she recovered her sangfroid and spoke casually as she stepped sprightly back behind the counter.

'Oh, good day to you. It's Sean, isn't it? Is it ciggies that you're after?'

He was looking around the shelves and then focused back towards Nora.

'That's me. Sean O'Callaghan, all the way from County Kildare. The town of Athy to be precise! Indeed, I'll have sixty Sweet Afton if you have them. If you haven't any Sweet Afton, give me Players Medium, please.'

Nora reached round into the tobacco cupboard and brought out three pristine yellow packets of Sweet Afton. Sean was again looking around the shop when she turned round and laid them on the counter.

'Is there something else you are wanting?' she asked.

'Yes, I'm needing some writing paper and envelopes. Is that something you would have?'

'I'm sure we can find you something,' Nora answered. 'Would you be looking for something fancy like, or more plain?'

He had to think for a moment and then he said, 'Plain would be grand. It's just that I've a letter to write.'

Nora smiled inwardly. She had not thought that he wanted the stationery for kindling.

She felt emboldened and began to chat.

'So, how are you liking it down the country with us Clare folk? Are you missing home?'

'I'm liking it fine here. I'm kept very busy with the Colonel, but that's grand. I'm staying up at Mrs O'Rourke's and she's like my own mother. Waiting hand and foot on me. Of course, I miss them all back home – ma and da, and I've four brothers and two sisters. And nephews and nieces, a new one every year.'

He laughed. 'How about yourself? Do you ever think of travelling?'

Nora instinctively looked towards the back door before

she answered. She did not share all her thoughts with her mother and father. Maybe she could do so more easily with a relative stranger. And someone more her own age.

'I've got a full time job here minding the shop. It's a lot for father nowadays on his own. Trying to keep up with everything. I used to think about going to the teaching college when I got my Leaving Cert. But, you know,' and she laughed to signal a joke, 'I'd have to end up an old spinster if I wanted to keep a teaching job.'

Sean laughed along with her.

'That wouldn't do at all, now,' he said.

In a slightly more hushed tone, Nora went on, 'I often think about what it would be like to go to England or America, don't you? You hear all the tales of the bright lights. It sounds so exciting.'

She stood gazing upwards, in a half dream. Then she sighed, 'Maybe I'd miss the old country though.'

As she said it, she was already doubting her words. What were her prospects in North Clare? It was true that she did not really want for anything materially. The business provided a good living for the whole family. The basics in life were well catered for. Food on the table, peat in the fire. They were certainly one of the better off families in the district. Living in a good big house, father driving around the county in his motor car. She had a good education. Could she really be discontent? Nora was young, energetic, strong-willed, and intelligent. There was something continually gnawing away at her, telling her that she could do more with her life. She looked around her, at the way of life that seemed never to change. She was hungry for new experiences. She could still be here running the shop in fifty years time. Or worse, she could be pitched headlong into some loveless marriage. Sentenced for life. Incarcerated by expectation. Making the best of a bad job playing out the role handed to a woman in these parts, her own true self unable to find expression. And in the meantime, she still had the stifling control and misery of her mother to contend with. The idea of getting away somewhere, anywhere, was the thing that consumed a lot of her waking hours.

'Maybe the old country would miss you more,' Sean replied seriously.

Nora said, 'It's a big step, of course. And I've got my sister Kathleen here too.'

'You've a sister? Just the one?' asked Sean.

More hushed than ever, Nora said, 'Well, there were other babies but they didn't live. So, it's just myself and Kathleen.'

Even as she spoke, she was surprised at herself for revealing so easily such intimate family details, and to a relative stranger to boot. Was she mesmerised by him? She could already hear her mother chastising her for daring to speak of such things in public.

'I'm sorry,' said Sean, 'I didn't mean to pry.'

There was a noise from the back of the shop and he looked up.

'That'll just be my dad coming in the back way,' explained Nora.

'Ah, yes, of course.' Sean moved forward to pick up the cigarettes and stationery.

'I'd better be paying you before I forget,' he said. Then he added, 'Here, I think I'll have a quarter of those mints.'

He pointed across the counter at one of the tall glass sweet jars.

Hughie Gallagher put his head round the back door, shouted something, and then disappeared again.

'He's a busy man, I can see that,' said Sean, as Nora weighed out the mints.

'Now, is there anything else for you?' asked Nora.

'That's my lot, thanking you.' Sean dug into his inside pocket for his wallet and handed over a ten shilling note. Nora counted out his change.

'That's grand,' he said. 'And would you see if you can keep me some Sweet Afton for the next time?'

And with that he was gone.

Nora went back to counting the papers. She wondered about a next time.

Day Two - June 1975 - Reims

Matthew was suddenly aware of daylight even with his eyes still closed. It dragged him out of his unconscious sleeping state. He opened his eyes and puzzled for a second until he remembered where he was. The unfamiliar room, the dark wallpaper, and the large window looking out on the street. He checked his watch. It was just after seven. The room was warm and the air felt stale. There was no sign of his dad who had been sleeping in the other bed. Matthew was not overly surprised. He knew him as an early riser and he expected that John had gone out for a wander and a smoke.

As he pulled off the covers to get out of bed, the door opened and in came John puffing on his pipe.

'So you're out of the land of nod,' he commented. 'Beautiful day out there. Had a walk back to the square. Plenty going on. The car's all right. It's still where we left it. And it's still got the wheels on! That café we were in last night is already open. They've got workmen and all sorts in there. Drinking spirits at this time of the morning, from what I could see!'

'Can you see if the bathroom is free?' asked Matthew.

'Well, your aunt's in there just now, and then it will be your mother. You'll just have to wait. The toilet is a bit peculiar although there looks to be a very good shower.'

'What do you mean "looks"? Did you try it?' asked Matthew.

'No,' said John, 'I just had a good stand-up wash at the sink.'

Matthew sat on the edge of the bed and reached over for his bag. He sorted out a fresh T-shirt and underwear. Then he lay back again on the bed, thinking about the day ahead. He had left his little notebook into which he had scribbled the route plans in the car. They would need to fill up with petrol and he should check the oil, the tyres, and the water.

John sat in the little armchair, which he pulled over to look out of the window, sucking occasionally on the now unlit pipe. He was fascinated, watching as the town came to life. Different clothes, different buildings, different language, but maybe similar underneath.

After a while, he asked, 'Will we have some breakfast or just be heading straight off?'

'It's going to be a long day in the car so we shall definitely need something to eat before we start off,' replied Matthew. 'How's the bathroom doing? Can you have a look?'

John got up and went to see. He returned with the news that it was all clear. Matthew sprang out of bed. He needed the toilet and he wanted a good shower to freshen up.

By quarter to eight, the little party was assembled, bags re-packed and ready to go. There did not appear to be anyone else in the house so they slammed the front door behind them and headed off to find the car. The money for the rooms had been handed over the previous evening when Gaston and the grandfather had brought them over. So, there was no further settling up required.

Once they had managed to stow all the bags in the boot, they made their way over to La Renommée once more. There were a few men standing at the bar with tiny cups of coffee, one or two with a glass of brandy, sharing the day's laughs and woes with the barman. Most of the tables were free and they chose one by the window. It was a different waiter from the previous evening that approached them. He started in French, then hesitated.

'Anglais?' he enquired.

Matthew nodded and simply said 'Breakfast? Petit déjeuner? S'il vous plaît?'

'Très bien, monsieur. Café pour tout le monde?' and he pointed at each in turn.

Matthew quickly interrupted. 'Thé, please, s'il vous plaît.'

And with a smile, the waiter retreated to the kitchen. Within a minute, he returned with a basket of fresh crusty baguette, a plate of croissants, butter and jam. Then he came back with four cups of tea. He looked at the four of them looking at the tea. Suddenly it dawned on him what was wrong.

'Bien sûr,' he exclaimed. 'Ça vous manque du lait!'

And off he went for some milk before they could respond.

'Not exactly a fry up, but it was nice all the same.'

This was Nora as they resumed their places in the motor.

'So where are we off to today?' joked Kathleen.

Matthew sat behind the wheel wearing a white T-shirt and jeans. He was looking at his notes and getting an idea of where he hoped to land by the evening. He was thinking it would be very good if they could reach somewhere on the outskirts of Lyon. It was a good three hundred and fifty miles to Villefranche-sur-Saône, and he had no idea what the roads would be like. It was about the distance that the car could do on a full tank and it was, he thought, probably as much as his passengers could cope with in a day.

'Are you all sitting comfortably in the back?' he said.

Murmurs of satisfaction all round. He turned the key and the V6 engine growled into life. He gave it the few extra revs he always did when he started the engine. He liked to hear how it sounded. He thought it was good to give it a bit of a warm up. He wanted to feel the smoothness and the power of the engine. He did not need to check the fuel gauge to know that the tank needed filling up. As they took off with a last look at the square and La Renommée, Matthew had John primed to look for signs to the N44 for Cambrai and on to Reims. Matthew himself was hoping to see a garage and it was only a few minutes before he spotted a forecourt with several pumps proclaiming "essence" and sporting the Elf brand. He drove up to the second pump on the left and got out. A teenager quickly appeared from nowhere and asked sullenly, 'Combien?'

Matthew thought for a moment, couldn't think of the right word so just mimed what he thought was "full" with his hands stretched low to high. It seemed to be understood and the boy went to work. Matthew watched the pump clocking over, trying to remember how litres matched up with gallons. The clock stopped at 58.3 litres, the price showed 131 francs and 76 centimes. Matthew thought it seemed a lot but he counted out 140 francs in notes and handed them over. When the boy came back with the change, Matthew pointed at the tyres. The boy understood and showed him where the air line was. John was already out of the car and they lifted the bonnet. The oil was on the mark and the water in the radiator was fine, so nothing to do there. Matthew went round the tyres and they all checked out ok. Back in the car, with everything settled, Matthew gave it a few more revs on the accelerator, engaged first gear and moved out smoothly onto the main road. He hoped that they were in the right direction for the N44.

Two and a half hours later, they were past Reims and the next target was Châlons-sur-Marne. The talk had been mainly between Kathleen and Nora sitting comfortably in the back. Matthew was concentrating on the road. John was watching the signs and enjoying the green landscape they were passing through. Nora was more herself today. Not withdrawn and not subdued as she had been in the last few days, especially yesterday. The tension she had been feeling in the weeks leading up to the trip finally seemed to be dissipating. She felt relaxed, able to think normally, her facial muscles were able to find a smile rather than sit permanently fixed in a frown. She had enjoyed the previous evening, the meal had been an unexpected pleasure, and she had slept perfectly.

'Do you think we'll be able to get our hair done when we get there?' she batted to Kathleen.

'Surely to goodness they'll have a place for a quick shampoo and set,' responded Kathleen.

'We'll need to look our best on Sunday,' said Nora.

'I don't imagine anyone will be paying us that much attention,' quipped John from the front.

'And you could do with a trim as well. Just look at the state of you,' said Nora. 'You're a holy disgrace.'

John smiled away although he knew she was right. Maybe he would find a little barber on Saturday. Mind you, he was wondering what he would ask for.

November 1948

John's hands were frozen. Winter had descended viciously as the last days of November played out. It was still dark at seven thirty as he trod over the rutted entrance to the site. There was ice on the ground, some flurries of snow blowing in his face. He pulled the dark donkey jacket tighter around him. His body craved the warm bed he had been laying in no more than an hour ago. He could still get the stale taste of old beer in his mouth from the pints of Guinness he had drunk in the King William IV the night before. That was another Sunday over. The summer was long gone. His life back in Ireland was a distant memory right now. The reality of this new existence in England had quickly replaced his imagined idyll. What you could dream of and hope for from afar was, it would appear, never how things worked out. Still, he thought, it could be a lot worse. His inner strength of purpose kept him going. His youthful energy and enthusiasm were boundless, and he kept a good humour.

It was having to get used to these freezing dark mornings that took the shine off things. At least, that is what he told himself. And they wouldn't last forever, would they?

It had been a big shock to arrive in a Coventry still massively scarred from the bombing raids of the German Luftwaffe. In neutral Ireland, the war had mainly existed for John as a radio commentary. He had no tangible experience of what the war had actually been like for those living through it. It had been known at home euphemistically as "The Emergency". The Irish had a way with words. It was ironic as well given that the Irish predilection for procrastination meant that few people really had any kind of understanding of that concept. The bombed sites, the broken houses, the damaged roads – John had never seen anything like it before.

Walking from the station back to the house in Blythe Road on the day he arrived in August 1948, he made the sign of the cross several times and hurried through some prayers. He wasn't devout in any big way normally, but he reckoned that this was a time when prayer was needed. All the souls lost. All the misery that had been wreaked on the city and its people. John could not comprehend it all. He just felt the shadow of it all around him.

It only took him a few days to get on top of it. Helped greatly, it has to be said, by the welcome for him from Tommy and his uncle Owen. They fed him, they gave him drink, and found him his own room. The house was a rambling terraced house with a succession of small rooms. An older couple, Harry and Brenda, rented the house from an agent, and in turn let out rooms to lodgers. They had been taking lodgers for years and it was now a way of life for them. With the arrival of John, there were four lodgers – Owen, Tommy, John, and another man called Peter who worked for Herbert's machine tools at the Butts. Brenda gave the men a breakfast and an evening meal and took care of their washing every week. It was a friendly set up, and the men were made welcome, having the living room at their disposal. For Owen and Tommy, it felt like they had landed on their feet with this place. Father and son had come over originally in 1946 for a temporary working stay. But the work had kept coming, the money was decent, and there was no proper work for them back in Ireland. So they had stayed on. Sending money home every few weeks and taking their turn to have a week or two back with the family at every major holiday period. They had tired of temporary digs – no more than doss houses – after a year and searched hard to find more homely rooms and a landlord that was happy to rent to them. Here they had found a level of comfort and homeliness, and it was worth every penny to get a good dinner and clean clothes without having to think about it. Owen's foreman had provided a reference and the deal was done. It was not a palace but it was a good substitute for a home from home, all things considered.

Owen had only ever worked on the land back in Ireland, but he could put his hand to all sorts of things. It was a case of "needs must" when there was no alternative. He could fiddle about with engines, he could build walls and fences, he could put a roof on a barn. He was quick-witted, strong and fit, and a good worker. He had very quickly found work with a scaffolding gang which was formed mostly of Paddies. Lifting and carrying at the start, eventually graduating to the job of actually fixing the scaffold pipes. Tommy was time served as a mechanic in Ireland, and his skills were in demand. He was working as a fitter at the bus depot. It was a steady job. The money was reasonable because there was a night shift every other week and always lots of overtime. It was Owen who had got John a start on the buildings. The job was a large housing estate being constructed to the west of the city. Owen had spoken to one of the gangers doing the ground works. He knew that anyone recommended by Owen would be all right.

John had not envisaged that he would be wielding a shovel in the land of hope and glory. It certainly was not completely new to him. He had helped out enough on the farm back home. There the scenery was green fields, hedges, trees, and the little stream at the end of the big field. Here it was mud and more mud. He was surrounded by piles of heavy clay drainage pipes, huge mounds of sand and gravel, and stacks of bricks dumped in awkward spots. It took him a few days to adjust to the workplace, and a bit longer to get used to the work. The ganger was reasonable enough, giving him fairly clear instructions. He was basically to dig holes and trenches where they told him, moving earth, creating mounds, and then often moving it again. It was demanding physically, and it took a couple of weeks for his muscles to be sore and then to strengthen up for the task. He learned quickly how to pace himself in this new job which was very different to working in the garage at home. There you had to work physically some of the time, but you also had time to puzzle over a problem or to stand working quietly at a bench to fix something. Here the trick was always to look busy if the ganger or any other boss was around, and then take the chance to ease off when no-one was there to notice. As long as the work got done. And always to have a shovel in your hands.

John had sent a telegram home the day after his arrival at Blythe Road. Then he sent them a letter after a week. He'd had one back in which his mother and sisters had each written their bit and sent him their fondest wishes. There was no real news of any import. Life was proceeding as it ever had been, it seemed. Well, that was comforting at least. The letter writing had then proceeded on a less regular footing, every two or three weeks. In his most recent letter, he had enclosed two crisp £5 notes. It was the least he could do, to give them something to fall back on at Christmas as well as to demonstrate tangibly that he was doing fine – even if he did not always feel it. It was a lot of money but he was earning every week and he was finding that he did not have to spend a great deal. He had a drink at the weekends with Tommy, and he had started to attend the dance on a Saturday evening in the Trinity Hall. That was about all. He did not want to get into the habit of visiting the pub every night of the week. He liked a drink now and then. A lot of his fellow workers, especially his Irish compatriots, were putting away the pints every evening. It was tempting, of course, but he knew it was a slippery slope that he had no intention of stumbling onto. He'd seen enough ne'er do well drunks back home not to have any ambition for that path.

One thing he had omitted from his most recent letters was the fact that he had begun to form a friendship with one of the girls from the Saturday dancing. It was a girl called Margaret. She would go to the Trinity Hall dances every week with a group of friends. Tommy knew one of them vaguely because she worked in the office at the bus depot and this gave Tommy and John an entrée into their company. Casual conversations, plenty of laughs and jokes, and the occasional dance. John was no dancer, but he tried hard. Of all the girls, Margaret seemed to be spending more time talking to John and laughing off his efforts to foxtrot. He liked her a lot, not least he liked the warmth of her company, feminine and elegant and graceful. It was much in contrast to the rough and ready masculinity of the building site and life in Blythe Road. He was wondering what the next move would be and had yet to work it out.

Day Two - June 1975 - Dijon

The car dutifully ate up the miles. They were not on motorway roads but these N roads were generally pretty straight and Matthew could keep up a decent 50 and sometimes 60 miles an hour. It was manoeuvring around the bigger towns that slowed them down. And he had to stop every two to three hours for at least a toilet break to satisfy the needs of his touring party. They managed to get some lunch at a roadside eatery on the way out of Vitry on the N4. Hardly more than a wooden shack in a large car park, it had nicely laid tables and a wave of enticing food smells swirling out from the kitchen behind the counter. Matthew had thought that omelettes might be an easy thing to order and they were duly served with salad and pommes frites and a basket of bread. They all then risked café au lait, and were more than satisfied as they got back on the road.

The weather was bright and sunny, and it was warm in the car. Matthew kept fiddling with the vents to try to ensure a flow of air. They were travelling too fast for it to be comfortable with an open window, especially for his mother and Kathleen in the back. No-one complained about the heat or the stuffiness, he just felt it was draining him more quickly than he would have wanted. Still, the car was performing nicely and he was starting to get used to driving on the right. He had decided that overtaking was least risky if he waited for a left hand curve in the road as it gave him the best chance for a quick look ahead of the vehicle in front. Other than that, he had to rely on John doing the looking and telling him if it was safe to pull out. It wasn't that he didn't trust his dad, more he didn't trust himself. He just liked certainty, especially when travelling at speed.

The afternoon trailed on. John and Matthew were talking about the price of a pint in London, the troubles in Ireland, Lord Lucan, and the decorating that Nora wanted when they got home. In the rear, the ladies fell off into a doze and it wasn't until they were skirting round Dijon just after four o'clock that Kathleen woke up complaining of feeling sick. Matthew viewed this as an emergency. He didn't want anyone being sick in the car. He pulled off the main road and looked for a safe place to park. He went round to the rear passenger door and helped Kathleen out. She stood a bit queasily on the bit of pavement that Matthew had parked beside. Nora got out as well and came round to support Kathleen.

'Get a bit of air, Kathleen,' she said. 'It's very stuffy sitting in the car all day, and in this heat. Here, do you want some of this orange juice.'

'That's the last thing to give her,' shouted John. 'It'll curdle her stomach. Here, Matthew, is there anywhere we can get her a drink of water?'

Matthew looked around and couldn't see any sign of a shop or a café. To hell with it. There was a house just opposite where they had parked. He went and knocked on the door. After a minute or two, a young boy answered. He could only have been about fourteen years old. Matthew was struggling to think what to say, or more how to say it.

'Water,' he started, 'could I have a glass of water for the lady over there? Not feeling well. Water?' Then he remembered. 'Eau, s'il vous plaît?'

The boy looked nonplussed, and then disappeared leaving the door half open. Then he returned with a man in his forties. Matthew repeated his attempt to communicate the request. The man looked across at the car. He saw Kathleen leaning on the car and being helped by Nora. He seemed to understand and said:

'Attendez. J'arrive.'

And a minute later he came back with a large bottle of water and a glass. Matthew expressed his gratitude and within a few minutes Kathleen felt restored with the slow sips of cold water that she passed over her lips. Matthew returned the glass to the man still standing at his door.

'Merci, monsieur. Merci beaucoup,' he said in his best accent.

The man smiled and in a soft voice simply said, 'Bonne chance!'

'Bonne chance' indeed, thought Matthew. He had driven towards the centre of Dijon to find a shop where they could get water and some provisions for the road. He found a very large supermarket eventually and drove into the busy car park. They all got out to stretch their legs and went inside. It was absolutely huge with a fresh butcher's counter at the front of the shop and a separate fish counter next to it. They all marvelled at the piles of shellfish sitting on ice on massive counters. You did not see that at the Co-op back home. Kathleen looked fondly at the variety of fish and the crustaceans. She had lived by the sea and from the sea for three years. Her Peter had brought home all sorts of catches when he'd been alive. He would have loved to see this lot. She said nothing, just kept her thoughts inside her. Time did heal, as so many people had been keen to tell her, but it didn't mean that you weren't left with the scars. Her loss of Peter had emptied something inside her. Over the years she had replaced some of it and she had grown stronger again. The deep sadness she had experienced was largely suppressed these days by holding onto the good memories and the love they had shared so long ago. She smiled inwardly and then abruptly said:

'I could murder a cup of tea. I think there's a little café over there, look!'

'I feel a lot better,' said Kathleen as Matthew finally found the N74 going south out of Dijon. It was just gone five o'clock.

'I want to go about another hundred miles this evening and then we'll see about stopping and finding a place for the night,' said Matthew.

'You're doing grand, Matty,' said Kathleen. 'I never

thought I'd be chauffeured all the way to Rome. You just tell us if you want anything.'

'Are you back to yourself, aunty?' asked Matthew.

'I think it was falling asleep and the heat of the afternoon that hit me for six earlier. That cup of tea has revived me. Maybe it's the excitement that got to me after all!'

Nora looked knowingly at her sister. She was feeling excited now as the journey progressed. There was the strangeness of a foreign land, the different language, the shops, the food, and the people. It was exciting to travel such a long distance, passing through so many places she had never known existed. The fields growing strange crops, the cows looking so different, the quaint buildings like the ones they had just seen in Dijon with the funny coloured tile roofs. Now they were on a road with vineyards either side stretching for mile after mile after mile. She had never seen vines growing before, certainly not like this. And, at the back of everything, they were travelling with a purpose. They had a date in Rome in four days' time.

December 1948

Nora was getting ready. Earlier, she had soaked in a hot bath, one of the genuine comforts that the Gallagher household enjoyed. It was the first weekend in December. It was Sunday, a day of rest. The store was closed for the day. More often than not, there was plenty of catching up to do like cleaning or sorting out the paperwork, but not today. Once the morning duties at church were over, Nora had retreated to her room. She was half way through *Tess of the d'Urbevilles* and was desperate to plough on with the story. The house was still. Mother and father were taking their customary Sunday afternoon nap. Kathleen had gone to the coast for the day. She was still grieving for her lost husband. Being with his family seemed to provide a crumb of comfort. Nora wondered if Kathleen would ever get over it.

It was well into the evening when she put down the book and began the customary struggle with her hair.

She longed to achieve the look of a Coleen Gray or a Rita Hayworth or an Ava Gardner. She had the long hair all right, but she could not seem to control it. She wanted it swept back, a neat parting and elegant waves trailing down behind her shoulders. But it never looked right. She put on the blue dress that she liked. She had found the material in McKendrick's in the town. Mrs Garrahy in Monastery Lane had fashioned it for her. She was a talented tailoress who kept up with all the modern styles. Nora always felt good in that dress. The hair would have to do.

It was nearly half past eight when she emerged from her room and made her way downstairs. Her parents had already stirred. They were down in the large kitchen cum living room that served all the daily needs of the household. There was a parlour but that was only for guests. Mother was fidgeting about at the range. Father was sitting at the table eating some supper and listening to the radio. A large mug of tea steamed away in front of him.

'Is that you off gallivanting again?' It was less a question than a condemnation from her mother.

Nora took it in her stride and ignored the jibe.

'Bridie and Lizzie will be along here any minute now,' she said with a big smile. 'It's a modern dance tonight with the Mulligan band. They're meant to be fabulous.'

'Fabulous, is it?' was all her mother could reply.

'It's the GAA organising the dance at the Hall tonight. I'm sure Uncle Joseph will be at it. He's usually counting the money.'

Nora was becoming adept at answering back. She had more to say.

'And if you don't mind, will you not be scowling at my friends?'

For the first hour of the dance, it seemed as usual like it was a girls' only night. The four piece band played a range of standards, reproducing a host of styles with amazing versatility. The girls congregated to the left hand end of the hall. There was quite a variation in their ages. The younger ones tended to dance to everything, trying out their steps, enjoying the freedom to express themselves physically, even if they were partly constrained by the conventions of the particular dance. The latest gossip was shared, family members were talked about – clothes, hairstyles, the latest film. There was always a laugh to provide a lift from the routine of day to day. Occasionally, there would be a mass movement onto the dance floor and the band raised the volume. By ten o'clock, the other end of the room was beginning to fill up. Younger boys arriving as if to a game of football while the older ones swaggered in from Linnane's or McInerney's with a drink in them.

No-one really understood how these dances suddenly took off. It could have been a particular tune or song that the band struck up. Or it could have been a predestined signal from nature. All that could be said was that suddenly the floor was awash with boy-girl couples waltzing and fox-trotting, some very ably and many stumbling their way through each number. It hardly seemed to matter if they were enjoying themselves.

Nora was never short of boys asking for her hand in the next dance. She enjoyed dancing and she never turned anyone down. If she got tired, she would simply keep out of the way for a couple of numbers. For the fourth week in a row, she was hoping that one person in particular would be there and ask her to dance. Try as she might, she struggled to keep her mind away from that Sean O'Callaghan. During the twenty minute interlude, Nora and Lizzie fetched glasses of lemonade and some sandwiches from the bar. There was no alcohol on sale, of course, although that hardly bothered Nora since she had no desire for it anyway. As they stood by the bar, Nora spotted Sean heading in their general direction. She waved at him instinctively, and immediately felt embarrassed. He smiled back and made his way over to join them.

'It's a grand night, isn't it?' he said. 'Mrs O'Rourke has let me out for the evening,' he joked. 'How about you girls? Are you enjoying yourselves?'

Looking at Lizzie, he went on, 'Nora here has been a godsend, making sure I get my cigarettes every week. I don't know what I'd do without her.'

He pulled out a half empty packet of Sweet Afton from his suit pocket and offered them round.

'This is Lizzie, by the way' said Nora, 'Lizzie Coleman. Her dad's the local Guard.'

'Aha, I'd better watch my Ps and Qs, then,' he laughed.

Then he asked, 'Are you wanting a drink or something?'

'We're grand,' said Nora. 'We'll let you get served.'

And she ushered Lizzie and herself away back to the girls' end of the hall.

'What's the hurry?' muttered Lizzie. 'That was your chance to speak to him.'

'All in good time,' said Nora.

Half an hour later, the band was at full throttle and the floor was invisible beneath a bobbing flotilla of dancers. Nora was sitting this one out. Sean appeared beside her and started to speak. It was difficult to hear themselves talking above the band. Then Sean offered his hand and they made their way onto the floor. It was a waltz. He held her firmly and confidently, and she was pleasantly surprised at his agility. She was extremely competent herself, so they made a good couple. The congested dance floor was the only thing holding them back from ever more exuberant swirls and twirls. Nora needed to remember herself. This was their first dance. They stayed on for a second dance and then she excused herself, not wanting to give out the wrong signals. She was elated, and she could have danced with him all night. But things like this had to take a slower course.

Day Two – June 1975 – La Saône

—∞—

After the hold-up in Dijon when Kathleen had felt unwell, Matthew was trying to make up for the lost time and pressed on down the N74 following the Côte d'Or as far as Beaune and then moving onto the N6 heading for Chagny, Chalon and Tournus. It was slow going at times, stuck behind trucks or the occasional tractor and just having to be patient. He was getting tired and could sense the day fading away. They needed to find another stopping place for the night. Despite the great success of the first evening, Matthew was feeling anxious that they had to do it all over again. He was just hoping they would be lucky.

As they passed through Tournus with the clock showing a little after seven, he decided that it was time over the next half hour to call a halt and get in somewhere for the night. He spoke quietly to John.

'Can you keep your eyes peeled for anywhere that looks

like a bed and breakfast or small hotel? I think it's time we got settled somewhere.'

As John was nodding his assent, Nora quietly spoke.

'Thank you, Matty. That would be grand. It's been a long day. You must be exhausted. I know we are in the back here.'

'Let's see what we can find, then,' said John. 'Douai will take some beating, though, don't you think?'

'I've said a few prayers already,' replied Nora. 'We'll put our trust in Him.'

Matthew was following the signs to Mâcon which was now about another fifteen miles away. They must have been close to a river on their left hand side because Matthew kept seeing signs pointing to it. The name was given as the Saône, although he wasn't sure how to pronounce it. One thing he was sure about, however, was that they wouldn't go any further than Mâcon today. If they didn't find anywhere before they reached the "centre ville", they would just have to try their luck in the town. With a few miles to go, they all registered a large roadside hoarding pointing straight ahead. *À 100 Mètres. Bar – Restaurant – Relais.*

'Well,' said John, 'that place seems to be offering at least two out of the three things we want. Food and drink.'

'I'll bet a pound to a penny that they'll have a bed for us as well,' chipped in Kathleen.

Matthew was hoping she was right and that this "relais" thing was yet another French way of saying hotel or guesthouse.

'Let's find out,' he said and swung the car across the carriageway into the gravel forecourt fronting a plain, old stone building with a simple sign proclaiming "Le Relais Lamartine". It had the look of the classic house that any child would draw, a simple rectangular block with a pitched roof and three large windows on the first floor. The real difference was the ground floor. It had a doorway to the right hand side and then three giant plate glass floor-to-ceiling display windows to the left. There looked to be a small bar just as you entered. That seemed to be quite brightly lit. Then stretching across to the left hand side, the broad windows revealed a warmly lit dining area with lots of tables already laid with table cloths, glasses and cutlery.

'Here we go,' thought Matthew as he pushed through the door with Kathleen close behind. Nora and John were bringing up the rear, whispering together a few yards further back across the forecourt.

'Come on, then,' called Matthew. He walked on in and could see that the bar was really just an extension of the dining room, with a few stools lined up at the bar itself and a few small round tables crowded into that end of the room. It was very quiet. There was no-one behind the bar. Two older men sat smoking pipes in the far corner. The restaurant was empty.

Matthew walked tentatively towards the bar. One of the old men offered 'Bonsoir' and Matthew responded in kind.

'Pascal,' the old man shouted loudly. 'Il y a quelqu'un.'

A muffled response came back and then suddenly the door behind the bar opened and a short stout middle aged man sporting a huge handlebar moustache emerged. He had on the apron of a bartender or waiter, and very much looked the part. There could be no doubt that they were in France now.

'Bonsoir, Messieursdames ...'

Matthew broke in before too much more French was flung their way.

'Pardon, monsieur,' he began in his best accent. 'Anglais? Vous parlez anglais?'

'Pas beaucoup, monsieur. Desolé.'

Matthew persisted. 'To eat ... manger,' he mimed eating with knife and fork. 'Rooms? Chambres d'hôtes? Pour la nuit.'

The bartender looked inscrutably at the four of them for a long second and then broke into a smile, wrapped his arm around Matthew's shoulders, and motioned the group through into the dining area to a table by the window.

Then, returning to a more grave and serious tone, he said:

'Combien de chambres?'

There was some confusion for a few moments. Matthew couldn't quite get the meaning to start with. Then it clicked. He managed to explain what they needed. Pascal, the bartender, ushered Matthew away from the table and through to the stairs. They went up and Pascal proudly showed Matthew two bedrooms – each with a double bed – and a spartan shower/toilet at the end of the corridor.

'C'est soixante-dix francs pour les deux.' Again, Matthew struggled to understand. He froze temporarily. He knew that they were now talking about the price, he just couldn't get the number. Then he mimed writing in the air. The bartender obliged with a slow 7 and 0. Smiles all round.

Matthew offered to pay there and then but the bartender raised his hands as if to say we can take care of all that later.

They descended back to the dining room. Orders for drinks were taken as Matthew confirmed that they were in for the night. John and Matthew ordered beer. Kathleen looked hard at Nora, and quickly they agreed that they would like to try a glass of wine. Matthew confirmed "vin rouge" for the ladies and he waited to see what would arrive. No-one was disappointed. The beer was cold. The wine was soft and fruity. They were old hands now at ordering food. The table d'hôte was the clear choice. And they were still sitting at table two hours later finishing their last drinks and feeling very mellow. It was difficult to have any real conversation with their French hosts but by the end of the evening it was striking how much they had shared together. They had learnt that the bartender, Pascal, was the owner. He ran the place alongside his wife, Edith. They did everything between them - waiting, cooking, serving drinks, clearing, and cleaning. They were open all day from early till late. The daytime was the busiest with lots of truck drivers and other motorists making it a favourite stop. Pascal and Edith were locals, born and bred in the little commune of La Salle. They had barely moved from where they had grown up. They seemed utterly content with their own station in life, exuding a gentle confidence and worldly wisdom. They eventually managed to understand about their guests' trip to Rome, and it was clear that they felt honoured to have them on the premises. Matthew sorted out the payment for everything. Pascal seemed inclined to leave it all until the morning but Matthew wanted to get it out of the way and be able to go to bed with a clear conscience.

And so to bed. It was the same arrangements as the night before. Matthew and John were in one room, Nora and Kathleen in the other. The men hardly spoke. Too tired, perfectly satisfied with their meal, pleasantly soothed by their beer. The ladies were a bit different. They were also happily replete with the lovely meal, but more awake now than in the car, lively and animated. They were both excited by the unfolding adventure, loving the experience of meeting new people even if the language barrier made communication hard. They talked for an hour before finally slipping into deep sleeps.

April 1966

—⁂—

'Hoolahan, can you stay back at the end of class, please?'

'Yes, sir.'

This was Mr Pearson, the English teacher. Matthew had no idea what he wanted. Mr Pearson, like most of the other teachers, had a nickname. His was the relatively affectionate "Dylan", probably because he had arrived in the school in the summer of 1963 just around the time that Bob Dylan was beginning to have an impact in Britain. And also because he fitted the folk poet image quite perfectly with his donkey jacket, Aran jumper, and denim cap. Dylan was one of the teachers Matthew actually liked and respected. He hoped that he hadn't done something to upset him without realising.

The English class was always good fun, especially with Dylan. They were reading *The Third Man* by Graham Greene. Matthew could lose himself in the thrill, in the excitement and intrigue. The immorality, the struggle between good and evil, pricked his conscience without him really knowing it. They had been given a spin off creative composition to write for homework using the type of atmosphere created by Greene as inspiration. Matthew didn't always apply himself to homework, but for English he usually tried. He found that he enjoyed writing. For this composition, he had crafted a three page story over two lunch breaks in the school library. Not that it was easy working there with people interrupting every two minutes.

The lesson ended at a quarter to four. It was the last class of the day. Matthew lingered at the back of the room as the others trooped out. It was the second week of the summer term. The weather was picking up, and it was staying light till nearly eight o'clock. Matthew was looking forward to getting out on the park for a game of football and general mucking about. What did Mr Pearson want?

'Right then, Hoolahan. Come and sit down at the front here. It shouldn't take long.'

'All right, Mr Pearson. Have I done something wrong?'

Matthew moved down the aisle of desks to the front where the teacher's table sat in the middle of the floor. Mr Pearson picked up a chair from the front desks and brought it over to the table for Matthew. They sat down at right angles to each other.

'Look, Hoolahan, the first thing is that I've been marking this week's homework. I haven't finished the whole class so I've not given it back yet. But I can tell you that I think your story is outstanding. A few things to sort out – grammar and spelling, that is – but you have clearly got a very able mind and a very creative imagination.'

Matthew was a bit embarrassed. All he could mutter was, 'Thanks, sir!'

'The point is,' went on Mr Pearson, 'the point is that I've heard a story from the Head of Department that you are set to leave school at the end of this term. Is that right?'

'Well, I'm already fifteen and I'm entitled to leave. And I want to get a job and start earning money.' He had been telling everyone this for months and he had it well rehearsed.

'Ok. Let's have a think about this. Am I correct in thinking you don't much like being in school?'

No-one had ever put it so bluntly before. It made Matthew think before he answered. 'Not really, sir. I mean, I like your class, sir!'

'No need for flattery, Hoolahan. Tell me what's going on in that head of yours.'

'I do mean it about your class, sir. I like English. And you're fair.' Matthew paused, stuttered a little, and dried up.

Mr Pearson drew breath.

'Look. I'll come to the point. And this is just between you and me. Got that?'

'Yes, sir.'

'I think you can do better than leave school in a couple of months, with no qualifications and, most likely, a long term regret about your time spent here. Believe you me when I tell you, I know life here has not been easy for you. But let me tell you something. Life is not easy anywhere. And it doesn't get easier when you leave school.'

'Yeah, but I'll have money and I won't be looked down on by …' He tailed off, not wanting to reveal too much of himself to the teacher.

'Hoolahan, perhaps I am overstepping the boundaries here. What I mean is, perhaps I shouldn't be having this conversation. However, as a teacher, I think I have a responsibility to offer some guidance when I think it is appropriate. I just want you to give this some thought. Firstly, I am confident that you will pass English O level if you stay on next year, and if you do the work. Secondly, I have spoken to your form master Mr Gibbs, who also happens to be your maths teacher. He believes that you are more than capable of getting your Maths O level. But that will also need you to do the work. You may not know this but achieving just those two O levels could open a great many more doors to you than if you don't get them. You may not like it at this school, you may not be happy here, but with a little more effort and by staying on for the fifth year, you could end up with something very valuable out of it.'

'I don't know, sir.' Matthew did not want to say no outright, but that was what he was thinking.

Mr Pearson let the air settle for a few moments.

'Well, go away and give it some more thought. If you want, I am happy to speak to your parents about it. We'll speak again this time next week. Is that ok?'

'Thanks, sir.'

The conversation was over. Matthew replaced the chair he had been sitting on in its normal spot, his mind racing. He stepped quietly out of the room muttering a goodbye to Mr Pearson. How was he going to get out of this?

Day Three - June 1975 - La Salle

The next morning, Matthew woke to find John up and dressed and sitting looking out of the window, watching the steady stream of trucks and cars heading into and out of Mâcon. It was just after seven o'clock. He felt surprisingly refreshed, ready for the next leg of the journey. He just needed to look through his notes and check the map to remind himself of the route and the intended destination for day three. So far, so good.

'Kathleen's been sick in the night.' John spoke calmly, trying to ease across the information without causing Matthew undue alarm. He knew Matthew's inclination to want things to be perfect, to fret until any problems or difficulties had been overcome.

'What's wrong? Is she all right?' asked Matthew.

'Your mam woke me at four o'clock this morning. Kathleen was as sick as a dog. I think she's still in her bed sleeping it off.'

'Was it the food? Or the drink?' wondered Matthew. His head was working overtime thinking about how this would affect all his plans for the trip. He suddenly felt guilty for not concentrating on how Kathleen herself was feeling.

'I'll go and knock the door in a wee while to see how they're doing,' said John. 'Maybe she'll be fine.'

They left it until eight o'clock before they went along to see what the situation was. Nora was dressed and busying herself with the suitcase. Kathleen was still in bed, looking pale and worn out.

'How are you feeling, Aunty Kathleen?' asked Matthew as delicately as he could. She was usually such a formidable woman but she looked weak and fragile as she lay propped up against a couple of pillows.

'Not so good, Matthew. I don't know what's come over me. I'm aching all over. I feel sick. I couldn't dream of eating anything. And the thought of sitting in the car …' She tailed off.

This had not featured in any of Matthew's plans. He hadn't envisaged a medical crisis en route. Problems with the car – yes, that was always possible. Indeed, that had been foremost in his thoughts. He had planned as well as he could for that. The car had been thoroughly checked over the week before, oil changed, radiator and hoses checked, tyres checked and a couple of new ones fitted on the front, windscreen washer checked, and even had new window wipers put on. It hadn't occurred to him to think beyond that.

Nora took control.

'Now, Kathleen, are you sure you wouldn't want to freshen yourself up with a little shower? And then see how you're feeling?'

Before she could say anything, Nora continued:

'Matthew, you and your dad, why don't you head downstairs and get yourself some breakfast. I'll join you in a bit.'

Matthew and John took their cue and quietly stepped out of the room.

'Come on now, Kathleen. What do ye say? Will ye try?'

Kathleen sat up a little. She moved the bed covers away and shuffled herself round so that her legs were dangling over the side.

'I feel that weak, Nora. And I've a terrible pain in my side.'

Nora was patient and held her hands. 'Come on, I'll give you a help. You've maybe eaten something that doesn't agree with you. Maybe it's the wind.'

Kathleen forced herself up, having to steady herself against Nora. They walked gingerly along the corridor to the bathroom. Nora brought a towel and soap.

'Will you manage yourself?' she asked Kathleen.

'I'll be all right now. Just wait in the room for me.'

It was a long fifteen minutes later that Nora heard the bathroom door unlock and Kathleen padding along back to the bedroom. She came in and flopped to sit down on the side of the bed. She looked much fresher in the face, but it was all relative.

'What are you thinking?' asked Nora.

'I've been praying all night for this to be lifted off me.

But I'm not right at all. I've no appetite. I feel like I need to vomit but there's nothing there. This pain in the side keeps coming back. It's not all the time but when it comes it grips really terrible.'

'What in God's name will we do with you?' Nora was smiling. Not laughing at Kathleen, but at the situation.

'You never have a day's illness in your life and you wait till we're in the middle of France to be poorly!'

'I'll never take another glass of wine in my life,' said Kathleen.

'Now, you don't know it's anything to do with the wine. Would you take a cup of tea?' asked Nora.

'I want nothing.'

Nora eventually left Kathleen lying on the top of the bed and went to join Matthew and John downstairs in the dining room.

'She's not in a good way,' Nora said. 'I think she needs the doctor.'

'How are we going to get her a doctor here?' Matthew was thinking out loud.

John spoke up. 'If she needs a doctor, she'll get a doctor. Can we not ask Pascal and Edith?'

The Relais was busy but eventually Matthew managed to summon Edith and between them they explained that Kathleen was "malade". The phrase book was turning out to have its uses, after all. Once she understood, Edith went straight away with Nora to see Kathleen. There were no Gallic histrionics, just concern and sympathy and decisiveness. They would need to send for the doctor. Edith would arrange everything. In the meantime, she made

Nora join John and Matthew back in the dining room for her breakfast. Nora found herself drinking a huge soup bowl full of hot milky coffee, with a crispy croissant and French crusty bread and jam. She had only ever drunk tea at breakfast before!

The doctor was expected to come about ten o'clock. Nora went and sat with Kathleen. The men went outside. John puffed on his pipe. Matthew checked the car over. The oil was quite a bit below the mark on the dipstick. John took the can of oil that was stowed carefully in the boot of the car and, with his practised eye, poured about a third of a pint in. The tyres looked fine, as did the radiator. Matthew sat in the driver's seat with the door open. He fiddled with the radio, finding the odd crackly French station. Lots of British pop music being played amongst the fairly recognisable archetypal French accordion or jazz sounds. He had his map and notes and he was trying to work out what the new plan was going to be.

John came round and stood by the door. 'How are we doing for time, do you think?'

Matthew told him that he was just having a think and trying to re-calculate. They did have some time to spare, so there was no panic. Yet! It all depended on what the doctor said.

Christmas 1948

—∾—

John woke later than he had intended. It was already half past nine and he was intending to get up for ten o'clock mass. The house was empty apart from himself. Owen and Tommy had left on Thursday, catching the train to Holyhead and hoping to be back sitting by the family hearth at Kilfenora by Friday teatime. The landlord and landlady, Harry and Brenda, were away for a couple of nights visiting her sister in Birmingham. Peter, the other lodger, was also missing. He had family in Scotland and he would be up north for the week. John had finished up from work on Friday lunch time and the site would now be closed until New Year's Day. He had thought about going home but he finally decided to stick it out in England. He would have been very happy to see them all back home but he dreaded the idea of leaving it all behind again after just a few days.

He was not going to be alone for Christmas, however. Firstly, he had been given an invite from one of the ground gang on the job. He was an older man, known always by his surname O'Brien, who was married with grown up children. They were all away from Coventry in various parts of the country bringing up their own families. When John had told him that he was staying put over Christmas and New Year, O'Brien had come in to work the next day to say that he and his wife would be very glad if John would join them for Christmas dinner. None of their own children would be able to be with them. It was just too much for them with all the expense of travelling and presents to buy for the children.

The invitation was very kind and John didn't know how to respond because he had also had an intriguing invitation from Margaret to eat Christmas dinner with her family. This had been totally unexpected. John was excited and frightened at the same time. Why would she invite someone, him, into the house? It would be unlikely to happen back home. In truth, he hardly knew the girl. He definitely had feelings for her. Perhaps it was just a simple desire borne of the celibate bachelor life he was leading. Perhaps it was more than that, something a bit purer. He wasn't sure. His mother and sisters, along with the school, had taught him enough social graces to get by in most companies. He was not so sure though about being thrust into the company of a strange family at Christmas, in the role it would seem as suitor of the daughter of the house – and having never yet met the mother or father. And indeed not having even properly started to court the daughter.

Perhaps that made it better. Perhaps he was not a suitor at all, just a friend from Saturday nights that they were taking pity on. This was England and the English after all. It was still early days for John in finding out how things were here, how the people lived, what the norm was, and what was beyond the pale. He had not expected the people to be any different from home. Time would tell.

John had thought hard and found what he hoped was a good compromise. He had agreed with O'Brien to have dinner with them but insisted that he would take his leave in the early evening to let them enjoy the rest of the day themselves. O'Brien had readily agreed. Then, last Saturday, John had explained to Margaret that he had already been counted for dinner with Mr and Mrs O'Brien and he couldn't let them down. Would it be ok, however, if he came along to hers in the evening? If Margaret had been disappointed, she hid it well. In truth, it was probably a relief. It might have made for a very tense dinner. The evening would be more relaxed and she would still get to see John.

It was a busy day ahead. John made it to mass just before the Gloria. He stayed well at the back, perched at the end of a row. It was a cheerful session for once, the tidings of great joy rubbing off on both priest and congregation. Then he went back to the house and fried himself some bacon and eggs. He was due at the O'Brien house at one o'clock. As he had been rushing for church, he now had a proper wash and a shave and spruced himself up in his best suit. He had four bottles of stout and a bottle of sherry to offer his hosts. Mrs O'Brien busied herself in the kitchen while the men had a drink in the middle room. John felt relaxed, half listening to the radio in the background, telling the O'Briens some of his funny stories from back home in Clare. It was the best dinner he had eaten since he had left home. A lovely tender roast chicken, crisp roasted potatoes and Brussel sprouts, covered in a rich gravy. This was followed by a sherry trifle, then cups of tea and fruit cake. The radio remained on throughout, crackling away in the background bringing messages of goodwill from around the Empire and from the king himself. The three talked away, and when something caught their attention from the radio, it provoked more amusement than anger to hear the 'empire' mentality still being propagandised with customary arrogance. They had plenty to thank England for, which tempered any grievances that they might have harboured. John was aware of the many hot-headed republicans that wanted to continue the fight for a united Ireland. It was not a fight that he had a lot of interest in joining. He had a life to live, and there was more to life than politics and war. Hadn't they all seen enough fighting by 1945?

By six o'clock, with the O'Briens nearly dozing off in front of the blazing coal fire, John was able to take his leave expressing his fulsome thanks for a lovely dinner and a very happy occasion. He had to pass Blythe Road on his way to Margaret's house, which was a good forty minutes away. He picked up the second set of beer and sherry that he had bought at the off licence. He couldn't go empty-handed to the Pickerings, and he had no idea what else he could take to them. He had only learnt Margaret's surname last week when she was telling him the address and how to find the house. He had an idea where Clayton Road was. He knew that it was a long walk up Holyhead Road. He felt the poignancy of that. He was literally on the road home but he would not be going quite that far today.

The street was in darkness and he hoped he had the right house. Perhaps this was a mistake. Should he just go and forget it? He knocked. It seemed a long time before a light came on in the hall. He could imagine the flustered whispering and re-arranging that must have been going on when the knock was heard inside. He had seen how his mother acted in similar situations, when a stranger was coming into the house. He had no choice now but to stay the course. The door suddenly swung open and Margaret stood there, grinning broadly and pulling at his hand to bring him into the house. She was wearing a bright red dress and was awash in a lovely perfume. John smiled and held her warm hand for just an extra moment.

'Come in, John, come in. Everybody's dying to meet you. Happy Christmas!' And she gave him a peck on the cheek. He blushed a little. They had never kissed before. This was no romantic kiss, but it felt to him like Margaret was getting a bit closer than just being the friends that they had become over the last few weeks.

The door to the front room opened and Celia, Margaret's younger sister appeared.

'Is this him?' she said in her amusingly blunt schoolgirl manner. 'We're all in here. Come in and meet everyone.'

'Come and get yourself a seat,' said Mrs Pickering. 'You're very welcome. Happy Christmas! Come in and tell us all about yourself.'

John shook hands with everyone in the room. Mr and Mrs Pickering, Celia, the brother Robert, and Margaret's aunt and uncle, Flo and Bill. There was an empty armchair that he was ushered into. A glass of beer was placed in his hands, and the floor was all his. Margaret knelt on the floor beside John, filling in some of the parts of his stories that she had already heard. He didn't think of himself as much of a raconteur and yet his audience seemed very appreciative.

'You have a beautiful way of speaking,' exclaimed Flo. 'You've got that lovely Irish lilt.'

The Pickering family could not have been nicer. John had come across quite a bit of prejudice against the Irish in the few months that he had been in England. There did not seem to be any prejudice in this household. They were a solidly English family, reasonably comfortably off. Mr Pickering had a good job working in the Council offices in the housing department. He was very interested in John's work on the Canley estate. At one point he said that they would never get anything built in England if it wasn't for the Paddies, and he seemed to mean it. John also felt at home seeing a picture of the Sacred Heart on the wall. He knew well that Margaret's family were Catholics. In fact, it was through her friendship with some of the Irish girls from the convent that she had been introduced to the regular dances at the Trinity Hall.

To his surprise, as he walked the long stretch home, John could not remember a happier Christmas Day. He was still tingling from the brief embrace with Margaret when she saw him off the premises at midnight. Her perfume lingered in his senses, the touch of her lips, and the warmth of her body against his. He smiled all the way home.

Day Three - June 1975 - Relais Lamartine

There was no sign of the doctor at ten o'clock. Nor at half past ten. By a quarter to eleven, Matthew was getting twitchy. Finally, at ten past eleven, an old green Peugeot 404 rolled into the forecourt. A smartly dressed older man, possibly in his sixties, got out of the car. He carried the type of bag which told them that this was the man that they were waiting for. He had spotted the British car and approached John and Matthew.

'Bonjour, I am thinking that you are the English people who need the doctor.'

'Yes, it's my aunty who is not well. She is upstairs,' Matthew responded eagerly. He was half thinking that Kathleen would not have been happy to hear herself described as English. John and Nora were less prickly on that subject – just occasionally did it seem to come to the fore with them. Matthew was so relieved that the doctor had spoken in English. Actually, pretty good if heavily accented English.

'Eh bien, allons-y! Let us go!'

The doctor made a thorough examination. Nora stayed and was impressed. Kathleen would have been impressed if she hadn't been feeling so unwell. Nevertheless, she was glad to be poked and prodded if it could help to make her better. The verdict was:

'Pas grave. It is not serious. But you have an infection which may last one or two days. You must rest and drink fluids regularly. The pains in your stomach should ease in the next twenty-four to forty-eight hours. I will give you some medicine. You can take if it gets very painful. No more than one tablet every four hours.'

'Is it something that she ate, doctor?' asked Nora.

'Mais non. No. It is something, comment dire, in the air. It is a bug, a virus. We cannot say where it comes from. They usually last only a short time.'

'Oh, thank you, doctor. That is good. So, nothing really to worry about. She doesn't need to go to hospital?'

'Pas du tout. Not at all. Rest and fluids. She will be fine in a few days.'

Nora followed the doctor down stairs.

'We need to pay you, doctor. What do we owe you?'

The doctor reflected for a brief instant. Then he pronounced. 'It is nothing. Edith has explained where you are going. And the reason. It is wonderful. I am only glad to be able to help in a little way.'

Nora was embarrassed. This was real kindness she wasn't used to. She suddenly had the feeling that some of the privileges in life that had passed her by for most of her time on earth might be starting to come her way for once.

Her luck was in! God was looking after them. She cleared her throat. She did not know what to say but decided she had to say something.

'Thank you, doctor. I really don't how to thank you. We are much obliged to you. Much obliged. I'll say a prayer for your good health and your family when we are in Rome.'

The doctor smiled happily. 'Merci, madame. That is perfect. Parfait! Au revoir, et bonne chance!'

And with that he swept out through the main door with a brief wave towards the little group of John, Matthew and Edith who had been waiting in the dining room. Nora watched him as he walked over to the green Peugeot. He opened the car door, slid into the driver's seat, reached over to place his bag in the passenger footwell, revved the engine, and drove smartly off. Nora was still swooning a little as she regained her sense of the three heads watching her.

'Well,' said John. 'What's the verdict?'

'Oh,' said Nora, pausing to collect her thoughts. 'Well, she's poorly all right, but nothing too serious. He says it's a bug, an infection. She needs to rest and take plenty of fluids. Plenty of water. Tea is all right. She should be better in a day or two.'

Matthew was waiting to ask the critical question.

'Can she travel?'

Nora looked blank. Her concerns had been purely about what was wrong with Kathleen. She had been convinced that it was something serious, that she might need to go to hospital, to have an operation. Nora had not been thinking about the journey at all until Matthew raised it now.

'I,' she stumbled a little, 'don't really know about that. I wouldn't think she is in a fit state for sitting in a car all day. The doctor didn't say anything about that. And I forgot to ask him.'

Matthew sighed heavily. 'For Chri …' he began, but stopped himself before it all slipped out. 'Well, can we go and have a word with her and find out what's what? We're going to have to decide what to do.'

'Steady, Matty,' muttered John. 'One thing at a time, son.'

On impulse, Nora went and held Edith's hands. She wanted to embrace her for all the help she had given them. She felt a little overwhelmed with the kindness coming her way. Nora was not the demonstrative type. Her Irish upbringing had instilled modesty and restraint. She couldn't bring herself to public displays of affection. She tried to make up for it with a warm hand, smiling eyes, and a sincere look.

'God love you, God love you, you're a saint,' she murmured. Edith got the message, shrugged her shoulders and promptly gave Nora a hug and a kiss on the cheek.

John smiled wryly and thought, 'You got more than you bargained for there.'

They assembled around the bed, Kathleen sitting up with pillows behind her. She looked a little brighter, but John could see immediately that she was no more than fifty percent.

'Did he say anything else?' asked Kathleen. 'You've been down there an age. Has he got me written up for something you're not telling me?'

'Not at all, not at all,' said John firmly.

'Kathleen, you heard what the doctor said.'

This was Nora, trying to settle Kathleen's nerves. Kathleen might be a formidable woman but Nora knew that anything medical could throw her off kilter.

'He says you have caught some bug and it should be away in a day or two. You're not dying, although you might feel like it. You'll be as right as rain before you can say Jack Robinson.'

'Are you wanting anything, Kathleen?' asked John. He was on his best behaviour, surprising all of them with his genuine solicitude.

'Oh, you're all right, John. I'm not feeling up to anything. I'll just have a sip of that water. There. That's it. I feel like I've been ten rounds with Cassius Clay.'

'I wonder how Cassius is feeling,' retorted John.

'Now, don't make me laugh,' said Kathleen. 'My side is aching as it is.'

'Never you mind, Kathleen,' said John, 'when your number's up, you won't know anything about it anyway.'

It was always a bit of a shock to Matthew to hear this kind of dark humour. The Irish in particular, his parents and their generation more generally, seemed to relish laughing about life and death in a way that he had clinically sealed himself against. He wished that he could loosen up but he felt taut and tense in these sorts of exchanges and always looked for an opportunity to move the talk on. Now he intervened, trying to get back to the thing that was uppermost in his mind.

'I don't suppose you're up for a spin in the motor, aunty?' he asked jokingly, but with a serious point to get cleared up.

'My head's spinning, Matty. My stomach is heaving every few minutes. I'm as weak as a mouse. I just couldn't dream of it today.'

'Ok, that settles that. We'd all better have a think about what to do. I hadn't thought of having a Plan B. But now we really do need to look at our options. We've still got three days before Sunday. Well, more like two and a half now. Anyway, we have some leeway. Any ideas on what we do from here?'

New Year 1949

It was the first week of the New Year. Hughie Gallagher had been impatient to open up the store again after the Christmas holidays. He had had enough of sitting around and he had money to make. He was thrown completely off course on the first day back in the shop. News arrived that his cousin Danny up in County Mayo had died suddenly on the Sunday. So it was that Nora was left in charge while her father and mother went off for a number of days to the wake and the funeral.

Kathleen had already started back at the linen mill and was not able to offer any help. Nora did not mind, in fact she enjoyed the freedom it gave her. The General Store was as busy as ever on the first day of opening up but the subsequent days hardly saw a dozen customers coming through the door. This was January, the long dreary month when every day seemed longer than the previous one. The bleak weather of midwinter dampened the spirits and drove folk to stay deep in their burrows. It was a dramatic fall from the heights of the Christmas festivities. The weeks of anticipation and the excitement that had gripped like a fever. And then it was all over, and the realisation sank in that Christmas was just about as distant as it could ever be.

Even if January had arrived to spoil the party for most people, there was a vitality and sparkle still bursting through Nora. She had energy and strength for three people, her mind was racing with a host of ideas and possibilities. She was singing away to herself as she hurled herself into a reworking of the shelves and displays in the shop. There were things at the back of shelves and hiding in corners that had seen several previous years come and go, and it was time that they were ditched. This was her opportunity. While Hughie Gallagher was elsewhere, he would never know.

The source of Nora's soaring spirits was her developing thoughts about Sean O'Callaghan. Since the first day that she had seen him, there had been something appealing to her senses. In the course of him coming into the shop and then meeting him at the dancing, she had started to experience feelings about another person that were completely new to her. She had, of course, revealed nothing of this to her mother. What was there to tell anyway? It was just a friendship, was it not? Kathleen had an inkling that there was something going on, but she did not pry. Her own sadness sometimes overwhelmed her too much to take a real interest in others. Marie Gallagher, the mother, wondered if she saw signs of something changing in Nora, but had not yet confronted her daughter. In the meantime, Nora was wondering how her "friendship" might develop and what, if anything, she could do about it. To make it go the way that she was hoping it would go. There were so many constraints within which her world operated that you could justifiably feel a little helpless at times. You might wonder how two people could ever find themselves cementing a relationship when the very idea of courtship appeared to be an unspeakable notion. The Irish approach to many things – "say nothing" – was at its zenith in matters of romance and love.

It was over two weeks since she had seen Sean. He had made an excuse to come into the shop on the Wednesday before Christmas. He was going back to Kildare to spend Christmas with his family. He was his usual jovial self, sporting a broad smile and filling the shop with his presence. He had on his over-sized grey overcoat. His big leather boots trailed mud across the floor. He had come into town from the job out surveying for the new road along at the Point. Nora had been impatient to see him again after Sunday night at the dancing. Their conversation was still very much at the getting to know each other stage though. They swapped snippets of information, chatted about the dancing and the people they knew, and about what was happening around and about the town. The only elements of the chit-chat that came close to being more personal consisted of family trivia. He told her all about his nieces and nephews. And he remembered that he would need to have a bundle of presents in order not to disappoint them. So Nora helped him choose some boxes of chocolates and toffees that would suit the older ones. Then she told him about the preparations in the Gallagher household and about the turkey that Tommy Herlihy had handed in the day before, all plucked and ready to be roasted. It was in lieu of some of his never ending line of credit. It was the same every year. Nora's heart leapt when Sean wondered if she would see him off on the train the next day. If she could get an hour away from the shop, they could have a cup of tea and a cake at the Cascades Hotel, and then he would board the midday train.

Indeed, that is exactly what happened. Nora told her father that she had to go out for an hour at eleven. She made it clear that he should not ask why, and giving him to believe it was something to do with Christmas. It was always a good excuse for being secretive. Then she wandered along Main Street hoping that she would see Sean before she got to the hotel. When he did not appear along the street, she decided not to wait outside for him. In fact, she realised that this might actually work out better as far as the likely local gossip was concerned. So, she stepped smartly into the lounge and quickly gave her order, making it known to Betty the waitress that she was having a quiet half an hour in between all the Christmas hustle and bustle. Before her pot of tea arrived, Sean appeared. Although there were several free tables it did not seem strange for him to join Nora at her table. To the casual observer, it would have seemed like nothing more than a friendly encounter between two young people who were acquainted.

They chatted freely. Nora regaled him with all the gossip that had come her way over the last few days. Sean told her about another surveying project that would be starting in the New Year. They drank their tea and ate their cake. At one point, Sean seemed to have gone very quiet. Nora filled the void with her nervous chatter. She wondered what he was thinking about. Had he something to say? He snapped out of the reverie and reignited the chit-chat, telling her about some of the people he would have to call on when he was back home. He would enjoy going to his cousins in Moone where he would be fed and watered, and there would be a good laugh and a sing-song. The aunt with all the airs and graces in Crookstown was a different proposition, but he would do his duty anyway.

As the time drew near for him to head over to the station, he told Nora how nice it was for her to come to see him off. And he would look forward to seeing her when he came back in a couple of weeks on the 6th January. Nora walked across the road with him. They were like brother and sister. They said their formal goodbyes and a simple "Happy Christmas" to each other. He lit a cigarette, picked up his suitcase and boarded the train. Sean waved from the window and Nora waited till the train was out of sight. Maybe she was expecting a little more intimacy to have developed. Even so, this was another little step in their friendship, and it kept alive her hopes of more to come.

Throughout the Christmas period, Nora was at peace with the world. She imbibed the joy of the season and was attentive to Kathleen and her parents. She became the chief instigator of the entertainment within the family. With the New Year, she had remained cheerful and bright. When the news came of the death of her father's cousin in Mayo, she had taken charge and organised her mother and father for the trip. Now it was 7th January and she knew that Sean should have arrived back from Kildare the night before. She was longing to see him, to be in his presence, to talk to him. Her head was turned upside down with the possibilities of him.

So when he walked into the shop on the Friday afternoon, she was delighted and relieved to see him.

'Happy New Year, Nora! Did you enjoy the Christmas?' he asked.

'Oh, we had a nice quiet time of it in the family. I ate until I could burst.' She half regretted being so honest but ploughed on. 'Meself and Kathleen went a trip to the Burren on Saint Stephen's Day. Da let Lizzie's brother, Thomas, take the car for the day. I think he was glad to get us out of the house. So we had a grand day getting blown about and then we stopped off in Liscannor on the way back. And how was it in Kildare?'

'It was great to see everyone, especially the little ones, and them getting so excited. They had me playing at all sorts of things. I've been sleeping on the floor for a fortnight though! Now I'm back here and I need a good rest!'

'Have you been out with the Colonel already?' asked Nora.

'Well, I've been out surveying some land up near Kilshanny since nine o'clock this morning. The colonel's hobnobbing with some grandee up in Galway and has left me to it. It'll be dark soon and I've done as much as I can today.'

On the spur of the moment, Nora said:

'Would you like to have dinner with myself and Kathleen? My folks are away up in County Mayo for a funeral, and we've a good stew in the pot.'

'Well,' said Sean, 'that would be very tempting. But I know that Mrs O'Rourke is expecting me and I don't think I dare to let her down.'

Nora was a little deflated but kept smiling. Sean went on.

'I have a little idea, though. I'm going to be driving up to Ballyvaughan on Sunday to pick up some drawings from John Donohue, the Colonel's engineer. How would you and your sister like a run out for the afternoon?'

Nora would have agreed to any opportunity to spend some time with Sean. This was a very unexpected development. There might be some ructions at home to sort out first. Would Kathleen agree? Would her parents be back in time for her mother to object? Nora ignored the potential problems. It was agreed that if the girls were going, he would see them after the eleven o'clock mass on the Sunday.

Day Three - June 1975 - Mâcon

Between John and Matthew, a new plan began to emerge. From the start, Kathleen was adamant that they should leave her exactly where she was and continue on the journey without her. However, Nora would not entertain leaving her sister in the middle of a foreign country by herself, unwell and, as far as she was concerned, unable to look after herself properly. Matthew was used to handling a set of variable parameters in his job. Albeit in the mundane logical workings of a computer program as opposed to the drama that included feelings and real people. Even so, he could step back a little from the emotion and focus on the goal.

It seemed to him that the most important thing was for his mother, Nora, to be sitting in that basilica in Rome on Sunday morning before nine o'clock. John should be there too, but that was of slightly secondary importance. It was also the case that Kathleen wasn't going anywhere for at least the next twenty four hours. Moreover, and finally, none of them wanted to leave Kathleen on her own.

It was John who casually said: 'I wonder if there's a train somewhere.'

This reminded Matthew of something that his history teacher – something of both a train buff and a Francophile, it seemed – had told them. The French railways were meant to be very good. It was a big country and the French had always put a lot of emphasis on the economics of a good railway system. He looked at the map and could see the thin grey lines denoting the rail tracks. Of course, he could visualise it now. They had seen a train and tracks at different points along the N6. There was actually a line passing close to where they were currently sitting which headed into Mâcon. Then Mâcon to Lyon, and from Lyon across into Italy and Turin.

'Right,' said Matthew. 'I've got an idea.'

'We're not leaving Kathleen behind,' interrupted Nora. 'Whatever happens, I'm staying with her.'

Matthew paused. Then he spoke slowly but firmly.

'Mam, let's stop a minute. Why are we here? I don't mean … you know what I mean. Why are we in the middle of France?'

He took in a breath. 'We're on our way to Rome. More specifically, you and dad have an appointment in Rome. You need to be there before Sunday. You cannot miss it.'

'Well, I suppose,' mumbled Nora, her mind not fully focused.

'Whatever happens, you and dad need to keep on the move. It's not the same for me. Don't get me wrong. I want to be there too. But you are more important.'

'What are you thinking, Matty?' asked John encouragingly.

'Well, you said it, dad. What about the train? I reckon that you could get a train all the way to Rome if need be. We'd need to check it all out but it looks on the maps like there is a railway line from Lyon into Turin. And once you're in Italy, you're bound to be able to get to Rome.'

'But what about yourself and Kathleen?' asked John.

'That's the beauty of it, see,' said Matthew. 'I've got the motor. I can stay here with Kathleen today. Hoping she makes a recovery overnight and we can set off again tomorrow. If need be, I can drive through the night and still get to Rome in plenty of time.'

It was a hard sell to Nora. The apple cart had been truly upset. There were too many imponderables. Were there any trains? How would they manage with the language? Where would they stay overnight? What about the suitcases?

Eventually, she came round a little, at least to the point where Matthew would ask Edith for some advice. The advice was very positive. Edith telephoned one of the travel agents in Mâcon and checked out the trains to Italy. It turned out that there was a train from Lyon to Turin leaving at five o'clock that afternoon. They could get a train to Lyon from Mâcon, or Matty could drive them. The travel agent could sort out rail tickets and an overnight pensione in Turin. She could even book them on the morning train to Rome.

It was Kathleen who came to the fore and made the decision for them. Although diminished temporarily by the illness, her decisiveness had not left her.

'I'd prefer it if you all just got in the car and drove off leaving me in a bit of peace. But since that prayer isn't being answered, I want you to get your bags sorted out, Nora, and get on that train. Matty can keep me company and we'll see if I am back to fighting fit in the morning.'

And with that it was settled. Nora knew when to concede. And she did really want to get to Rome. She had to get to Rome. They had time to re-arrange the bags so that John had two of the smaller cases which were easier to manage. Nora had her handbag. She had the passports for the two of them. She also had an array of francs and lire. Matty had tried to give them both a quick lesson on the currency. He was not confident that it all went in. But then these two had Irish blood in them so he should not have any qualms about them being able to manage the money. Hadn't his mother run the family shop back home? That's what he'd been told, anyway. He ran them down into Mâcon and stood with them on the platform until the 15:09 train to Lyon began the odyssey anew for Nora and John. Matthew waved them off, head in a swirl. It wasn't meant to be like this. He found the car and dawdled back up the N6 to Le Relais Lamartine at La Salle, where Kathleen was now in residence. Edith and Pascal had said that they could have the rooms as long they wanted. Matthew hoped that they would not need them beyond tomorrow. While Kathleen rested, Matthew sat at one of the outside tables and enjoyed a couple of bottles of beer. It was freezing cold and it tasted strong. At six o'clock, he checked on Kathleen. She was awake but did not want to get up. She agreed to try eating something. So he got Pascal to make a ham sandwich and a cup of tea for her. He brought it up to her and stayed while she pecked at it.

'I'm frightened to eat it in case it sets me off again,' she said. 'I'll do what I can. That tea's lovely, though. Something hot.'

After a while, Kathleen motioned Matthew to go. 'You don't want to be sitting up here all night. You go and get yourself a meal and I'll see you in the morning.'

Matthew heeded the advice. He sat quietly in the dining room and worked his way through that day's table d'hôte dinner. And by nine o'clock, he felt it was not too early to go up to bed. If things worked out as he hoped, there would be a long day of driving ahead. He suddenly realised that he had forgotten to fill up with petrol. It would have saved a bit of time in the morning. It was too late now. He lay for a good while wondering how his mum and dad were getting on. Had they managed to change trains at Lyon? Had they arrived in Turin? Had they found the pensione? There was no way of knowing. He would simply have to have some trust. And with that easing of his mind, he drifted off into a welcome sleep.

June 1966

—~—

'Come on Matt,' said Dave Roberts. 'Give us sixpence and I'll have enough to buy a packet of five.'

'I'm skint,' was all Matthew could offer. 'Go round to Fairfield's and they'll sell you a couple of Park Drive for four pence each.'

'Hey, Danny, you got any money on you?' Dave was not giving up immediately.

Danny Kowal picked up his blue nylon tracksuit top from where it was lying on the grass forming a goal post. He unzipped the small inside pocket and took out a shiny silver sixpenny bit.'

'I want a couple of fags for myself,' he warned Dave as he handed the coin over.

Dave grabbed the money and set off for the shop. Danny and Matthew played at close passing, knocking the ball to each other with alternate lefts and rights. They gave up after a few minutes, tired from the take-on they had played with another bunch of boys earlier. They sat down on the grass to wait for Dave to return.

'Won't be long now,' said Danny seriously.

'I know that,' said Matthew. 'The shop's only five minutes away.'

'No, I mean, we'll be leaving school in a couple of weeks. I can't wait.'

Matthew had been trying to put this out of his mind. He was in a dilemma. He had been so certain that he was going to be finished with school and get out into the world. Start earning. Have some money to spend for once. Have something to give his mother.

'You got something lined up?' asked Matthew.

'Yeah, me dad's come home tonight and said he's fixed me up in the stockroom at Leah Bros down St. Catherine's Street. His mate got me in. Start the middle of July when they're back off holidays.'

'What will you be doing?' asked Matthew with interest.

'No idea really,' said Danny. 'Me dad reckons it's shifting rolls of fabric around. They come down from the knitting floor. Shouldn't be too difficult. Put a bit of muscle on, won't it? Can't be bad.'

Matthew tried to imagine what Danny was letting himself in for. It might not be difficult, but it sounded bloody boring. He had already asked Dave Roberts the same question. Dave was very proud to recount how he had been out to the big shoe machinery company on Melton Road for an interview. He'd got the job!

School Leavers wanted. Strong, adaptable youths required for factory floor operations. Opportunities to train for skilled and semi-skilled roles in the future.

What did it really amount to? Matthew guessed that it was really just a labouring job, at least to start with. He supposed that you had to start somewhere. The question was what it might or might not lead to. And what would it be like in the meantime? He looked at the example of his father. John Hoolahan was a skilled engineer. It seemed to Matthew that he had a reasonably good job as far as work in his line went. It was a job that continued to interest him every day. But that was after years of apprenticeship and continuously proving himself. And not always in the best of workplaces. Faced with the cold impending reality of having to make a decision, Matthew was beginning to realise that he actually wanted something different. Given a choice, he would not take a job in a factory. Given a choice, he would not pursue a career where you worked with your hands. Did he still have a choice?

On Sunday, Nora was up at seven o'clock, cleaning and tidying the downstairs. The small kitchen, the living room, and also the rarely used front room were the focus of her energies. She would deal with the tiny bathroom later after all the family were well out of it. Visitors were expected later in the day. It was the last thing that Nora wanted. She felt it was like an inspection. There was no way of avoiding it, however. They had received a letter two weeks before from John's brother, Joe, who lived in London. It was to warn of one of Joe and Agnes' periodic visits to see them. Nora was sure it was meant from kindness and a genuine wish to keep the family connections intact. For Nora, it was the constant burden falling on her shoulders to make things presentable, to maintain hers and the family's pride. She wanted to show their situation off in as favourable a light as she could, even when the reality was something much less.

The visitors would arrive about half past twelve. There would be time for the family to go to ten o'clock mass, have their Sunday morning fry-up, and for Nora to clear up again ready for the visitors to descend. The logistics of these visits were always a nightmare. What to feed them, when to serve up? Which room to sit in? Nora had worked out the arrangements this time well in advance. She was going to feed the children first, her own and any of their three that came with Joe and Agnes. Her mother would never have done it this way. The children would have been last. Times changed, however. Once Nora had got the children out of the way, she would serve the four adults in a more leisurely fashion. The shoulder of lamb was already on a long slow roast in the oven, its aroma filling the whole house. It was lucky that she had had a couple of weeks' notice. It meant that she had been able to manage the money to pay for the extras this week.

The red and silver Vauxhall Victor pulled up in the street at ten to one. It generated much interest from the neighbours, a few of the younger boys inspecting it closely and asking Joe how fast it went. It was just the middle son, Paul, with the parents today. The oldest, Mary, had not yet returned for the summer from her teacher training course placement. The fifteen year old, Jane, had stayed behind as she was rehearsing with the youth orchestra that she belonged to. Nora admitted to herself it was good to see them and the conversation flowed spontaneously and easily. Joe was generally the serious, earnest type. He liked to talk about politics and the big issues of the day. For all that, he also liked to tell a joke and could see the funny side of things. Agnes was a very warm motherly type, interested in the family, and ready to get her hands dirty in the kitchen. The one thing that irked Nora was the element of boastfulness that would rise to the surface at some point during any visit. Nora conceded that it was healthy to have pride in your children. But why was it necessary to show off in public about this exam and that certificate. Nora did not have anything to boast about.

At least, Agnes was happy to help Nora dish out the food for the children. Meanwhile, John and Joe disappeared for half an hour to the pub. It was a chance for the brothers to have a chat by themselves. Nora hoped that there was not bad news from home that this visit was about. A couple of drinks at the Black Horse and that was it. It was last orders at two so they were back and eating the Sunday roast by two thirty.

'Nora, I have to say that you always serve us the finest Sunday dinner.' This was Joe giving his compliments to the chef. 'The lamb was as tender as anything, and you should put a patent on your gravy.'

'Well, it'll fill a hole anyway, I hope,' said Nora, trying to deflect any praise.

'How's young Patrick getting on?' enquired Joe.

'He's going on fine, according to what they tell us,' answered Nora. 'He's just finishing the second year at the college and he'll be home at the end of the month. We went up for a visit last month. He's well settled. Loves his books.'

'It's such a blessing for all of us,' joined in Agnes. 'Imagine! A priest in the family!'

'Better not be getting ahead of ourselves.'

This was John, cautious and never wanting to tempt fate.

'There's a long way to go before he gets anywhere near Rome.'

While the parents were having their dinner, Matthew knew his task was to get all the kids out of the house for a while. Sean had already disappeared. He was almost never in the house unless it was meal time. Geraldine was playing happily in the street with her little girl friends. There was just the six year old, Martin, to keep an eye on. Matthew's default option was the park. It felt sometimes like he lived on the park. All life was there. Today, there would probably be some cricket on, as well as the informal games of football. And there was the swing park for Martin. Even though Paul was a good two years older than Matthew, he felt comfortable enough with his cousin. It was clear that Paul was happy to do anything if it got them out of the house. The three headed off. Martin skipped backwards and forwards, kicking the flyaway plastic ball that Uncle Joe had brought for him.

Paul was chatty, talking about football and the World Cup starting the following month.

'Do you think Greavesie will be playing?' he asked Matthew.

'You seen him at Spurs?' Matthew countered.

'Yeah, him and Gilzean. You want to see 'em.'

'Do you go every week?'

'Nah, I'd like to though. Been a few times this season, as it happens.'

'Are you gonna be a teacher like Mary?'

'You're kidding,' laughed Paul. 'I'm thinking about the Civil Service. But I'd really like to join the Police.'

'What does your dad think of that?'

'He wanted me to do Maths and Physics and become an engineer like him. I just scraped my Maths O level. I wouldn't know one end of a slide rule from another.'

'You're doing A levels, though, aren't you?' asked Matthew. He was keeping an eye on Martin who had wandered a good bit ahead chasing the ball.

'I'm doing Geography, History and English. As long as I pass two of them, I should be all right.'

'Do you enjoy it?' wondered Matthew.

'I just do what I have to,' said Paul. 'I've got all the crib books for English. Haven't actually read any of the Shakespeare plays. Just learn a few quotes. Geography is ok. I can do the drawings and colour in tables easily enough. History is a pain in the backside. I'll be lucky to get an E in that.'

Matthew was mulling all this over as they stood watching the cricket and occasionally looking over to where Martin was playing on the swings. They were standing more or less in line with the stumps of the match taking place on the main wicket. There were plenty of onlookers skirting the boundary. Paul seemed more interested in watching the girls out strolling for the afternoon. Then he suddenly darted off, making a bee-line towards the swing park. Matthew had been watching the bowler running up and delivering to the far end. He turned to see Martin in floods of tears. Paul was remonstrating with two kids about twelve or thirteen. He had the flyaway ball in his hands and he was giving the two a good bollocking. They looked scared. As soon as Paul turned away from them to check Martin, they ran.

'It's all over,' said Paul, crouching down and speaking kindly to Martin. 'Here's your ball. I've sorted those two b's out. They won't be bothering you again.'

Martin had dry eyes now and was smiling again. He pulled Paul by the hand. He wanted to go on the grass now and kick the ball with him. Matthew came over and joined in the kick about. Jimmy Greaves was nowhere to be seen.

Matthew reckoned Paul was ok. He was a good cousin to have. He obviously had a good heart, he was confident, and he was pretty sociable. It struck Matthew, however, that Paul was definitely not the brightest person he had ever met. There were loads of kids at school who were much cleverer. Paul definitely had something. Maybe it was that self-belief of his, pure and simple. He would get into the Civil Service if he applied. Or more likely, he would succeed at what he really wanted and be accepted into the Police. And what about himself? If Paul could contemplate passing some A levels, surely Matthew could manage a couple of O levels.

By the time they returned to the house, Martin was full of how Paul had seen off some horrible boys who wanted to steal his ball. He was the hero of the day. He got an especially large piece of cake from Nora for his troubles. Plus a good pat on the back from his uncle John. The visitation came to a close shortly after half past five. Nora breathed a sigh of relief as the car pulled away. When it had finally disappeared around the bottom corner, they all went back inside for the post mortem. John disappeared swiftly for a very late afternoon siesta. Nora flopped back on the sofa. Matthew stayed to talk to her while Geraldine and Martin went back out onto the street to play. There was no sign of Sean as usual.

'Are you all right, mam?' asked Matthew.

'I'm fine,' said Nora. 'They were very nice. We had a good craic about the old days and the shenanigans at home. It's just the thought of them coming. That's the worst part of it.'

'Uncle Joe gave me five bob before he left.'

'He's always been very generous to us.'

'I've been thinking,' began Matthew. 'I've been thinking about school.'

Nora perked up at this. Matthew hardly ever wanted to speak about school.

'And?' she looked hard at him.

'Well, how would you feel if I stayed on next year to do my O levels?'

'Praise be to God! Whatever has come over you? That's what I've been praying for this last year. All that talk about leaving and getting a job. It wasn't agreeing with me at all.'

'But I still won't be earning anything and you'll have to keep me.'

'Don't you be bothering your head about that. We've managed this far and we'll be grand.'

Nora sat back and closed her eyes. This moment of inner contentment was one to be savoured. She would be back in the fray soon enough.

Day Four - June 1975 - La Reprise

Matthew turned over in the bed. What was that? He heard it again. It was a knock at the door. He instinctively threw off the covers and went over to open it. It was Kathleen.

'Can I come in and speak to you?' She bustled past him and flopped down on the little side chair by the window.

'Look, Matty, I wanted to tell you. I don't want to hold you up,' she began. 'I'm definitely on the mend. I've kept that sandwich down from last night and I'm starting to feel a good bit less achy. But I'm nowhere near A1 at Lloyds.'

'Do you think you'll be ok to get back on the road?' asked Matthew. He had not quite grasped what Kathleen was leading up to.

'The way I'm feeling,' she said, 'I wouldn't be wanting to travel hundreds of miles in the car. I think that age has caught up with me at last. I'm well past my prime, if you didn't already know it. I would dearly love to be in Rome on Sunday, such a proud occasion, such an honour. I've had plenty of time to think this through. I've just come to accept that it's not meant to be. There's been a lot worse things, so don't you start. It's not the end of the world. And sure, can't I be there in spirit if not in the flesh?'

'What are you saying, Kathleen – I mean, Aunty Kathleen? I'm not leaving you here on your own. Mam would kill me. And you don't want that on your conscience, surely?'

'I'll deal with your mam when and if I have to,' replied Kathleen, her normal determination returning for this conversation. 'I'll tell you what's to be done. I'm staying put, confined to barracks. I've got that book your mam gave me to keep me company. I've got a lovely bed to rest up in. I've got Edith and Pascal waiting on me, hand and foot. You need to get in that car of yours and get yourself back on the road to Italy. I'm sorry I can't keep you company and that you'll be on your own. I know you well, though. You'll be as happy as Larry, out on the open road. You're sensible and smart, and a good driver.'

Matthew was sitting on the bed. He hadn't expected this. Could he just up and leave? Nora would say no. Then there was the prospect of completing the drive on his own. In truth, driving alone was one of his special delights. However, there was still another six hundred and fifty miles to go, and he hadn't even seen what the Italian roads were like yet. He looked at his watch. It had only just turned a quarter to seven.

'Are you adamant that you can't go on?'

'You've hit the nail on the head, Matty. I am adamant.'

'It's still early. Are you sure you wouldn't want to get freshened up, have some breakfast and see how you feel then?'

'You said it. I am adamant.' And she laughed at herself. 'Just look at the cut of me. I'll be back to normal in a day or two, with the help of God. Just not today.'

Matthew showered and went downstairs. He was starving. Over the course of filling up on coffee, croissant, bread and jam, he tried to explain to Edith what Kathleen was proposing. Edith did not seem unduly surprised. She made it clear that Kathleen was welcome to stay with them for as long as it took. Matthew needed to be with his parents on Sunday, so of course he should move on. Matthew sorted out payment of what they owed so far with Edith. It all seemed so reasonable when you paid in francs. He went back upstairs, sorted out the suitcases, and was ready to leave by half past eight. He went along to Kathleen's room. Kathleen was sitting up in bed, book in hand. Matthew could see it was one of his mother's little collection, *The Last September* by Elizabeth Bowen.

'Any good?' he enquired, more out of politeness rather than any real interest.

'Your mam says it is fierce,' she replied. 'Nora knows a good book when she sees it. I've only read a couple of pages so far but I'm sure I'm going to love it.'

'I've come to see if you have changed your mind,' said Matthew.

'I have not,' retorted Kathleen. 'Now get along with you. I'm expecting you to come back for me, of course! Any idea when that might be?'

Matthew had to think. 'Yeah, of course we'll be back. If we get away ok on Tuesday and the roads are ok, we should be back here on Wednesday evening. Ready to roll on Thursday.'

'I'll be speaking the lingo by the time you get back,' laughed Kathleen. 'Or I'll be a goner.'

'That's not funny. You better look after yourself or it will be my head on the block.'

Kathleen looked at Matthew. Then she remembered.

'Can you remind me about the money here, Matty? How much have I got?'

He quickly went over all matters "francs" and explained how much the room and the meals were costing in Le Relais. Kathleen had been saving up for the past year for this trip. As ever, she had not stinted when it came to something she thought important. She never wanted to be short in public. So there had been a lot of currency exchanged. The only problem was that she had a lot of lire as well, which wasn't going to be much use in France. When it came to it, though, Matthew was certain she had more than enough French francs to keep her going for the next six days. Unless she started giving it away – which was always a possibility with Kathleen.

'Now, you be watching out for yourself. You hear plenty of tales of robbers in these parts. Italian bandits, crooks the lot of them.'

Kathleen pronounced the *I* in Italian as the first person pronoun *I* is sounded.

'And don't be getting involved with any of those dolly birds with their skirts barely covering their backside. Excuse my language! You remember where you're going and say a prayer to St. Christopher to keep you safe. And St. Anthony while you're at it – he'll keep you on the right track.'

Matthew was holding back his blushes. His mother would never speak to him like this. Aunty Kathleen was kind and generous and loving, and she also spoke her mind without fear or compromise.

'I'd better get moving. You can see me off from the window. Make sure you look after yourself.'

There was no embrace, no hug, and no little kiss. They just didn't do that. And he was gone.

January 1949

—⁓—

It rained all night on the Saturday. There was a storm blowing off the sea, firing a continual barrage of heavy gusts at the house. The solid stone walls remained unmoved, but the wind found its way in through the crevices at the roof and windows, playing a series of low semi-musical notes just about worthy of a piper warming up his instrument. The rain lashed across the windows. The darkness was all consuming. Inside there was a good peat fire glowing in the fireplace, radiating warmth and giving off its heady scent. Kathleen and Nora were oblivious to the weather. They were used to west coast life. All they were hoping for was that the storm would blow itself out by the morning so that the planned trip out to Ballyvaughan could go ahead. It would be no fun driving up there in a gale.

It had not taken much to get Kathleen to agree. Nora had made out that it was just a chance for the two of them to get away from the normal humdrum for a few hours.

Kathleen sensed that there was more to it than that but said nothing. She was happy to go along with her sister. From a selfish point of view, she knew inwardly that she should get out more. She had sunk into a deep pit of melancholy and she was capable of so much more. Kathleen needed to take these chances when they arrived, even if it was just an innocent drive in a motor car. The parents were not due back until the Monday, so any objections that they might raise would have to be made in retrospect. Nora smiled as she contemplated this.

Once they had eaten their meal and were sitting back in front of the fire with a cup of tea and the remains of the Christmas cake, the girls drifted from small talk about the shop and the factory into a more serious conversation. As mature and worldly as she thought herself, Nora was jolted upright as Kathleen, without any prompting, started to muse about the future.

'Do you ever think about leaving this old place? Seek your fortune in distant lands?'

Nora was not sure whether Kathleen was just trying the idea out on herself, being deliberately provocative, or deadly serious. She waited to hear more. Kathleen continued to ponder on the subject. It was almost as if she were talking to herself.

'I look at myself. A widow woman at twenty-four. A factory hand. What are my prospects? You tell me.'

Nora had to think quickly how to reply.

'Don't be so hard on yourself. You've had terrible hard luck. I can't know how much it hurts losing Peter. But I know you. You are strong. You're young. You're not just a factory hand. You'll be running that place one day if you want to.'

'I suppose that's the point,' said Kathleen. 'Do I want to?'

The noise of the storm outside and the crackling of the fire inside could not mask the silence that fell between them. Then Kathleen went on.

'I'm telling you this now but you're sworn to secrecy. D'ye hear me?'

Nora nodded, wondering what was to come next. Kathleen pressed on:

'I've been thinking about this for a while now. You know I've been writing on and off to Mary Lavelle, Peter's cousin. She went over to Leicester last year with her big sister, Pat. We were good friends down in Liscannor. She keeps telling me how good it is over in England. They're crying out for workers, including women. Pat's the clever one and she's working in a lawyer's office. Mary herself walked straight into a great job in one of the engineering factories. She's earning good wages and is loving it. They're still on the rationing over there, of course, but she said everybody has ways round it. She keeps saying I should get on the boat and join her. I'm not kidding myself that everything would be perfect. The grass is always greener, so they say, but I'm not an eejit. To be honest, I'm beyond caring. I just know that I have to move on from this, from what I've become. If I don't do something, I'll slowly suffocate. So, my mind's made up.'

Nora was concentrating, staring at her sister, taking it all in. Finally, she knew what to say.

'I would never have guessed what you were thinking. And now that you've said it, I know it makes sense. I – we – what will we do without you?'

Nora was starting to smile and giggle as she said this.

'What an adventure? What an excitement? And what will "they" say? Anyway, that's not your problem.'

Kathleen took this up.

'Ma will not dare say anything to me. She knows that I'm beyond all that. Da will worry but he'll give me his blessing.'

'Have you decided when?' asked Nora.

'Probably in a month or two. Mary says it will be better to wait till the Spring. And I need to make all my arrangements. So, not a word of this to anyone until I say so.'

'I won't tell a soul,' said Nora.

The fire was burning low. Kathleen stood up and threw in a turf with a feeling of satisfaction and renewed vigour running through her.

Nora changed the subject deftly.

'You've not changed your mind about tomorrow?'

'Certainly, I have not! It'll do us both good to get out of the house. As long as the Sean one is a decent enough driver.'

'I can't guarantee that,' laughed Nora.

The next morning was a scramble in the Gallagher house. Nora was up early, getting herself ready, changing her outfit twice before finally settling on her practical tweeds and old rain coat. The weather had improved from last night, but this was Ireland in January. Kathleen ate her breakfast leisurely and would not be hurried. They made it into the third row from the back just as the priest began to intone 'In Nomine Patris …' Nora would not remember any more of that mass until she heard the farewell 'Ite, missa est'. Then the slow exit amongst the crowd of worshippers, several greetings from friends, relatives, acquaintances. The casual drift down the hill away from the church, seeing Sean on the corner of Monastery Lane, cigarette in mouth, leaning back on the bonnet of a muddy black two door Ford Anglia.

'How are you?' he called over to them. 'You must be Kathleen.'

And then as an after thought, 'What did you think of yer man?'

Kathleen liked the question. She had little time for Father Rodgers, who seemed to like to make everybody's life as much a misery as his own.

'He's what you'd call an acquired taste is all I'll say. I don't want to be hearing about nuclear bombs killing us all off so we'd better get praying now! Not every Sunday.'

'You're right about that,' said Sean. 'Let's get moving and we can talk about more pleasant things.'

They got into the car. Kathleen squeezed into the back seat, Nora taking up the front passenger berth. Sean fired up the engine, lit another cigarette, took a draw and pulled off down Main Street heading towards Kilfenora.

'I thought we'd take the country roads on the way up to Ballyvaughan. And if the weather stays calm, we can come back the scenic route by the coast. How does that suit you?'

'That's grand,' shouted Kathleen from the rear, before Nora could get a word in.

Kathleen then proceeded to fire a series of questions at Sean, and he answered readily and with good humour. How old was he, what school did he go to, how many brothers and sisters did he have, what did his father do for a living? And that was just for starters. Nora sat quietly, at moments feeling some embarrassment at the onslaught, at other times acutely interested to find out things that she did not yet know about Sean O'Callaghan. After a while of this, Kathleen seemed to be satisfied with the answers and started on a different tack.

'Do you remember the family Kelleher from along the Kilcornan Road? There were the three girls and the young boy? The father was a decent man but he just couldn't make their bit of land pay. Even mother felt sorry for them. I remember she handed some of our old rags to the missus one Christmas, and they were delighted. Can you remember them?' Kathleen repeated, wanting some acknowledgement before she went on.

'I do, I do,' said Nora. 'The little boy had the real red hair. What ages would they be, those girls?'

'I think the oldest would be about seventeen,' said Kathleen. 'Anyway, let me tell you. They packed up everything and went off about two years ago. Peg from work was telling me. She heard from her own cousin who's away in Leicester. Anyway, that's just where the Kellehers have settled. Kelleher himself has a job in a knitting factory of all places. The two oldest girls are both working as well, and the mother has a small job in a school kitchen. So, according to Peg, they're raking it in. And good luck to them!'

'Indeed, good luck to them!' repeated Sean. 'It's heartening to hear a story like that. Sometimes you've to take the bull by the horns, haven't you?'

Nora knew the undercurrent to Kathleen's story. It was another step towards convincing herself that she should also be taking the bull by the horns. And it was a good story. Making good in a foreign land. A lot of people dreamed of it.

They were well past Lisdoonvarna and in the vicinity of Toomaghera. Sean proudly pointed out where he had helped in the job of straightening out a bend in the road the previous year.

'That's what I'm good at,' he cackled, 'straightening things out.'

'Well, I wouldn't mind straightening my legs,' said Kathleen. 'How much further would you say?'

'Just another six or seven miles,' said Sean. 'We'll be at Corkscrew Hill shortly and then it's another ten minutes. Donohue said he'd come down to the hotel about half past one. We can kill two birds with one stone. I can speak to Donohue and get the blueprints from him. And then I'm looking forward to treating you girls to a nice lunch. How does that sound?'

Before Nora could say anything, Kathleen jumped in.

'Now that sounds like a good plan.'

Donohue had joined them for a drink and a sandwich lunch. He was older than them, about forty, in between their parents' generation and their own. A dry sense of humour, and a fountain of funny stories. Kathleen could hardly contain herself. For the journey home, Nora took the back seat to save Kathleen's complaints. Sean decided that it was a bit late to go back via the coast. He did not want to risk losing the daylight on the wild wintry roads. So, the compromise was to return the way they had come towards Lisdoonvarna, and then head out to the coast at Doolin. There they were able to stop off for half an hour to stretch their legs and wonder at the crashing waves washing in from the Atlantic. Hair blown everywhere, cheeks rosy red, the girls piled back into the car. They were back through Kilshanny and into Main Street before they had got their breath back.

The daylight had faded now and the car's headlights struggled to pierce the growing darkness. Sean stopped at the corner of Monastery Lane. Kathleen was telling him what a great day it had been. She stepped out smartly, telling Nora that she would hurry on up to the house and get the kettle on. And with that she was gone. Nora shuffled around in the back seat, making to get out of the car. Sean turned to her and said:

'Nora, there's something I want to say to you. Will you come in the front here, it'll be easier to speak.'

Nora was wondering what all this was leading to. Was it really happening? She changed seats, heart pounding, head in a swoon.

'I've wanted to tell you this for a while,' said Sean. 'I was trying that day you saw me off on the train.'

Nora could only mutter, 'Go on, go on.'

'Do you remember that time I was getting writing paper in the shop?'

She nodded.

'I'm not sure how to say this.' He was stumbling a little, a flush on his cheeks.

'Look, I'll just spit it out. I've been accepted to All Hallows College in Dublin.'

Nora's brain went into overdrive. All Hallows. She'd heard something about it. Wasn't that a seminary? My god, she thought, he's going to be a priest. She was all mixed up. Those feelings that she had been harbouring. Now they suddenly felt wrong. How could she have? But they were real. And she could not escape an intense disappointment. Her dreams were thwarted. An axe had been taken to them. What could she say? She composed herself. She started to distance herself.

'Sean, I'm lost for words,' she said, honest and true to herself as ever. 'I had no clue.'

Sean looked straight at her.

'Nora, I'm not stupid. I have an inkling that you have had feelings towards me. And, I'm no saint either. I confess that I have had feelings for you. I have feelings for you. For whatever reason, you have come to mean a great deal to me. I think it is a love of some sort. But I'm no expert in these things. And the truth is that I have been called to the priesthood. I don't know how or why. I was never interested in it when all those boys at school were taken off to the colleges. Something has happened to me. I can't explain it. I just hope that you will understand.'

Nora was close to tears. Even with her own hopes smashed to pieces, she could not help feel a new sort of love for this vulnerable courageous man. She took his hands in hers and said softly:

'Sean, you have to do what you have to do. I'll say my prayers for you. This is my one chance to tell you that I have felt a love for you that I have never felt before for anyone. That love will never flower now in the way that I might have hoped. I'll still love you but in a different way. You'll still be a dear, dear friend, will you not?'

She was making it easy for him, and he knew it.

'Of course, Nora. Of course. I would want that, of course.'

Day Four - June 1975 - Lyon

'Hello.'

It was a long drawn out "Hell-ohhh".

'Hello, there!'

It came again. Matthew looked up from under the bonnet of the car. He was on the forecourt of a petrol station. A few miles south of Lyon. He had had the car filled up with "essence" and he was just having a quick check to see whether there were any obvious signs of oil leaks or water dripping from the radiator or hoses. He wasn't sure what he would do if he found anything. He would get some comfort though if it all looked ok.

A yard or two away towards the driver's door stood a pretty girl. Long brown hair. Slim. Fresh-faced. Smiling. Average height, he thought, about five foot four. She was wearing a white T-shirt with some writing across the front, faded blue jeans, and brown leather sandals. Matthew's first thought was "student". Certainly not one of Aunty

Kathleen's dolly birds.

Matthew debated in his head whether he should think of her as a "girl" or a "woman". The language mattered. He knew that from reading the Sunday papers. He couldn't make his mind up. His mates usually talked about meeting "girls". The London lads spoke familiarly about the "gels". On the other hand, his cousin who had been to university only ever spoke about the "women" at college. In his own mind, in this instance, he was tending to favour "girl" to describe the person talking to him. It wasn't intended as a put down. Precisely the opposite, in fact. "Girl" was good. It emphasised youthfulness, openness, a woman at the start of her adult journey. Matthew did not have a problem using the word "woman". It was simply that for him "woman" felt more appropriate for an older person, a more obviously mature female. What did he know? The person in front of him was what might otherwise have been described as a "young lady". She was a fully grown adult. Not a child. But a young, youthful adult. "Girl" or "Woman". Take your pick.

'Are you English?' she said. 'I saw the number plates on your car and I was wondering …' she tailed off leaving Matthew to answer.

'Yeah, you're not wrong.' And as soon as he said it, he wished that it had come out differently. It did not sound very friendly. It was an attempt at light-hearted humour. Maybe not everyone would appreciate it. Even so, she was still smiling and continued her friendly enquiry.

'Where do you hail from?'

Even a little word could tell someone a lot about you, thought Matthew. He knew what she was asking but it struck him that he could hardly think of anyone who would use the word "hail" nowadays. Apart perhaps from the manager of his bank, an old public school military type. He smiled inwardly, glad that he had acquired a half decent vocabulary through the grammar school, his love of reading, and his experience of mixing with a few different types at work and in London.

'I'm originally from the Midlands – Leicester – but I've been living in London for the last few years. What about yourself?'

'I'm a student at uni. Oxford actually. My parents live in Hampshire.'

'Are you on holiday or something?' asked Matthew.

'Yes, that's it. Actually, I'm with a friend from college. We've had a couple of weeks in France. Mostly in Paris. What a dream? All the museums and the galleries. And, of course, the "ambience". We had a couple of days in Lyon and that has been marvellous. Now we're making our way to Italy.'

She was gushing. Plenty to say. Full of energetic enthusiasm for everything. Matthew scratched his head. He knew what was coming next. Was he ready for it? Did he want two strangers in the car for the next several hundred miles? Especially if they were rather posh ones. On the other hand, wouldn't it be very pleasant to have the company of others, particularly if the company was female? He knew he shouldn't think like that, even though he knew it was perfectly natural. He suddenly wondered about "the friend".

'Where is your friend, by the way?' he asked.

‘Oh, we’ve been having breakfast in that little café and Katerina is paying a visit to “les toilettes”. She’ll be here any second now.’

So, he registered that it was two girls rather than a boy and girl.

More or less on cue, a second person emerged from the café that formed a part of the service station shop. The first thing that struck him was the large thick-soled walking boots that she was wearing. Along with denim shorts – hand cut from a pair of jeans – and a check blouse or country style shirt. She was taller than the first girl, and had a fuller figure. Long thick dark hair, attractive tanned complexion, a warm engaging smile of perfectly formed white teeth. She marched over with her hand held out to shake Matthew’s hand. She seemed full of self-confidence. A lot more than Matthew felt he could ever muster. And he wasn’t exactly a shrinking violet.

‘I’m Katerina, and you are?’

For a brief second, Matthew had the same feeling of awkwardness that he had frequently experienced with assertive types when he was younger, especially early on at the grammar school. He had grown up a lot since then and could usually handle himself in most situations. The fact that it was a young attractive woman – or possibly “girl” – made this situation a little different. Was he simply lacking the worldly experience or conditioning to deal with these strong types of entitled women? Was it perhaps an instinctive deference to class that had kicked in. He wasn’t used to joshing along in the company of the more privileged classes. And certainly these were not the kind of girls that he mixed with back home, even in the briefest encounters in pubs or clubs. He felt some strength at least in the fact that he recognised who he was dealing with.

'Oh, I'm Matthew. Pleased to meet you. I've been talking to your pal, your friend here. Actually, I didn't get your name.'

They both said, 'It's Emily.' And then burst out laughing.

Katerina stopped laughing and began in a more earnest tone. She had a deep and slightly husky voice. She enunciated her words loudly and clearly.

'I say, Matthew, is it possible that you are heading south? And if so, could we possibly trouble you for a lift?'

'Where exactly are you heading?' asked Matthew.

'We're pretty flexible, actually,' jumped in Emily. 'We've not got any set deadlines. We'd like to get to Rome in the next week or so. Meander down Italy, see Florence, Pisa. Maybe Venice, although that's on the other side. And they say it is ultra expensive. We are the epitome of flexibility really.'

Matthew already knew that he wasn't going to turn them down. He wanted to get moving so he explained quickly where he was going.

'I'm heading to Rome and I hope to do it in the next two days. The plan is to get past Turin today and then drive another full day tomorrow down the main A1 via Bologna, Florence and the rest. You're welcome to go all the way if you want.'

They both giggled and Matthew realised how that had sounded.

'You know what I mean,' he said a little coldly.

It was Katerina who quickly gathered herself.

'That sounds absolutely splendid. It gives us lots of options. We'd be ever so grateful.'

March 1949

—∾—

Margaret Pickering was giving John a last hug before the train departed. He held her firmly and spoke quietly.

'You're so lovely. I could take you home with me right now. And never let you go.'

She smiled joyfully as she repeated the hug.

'I think I am in love with you,' she said softly, almost to herself.

Since Christmas, they had moved on from being just friends within their broader social circle. They had become girl friend and boy friend. They still only saw each other once or at most twice a week, but they were being drawn ever closer in a romantic swirl around each other. They liked each other very much. John was touched by Margaret's genuine goodness, her free spirit, her openness. Margaret loved his wry sense of humour, his quiet confidence, and his caring nature. She was also excited to touch him and feel his strong muscular body, but she tried hard to dampen these new and unexplored feelings in case she was struck down by a bolt from heaven.

'Come on, then, you'd better get on the train. It's about to leave.'

'I'll be back next Friday and I'll see you on Saturday.'

'I hope you will be all right. It's a horrible thought to be going to a funeral.'

'Ah, it cannot be undone. She's gone, and that's all there is to it. I'll be fine.'

With that, he climbed up the step into the carriage, touched her hand one last time, and pulled the door shut. The whistle sounded, the steam rose, and the engine staggered into life, chugging with deep breaths as it pulled the long train slowly out of the station. Margaret stood and waved till it was out of sight.

John found a compartment with an empty seat. He threw his case onto the rack and sat back. Eyes closed, thinking about Margaret, thinking about his mother and father and all the rest of the family that he would be seeing very soon for the first time since he had left for England. The circumstances were not the best. His grandmother had been unwell throughout the winter and had finally succumbed just when the weather was picking up. She had lived to a good age, and yet it was still a sad end. He had been frightened of granny most of his life. He wasn't exactly sure why. He respected her though, and latterly had understood better how hard her early life must have been. And she had always had a devilish sense of humour which was fine when it was not directed at you.

When he came out of his swoon, the guard was asking for his ticket. John asked him how long to Holyhead. It was another hour to the boat, one more step in the tortuous journey ahead. The prospect of a night sailing, arriving in Dun Laoghaire around six in the morning. A ride into Dublin's main station and then hopefully the nine o'clock train down the country to Athenry. Another train to Ennis. Finally, the ambling West Clare line around the houses to Ennistymon and Lahinch.

Just after eight o'clock the next evening, he stepped onto the platform to be greeted by his sister Theresa and brother Paul with the pony and trap. They embraced each other, half in joy, and half in sadness at the thought of granny lying in the house waiting to be buried in the morning. Theresa broke the silence and asked John a dozen questions before he could answer one. It would be a long night for his homecoming.

At the wake, the house was full of the neighbours plus family both close and distant. There were murmurs of disapproval that his eldest brother, Joseph, had not made it back for the funeral. That put John in something of a good light. His mother held onto him in the scullery, tearful with the joy of his return. The rest of them took comfort in being able to divert the gloominess of the occasion into a more joyful line of conversation, asking him about England and Coventry, work and money, drinking and dancing. His father took him to one side and asked if he was getting on all right. This was a rare event as the father normally had little conversation. There was no acrimony between them. Simply, the father was a man of few words altogether, and the relationship was mostly one of filial deference. John was not a natural rebel. His chosen way through life – whether pre-determined for him or acquired from his experiences – was quiet determination, a readiness to compromise to save relationships, and a reluctance to burn bridges even if he sometimes really wanted to. Father and son understood each other well enough without having to speak. John reassured the old man that things were going fine over in Coventry. And that was that.

Only Theresa and his other sister, Patricia, were bold enough to ask if he had a girl yet over there. The men were too shy, embarrassed or probably not interested enough to follow this line. They wanted to know about the jobs, the pay, and the drink. The girls, on the other hand, seemed to have a sixth sense. John gave nothing away. He just said he had a habit of going to the dancing with Tommy and a few other boys on a Saturday, and he tried to leave it at that. It was nearly the truth. Then Patricia and Theresa wanted to know what the girls wore at the dancing, what were the latest dresses they were wearing, what about the hairstyles, and the shoes. John thought that they must be getting carried away with seeing too many films from America. Eventually he convinced them that he had exhausted all his knowledge of women's fashion in England. This proved to be very little and a bit disappointing for them.

The funeral had taken place on the Saturday. John had booked to start his return to England the following Thursday. He had not wanted to rush away, especially as he had not been home since August. So he had a few days to relax and remind himself what he had left behind all those months ago. On Sunday, the family went to eleven o'clock mass. He met some of his old school pals outside and they chatted away, laughing at some of the antics they had got up to and their general stupidity at school. He learned that one of his old classmates at the secondary, Tommy Fenlon, was planning to emigrate to Canada. He had some family already over in Newfoundland. A much older second cousin was running a timber yard and he was going to get Tommy started there. Timber must have been in the family genes because Tommy had been training as a carpenter. John wished him all the best and insisted that it would be a good move.

Mr Lynch, his old boss from the garage, made a point of coming over to speak to John. A few months earlier, John would have found it difficult to be civil. It had been a big shock when he had found out that they were not going to keep him on at the garage when he had served his time. However, in a fairly short matter of time he had come to terms with the situation and he was now secretly glad. Although the situation in Coventry was not perfect, John had experienced so much in the last few months that he would never contemplate turning the clock back. It was not all good experience, but what he had really found was an independence that he didn't know he was entitled to.

Hughie Gallagher, who ran the General Store in Main Street, also greeted him warmly. Mr Gallagher had a bit of money, although he did not brag about it. He knew John as he ran an old Ford motor car that had often spent time in Lynch's garage. Mr Gallagher confided in John.

'You know, John, that car has never run the same since you left the garage. Anyhow, I hope you are making your fortune over yonder.'

'Thank you, Mr Gallagher.'

'John, you'll be acquainted with my wife, Marie? And my youngest, Nora?'

'Pleased to meet you. Yes, I know Mrs Gallagher from the Store. Is Nora about ages with my sister Patricia? Would that be right?'

Nora, who had been looking a bit sullen, piped up. 'Yes, we were in class together at the primary. Then I went on to the nuns, and Trish went to the vocational secondary.'

'Yes, Nora's got a good head on her,' Mr Gallagher went on. 'She has her Leaving Certificate, you know. She's a mighty appetite for the literature. And she's a dab hand with the other kind of books – you know, the important ones with the money!'

He chuckled and took a large draw on the cigarette burning away in his right hand.

'You're helping me out in the Store, aren't you Noreen?' playfully teasing her with the diminutive form of her name.

'What am I saying? She'll be running the whole damn show before I know it. Well, it's very good to see you, John. Take care and please give our sincerest condolences to your mother and father.'

John watched them walk away. He could not stop himself from looking at the trio as they walked down the road. Particularly the Nora one. He could only remember her as one of the many kids in Patricia's class at the primary school. She had certainly grown up. She was very pretty, you might say really handsome. Beautiful perhaps. A fresh West coast complexion, a broad strong face, long glossy dark hair, full lips, and an innocent honest smile. And a shapely figure despite the limitations of the rather heavy drab cloth that made up her Sunday best outfit. He quickly turned his mind to Margaret back in Coventry, waving him off a few days before. He would see her soon enough.

Day Four - June 1975 - Grenoble

And so it was decided. It was already well past ten o'clock now. The girls each had a large unwieldy rucksack which Matthew managed to shoehorn into the boot. Katerina took up the navigator's seat. And they were off.

After the initial uncertainties of the encounter and the necessary re-organisation to accommodate his new passengers, Matthew was trying hard to focus on the driving. He could feel that he was distracted by the unexpected turn of events and he hoped to re-find his composure from the comfort of the driver's seat. For the first thirty miles or so, he switched off from the hubbub of voices surrounding him and concentrated on the road, his speed, the other traffic, and the passing countryside. The car was driving beautifully. The engine was giving out that lovely bass V6 thrum of noise which always gave him the impression of limitless power and energy.

Beside him and from the rear seat, the girls were full of

chatter. Matthew only half listened while they sorted out various practicalities involving shared expenditure and who had paid for what. It let him focus on making sure he correctly joined the N85 from the N6 at Bourgoin-Jallieu. This was the road to Grenoble and what the book described as the "gateway" to the Alps. Matthew was still unsure what to expect. What would the road be like? Would it be very steep gradients? His only experience of mountain country consisted of a day trip to Snowdonia with the school when he was fourteen. And then he had seen little to excite him through the rain splattered windows of the bus. The Alps was just something you heard about on the television or in the papers when there was an avalanche.

In the background, the chatter had drifted into some arcane talk amongst Katerina and Emily about their "vac reading lists", "end of term collections", "hall", and some mysterious thing called "the JCR". Matthew did not register a lot of boyfriend talk although there was a steady flow of bitchiness and supercilious comments about what he supposed were friends, or friends of friends.

Matthew was more relaxed by the time that the road signs started to show Grenoble as the principal destination. The latest one told him that it was another sixty three kilometres. That meant it should be under an hour away given how the roads were looking. Eventually his curiosity got the better of him. He also realised that he should try to be a bit more friendly to his fellow travellers. He tentatively began a conversation when there was a brief lull in the girls' verbal sparring. He was actually interested to know what they were studying. The girls were delighted to entertain him. He learned quickly that Emily was "reading" foreign languages, specifically French and Italian. Matthew smiled to himself when he heard this. It was something of a bonus. His Italian was non-existent. He had been wondering how he would manage when they got to Italy. A bit of help was now at hand. He immediately felt pleased that he had taken the girls on. Katerina was studying English.

They were both aged twenty and had just completed their second year at Somerville College. Emily's background was comfortably middle class. Of course, she herself did not think of it like that. Her dad was a doctor, her mother had been a midwife. Emily had gone to a very good "all girls" school somewhere in Hampshire. Actually, a convent school. That was interesting. Every where you went you could find a Catholic. Shared religious culture was a powerful bond but Matthew was wise enough to know that there were lots of different types of Catholic. In his head, a major area of distinction could be put down simply to different ethnicities – to start with, Irish versus English. At the same time, he knew well that differences existed between different social classes. He only had to think of some of the wealthier in the congregation back home. And, more obviously, between the intellectual Jesuits at the Sacred Heart in the centre of the city and the more humble parish priests in the likes of St. Patrick's and Our Lady's in the suburbs.

Still, he felt an immediate warming towards Emily as they would inevitably have some common understanding you might never get with a non-Catholic. It also transpired that Emily played the violin and had been a member of the county youth orchestra. She had a quiet innate awareness of her own value and worth. Matthew had seen this before in the affluent classes. She wasn't brazen about it but she was all the same clearly not one to hide her light under a bushel.

Katerina, it appeared, had an even more privileged upbringing in the West Country, from which flowed a relaxed self-confidence mixed with a steely determination. Or maybe it was just selfishness. Her parents were both senior members in a law firm, apparently from a dynasty of lawyers with landed gentry connections. She had attended Cheltenham Ladies' College. Matthew had heard of that. The pressure for her to follow the law was lessened by her older brother doing just that. She clearly had a flair for the arts that her parents did not really understand. They were indulgent enough to allow it to flourish though. Matthew thought back to what he was like at twenty years old. These girls seemed light years more mature than him. They were already behaving more like matriarchs than any other girls that he could think of. They were twenty going on fifty, it seemed. Matthew was inclined to think that what they said and the way they spoke was a well practised imitation of their mothers. They switched topics of conversation effortlessly. From the mundane cost of yesterday's baguette to the finer points of German Expressionism.

Matthew listened intently. He did enjoy meeting new people, having conversations, hearing their stories. It often took him a while to warm up, especially with people of a certain social order. He was also acutely conscious that he tended to be much more relaxed in the company of men rather than women. He couldn't put his finger on it. He had had a few different girl friends over the years, none that developed into anything very serious though. At work he had colleagues who were friends and who happened to be women. He did actually feel comfortable around women most of the time, especially once he got to know them. He wanted to think of himself as reasonably experienced. But maybe the reality was that he was quite inexperienced at least in some aspects of life. There was definitely some innate deference to the fairer sex, something in his makeup which tended to place women and girls on a bit of a pedestal or a little beyond his reach. Was it the nuns at junior school, or the Irish sub-culture, or the all boys' grammar school that had marked him in this way? Probably all of them if he thought about it long enough.

He fiddled with the air vents. He thought the car was getting stuffy. The sun was bright and it was hot inside the car. He got some more air circulating. He did not want to open the window. They were travelling quite fast and he hated road noise. He had noticed that he was getting a musty body odour smell every time he looked to his left. He suddenly felt emboldened.

'Do you mind if I ask you something?' he said directly to Katerina.

'By all means. Fire away.'

'Well, don't take this the wrong way. But how many days have you been wearing that shirt?'

Emily burst out laughing in the back.

'I told you,' she screamed. 'She's what we call a bit of a tramp when she wants to be. Aren't you, my dear Katerina? Ask her how long she's been wearing some of her other garments.'

Emily could hardly contain herself. She managed to splutter some additional advice amidst a fit of giggles.

'I wouldn't risk being in the same room as her when she takes those boots off!'

Katerina was unmoved, completely unruffled.

'Are you getting a bit of a whiff?' she asked. Then she laughed. 'It's probably just the pheromones.'

That went over Matthew's head. He wanted to keep this light but make the point.

'More like old sweat, you mean. It reminds me of the changing rooms at football on Sundays. I would normally offer the "LifeBuoy" recommendation.'

Everyone laughed at that.

Katerina admitted. 'Ok, I get it. But people shouldn't be so picky. It's just staying close to nature. It's all about natural body oils. A bit of muck and sweat never hurt anybody.'

'Not so sure about that,' commented Matthew. 'My olfactory glands have been taking a bit of a hammering.'

'Goodness, that's a very big word,' said Katerina.

Matthew thought she had probably added 'for you' in her head.

Then she continued, 'If you must know, I was thinking of doing a bit of washing tonight.'

Emily giggled, 'That will be a first. Is it your body or your clothes, by the way?'

Katerina made a face back but let it go and they changed the subject. The girls were starting to get hungry.

June 1949

Kathleen was downstairs in the kitchen helping Mrs O'Dwyer with the washing up. Nora could hear her gabbling away even two flights of stairs away. It was only a few months since that trip to Ballyvaughan. Things had changed dramatically. The old Kathleen had come back to life, full of fire and energy. It seemed finally that she was emerging from the desperate sorrows that had been pulling her down for so long. Rather than sitting and moping about the past, something had stirred Kathleen back to the present. And in practical terms, her hopes were pinned to the idea of rebuilding her life over in England.

Kathleen had set about planning the move carefully and with determination. She was mature enough to know that there were risks. It might be a case of "jumping from the frying pan into the fire", as her father was often inclined to quote. So Kathleen did her homework. She corresponded at length with her friend, Mary Lavelle, who was already settled in Leicester. And when the older sister, Pat, had come home to Liscannor for Easter, Kathleen had plugged her for all the information she could get. Where to look for work and where to find a place to live? These were the key questions. First hand information was priceless.

And while all this planning was going on, Nora in contrast had taken a backward step. She had lost Sean O'Callaghan. That was the plain fact of the matter. It was a total shock when he had told her. She could never have imagined that. She kept going over it in her head. It was just so sad. For a few brief weeks around Christmas, she had had the temerity to hope that perhaps something special was happening. And then before any meaningful relationship had begun even to bud let alone flower, it was all over. She knew it was wrong to think of it like this. In other circumstances, his vocation would be something to celebrate. But it was all too personal for Nora.

Those last months of the winter were hard. Nora was withdrawn. She carried out her duties at the Store competently but with little gusto. She stopped going to the dances on the Sunday night. That pleased her mother. Hughie Gallagher was more astute and realised that something was not right. He did not know what to do about it. Then, the bombshell came from Kathleen. That was an unexpected shock for Marie Gallagher. As Kathleen predicted, though, the mother knew that she had no power over Kathleen any more. As for encouragement, all she could offer was:

'You wouldn't be travelling all that way by yourself? Surely not?'

Kathleen had waited until the week after Easter to tell her parents. By which stage, she had answers to most of the questions that came her way. Not all the answers, as she was acutely aware, but enough to make it sound as if she was in control of her destiny. Once the secret was out, and the initial shock had subsided in the household, Kathleen's imminent departure suddenly became real for Nora. Her imagination wandered. There was the promise of a new beginning, of meeting new and different people, the unknown. It was very appealing when she thought of the dullness and complete predictability of her own life. And she kept hearing her mother's words: 'You wouldn't be travelling all that way by yourself.' Maybe for once, Marie Gallagher had got it right.

Nora confided in Kathleen. She wanted to go to England with her. Would she agree? Kathleen was reticent, knowing that this would cause a major row in the Gallagher house. She tried to talk Nora round. Kathleen had her reasons for making the move. She thought Nora had better reasons to stay put. She knew the family business inside out and there was almost an unspoken assumption that she would take it over in time. Nora was a single, attractive young woman who would find a decent husband in time. Unlike the old widow that Kathleen herself had become. What Kathleen left unspoken was the fear shared by both the girls of leaving behind their parents. That might just be too much of a blast for them to ever recover from. Nora listened patiently, but also calmly made her case. She was not starving or lacking in home comforts. But she knew that she was not settled in this way of life. Actually, she was "settled", that was the problem. She was settled in a rut. She was not content with what lay before her. She struggled constantly with her mother's overbearing control. She wanted her independence, her freedom. In the end, Kathleen gave in. They would make the journey together.

They landed at Holyhead on 19th May. It was a relief to escape the acrimony that had enveloped the household once Nora had made known her intentions. Hughie Gallagher had tried his hardest to talk her into staying. He was bereft at losing one daughter. Losing two was heart-breaking. Marie Gallagher took a more combative approach, taking every opportunity to make Nora feel guilty, pricking her conscience about deserting her parents.

When the day inevitably came round, the tension finally eased a little. Marie Gallagher was superstitious enough not to want to see her daughters off in a state of animosity. Apart from anything else, it would not do for the neighbours to see the family as other than whole and happy. Marie made her peace offering, giving the girls medals of St. Theresa and a set of rosary beads each. She also prepared a pile of sandwiches for them to take for the journey.

Hughie drove them down to Ennis to catch the train. There were brief hugs before they boarded. Few words. Hughie struggled to hold back tears. He masked it with pleasantries, telling Nora to look out for his letters when he could not find something in the shop. He was trying to hold onto something. Kathleen and Nora felt the deep sadness of the moment in themselves and in him. That step up into the train was the hardest. Once they were in their seats and the train had pulled out beyond the station, chugging along through the countryside, the sadness began to lift. They watched silently out of the window for most of the journey up to Athenry. This was the world they knew, the little towns and villages, the people. They were saying goodbye to it. They did not know when they would see it again. As the journey progressed, the feelings of sentimentality and nostalgia began to dissipate. An adventure was beginning. It was time to look forward.

Two weeks on from their marathon journey, Kathleen and Nora had established themselves at number 96, Moore Road. Their landlady, Mrs O'Dwyer, was a motherly sort and had immediately taken to them. The house was a large terraced villa on three floors, overlooking a beautifully kept park. Mr O'Dwyer remained in the background while Mrs O'Dwyer was front of house. She and her husband were originally from Meath and had come to England before the war. Their lodgers were exclusively of Irish extraction. Not through any particular prejudice, it was just the way things worked out. It was Mary Lavelle, Kathleen's friend, who had asked a friend at the local church, Holy Cross, if she knew of any rooms going spare that would suit two girls coming over from Clare. And via a circuitous route, the connection with Mrs O'Dwyer was made. Her reckoning was that two well brought up girls from Clare would suit her fine. And she had not been disappointed. Especially with that Kathleen one. She kept Mrs O'Dwyer laughing about all manner of nonsense. The Nora one was a bit more serious, but not an ounce of trouble. So far.

It was Sunday evening. Work tomorrow. They were already starting their second week in new jobs. That was one thing that was true about England. They were crying out for workers. They even had the Labour Exchange here where you could see what was on offer. Both girls could have had their pick of any of ten jobs on the very first visit. It was agreed that neither of them wanted to work in a shop, even one of the big department stores. Kathleen had it in her head that she would try to get a job in one of the engineering factories like her friend, Mary. In Leicester, it seemed that they made all sorts of things big and small. From lifts, cranes, transformers, generators, laundry and bakery equipment, through to typewriters, fountain pens, watches, and lenses. It all sounded interesting, even if she had little clue what a job in one of these places would entail. If it suited Mary, it would be all right for Kathleen. Sure enough, she got started almost immediately at Gents' where they made a range of electrical equipment. She arrived at nine o'clock on the Thursday morning for what she thought was an interview. By a quarter past nine, she was sitting at a workbench learning her first assembly job. Within a week, Kathleen had already made a dozen new friends, and possibly the odd enemy.

For Nora, there was an even wider choice of jobs. Not just on the factory floor, but in one of the many offices. She went for three brief interviews, was offered a job in each case. Spoilt for choice, she sought Kathleen's advice. She ended up taking a job as a trainee bookkeeper for Gimson and Company. She was hoping the work would suit her. And there was an allure about the whole enterprise. It was all so new and strange to her. It was a million miles from the green fields of County Clare. Gimson's engineering works included a large foundry for making heavy equipment. The imposing red brick edifice rose up to an impressive four stories. Nora immediately sensed the air of confidence exuding from the building. It was a solid Victorian structure, almost a monument to power and industry. And at the same time it had real style. She loved the sweep of the rounded corner giving a hint of grandeur. And the biggest surprise of all, the clock tower that would grace a cathedral. Nora was utterly taken aback by the heat and the smell, the noise and the sheer ferocity. What the engineers were able to create was beyond her comprehension. How did anyone ever imagine the world on such a gigantic scale? As Nora saw it, they were grappling with the forces of nature, and winning.

Fascinated as she was, Nora was nonetheless happy to be in the office. She was thankful for her education. Maybe her time at school would not be wasted after all. This was perhaps her chance to exercise some of the brain power that was lying fallow. There were half a dozen girls about her own age and a couple of older women. They were all friendly enough. However, it did not take long for Nora to be fed up hearing:

'Oh, say that again, luv. You've got such a lovely accent.'

This usually meant that they could not understand a word that she was saying.

It was worse when they tried to imitate her. Still, all in all, things were definitely on the up. The job was turning out to be quite varied, involving a lot more than just keeping account books. She was learning something new every day. And while one girl in particular would laugh heartily when she did something wrong, there were enough nice ones to keep her on the right track. Nora was earning four pounds ten shillings a week. Every week! Not a king's ransom, but it was good money for a single woman. Kathleen could actually earn a bit more if there was overtime. Between them, they were paying thirty five shillings a week for the room and another fifteen shillings each for their breakfast and evening meal. They had money to spare. They could save or spend it as they wanted. For Nora at least, she was getting that taste of freedom that she had craved. For Kathleen, it was the chance to confront her pain. Not to forget it, but not to be defined by it. And so, to start to be herself again.

Day Four - June 1975 - Claviere

Matthew had wanted to avoid stopping before they got past Grenoble. By around half past twelve, he had managed to negotiate the Grenoble traffic, head south on the N85 for a few miles and then make the turn east onto the N91. They were heading past Viziville on the way towards Briançon. He had found a large lay-by services with all the basic facilities. Everybody needed to "pay a visit". Katerina was blunt in her carefree way with 'I need to pee.'

There was a glorified hut doubling as a café selling sandwiches and coffee. Its mainstay was the "sandwich au jambon". In this case, a sandwich was a long crusty roll filled with ham. There was a bit of variation – they also did a ham and cheese sandwich. Or there was a greasy looking thing which Emily explained was called "croquemonsieur". He settled for the French version of a ham sandwich and a coffee. It was not an uncommon lunch for him back in London when he was working in the city. Katerina was bemoaning the prices. It rankled with her that she could have bought bread, paté and tomatoes at half the cost in the supermarket back in Lyon, and then fashioned her own more nutritious and wholesome picnic. Emily quietly bought a bottle of water and risked the croquemonsieur. She was clearly one of those sinewy, athletic, calorie burners who never put on an ounce of weight. She probably needed the fat simply to maintain her constant high energy levels, thought Matthew.

There had been no real indication yet of how far the girls were going to travel with him. After they left behind Briançon, with Turin the next major landmark, he felt he would have to ask.

'Any thoughts yet on your itinerary?'

He tried to ask it in the most neutral way possible. He made the pretence to himself that he had no feelings either way. In reality, he was enjoying their company.

It was Emily that replied.

'Didn't we say? If it's all right with you, we would love to stay with you all the way to Rome. We've been thinking that we might as well take the chance to get there while we have it. And then maybe we'll work our way back north this time next week to see some of Tuscany and the big cities.'

Matthew was inwardly pleased and made no objection.

'Ok, that's fine. Brilliant, in fact. Makes sense. You don't know when you'll get your next lift. You've struck it lucky with Matthew Hoolahan and his plush motor.'

He added quickly. 'Just joking.'

'We do seem to be a rather good team, don't you think? And you're a super driver, Matthew,' joined in Katerina.

Matthew wasn't sure if he really wanted to be on any team with Katerina. He thought that she would always want to be the captain, the leader, the boss. However, if she wanted to be on his "team", he would go along with it.

They crossed the border into Italy at Claviere at ten minutes to three. So, this was the Alps. This part of the journey was proving the most scenic to date. Climbing into the mountains through the Col de Montgenèvre, there were continual twists and turns of the road with tantalising views of the peaks. There was still some snow to be seen even this late into the warmer months. The air was so much sharper. There were pine trees in abundance from the roadside stretching away into the hills and down the valleys. There were signs for "Col" this and "Col" that. This was mountain pass country – Emily filled him in on the meaning. The chalet style buildings along the route bore witness to the skiing resort credentials of the area.

Matthew was thinking ahead. How far would they get today? Where to stop? If he could reduce tomorrow's target to under about four hundred miles, they would be in with a good chance to be in Rome by six o'clock on Saturday evening. So he pressed on, winding his way along the S24 and the S25. It was exhilarating and a bit exhausting. It wasn't that there was a huge amount of traffic, just that the road needed a lot of attention. There were a few trucks and the odd caravan that were difficult to get round. There was the constant stunning landscape to gawp at. He remained patient.

At the border, they had taken the chance for another quick toilet break as there were facilities readily available.

This was where Matthew had pored over the maps again for a full five minutes to make sure he knew where he was going. His specific aim was to be able to skirt round Turin. In the event, the closer they got, the more they were sucked into the city. They had probably missed a key sign post. Once in, it was a bind to get out. There was heavy traffic, just at the wrong time of the day. The girls had been dozing for the last hour but were wide awake again and taking in the sights. There was clearly a splash of glitz and glamour in the shops and the buildings. There was a certain style in the clothes of the people they could observe going about their business, on a shopping trip or simply out for a stroll and an early evening aperitif.

Eventually, after a good forty-five minutes of seemingly going nowhere, Matthew saw a way out to the north of the city and effected their escape via the very welcome S10. This took them eastwards and within fifteen miles they were able to join the A21 heading towards Piacenza. With the time that had been wasted in negotiating downtown Turin, it was already nearly six o'clock. Matthew felt himself flagging. Emily and Katerina had gone quiet again. He would have to stop soon. Give it another hour and try to eat up a few more miles.

'How are you doing, ladies?' he enquired, feeling it would be good to talk to help stay awake. He needed to find out what they were thinking about accommodation overnight.

'Very nice and polite of you to think of us as ladies,' said Emily jokily.

'Just a turn of phrase,' replied Matthew with a laugh. 'I

am thinking about stopping in the next hour or so. You ok with that?'

'Any time you like,' answered Katerina.

Emily said, 'We shall need to book in somewhere for the night. We'd prefer a youth hostel if we can find one. Or I suppose we could see what bed and breakfast will cost in a pensione. What about you? Do you know where you are going to stay?'

'Far from it. I'm making it up as I go. We have a decent chance of getting to this place called Alessandria in the next hour. Let's look at the options when we get there or thereabouts.'

Matthew felt that he needed to look after his own interests at the same time as feeling a certain amount of responsibility for the girls.

'My guide doesn't say much about Alessandria, I'm afraid,' said Emily after a few minutes of studying the book. 'It's really only any use for the bigger, more famous places.'

Emily continued to thumb through a grubby inch thick hardback tome.

'I've been lucky so far,' said Matthew.

'I think we've been lucky too. Meeting you, I mean,' said Emily. As she said it, a certain bashfulness seemed to creep up on her. She added for clarity, 'This lift has been absolutely brilliant.'

March 1967

—∾—

It was the first Monday of the Easter holidays. Matthew had spent the morning in bed trying to shut the world out. His mother tried half-heartedly to rouse him every half an hour. Asking him if he had homework and about the exams coming up in June. The two youngest were outside in the street playing with their friends. Sean had been up early and would be at the park for most of the day. It was the noise from the vacuum cleaner, as Nora did her weekly clean of the stairs, that finally drove Matthew from his bed. He filled his bowl from the box of cornflakes and splashed milk over them. Nora brought him a cup of tea and some fried bread.

'Don't be expecting me to be making breakfast for you at this time every day of the holidays.'

'Ok, mam,' said Matthew, yawning and stretching. 'It is the first day, after all.'

'Well, mind now. I'm not your skivvy.'

'Are you working tonight?' asked Matthew.

'I am indeed,' replied Nora.

This was a very new development in the Hoolahan household. Through one of the neighbours, Nora had found a little job in the evenings working from four till eight o'clock. It was a small warehouse a few minutes from their street where they weighed and bagged up fruit and vegetables for sale in some of the local supermarkets. It was menial work and the pay was poor. For Nora, though, it was a release after all the years stuck at home bringing up the family. She had some adult company for a change, and she was enjoying the laughs and the different stories she heard every day from the other women. She was a married woman with five children but she still had a lot to learn about the way some people lived their lives.

'So, will you make sure you are here until your dad gets home at six?'

Matthew assented. It hardly affected his plans as he would not be going out until after six anyway. While the going was good, he decided to declare his hand in advance in order to stave off any further nagging today.

'By the way, I said I'd meet up with Finn and Jonesy this afternoon. Jonesy wants to look at guitars in Schneiders on Melton Road. But I'll be home in time before you leave.'

'And what about the school work?' enquired Nora patiently.

'I'll get started tomorrow. Don't worry. It's all under control.'

Matthew said it confidently enough. He wished it was true. Anyway, tomorrow was another day.

The rest of the morning and the afternoon passed by pleasantly enough. Matthew was an observer only when it came to the guitar shop, albeit a very interested one. When he met up with Jonesy after tea, he was keen to find out whether a purchase was in the offing.

'What you thinking then, Jonesy?' said Matthew. 'Gonna get that twelve string?'

Rob Jones was a friend from the grammar school, one of the few that had integrated seamlessly with his other friends. Rob was an only child. He lived in a big house in Knighton. His dad was a lecturer at the Poly and his mum was a music teacher. He had inherited his mother's passion and talent for music. Already grade six on piano, he was now learning guitar. Matthew had no pretensions to playing an instrument himself. He was fascinated, however, with the ability that someone like Jonesy had in his hands. Even the owner of the shop had warmed to Rob as he improvised a few different tunes on the two guitars he was considering.

'Not sure, Matt,' quipped Rob. 'It is a beauty, no kidding. The other one might suit me better though. I don't know.'

They were heading down the Walk towards town. There was a little park by the museum where a bunch of them had taken to meeting up. It was where they talked about girls, about football, about their latest records and the films they had seen. They talked about money too, or more often the lack of it. Sometimes the talk could be more pretentious, ideas gleaned from writers that someone had heard something about. Like Albert Camus, George Orwell, and Dostoevsky. Or from revolutionaries in history like Lenin and Trotsky, or contemporary activists like Martin Luther King in the States. They could make a cigarette last for hours as they tested each other out, played cards, and dreamed their dreams.

When Matthew and Jonesy arrived at about quarter to seven, there were only three other boys at the benches in the far corner of the square. Matthew knew Eric from playing football on Victoria Park. The other two were recent additions to their crowd. They came from Evington and had gone to different schools. The link had been a mutual pal, David Bell, who knew them from his local youth club. The talkative one was called Seely – otherwise known as Piotr Zielinski. He was already seventeen and was an apprentice electrician. He was short and stocky, strongly built, cocky, with no fear. He was forward with the girls, and the other boys had no reason to believe he was boasting when he recounted some of his exploits. The quieter one was Birdman – John Bird – who, it turned out, shared Jonesy's interests in music. They had taken to dreaming about forming a band. Matthew was not holding his breath.

'What's the deal?' said Seely. 'Don't wanna stand around here all night getting cold. Any ideas?'

'Let's go down town and see if we can get served in the Churchill,' offered Eric. He was tall and athletic, and was already having some success in pubs.

'Ain't got no money,' said Birdman. That was not unusual.

'You can owe me,' said Seely, warming to the idea.

Twenty minutes later, Eric and Seely were ordering five pints of Double Diamond in the dingy basement bar of the Churchill pub. The other three had found a little haven as far away from the bar as possible. A dark corner, the eerie red lighting helping to mask rather than illuminate the underage drinkers. For extra safety, they sat with their backs to the other tables. Dotted around the room were a few courting couples in their twenties having an intimate drink. There was no problem getting served and the pints arrived at the table. They played the jukebox loud in the Churchill and it attracted a younger crowd. Cat Stevens was singing "Matthew and Son". Birdman mimed, lost in his performance. Then the volume cranked up as "Let's spend the night together" came on.

'That's more like it,' said Seely. He was looking around, casting his eye over the ladies even if they were already fully accounted for. 'Not much going on here,' he concluded after a while.

Matthew sipped the beer. He did not know if he liked it or not. As long as it did not make him sick. They managed to make the drinks last for half an hour. There were some good tracks on the juke box and Matthew was impressed with the entertainment. They eventually got a shifty look from the barman who came round looking for empty glasses, although he did not say anything.

'Time to go, I think,' said Eric.

If Seely had all the bravado, Eric seemed to have the ideas and the plans.

They emerged onto the street to find it was raining. Eric gave one look and said, 'I'm not staying out in this. I'm going for the bus.'

And without any further elaboration, he started running off towards the bus stands by the Clock Tower. Matthew would have willingly called it a night as well but the chance was gone.

'It's only a bit of rain,' said Seely. 'Let's go round the Revolution and see if we see anyone.'

Revolution was a night club. They would never get in there. Firstly, because of their age. And secondly, because they were not dressed for it.

'It's only nine o'clock,' said Jonesy. 'There'll be no-one there. And we won't get in anyway.'

Seely smiled. 'Yeah, I know. But the girls get there early. We can chat them up before they go in.'

Matthew had to admire the confidence. Maybe Seely could pull it off. He shivered with embarrassment at the thought of himself, a gangly teenager, trying to chat up a twenty year old woman in the middle of the street. The consensus was to give Revolution a miss. So they walked up London Road, trying to shelter in doorways and under awnings as they went. They lost Seely, or at least he disappeared for ten minutes. Then, as they were about to go their separate ways, a car pulled up beside them. The engine was revving. A shadowy figure leaned across the front seat and wound down the window. It was Seely.

'Come on, don't muck about. Get in.'

'What you talking about?' said Jonesy. 'Where'd you get this?'

Birdman, Jonesy, and Matthew stood there frozen. Then Birdman made a move.

'Might as well,' he decided.

Matthew and Jonesy looked at each other. They hesitated. Then, almost in a trance, they followed suit. They were in the back, Birdman sat tight to the passenger side door on the front bench seat. Seely crouched over the steering wheel. He revved the engine hard and it shot off up London Road. He was doing 35 before he got it into third.

'You know what this is, don't you?' said Seely, totally consumed with the thrill of the moment.

'A car?' suggested Jonesy, trying to expel some of his nerves.

'A 1500. A Cortina 1500. These don't 'alf go,' shouted Seely over the engine noise.

Matthew conceded that he seemed to know how to drive. They were past the race course already and Seely was totally transfixed. Jonesy broke his concentration.

'Here, we don't wanna end up in London, Seely. Take the next left up Stoughton Road. You can go back to Knighton and drop me off.'

'Yeah,' joined in Birdman, 'you can drop me in Evington on the way.'

Seely screeched round the corner into Stoughton Road, still feeling his way with the braking. There were some whoops from his passengers and laughs all round. Matthew was not comfortable.

'Have you passed your test, Seely?' asked Jonesy.

'Yeah, I did it a couple of months ago. Passed first time an' all. I've not had much practice since though. Making up for it tonight,' he laughed.

The roads were very quiet. Out at Stoughton, it was

like being in the countryside. Then gradually returning to the built-up environment, there were some nice detached houses and large gardens on the fringes and then a more obviously urban set of streets and buildings. Birdman jumped out at the golf course. A few minutes later, Jonesy got out at the corner of his street, just up from the Anglers' Arms. Seely motioned Matthew to get in the front. He was relishing his role as taxi man. He swung the car round and headed back across Knighton.

'I'm going to have to dump this somewhere but I'll drop you off first. Where do you wanna go?' He sounded like someone off a television crime drama.

Matthew suggested the top of London Road by the gates to Victoria Park. He certainly did not want to be dropped off in a stolen car anywhere near home. He did not care about getting wet, and in any case the rain had more or less stopped.

'Okey dokey,' said Seely. He knew the back streets well and avoided the main road until he had no option but to join it. They were just at the roundabout on Victoria Park Road when Seely slowed uncharacteristically.

'Rozzers up front,' he whispered.

Matthew saw immediately what he was talking about. A panda car about a hundred yards ahead on London Road. The Cortina was just approaching the roundabout and the intention had been to bear left in the same direction that the police car was going.

'Change of plan,' shouted Seely. He looked right as he got to the roundabout, and with nothing coming, he put his foot down and shot round to take the second exit down

Mayfield Road. Matthew briefly saw the brake lights of the police car coming on. It was not a good sign.

'I think they saw us,' said Matthew.

'It's all right,' said Seely, totally focused on the job in hand. They sped down the hill, round into Beckingham Road and then sharp left up Evington Road.

'We've got to get rid of this now,' said Seely.

Matthew was panicking. An idea came to him.

'Do you know Abingdon Road? It's up here on the left. It goes in, there's a bit round the back, and comes back out further up the road. Why don't you try there? Not many people know it. There's a little path that runs at the back of the houses.'

Seely nodded and raced the car up Evington Road. There was no sign of the cop car behind.

'Left,' screamed Matthew. 'This is it.'

Seely pressed hard on the brakes in time and swung round the narrow corner. Fifty yards in and it was a ninety degree corner to the right. There were a half dozen cars parked on the left hand side of the street. Seely crawled along and chose a narrow space between a Ford Transit van and a Ford Anglia saloon. His parking was not great but he eventually got it tucked right in front of the van. It would be more or less invisible coming up the street. They emerged stealthily, pushed the doors closed quietly, and Matthew made signs for Seely to follow him.

Once they were on the quiet footpath, leading well away from the scene of the crime, Matthew felt an enormous sense of relief. Seely was bouncing with excitement.

'That was some ride,' he said. 'Wow, I am buzzing.'

After a quarter of a mile, the footpath ended and they were back on Mayfield Road. As they turned the bend into Beckingham Road, a police panda car was heading their way about fifty yards away. Matthew froze. Seely gave him a tug and said, 'Let me do the talking.'

The car pulled across the empty road and stopped by them. Two police officers got out. The one who had been driving started.

'Been out, lads?'

'Yeah, been out for a bit.'

Seely was not going to volunteer anything until asked.

'Where you been, then?'

'Tried to get in at Revolution,' answered Seely.

'What, dressed like that?'

'Yeah, thought it was different on a Monday. Wouldn't let us in, though.'

'So, where are you going now?' This was the other police officer.

'Walking home,' said Seely.

'Your friend hasn't got much to say, has he?' This was directed at Matthew.

Matthew took the hint. He said as calmly as he could muster, 'Yeah, just on the way home.'

'And where is home?' asked the first policeman.

Matthew gave his address.

'Bit out of the way, aren't you?'

'Came up the Walk,' interrupted Seely. 'Bit safer that way. That's what we think, anyway.'

The two policemen looked at each other. They were not getting anywhere with these two. And the rain was starting up again.

'All right then, lads,' a more friendly approach being adopted. 'On your way.'

The policemen got back in the car. Matthew and Seely did not wait to see them off. They walked for a good half mile without speaking. Seely took his leave when they were a couple of streets away from the local cinema with a 'See you later, pal.'

Matthew had made his mind up. He was not intending to see a great deal of Seely in the future at all.

Day Four - June 1975 - Solero

When the clock turned past seven, Matthew felt immediately twice as tired as five minutes earlier. In truth, he was shattered. Psychologically, he had reached the end point for today. He would have to draw proceedings to a close as soon as possible. They were close now to Alessandria, just a few miles away. There was a sign to somewhere called Solero. Off to the right, only five hundred metres. It was a village of some sort. It was worth a try. Matthew swung the car over to the right at the last second and there was an audible "Ooooh" from the back seat. Katerina had probably seen it coming and was a bit more nonchalant.

'Sorry about that,' said Matthew. 'A bit last minute but when I saw the sign I couldn't resist. It looks a bit sleepy, though. May be nothing here.'

'These places often seem deserted but they can be deceptive,' said Katerina authoritatively. 'Keep driving down here. See that sign "Municipio". That's for the town hall. If there's any life here, that's where it will be.'

Katerina was effortlessly taking charge of the situation, alert and business-like.

They found what they were looking for at the end of a long narrow street. The space suddenly opened out into a dusty tree-lined square. There was a large public building at one end. The Parrochia di San Perpetuo took up half of one side of the square. In the opposite corner was the church of Saints Bernadino and Sebastiano. In between there were several three storey buildings, houses or apartments. There was a small shop next to a bar at one of the corners.

'This is a bit more promising,' said Katerina. 'Why don't you park up and we can ask in that bar if there are any rooms to be had. Actually, hold on a second. I see that there is a 'farmacia' down that lane. Look, can you see that green cross? I really need to get some things urgently. Emily, can you and Matthew see about the rooms and I'll see you back here in five?'

Matthew did not enquire and Emily did not volunteer any further explanation when Katerina had gone. The bar was empty save for one old man sitting outside accompanied only by an empty glass. Emily strode in and began speaking to the man who was fiddling with something behind the counter. Matthew was impressed. The conversation was lengthy and at times animated. It seemed like Emily really did know her stuff. Matthew couldn't understand the words but got some idea from the body language and the hand gestures. It didn't seem like plain sailing. After a good five minutes, Emily turned to Matthew and said:

'It's turning out to be a bit awkward. The bar here has one family room. It has a double bed and a single bed. The good news is that it's really cheap.'

Matthew was too tired for this. In other circumstances, he might well have been excited by the prospect of sharing a room with two very attractive girls. Not tonight. Not this week, in fact.

'I see what you mean. Well, that's not going to work, is it?'

'I suppose not,' said Emily sheepishly. She was so glad that it was him saying this and not her. It was the last thing she wanted, but she had been struggling to know how to tell him. She was glad Katerina was missing. Emily thought that she would almost certainly see things differently. Katerina would be happy to save some money and be totally unfazed by a potentially embarrassing situation.

'Can you ask him if there's anyone else in the village with a room for the night?'

Emily turned and switched back to Italian. The barman pondered for a moment. He went outside and into the shop next door. He came back a few minutes later. There was a solution after all.

When Katerina returned from the chemist's, Matthew and Emily were already seated at a table outside with a beer each.

'Cheers,' said Katerina. 'What about a drink for your team-mate?'

Now the chatter resumed at full pelt as the beer relaxed everyone. It was Matthew's turn to be thoroughly interrogated. They wanted to know all kinds of things. He was not untruthful but he did massage some of the answers. Particularly when, after the third beer, Katerina was more forceful than ever in trying to probe into his love life – and the rest.

They needed food. This was Italy. They were served a plate of cold meats and cheese, dotted with green olives. This was followed by a simple pasta dish served with crusty bread. They ate hungrily. Matthew smiled innocently at the tomato sauce drooling down Emily's chin. He was learning quickly how to fork up spaghetti after a tutorial from Katerina.

By nine thirty, Matthew was yawning and stretching. A room had been found for him above the shop next door. The girls were in the family room that Emily had negotiated with the barman. That was perfect for Matthew. He had enjoyed the day for the most part, and the evening. But now he needed some time alone. And he needed to sleep. His parting shot was that if they wanted to go to Rome tomorrow, they should be ready to leave no later than eight o'clock in the morning.

August 1949

—∿—

'There you are, me duck! One penny, if you please. And don't forget your biscuit.'

Kathleen liked this custom they had of serving tea in the Church Hall after Sunday mass. She could not imagine it happening back home. There was a real welcome here. Father Henry, the parish priest, was not like any she had come across before. Very English, very posh. He spoke like someone from the BBC. It gave her a real lift when he said the mass. His sermons seemed to find the good in humanity, to see the best in each individual. He even thanked them for being at mass.

Kathleen was already friendly with lots of the other women. She seemed to have left her inhibitions behind in Ireland. She was not afraid to tell people her life story. This was the new Kathleen. It had taken no time for her to volunteer for the rota to clean the church once a month. The older women appreciated her youthful energy.

Kathleen moved about the hall confidently, chatting to all and sundry. Nora tagged along with her, happy to talk and to get to know the faces, not wanting to get too involved.

'There you are now, the two ladies from the County Clare in the newly declared Republic of Ireland.'

It was Father Henry. He was tall, lean, and gangly, with a good head of greying hair, somewhere between fifty and sixty years old.

'Good morning, Father,' they both intoned respectfully.

'I have something of a surprise for you, I would hazard,' he continued. 'I have an introduction to make. Follow me!'

With that he marched off towards the hall kitchen. They quickly found a table to rest their tea cups and followed on behind, through the door of the kitchen and out into the courtyard at the back of the church. There was a brick garage on the left hand side. The double doors were wide open and a large black Humber Hawk was parked half in and half out of the garage.

'Good morning, John,' shouted Father Henry. 'I take it that is you in there?'

A voice called back.

'Good morning, Father Henry. 'Tis myself, of course.'

'Would you have a minute, John?'

'I'll be right there,' came back the voice.

Kathleen and Nora stood staring at the back end of the car, wondering what was going on. The voice had an unmistakeable Irish accent. That was not uncommon in these parts. What was Father playing at? A minute later, a figure slid round the side of the car. Wearing a dark blue boiler suit and sporting a greasy cloth cap, hands black with oil. The girls paused, taking a long hard look.

'Aha, now, here he is,' laughed Father Henry, highly amused with himself. 'I'd like you to meet John Hoolahan. I believe he is one of your own countrymen, indeed from your own dear County Clare.'

John recognised Nora instantly. He would not have been sure about Kathleen if she had been alone. Clearly, though, she was the big sister he had heard about. He took off his cap. Nora exclaimed:

'It's you! I thought I knew you. I can't believe it.'

She turned to Father Henry and said:

'John is from exactly the same part as ourselves. It's so good to see a face from home.'

'Well, well, well!' said Father Henry. 'It is a small world, indeed. I have no doubt that you will have plenty to catch up on. I shall leave you three to share your news. Toodle pip.'

Kathleen remembered the Hoolahan family. They were decent.

'You're Pauli's brother. And Joe's the eldest. Is that right?'

She knew she was right but that's how you had to put these things over. Pauli had once been up to mischief and stolen her bike. She remembered that all right. He was probably only ten at the time and she still reminded him any time she saw him.

They stood in the warm morning sunshine, throwing names backwards and forwards, one question leading to another.

'Look,' said John eventually, 'I'd be happy to talk all day but I'll need to get on and finish this job for his lordship. I think he's wanting to be going out in it this afternoon.'

'We'll not hold you back any longer,' said Kathleen firmly. 'Maybe we'll see you here next Sunday?'

'I'm usually at the eleven o'clock,' replied John. 'I think he's going to let me off this week,' he added with a grin.

'Right you are,' said Kathleen. 'We'll make a point of coming to the eleven next week. We'll get a proper chat then.'

As they walked back into the hall, Nora was whispering to Kathleen, 'What did you want to say that for?'

Kathleen said calmly, 'He's a nice feller and from a decent family. And he's one of our own. In any case, it would be rude not to make a proper arrangement after Father Henry has gone to all that trouble to introduce us.'

That put Nora's gas on a temporary peep. Did Kathleen see something in this John Hoolahan? He would be the first man she had looked at in a long time if she did.

Day Four - June 1975 - Torino

It had been a surprisingly relaxing journey the day before, especially once they had found the right platform and train at Lyon. It was such a huge station, everything signed in French, stretching John and Nora's communication skills to the full. John navigated by instinct. He had travelled on trains quite a lot in his younger days, journeying between his native home in Ireland and his new found domicile in post-war England. He knew that you needed to keep looking at the board, checking the destinations and the exact times.

After an initial false start, struggling to interpret "quai", they emerged onto a busy platform and there were enough signs to convince Nora that this was where the Turin train was to depart from. At the last minute, John remembered what Edith had explained about franking their tickets at the little machine at the entrance to the platform. The train had been very comfortable. You hardly knew you were moving. Some of the scenery had been spectacular. And there had been a very long tunnel. John wondered at the work that would have gone into digging it and the men who had accomplished it. It was a certainty that the odd Paddy would have been on the job.

Nora had encouraged John to have a bottle of beer – actually, a couple. He had bought them on the station in Lyon. There was a wild-haired teenager running a drinks trolley who had been doing a reasonable trade as he paraded up and down the platform. Nora had selected a strange chocolate bar and a tin of orange juice. There had been no problems at the frontier, their passports checked only cursorily by the relaxed border guard.

True to the travel agent's word, the hotel in Turin that had been booked for them was only two streets away from Porta Nuova station. But it took quite a bit of finding! The station was built on a majestic scale with arches and columns, glass and steel. They struggled to find their way out of the sprawling space. They had eventually emerged through the spectacular entrance hall onto the busy front avenue, Vittorio Emanuele, and then started walking in completely the wrong direction with no idea where they were heading. It took Nora to accost several people before finding someone with a smattering of English and more importantly who was a local and who knew the streets. It was a young man, about eighteen years old. He took pity on them and showed them right to the door of the hotel, taking a good twenty minutes of his time to do so.

The hotel was fine. The room was small, but what more did they need. It was only for one night and they would be up early. Neither of them had been bothered about a meal, more from the point of view of the time it would take to find a place, get seated and order. The journeying had tired them out and all they needed was a good night's sleep. Their train was leaving at 09:06 in the morning.

The knock on the door at seven was what they had asked for. It was superfluous given John's body clock waking him early every morning. He was already up and washed, and smoking a twist of tobacco while Nora got ready. There was breakfast downstairs and they were both ready for some nourishment. The Italian breakfast was not very different to what they had been getting used to in France. There was tea, albeit not exactly like at home. And they used warm milk for some reason. There was some fancy type of bread and a sort of cake. They boarded the Rome train feeling refreshed and ready for the final leg of their journey. In the previous twenty four hours, they had spent more time in just their own company than they had done in the previous twenty five years. Essentially, since Matthew had been born. After their first child, they had rarely been together just by themselves - or hardly, it seemed. Nora would not have had it any other way. She had been apprehensive at the thought of becoming a mother, the demands she knew it would make, and the responsibility it would involve. When it happened, she was a natural. Being a mother was an integral element of who she was. It is how she thought of herself, if indeed she ever did think about herself. It was in her subconscious anyway. She was nothing without her family.

Preparing for this trip had made her think about a lot of different things. Now, here was another set of thoughts swirling through her head. She was looking at John. She realised that she had not looked at him properly for years. Not for any other reason than that the children had taken over in their lives. They had both been playing second fiddle to the greater demands of their family. They were locked together. Relatively happily, it had to be said. Certainly, when Nora compared their situation to many of the marriages she had known as a child back home. The implacable fathers, the violent husbands, the drunks, or the conniving wives, the controlling mothers, the pious zealots, and the plain nasty folk. And then there was the obvious change over the years in many people's attitude to the idea of fidelity. Nora and John had witnessed it on the television, in the Sunday papers, through real people that they actually knew.

The swinging sixties, the nifty fifties. None of it was entirely new. Nora was well aware. It was perhaps simply that there was a more brazen approach to these things. There was a frankness and an openness that it still took some major effort to understand and accept. Nowadays it was not so much a case of covering up, more a case of flaunting it. It was not necessarily wrong. It might be for the best. Who had the right to say? Nora and John had somehow stayed their course. It was clear to Nora that they had an immutable bond. What Nora was thinking about was whether they had made the most of things. Were they missing out on something in all the past years of bringing up the family? Maybe it was guilt. What did she have to be guilty about? No, it came to her that maybe herself and John were now in the process of embarking on a new stage in their lives. What was past was over and done. It was the future that mattered. And now she and John would be more together than they had ever been. They would still need to work at it. It was with a mixed sense of longing, excitement, and some apprehension that she sat back in the window seat and put her left hand on John's right hand and said:

'It's just the two of us now, love. You'd better make sure and get us to that service on Sunday.'

John nodded slowly and squeezed her hand. It was as if he understood all her thoughts and doubts and worries, and was affirming that his strength was there for the two of them.

September 1949

The last days of September were keeping the illusion of summer alive with a late burst of sunshine and blue skies. Victoria Park was glistening in the heat. The trees were still abundantly green, the flower beds were ablaze with reds and blues and yellows. Children shouted and screamed as they played on the swings. Impromptu games of football struck up. Over towards London Road, a fully fledged cricket match was being played out, the players kitted out in their white flannels and shirts. Families strolled along the paths in the warmth of another Saturday afternoon in the sun.

Nora and John were walking along by the university. Every week since the surprise from Father Henry, Kathleen and Nora had spoken to John after mass on Sunday. It was a cup of tea and a bit of the craic in the Church Hall. It was a comfort to meet up with your own, especially so far from home, even if it consisted simply in sharing old recollections and the odd bit of news. The previous week, John had surprised them with a suggestion. Would they like to go for a fish and chip tea on Saturday? He was already a year away from the old country and John made the excuse that they could mark the first anniversary of his arrival in England. It was surely something to celebrate? The girls readily agreed without any qualms. They were not in the habit of treating themselves to meals out and this was a perfectly good reason to do something special. And if there was a hint of any ulterior motives, they were conscious that there was safety in numbers.

On Friday, Kathleen came home from work to declare that she was needed in the factory all day on the Saturday. Gents' had a big order to complete and it was already late. It had been so simple when it was all three of them meeting up. With just two, it became infinitely more complicated. Nora was in a dilemma. Kathleen had dropped her right in it. They did not even know where John lived so it was impossible to get a message to him.

'There's nothing else for it,' commanded Kathleen. 'You'll need to go and meet him and have your tea. And enjoy it. It can't be that hard.'

When Kathleen commanded, Nora did.

They were strolling slowly, casually. Nora had been nervous right up to the point that she found him waiting by the park gates at the agreed time of two o'clock. Within a few moments she had been able to relax. John did not really make anything of her being alone. He seemed to understand perfectly well that Kathleen could be called in for compulsory overtime. The factories just could not keep up with demand. It was a great thing, when all said and done. John spoke quietly, with a warm gentleness in his manner. There was still a countryman in him, a knowing respect for nature, a kindly outlook to the plants and the birds, even the mongrel that yapped around their feet. It was an interesting side to the oily figure that had emerged from Father Henry's engine pit.

'You never really explained how you came to be in Leicester,' began Nora.

This was true. For all the chatter and sharing of past histories and the story of their emigration, John had skirted around his landing in Leicester. He always spoke about coming over to Coventry, staying with his uncle and cousin. He let others surmise what they wanted, most probably that he moved on to Leicester for the work.

John stopped walking. He looked into the distance, across the long flat stretch of grass, beyond the avenue of trees leading up to the grammar school. He turned towards Nora and spoke hesitantly.

'There is something. It's a long story.' He sighed and she could tell that something was seriously wrong.

'Don't upset yourself,' said Nora. 'You don't need to say anything if you don't want to. I was just being nosey and I shouldn't be.'

'I don't know. Maybe …' he hesitated. 'The thing is, I don't want to burden you or anyone with it.'

Nora was cursing herself for opening up what was an obvious wound. In reality, there was no way back now.

'John, don't be bothering yourself. You can say what it is in your own good time. We can talk about something else.'

'Let's have a seat,' said John. They walked over to an empty bench.

'Nobody really knows any of this. Only Uncle Owen and Tommy. They've not said anything back home.'

Another pause. Then he went on. 'It's like this. When I was in Coventry, after a few months I met a girl. At the dancing. At the Trinity Hall. Margaret. Margaret Pickering.'

Nora listened intently, holding onto every word. What was he going to tell her?

'Well, we were becoming friendly like. I met her parents. They even asked me round at Christmas. That's another story. Anyway, in the March time, I had the word to go home for the grandmother's funeral.'

'That's when we saw you at mass on the Sunday morning.' Nora was trying to help him get his story out. 'I remember you and my dad speaking.'

'After the funeral, I stayed a few more days and I went back to Coventry on the Thursday. When I got off the train, I see Tommy was waiting for me. I was a bit suspicious but I thought he might just be wanting to go for a pint.'

John paused, taking a breath, screwing up his face before continuing.

'Tommy just comes up to me and says he's got some bad news. I thought he was going to say it was someone back home. And he makes me sit down and says he doesn't know how to tell me. He just has to say it. Margaret was rushed into hospital on Tuesday night. She was complaining of a terrible headache. There was nothing they could do. A thing on the brain. She saw me off on the train the week before. I never saw her again. God rest her soul.'

There was the hint of a tear in his eyes, but he managed to hold on. Breathing hard, unable to look at Nora for a minute.

'It's so hard to understand. I'm not sure it is something you can ever get over. She was a lovely girl. Just taken like that. The mother and father, the sister, the brother. Everyone was demented.'

Nora remained silent and motionless, save for gently placing her right hand over his left hand. It was an instinctive action to offer her understanding and consolation.

'I spent all my time with the family for weeks afterwards. They were kind to me but I came to the realisation that it couldn't go on forever like that. There was a chance to work through here on a new site and I jumped at it. It was true that the Coventry work would have ended sooner or later, anyway. I told Margaret's family and they were very understanding. I just had to get away.'

'I'm so sorry, John,' said Nora. 'That is a very, very sad story. I would like to have met Margaret. She sounds lovely.'

'You two would have got on very well, I'm sure of that.'

They let that settle in the air and walked on. John eventually perked up a little and continued with the story of his move to Leicester.

'You know I was only on the ground works in Coventry, just labouring, digging holes, fetching and carrying. I didn't mind, though, don't get me wrong. They had me doing the same here for the first couple of weeks. Then one afternoon the agent came to speak to me. I thought I'd done something wrong. But no! He'd had word from Ben the fitter that I seemed to know my way around engines and machinery. The funny thing was I'd hardly got to know any of the fellers on the site. I'd just happened to help Ben out one morning when the piling machine broke down. So the agent asks me outright if I wanted a job as the fitter's mate. And that's me. I'm back getting my hands black with grease every day.'

Nora smiled at the quiet intensity. There was more than one side to this John Hoolahan. The pride in his work was commendable. The inner hurt would take a long time to heal. John looked into the distance and said:

'Let's stroll over to the university, see where all the brains are hiding.'

They walked on, the mood lightened and John felt surprisingly better for exposing his grief, revealing more of himself to Nora. He had not wanted to put a burden on her. She seemed to take it in her stride. Nora seemed so level-headed and sympathetic. And he wanted to be honest with her. For her part, Nora was glad of his openness. His vulnerability was somehow an endearing quality. It was a tragic story. He might take a long time to get over it. He might never get over it. This was perhaps the start of some healing for John.

They could have continued walking until dusk, comfortable now in each other's company. Hunger intervened and they both agreed that they were ravenous. They made their way back over to the main gates of the park. Diagonally opposite, across the main road, stood the landmark Rialto. John and Nora crossed over and took a seat in the large open space of the cafeteria. The waitress brought them large plates of battered cod, chips and mushy peas. Bread and butter, and a large pot of tea. It was a glorious feast. They were both completely at ease, savouring the food, not embarrassed by any silences in the conversation. They felt good, they felt happy, they felt like they had known each other forever.

Day Five - June 1975 - Bar Piemonte

The sun was already piercing through the gaps of the shutters when Matthew woke with a start. He quickly looked at his watch. Relief, it was still early. Quarter past six. He was in a small room on the top floor at the back of the building. It was a narrow bed with a ropy mattress and just a sheet for a cover. Despite its limitations, he had slept very well. He lay awake for a few more minutes, thinking about the day ahead. He was fresh, alert and excited. He could hardly believe that it was already Saturday.

The facilities were no better than primitive. However, he managed a very thorough stand-up wash, including his hair. He certainly could not afford to lower his standards after teasing Katerina the day before. He put on a new blue T-shirt, one he had bought in a boutique near Tottenham Court Road tube station. It had that brand new factory smell. He felt good. He tidied up and stuffed the few things he had taken out back into his case. He checked round to make sure nothing was being left. And shortly after seven he descended the stairs and made his way out through the passageway that ran past the shop area. It was already open and the signora was sorting out her display of vegetables. She smiled and called out, 'Buongiorno.'

Matthew stopped and looked through the doorway. He was stuck for words and offered back, 'Hi, there. All right?' He could have added 'me duck' but that would have been playing the daft Leicester lad to excess. He stepped into the shop out of politeness. He had already paid for the room the previous night so there was no obligation owing. The woman seemed nice and friendly. She was probably ages with his own mum. He wanted to linger a little and show a bit of friendliness in return. He picked up an orange and, in made-up sign language, he completed the transaction. The signora spoke. 'Vuoi mangiare qualcosa?'

Matthew was clueless. 'I'm so sorry. I don't understand.'

She mimed eating, hand to mouth. And she came from the behind the counter and took him by the elbow. They went outside and into the cafe bar next door. It was surprisingly busy with what Matthew took to be workmen, possibly one or two farmhands judging by their footwear. They were sippping small cups of coffee, smoking, and chatttering away in a sing-song chorus. She sat Matthew down at a small table. Then she turned and gave her stern orders to the young barman who nodded affirmatively while he continued serving one of the other customers. Then she gently touched her hand across Matthew's head in a maternal gesture, smiled, and exited back to her shop.

Matthew wolfed down the bread, butter and marmellata that was placed on his table. The hot milky coffee was perfect. He couldn't speak a word of Italian and yet here he was sitting in the small "Bar Piemonte" at half past seven in the morning and getting on with a simple breakfast just like he was one of the locals. As he finished the final crumbs, he looked at his watch again. No sign of his passengers. Maybe they had decided to bail out after all. He'd already done them a big favour, so he should have no qualms. On the other hand, he did not like to think that they had had enough and were happy to see the back of him. That would not feel good. 'Que sera sera'. Maybe he did know some Italian after all. No, on second thoughts, wasn't that Spanish? Oh, who cared? He was leaving at eight o'clock come what may.

He got up and made the bill sign to the barman. He was waved away. Two hands flapping and it could not be clearer that his debts were all settled. Maybe it was included in the cost of the room. He picked up his bag and walked outside into the warm sunshine. He strolled over to the car, opened up and put the bag into the boot. He had a quick walk round to look at the tyres. The bodywork was covered in a film of dust. The windscreen was also grimy. He opened the glove compartment and pulled out the chamois leather that Aunty Kathleen had bought him for his first ever car. This was the fourth car now that it had graced with its presence. Matthew surprised himself sometimes at his sentimentality. He rationalised the fact that he had held onto it for so long. It was a damn good chamois, wasn't it? There was something else though. Maybe he kept it because it brought him luck.

He gave the windscreen a wipe. It probably made it worse. He decided to wait until they got to a garage where he could apply some water and elbow grease. Just as he was standing back to take in the view, he heard a voice calling. It seemed a long way off.

'Matthew. Matthew. Hi, Matthew.'

He looked round. It sounded more like Emily than Katerina. He could not see her. Then the voice again. 'Up here.'

He looked up to the second floor above the cafe. At an open window, Emily's head and shoulders were thrust out and she was waving over to him.

'Can you give us ten minutes? We'll be down right away.'

He waved back and shouted, 'Ok.'

Inevitably, there was a delay. Katerina possibly keeping her promise to have a thorough wash for a change! Matthew noted that she was sporting a different checked shirt at least when they finally emerged. Then both girls wanted to buy fruit for breakfast and provisions for the journey from the signora. Emily's purchases were straightforward. Katerina's were a level more complicated, involving a lot of translation work for Emily. In the end, it seemed that she ended up with the same stuff that Emily had bought anyway.

'We're here. Raring to go. Sleep well?' This was Katerina. 'So, Rome in a day!'

'That's the plan,' said Matthew. And he added, 'I don't want to sound like a nagging parent, but …'

Katerina looked puzzled. Emily laughed.

'Yes, Matthew,' she said, 'we are duly fed and watered! Avanti tutta!'

November 1968

Matthew was dressed in the blue suit that he had bought for his cousin's wedding a few months before. He had on a pale blue shirt and narrow navy blue tie, black shoes and black socks. He looked smart. He looked conventional. At ten o'clock in the morning, he felt overdressed and a bit uncomfortable. Still, for an interview, you had to make an effort. That was something he had learned quickly in the world of work. It went against his normal casual approach, but you had to play the game.

'Come in, Matthew.' It was Simon Hawkins, the Technical Services Manager. 'Please, take a seat. You'll see that Mr Peters from Personnel is sitting in with me on this.'

'Thank you,' was as much as Matthew could offer back.

'Well, now, you're here because you have applied for one of the trainee programmer posts that we have advertised internally.'

'Yes, that's right,' said Matthew.

Before he could say anything else, Simon continued: 'Good. Ok. I can tell you that we will not be asking any trick questions. If there is anything that is not clear, please speak up. And you will have a chance to ask any questions of your own at the end. And I can tell you that we will be making our decision today. All right?'

The first question was meant to be an easy one. It did not seem like that to Matthew.

'Ok, Matthew. Can you tell us why you have applied for this post?'

Matthew began hesitantly, his mind so full of thoughts that it actually went blank. He felt the sweat accumulating under his arms, the heat rising in his head. Then something clicked. There was a flash of a thought – his aunty and his mother telling him to just be himself. He relaxed, took a breath, found he could smile. He began to explain his motivation. He even convinced himself.

As the interview went on, Simon probed deeper into Matthew's technical knowledge. He found the limits but not before Matthew had been able to impress him with what he did know. As a callow youth, he had applied for a job at the building society's computer centre sixteen months previously, starting in the print and despatch department. Carrying and fetching to begin with, minding the big printers within a couple of months, and being pulled over to the computer operations section within six months. As an operator on shifts, he learned the basics quickly. Handling tapes, feeding job packs, scheduling work, dealing with error prompts. As a cheerful gregarious colleague, he made friends and contacts easily across the computer department. Within the technical team, several of the support and development staff recognised that he was a cut above the average. One or two had reason to be grateful for Matthew's help when their job submissions to the mainframe were faulty.

'Right then, Matthew,' said Simon. 'I'll just hand over to Mr Peters to see if there is anything else he wants to ask you.'

'Matthew, I'm looking at your application form and I see that you went to the City Grammar School.' Mr Peters was in his forties, slight, balding, wearing a light grey suit that had seen better days. 'Tell me about your time at school.'

It threw Matthew onto the defensive initially. He thought that school was past history. What was there to be said about it? He certainly was not going to tell the truth. Well, not all of it. He found a way to put the sort of gloss on it that he thought that Mr Peters wanted to hear.

'The grammar school was a bit of a shock at first, after junior school,' Matthew ad-libbed. 'So many pupils and so many teachers. I got used to it very quickly, though. We got lots of tests every week, and lots of homework. So I learned fast that you had to work really hard.'

What he did not say was that, while he had understood that hard work was needed, he himself had not necessarily practised working hard. That was not totally true. In the fifth year, having made the decision to stay on to try for some O levels, he had actually put a lot of effort in. There was a decent reward as well. From the prospect of leaving with no qualifications in the fourth form, he had ended up with five passes. An "A" in Maths and a "B" in English. He was secretly very proud of those two. When he had been told the results, he wondered if there might have been a mistake. "C" passes in History, Geography, and French. How he had ever passed French was beyond his comprehension.

'And did you play any sports or an instrument at school?' enquired Mr Peters.

'Yes, I played football for the school up until the fourth year. Then I got a Saturday job and I couldn't get to the games.'

Mr Peters seemed disappointed with that. He looked up from his notepad.

'And finally, then, what do you consider are your main strengths?'

This was another question that had Matthew twisting and turning in his seat. He managed to repeat something that he had said earlier about being a quick learner. With the confidence that gave him, he went on to emphasise that he was a hard worker. And finally, he explained a bit awkwardly how he felt he was friendly and helpful and could get on with other people pretty well.

'Ok,' said Simon, resuming control of the proceedings. 'Over to you, Matthew. Do you have any questions for us?'

Matthew strongly felt the urge to say that he had no questions. On the other hand, did they not expect him to want to ask something? On the spur of the moment, he decided that he had said enough already.

'Actually,' he said, 'I think you've told me everything I can think of for the moment. It would really be about the training, and you explained all of that earlier. So, really, there is nothing else from me.'

Matthew felt drained as Simon showed him out of the door. It was eleven o'clock and Simon suggested that he should go to the canteen and get a cup of tea. He was to come back at a quarter to twelve and they would give him their decision. The last thing Matthew wanted was to go up to the canteen where there would be dozens of the data prep girls on their early break. They could devour the strongest of men for their breakfast. In his interview suit, and with none of the usual colleagues for backup, Matthew would not dare risk it. Instead, he slipped downstairs into the basement. This was his old haunt – the print and despatch department. It would be quiet at this time of day. No-one would bother if he stayed around for half an hour for a chat.

At twenty minutes to midday, Matthew sat back down in the plastic chair outside Simon Hawkins' office. Had he done enough? Would Mr Peters from Personnel mark him down? Inadvertently, Matthew had referred to Mr Lockhart, the head teacher of the grammar school. When he said the name, he thought that he detected a nod of recognition, possibly approval, from Mr Peters. The fact that he had no time for Mr Lockhart and what he preached was neither here nor there. Maybe it was enough to say you knew him and imply, at least, that you had gained something from doing so.

'There you are, Matthew.' Simon Hawkins peered round his office door. 'Come in, please.'

Matthew sat back tentatively in the chair he had vacated forty five minutes earlier. There was no Mr Peters now. Simon Hawkins smiled graciously. Matthew thought that this could still go either way. He could not read what the signs were saying.

'I'm pleased to say that we would like to offer you the post of trainee programmer. How do you feel about that?'

Matthew wanted him to say it again. Had he heard it right?

'Fantastic,' exclaimed Matthew. 'Sorry, Mr Hawkins. I mean, that is great. I am very happy.'

'Good. Excellent, in fact. You are young and you've a good head on you. We need people like you. You won't let me down.'

That was a statement, not a question. It was something Matthew would remember. It was something that was becoming the hallmark of his behaviour, both at work and in his real life beyond work. Matthew sometimes looked back at the rebellious third former. Was that really him? Had Mr Pearson not intervened, what would he be like now? Matthew had seen the fifth year at school as a necessary evil, almost a punishment. He just had to get through it. He had no inkling that he might be re-inventing himself.

Once he had left school and started work at the building society, he felt very different. He suddenly realised that he had left behind the suffocating constraints of the grammar school. It was not so much the addiction to scholarship that was the problem. The issue was that it was just not accessible to very many people, including the likes of Matthew. He had certainly had the opportunity but struggled to make the best of it. Most people that Matthew knew never even got the chance. Worse than that was the smug satisfaction of the school establishment and the endemic middle class arrogance. Matthew had railed against that.

In contrast, work felt so different. It was a liberation for Matthew. There was a purpose to it. There was an opportunity to try different things. He enjoyed it. And you could go somewhere else if you did not like it. There was a hierarchy, of course, and you had to conform to certain standards. Perhaps it was a reinvention, or maybe simply a maturing process. He was ready to conform if it meant he could earn good money doing something he actually enjoyed.

In the sixteen months since he had started out at work, his in-built resilience had stood him in good stead. It was now being complemented by a determination to get ahead. He had the solid foundations of his natural charm and good nature. His sharp awareness of the real world gave him some in-built self protection. All that ducking and diving at school counted for something. His encounters with some of the wider boys in the street and at the park also made for invaluable life experience – not that he would be keen to elaborate too much to the likes of Mr Peters. One thing was certain, Matthew could get on with all sorts of folk. He found that he could speak to most people, including the bosses. It just came naturally. He was still an absolute beginner as far as romantic relationships were concerned though. That seemed like it was going to be a long term project. The thought both excited him and made him nervous. In the meantime, maybe he did owe the grammar school a bit more than he would like to admit.

Day Five - June 1975 - Piacenza

They were now back on the A21 and the first target of the day was Piacenza about sixty miles away. It had been a slow process getting out of Solero and through Alessandria. However, they had been fortunate to find a petrol station early on and Matthew had been able to fill up, check the oil and tyres, and give the windscreen a good clean. Katerina and Emily were happy to watch all this. They remembered their manners and did politely offer to help but there was nothing for them to do.

From the slowish start to the day's proceedings, the car was now cruising along at sixty very comfortably. There was throttle aplenty to pass anything that was too slow in front.

The girls were full of beans, it seemed. Were they more relaxed with him today? Were they just excited at the prospect of getting to Rome?

'So, Matthew,' Katerina began. 'We've been talking about you. Were your ears burning in bed last night?'

'Can't say that I noticed. I crashed out as soon as I got to my room. Next thing I knew it was quarter past six and the birds were singing outside my window.'

'Well,' Katerina continued in a conspiratorial tone, 'what we want to know is this. Who is Matthew Hoolahan? What is he really like? What turns him on?'

She left this in the air for a moment. Emily was trying to suppress a giggle in the back. Katerina ignored her.

'Oh, I mean, we're not asking about your sex life! Although you can tell us all about that if you want. No, we were saying that although we had spent all day yesterday with you, we had not really got to know you. So, today we can set that right, can't we?'

She finished her statement and sat back triumphantly. Emily was fluttering in the back and said, 'Don't listen to her. And don't answer if you don't want. You've already got a good idea of what she's like.'

Matthew was actually feeling on top of the world today. He had woken up with a renewed energy and buzzing optimism. The sun was bursting out of the heavens, the sky was a perfect blue. He had a good vibe. Nothing could upset him. The girls were a bit of an enigma. He would readily admit to himself that he was really enjoying their company. He had already grown fond of them in an essentially platonic way. Equally, he had to admit that he also found them both very attractive in their different ways. They exuded femininity, and being in their company was patently appealing and even exciting. It was something that was often missing from his day to day life. At home and at school, life tended to be male dominated. He did have a sister but she was years younger and basically from a different generation to him. At work, there were some female colleagues but relationships were strictly on a business and professional level. There was undeniably a thrilling aspect to meeting two vibrant intelligent girls in a random way, and getting to know them in the course of this long shared journey. On the other hand, it was obvious to Matthew at times that Katerina and Emily were not as mature as their confident demeanour and sometime bravado implied. There was an awkward childishness in some of their behaviour. There was the petty squabbling about paying for their drinks. The occasional sulk when a raw nerve was touched. There was a lot of talk about mummy and daddy. Matthew concluded that they still had a bit of growing up to do. Not on the intellectual or academic side of life. They were well ahead there. It was more on the emotional side, a broadening of their experience of people, getting to be a bit more worldly perhaps. It was no serious black mark, however, because he knew he had a good bit of "developing" to do himself.

'What can I tell you?' Matthew indulged Katerina. 'I told you that I was born in Leicester. My parents are first generation Irish, came over in the late 1940's. I've got three brothers and a sister.'

Katerina interrupted. 'Yeah, we got all that. What we want to know is, well, let's start with … what are your interests? What do you do in your spare time? What do you do at weekends? You must read a lot because you are clearly very bright.'

Matthew was flattered and, if somewhat embarrassed, it still felt good.

'Oh, I don't know. You don't have a lot of time to yourself when you're working. My job is in central London and I have to travel in and out every day. I don't get home till quite late and then you don't always feel up to anything more than watching the box. I do like a good book as well. Read a bit on the train.'

'Indulge me, then,' said Katerina, now taking up the role of class teacher and personal tutor. 'For example, what are you reading at the moment?'

'I just finished *Catch-22* last weekend. Have you read it?'

'Yes. It's ok. It's well written, of course. Not really my cup of tea, though. Anything else recently?'

'Yeah, I read *Portnoy's Complaint* a couple of months ago.'

As soon as he said it, he wished that he had kept his mouth shut. But all Katerina said was, 'Another American? Don't you read any English authors?'

Emily piped up and could hardly get her words out for laughing. 'Maybe he's read *Fear of Flying* too if he's into modern American literature?'

Katerina's complexion reddened just a little. She turned round to stare at Emily, checking to see at the same time if there had been any reaction from Matthew. He was looking hard and straight down the road and hadn't appeared to register what Emily had said. Katerina tried to move the conversation on.

'There are lots of great American writers, of course. Mark Twain, Hemingway, John Steinbeck, Henry James. The list is endless.'

'Oh yes, I've read *The Grapes of Wrath*,' volunteered Matthew. 'John Steinbeck. I never fancied it at all for years. Kept seeing it on the shelf at W. H. Smith and kept avoiding it. Then one day I decided I would give it a try. It's become one of my favourite books of all time.'

'How interesting,' said Katerina, sounding though not meaning to be patronising. 'You really do know a good book. I'm curious. Have you always liked reading?'

That was easy. Matthew could explain.

'My mother loves a good book. Actually, any book. Though she never had much time for reading when we were young. And she didn't have any money to buy books. But she joined the local library. And when we were old enough, she joined us as well. I never went a lot to start with. Then something happened when I went to secondary school. The first reading book we got was called *Rogue Male*. I remember the title but just can't think of the author. Anyway, the truth is that I was a bit overwhelmed by the new school at the start. All the new subjects, new people, different teachers, and loads of homework. I started reading that book at night in bed. I had my first experience of losing myself in another world. It was an escape. I hated it when I finished that book. But I soon realised that there were others to lose myself in. And that's how it started.'

Matthew had never spoken to anyone ever before about all of this. He almost felt like he had been to confession. It was a good feeling.

Katerina listened carefully and with great interest.

'So, would you say that it's the story that really gets you?' she asked.

'Yeah, I suppose so,' replied Matthew. 'A good story can sort of take a grip of you. Another thing, though, is humour. I like it when they make you laugh.'

'What about the way that someone writes? You know, the language? And what about what they've got to say?'

Matthew pondered for a few moments. Then he answered.

'I was trying to think what you meant by "language". All I can say is, I'm not very keen on a lot of flowery language. I prefer simple, direct stuff. Not a lot of long difficult words. I like modern writing. I can't get into Charles Dickens, even if he does tell a good story.'

'Do you think you learn anything from the books you read?' asked Katerina.

'Not really. Not learning as such,' said Matthew. 'You get feelings, I suppose, and ideas. You know, *The Grapes of Wrath* makes you think a lot about how the farmers treated the workers. You can get pretty wrapped up in the emotions. I reckon that is one of the things a good writer can do.'

Katerina was about to continue this tutorial but Emily jumped in to steer the conversation elsewhere.

'Right,' she said, 'we know about books. Now, what about music? What bands do you listen to?'

Matthew smiled outwardly but felt a little uncomfortable inwardly. He knew that he did not have a deep interest in music and his knowledge was shallow. Some of his friends were heavily into music. They bought dozens of albums, played them endlessly, could name all the tracks, knew the words to obscure songs, and went to loads of concerts.

Matthew's taste was broad but not very deep. How could he make his answer sound interesting? He never wanted to sound like a bore. And he knew that displaying a more discerning musical preference could earn a badge of respect among friends and acquaintances.

'I like a lot of folk music. You know, contemporary folk. And some traditional.'

It was actually true and he liked to tell people because it made him appear a bit different from the crowd. He could tell them that he loved the Beatles, the Kinks, Rod Stewart, 10CC and countless others. That was all true but would not differentiate him from the masses. He could not tell them that he liked Deep Purple, Pink Floyd, and King Crimson - because he had simply never been able to listen to them. Liking Richard Thompson, Al Stewart, Roy Harper, John Martyn, James Taylor - that was a bit different and he actually did know a lot of their music. It was not always the greatest chat-up material though, being a little out of the mainstream of popular musical taste. He had tried talking about folk music on more than one date in the past with the effect that any potential interest in him had immediately evaporated. In the current circumstances, this was not a relevant consideration. Here he was just keen on having an interesting and intelligent conversation.

Emily was fascinated. 'That's amazing. I thought you were going to say the Who or the Rolling Stones, or maybe Status Quo. I kind of know who you are talking about, but that's all. What about when you go to a party? What do you like to dance to?'

'Anything really,' he said. 'It's usually the latest pop stuff they play at discos, isn't it? Things like the Stones, the Who, David Bowie are all great. But you can't beat Motown for dancing. There are some brilliant records that you can listen to over and over again.'

'You're a bit of a dark horse, aren't you?' joked Katerina, but she was impressed with his eclectic taste.

'What about you, then?' asked Matthew.

Emily jumped in. 'Oh, I love Mozart and Haydn, and Schubert. I love Early Music too. I sing in the choir at college.'

'What about when you go to parties?' Matthew responded. 'Can't see you dancing to that lot.'

Emily was laughing. 'You'd be surprised. We had a party last Christmas where we sang madrigals and danced around to a viola, horn and tabor. I grant you, it was not exactly normal but a whole lot of fun. I do like some modern music as well. ELO are excellent, don't you think? And I love Bryan Ferry.'

'Yes, he is rather dishy,' joined in Katerina.

'I thought we were talking about music,' said Matthew.

They all thought that was hilarious.

January 1950 – Part One

'Do you ever think about returning home? To the old life?'

It was another Saturday afternoon walk. They had taken the bus out to Abbey Park for a change. They were standing on the hump-backed bridge that straddled the River Soar. It would lead them over to the ruins of Cardinal Wolsey's abbey. It was a freezing cold January day. A clear bright blue sky stretched out above them. They were both wrapped up in heavy coats, complete with hats and gloves. John could not help admiring Nora. She suited her navy beret, her cheeks blushed with the cold, the ready smile on her full lips. The water flowed fast below them. A pair of swans was patrolling near the left bank. The question came from John. Nora had to adjust her thoughts to answer. It was a question that never really left you, one that you tried to lock away in a drawer so that you did not have to keep looking at it all the time.

'Maybe, one day,' she replied a little uncertainly.

Then, with more strength, 'I couldn't say it would be any day soon, though.'

She went on:

'Kathleen and meself, we're just getting settled. She was dead set on coming over. I had my reasons to get away too. Look at us. We've nice digs, good paying jobs. England's not as bad as some of them make out over yonder. They have some strange ways about them, I'll grant you that. And there's a few that don't like us. I'm happy enough though, aren't you?'

John avoided the direct question, continuing to muse on his theme:

'What about the future? Do you ever think about that?'

Nora had already discovered that there was a deeper side to John than initially met the eye. He was certainly in a reflective mood today.

'To tell you the truth,' said Nora, 'I've not had time to think much further than the next week all the time we've been here. That's one of the best things, when I think about it. There's something different every day. New people, new places, new shops, new things to learn at work. No time to worry about the future.'

John listened carefully. Then another question was aired.

'Do you ever think about getting married one day?'

Nora moved off from the parapet slowly and began walking again, collecting her thoughts. Did John just mean this in a theoretical way, or was there something more pointed, more personal to it? He caught up with her and they strolled on side by side. Nora deflected the question.

'You sound like one of the old biddies coming into the shop at home. That's the sort of question my Aunty Rosie in Kilshanny would ask us every time we visited.'

'Oh, don't mind me,' apologised John. 'I'm wandering in my thoughts today. I'm not very good with words. It's just that I get to wondering at times about life, where it's all leading to. Especially since Margaret.'

'John,' interrupted Nora, feeling immediately concerned and protective towards him. She linked her arm with his and pulled him closer to her. 'You've every right to feel like that. I just don't want to see you upset. Everything will work out, you'll see.'

'You're right, of course,' said John. 'You've a wise old head on you.'

'Less of the "old", if you please,' replied Nora with a giggle.

They both laughed and picked up their walking pace to get their circulation going. They walked round the park, then joined the canal and eventually ended up back at the Clock Tower. They decided on high tea at the Oriental café by the market. At Nora's suggestion, it was agreed that they would take a trip to the cinema the following Thursday. Their Saturday ended quietly with this happy prospect.

Whisky Galore! sounded like a film they would both like, and by all accounts was very funny. They were to meet outside the Grand Hotel at half past six for the last house. The B movie was a western. Nora tolerated it. John enjoyed the good versus evil simplicity, and the action. *Whisky Galore!* had them both in fits of laughter. Some of it was a bit stilted, but there was an authenticity about the characters which brought to mind the wily folk of North Clare. Afterwards, John walked Nora home and they spoke over the film and the antics of the whisky vagabonds. Nora was feeling bold. She was skipping along keeping up with him. It had been in her mind since Saturday. She could not get it out of her head. She picked her moment and threw John's question back at him.

'Remember on Saturday? You were talking about the future? You never said what you were thinking?'

John did not need to think about his answer. He stopped, gently tugging her arm to coax her to stop too. In his quiet, placid way, he just came out with it.

'Well, that's an easy one. All I can say is I'd be happy if I could be with you. Just the way you are. I don't know, these last months, I've got to know you so well. You're more than a friend. My best friend. Even more than that.'

Nora's heart was beating fast. She could hear her pulse pounding in her ears. Here was a man who had barely given her a peck on the cheek, who was declaring his love. She was not mature in these matters. Far from it. But she recognised that, at least. This was more romantic than any book she had read.

'You've a silver tongue in your head, and you don't realise it.'

Nora wanted to say so much. In the months since that first afternoon walk with John back in September, Nora had been happy to meet up with him every other week. They would walk and talk, and have their tea in a café. She liked his company, and he made no demands on her. It was a nice innocent friendship. She did not lack for other social outings, with new girlfriends from work and being roped in for helping in the Church Hall. She had also gone with Kathleen to the dancing at the Irish Club several times. And she had met lots of young Paddies over in England making a new life. John had told her that he had given up the dancing – it brought back too many memories of Margaret. She knew from others that he never made an appearance at the Club. After the debacle – as she saw it – with Sean O'Callaghan, Nora had repressed those perplexingly exciting feelings that she had allowed to surface in her. The sensual longings that she had wallowed in briefly the year previously were banished to the sidelines. And she had kept them under lock and key until the last few weeks. At Christmas, she had found herself thinking more and more about John Hoolahan. Since Saturday, she could hardly concentrate on anything else. And, if she was just a naïve immature young woman, she did not care. She would make her own mistakes if need be. She would make her own mind up. She would grow up doing so.

'Hush now, and come here!' She took his two hands and pulled him tightly into her. She looked up into his eyes. They kissed properly for the first time. And then again. He held her close, no words being spoken. It seemed to last a lifetime. Neither wanted to let go. Eventually, Nora whispered to him.

'You're so lovely, John. You're perfect. You can be with me forever if that's what you want.'

'That's what I want. Exactly.'

Day Five - June 1975 - Bologna

They stopped at a service station on the A1 on the outskirts of Parma around ten twenty five. They were making good time. Matthew surprised himself by finding that he was quite enjoying the interrogation mounted by the girls. It was all harmless talk. They were different today. For all the pushy, bubbly front that had initially met him the day before, he had felt a certain coldness from them. It was completely understandable really. They were young women getting into a stranger's car in the middle of a foreign country. It was wise to exercise some caution. He had felt something similar himself. He did not relish the possibility of being eaten alive by two female predators. The distancing and cooling off overnight had relaxed everyone and there was now a friendly camaraderie amongst them. And the collective end goal of reaching Rome was tangible.

Matthew was feeling buoyant and insisted on buying the coffee and croissants. He did not have to insist too hard.

Nevertheless, the kindness was appreciated. The girls were not short on manners. Katerina was thinking out loud.

'Do you imagine we'll meet up with Rowena and her Trinity crowd?'

'You mean those arty-farty types she sees at the Ashmoleum?' asked Emily. 'I've never met them, actually, just heard about them.'

'You should absolutely get to know them, Caspian Fellowes and Hugo Smith-Dorrien ...'

She stopped mid-sentence as Matthew nearly splashed his coffee all over the table.

'That's a right mouthful, if you ask me. Caspian what, and Hugo ... He's got a street named after him in Leicester!'

'Caspian is a classicist, exceptionally clever. Hugo is reading history of art. I was hoping they could give us a whistle-stop tour of the museums and galleries.'

Katerina was relentless. Emily countered.

'That would be nice, I have to admit. However, from what Rowena said, they are a long way out of my league.'

'Nonsense, darling,' Katerina told her, putting on suitable affectation. 'They are charming, perfectly charming. They will adore you.'

'Yes, it's ok for you. With all your connections, your family, and your school, you can match up quite happily with the minor nobility and the Home Counties hierarchy. Eton and Harrow, I think Rowena said. They have their own dining clubs at Oxford, for God's sake. Remember, I'm just a poor GP's daughter from Hampshire.'

It was a small tirade and Katerina deflected the angst by simply saying, 'It was just a thought.'

They finished their coffee. It was time to move on. Visits to the services were essential for all before rejoining the car. Matthew was intrigued by the last bit of the girls' conversation. He was pretty well attuned now to differences in the class structure. He sometimes felt that he had been on a learning curve in class politics his whole life. He had not fully appreciated some of the subtleties that also existed within the class divisions. When he thought about that a bit more, he realised that he was actually very well clued in to the sub-divisions in the lower classes. Time-served tradesmen were the elite of the manual workers. Then there were the semi-skilled, factory operatives, warehousemen, and drivers. Manual labourers were near the bottom of the blue collar ladder, even if some of them like building or road workers, for instance, were able to earn good cash. At the upper end of the class scale, the Oxford girls were providing him with an insight into how the other lot thought about each other. Funny how everyone was equal when it came to needing a pee.

It was the A1 all the way now. A long way, make no mistake. The traffic was heavy. This was the main artery linking north to south. There was a lot to concentrate on and the miles went by, sometimes faster sometimes slower. The road markers counted out the distances. It was good to see the progress, sometimes frustrating when it was less than he hoped. Still, there was an air of anticipation in the car. Towards midday, they were nearing Bologna. Matthew was thinking about the next stop. He had it in his head that it would be somewhere near Florence around half past one. Suddenly, the tail lights in front were all turning red and he had to brake very hard to avoid ramming the car in front. They had not fully stopped but the traffic was only creeping along. There had been no warning of road works. He presumed that there had been an accident. Emily and Katerina were quiet, picking up on the tension that Matthew was beginning to display. After a while, he relaxed. There was nothing he could do. They would just have to wait their turn to get through. If it took till midnight to get to Rome, so be it.

After half an hour of start-stop in which they moved less than two miles, they could see the two lanes opening up again and eventually they got past the spilled lorry and back to normal speed.

'I think we could do with a break so I'm going to stop at the next services. Is that ok?'

'Sure,' said Katerina. 'You can read my mind.'

'Same for me,' said Emily.

The car went back to silence for the next ten minutes until Matthew saw a sign promising petrol and sustenance.

'Won't be long now. Could do with stretching my legs,' he reported.

It was all glass and metal in the space age designed cafeteria. Stylish. Expensive. This was not for the truckers. Katerina nearly had a fit when she saw the price of a bowl of pasta. Emily counted out her lire a little reluctantly but she was hungry. Matthew found the obligatory ham sandwich and he bought a bottle of coke to quench his thirst, the cold fizziness scarring the back of his throat in a short-lived moment of pleasure. Then he had an orange to mask the sugary after taste of the coke. A forty minute stop was enough to revive his spirits. And they were back on the road by one thirty. Matthew had roughly calculated the mileage remaining as being around two hundred and twenty. If the road remained clear, they could be in Rome by seven even with another couple of stops.

January 1950 - Part Two

Nora was in tears, her face flushed and her eyes inflamed with sadness. She had waited nearly an hour for him in their usual meeting spot at Victoria Park. He had not showed up. The bitter cold wind had blown right through her, freezing her limbs and numbing her brain. Eventually, she thought that she was going to keel over. Her body was shaking with the cold, she could hardly think. The intoxication from Thursday's whisky galore now gave way to a throbbing hangover. Emptiness, headache, and confusion. Now she lay on her bed. Kathleen was out for the evening. Nora had not told her the real reason she was so out of sorts. She just said that she felt unwell and had insisted that Kathleen should enjoy her Saturday evening.

Nora had just about held herself together until Kathleen had finally finished getting ready. When the door closed behind her, Nora crumpled into a ball and sobbed for a good half an hour. Her thoughts flitted from one thing to the next. It came down to this. She had better get used to being disappointed. Whenever her hopes of something good were raised, something came along to dash them, as if they were a precious ornament crashing onto a stone floor. Just when she was reconciling herself to her fate, she relapsed again into tears. She just could not understand why. Why her? What had she done to deserve this? And then the horrible feeling of anger welled up inside, choking her, tempting her. Then it subsided and she consoled herself with the monotonous routine of getting ready for bed. Emotionally exhausted, Nora lay back and slept.

Kathleen was calling out.

'Who is it?'

Nora turned over and opened her eyes. The reply came back.

'It's Mrs O'Dwyer, love. Is Nora there?'

'It's me, Mrs O'Dwyer,' called back Nora. 'What is it?'

Nora looked at the alarm clock on her bedside table.

'It's Sunday morning. It's only ten past seven. Are you all right?'

'Yes, dear,' replied Mrs O'Dwyer. 'I've got a young man at the front door. He says he's got to see you. Urgent like.'

Nora was already out of the bed. It was freezing in the room but she did not feel the cold. Nevertheless, she gathered her dressing gown and threw it on. She opened the door to Mrs O'Dwyer.

'Whatever is it?' said Nora, gathering herself, trying to remain calm despite feeling anything but. Kathleen was also half out of the bed. 'It's all right, Kathleen, I'll go and see what the matter is. I'm so sorry, Mrs O'Dwyer. I can't think what's happened.'

They made their way downstairs. Mrs O'Dwyer pointed Nora at the front door.

'You'd better bring him into the kitchen. He's not to go into my parlour with those working clothes on.'

And then she diplomatically withdrew back up the stairs.

Nora went to the door. John stood there. He was dressed in old baggy trousers, a heavy sweater beneath a black donkey jacket. She had never seen him like this in his working clothes. Only on that first Sunday when he was clad in the oily boiler suit. Nora didn't know what to say. She just stood looking at him.

'Nora, can I speak to you for a minute? Please?'

'You'd better come in,' said Nora. The anger and the misery of the previous night were being held in abeyance for the time being. He seemed to have something to tell her. He had better have at ten past seven on a Sunday morning.

Nora showed him into the kitchen along at the far end of the hallway. She motioned for him to sit, but he ignored that.

'Look, I had to come and see you. To tell you about yesterday. I don't know what you thought.'

Nora knew. She did not say. Not yet, anyway.

'I was in work yesterday morning and should have finished at twelve. The gaffer comes over to me first thing and says he's got a big problem. One of the pumps was out of action from the night before. You should see the water in the basement of the building. It was like a pond. Well, the pump was needing stripped and rebuilt. We had to drive over to Derby to see if we could get the parts. Anyway, the long and the short of it is this. I was there till ten last night and I'm starting at eight this morning. He wants the other pump fully serviced as well. With a bit of luck, we'll be finished with that tonight. But then there's a backlog of work now for next week as well.'

Nora was staring at him. She had already forgiven him, even before he had said a word. She knew as soon as she had seen him at the front door. There was an overwhelming feeling of relief, all the anger completely dissipated.

'Do you want a cup of tea?' Nora concentrated on the mundane in an effort to control her emotion.

John paused and then agreed. 'That would be nice. A quick cup, mind you. I can't be late.'

She lit the gas and placed the kettle down. As she turned to get the teapot, they brushed together. John touched her gently, his hands reaching to her shoulders and drawing her into him slowly. She started to cry. She had no other release. He hushed her, repeating his apologies over and over again. She smelt the oil, the swarfega, the sweat of the working man. She put her arms around him and pulled tight. It might only have been seconds that they held each other. It seemed like forever. The tears were still running in Nora's eyes but she was happy, unbelievably happy.

It was the longest week of her life. There were moments when she thought that she would burst with the anticipation, tantalised by the possibilities, anxious that it might all be illusory. John was going to be working late every day and it would be impossible to see each other before the walk they had planned for Saturday afternoon. Nora did her best to keep calm on the surface. Work was a great diversion and she was even more efficient than usual. The other girls noticed a spring in her step and were not slow to point it out. There was the occasional risqué comment made at her expense. Nora was wise enough not to deny anything and chose to simply laugh it off. The evenings were long and drawn out, and she was struggling to confide her innermost feelings even to Kathleen. She found herself praying while she lay awake before falling asleep. If you could call it praying. She said the words but her thoughts were like a badly edited film with different scenes randomly spliced together and running unexplained into each other. She slept but she seemed to be awake at the same time, her mind racing, her thoughts so vivid. It was in the calmer moments of dozing before getting up on the Friday morning that things suddenly started to make sense. She got up that morning with a feeling of serenity coursing through her. She had finally worked out the solution.

On Saturday, Nora busied herself in the morning with cleaning and tidying the room, sorting her clothes for the following week, and finally getting herself ready for meeting John at two o'clock. Her resolve remained firm.

'Hello, John,' called Nora as she approached the waiting figure standing by the park gates. He was here and he was not late this week. She was feeling bold now. Nora went right up to him, put her arms out to him, and stretched up to kiss him. It was a light and tender welcome. John was relaxed and gave her a hug.

'Where would you like to go?' he asked. 'The usual?'

'Yes,' said Nora. 'Let's just have a good long walk in our park.'

John took her hand and they began to stroll along the path towards the concert hall and the university beyond. They were both well wrapped up against the cold. John was wearing his heavy black overcoat, Nora had on a warm woollen dress coat, knitted scarf and leather gloves. John told her about work and how pleased the boss was with what he had done that week. He also recounted a letter he had received from his mother and sister. Apart from the snippets of family life on the farm, the big news was that his older brother Joe had landed a promotion in London. The folks back home were so proud of him. He wondered quietly what they thought about John. This was Nora's opening.

'John, of course they are proud of you. Why wouldn't they be? Look at you. You've made a new life for yourself in a foreign country. You've learned a new job in record time. You've become the man the boss can rely on.'

John smiled at Nora's speech in his defence. He already knew that she cared for him. He was beginning to realise how much.

Nora was determined. She had made up her mind. Everything was crystal clear in her youthful exuberant lust to live life to the fullest. She knew what she wanted and she did not want to wait. There were risks. It was not conventional what she had in mind. She was not going to be a slave to convention. She started to speak again.

'John, I've got something to say to you. I don't know if you'll like me saying it. You will think me very forward.

I just can't help myself. I think you know me well enough now to know that I am, what they might say in a book, a bit impetuous. That's what Sister Patricia wrote on one of my reports, anyway.'

'Well, Sister Patricia was probably right. But I won't hold it against you. Anyway, I'm listening all right.'

Nora motioned them over to a green bench at the side of the path. They wiped away the drops of moisture and pulled their coats beneath them to sit.

'I've been thinking about this a lot. It's all I've been thinking of, truth to tell. So, here it is. I really like you, John. Really like you. I think we get on great. I'm not one for beating about the bush …' At which point, Nora felt the gravity of her words.

John came in to help her out.

'I know what you are saying. I've been thinking the same myself ever since I first set eyes on you. Will we get married?'

The question reverberated in both their heads for what seemed like an age. Then, by way of an answer, Nora pulled John up out of the seat and tightly hugged him whispering softly, 'We will, John, we will.'

The next day, when the eleven o'clock mass was over, they approached Father Henry and asked if they could make an appointment to speak to him. Sensing their nervousness, and never one to procrastinate, Father Henry said he would see them in the church house as soon as the "after mass" gathering in the hall was finished. They mingled with the tea drinkers as normal until Father waved them over to the back door.

'Well, now,' he smiled cautiously, 'what can I do for you?'

It was Nora who took the lead.

'We want to get married, Father.'

'I had my suspicions,' said Father Henry. 'And I suppose it is all my fault,' he mused. 'After all, I was the one that introduced you to each other.'

'Not a fault, Father,' said John in a serious tone. 'We are very grateful.'

Father Henry held his silence briefly.

'Now, you've known each other for a few months only. Can I be indelicate and ask if there is any reason that you might be, shall we say, in a rush to get married?'

'Certainly not,' responded Nora curtly, knowing exactly what he was asking. 'It's nothing like that. We have just been fortunate to fall in love and we see no reason to wait to get married.'

'Splendid, splendid,' said Father Henry. 'You are a fine young couple. I think I knew that some time ago. Let me congratulate you. You are being called by God into the holy union of marriage. That is a wonderful thing. Wonderful. Wonderful.'

Nora thought he was getting a bit carried away with it all. Still, it completely filled her heart with joy to hear such compliments from the priest. It was some kind of affirmation that they were doing the right thing.

'Now,' said Father Henry, picking up his diary from his desk. 'Let me ask you. What date were you considering for the marriage?'

It was Nora again who took the lead.

'We have both decided that we do not want a big wedding. It will be too much for the family from back home to travel. So, we just want a quiet affair. As soon as possible, in the next few months.'

'These things are not to be too rushed,' admonished Father Henry gently. 'And in any case, it would not be advisable during Lent. Ash Wednesday is nearly upon us and Easter Sunday, according to my diary here is the ninth of April.'

He leafed through the diary. 'I presume you would want a Saturday wedding?'

They nodded. They had not really given much consideration to the details.

'Well,' said Father Henry, 'Saturday 29th April is free at the moment. What do you think of that?'

John nodded assent. It seemed a good enough date. It would give them a little time to find somewhere to live. They would also need some time to tell their respective families. Nora acquiesced, simply thanking Father Henry for being so understanding.

'I shall need your baptismal certificates, of course. Can you arrange for them to be sent?'

Nora blushed. That had not crossed her mind. Father Rodgers back home, always in league with her mother, might be very difficult about it. She decided to come clean with Father Henry.

'Father,' she said, 'I don't know how to say this. There may be a problem for me, at least. I've been baptised – and confirmed. The problem is that my mother was forever trying to marry me off to another man back home. Someone twice my age – and who I despised, God forgive me! The truth is … Well, it's one of the main reasons that I came over here. I don't know how co-operative the parish priest back home will be.'

Father Henry bristled with indignation. He might be a little old fashioned himself, but he disapproved totally of those fellow priests who seemed to think they were still living in medieval times.

'Don't you give it another thought! You leave all that to me.' And he took a note of who he would write to.

'And now, let me give you a blessing. Please stand.'

As they walked back along the road, both Nora and John felt that they were floating on air. She linked her arm tightly with his. They spoke little. They just melted into each other's company.

Day Five - June 1975 - Arezzo

The journey was dragging. The intense brightness of the afternoon sun made Matthew permanently squint at the road ahead. He had all the makings of a tension headache. The stifling air and the heat inside the car did nothing to help matters. At least there were no clouds of body odour wafting his way. In fact, there was a light lemon perfume emanating from Katerina which was quite refreshing. He tried the radio again. There were just some very scratchy stations fading in and out of the air waves. He turned it off.

Emily came up with a game for them to play. She started with one word, "Italy". The next person had to come up with a place name beginning with the last letter of the previous word. She would allow a country, city, town, region, district, or even a continent - the rules were extremely generous. Going clockwise around the car, Matthew went next. He struggled for a while, and pretended that he had to concentrate on the road. Then he came up with "Yarmouth". Katerina immediately said "Harpenden" followed by Emily with "Newbury" and then they both laughed out loud.

'So, I've got another "Y", have I?' muttered Matthew. 'Ok, "York" – I've actually been there once on a school outing.'

Emily butted in: 'You do have the whole world to choose from – not just good old England.'

And the game played out for the next fifty miles. It was good fun and a useful distraction from the relentless driving. Matthew kept himself in the game – just. The girls had played it before, of course, and they had developed their own library of place names to meet anything thrown at them. After the geography lesson, Matthew suggested that they change tack and run the game on the names of actors, film stars, comedians and the like. He started with "Albert Finney".

'There you go,' he said, 'you can try a "Y" for a change.'

Katerina was quick-witted and immediately came up with "Yul Bryner". Then there was some jocular debate about whether it was first name or last name. They agreed eventually to allow either. "Richard Harris" was the "R" from the end of Bryner. The game was constantly punctuated by discussions of films or shows that the actors had been in.

The gulf in their film and TV tastes was immense. There was surprising agreement on a couple of things though. One was the universal appeal of *The Brothers* TV show. Apparently, the whole of Somerville college turned out in the Junior Common Room on a Sunday evening to watch it. For Matthew, it was one of his mother's favourite programmes. He couldn't understand why but he tolerated it for that alone. It was one of those programmes which were peculiarly compelling even while he more or less despised the precious characters in it and found the story lines laughably banal. He did not tell anyone that he actually watched it. The other piece of common ground was *Young Frankenstein* which they all thought was hilarious. They discovered this from someone proffering "Marty Feldman" for an answer. The previous response had been "Alastair Sim". That had come from "Gina Lollobrigida". And before that … well, it was a long game. Where did all the names come from? Matthew's distant Sunday afternoons watching black and white films on the television was coming in handy after all.

The landscape was flat and stretched away into the distance. There was a hint of higher ground towards the horizon. The road ran pretty straight. Even the curves were gentle and you could see for miles. Alongside there was an abundance of green foliage from the thickets of trees planted to line the highway as if it were a fancy boulevard. It made the road feel enclosed and less exposed. They had put on another hundred miles and had passed Arezzo. The petrol was running low and they were all in need of a pit stop. The next services were large, a huge tarmac'd area of car park, a dozen petrol pumps, toilets, cafeteria, and a grill for the higher end clientele. Matthew parked up. Joints were stiff and they all stretched their arms and legs as they walked slowly over to the toilets.

'I'll see you inside,' Matthew said, pointing at the cafeteria. 'I need a cup of tea.'

'Yes, good idea,' said Emily. 'Buona idea.' She was delighted to be flexing her linguistic muscles.

It was not a great cup of tea, no more than lukewarm, and not very strong. Matthew thought of his dad's predilection for tea that looked more like stout than lager. Still, it was wet and welcome despite its limitations. Emily had a Fanta. Katerina got Emily to ask for a jug of water and she sipped that while eating a banana she had bought at the start of the day.

'So, this could be the last leg if things go smoothly,' said Matthew. 'Are you ok with that?'

Katerina was first to respond.

'Matthew, I've got to say this. You have been brilliant to take us all this way. It's the best journey ever. We'll never be able to thank you enough.'

Emily was nodding approval to all of this.

'Very kind of you, ladies,' said Matthew, wanting to move it on. 'I can say the same back to you. I mean, what would it have been like for me driving through half of France and Italy all on my tod? Without you girls to look after me, how would I have coped? No, seriously, it's been perfect. You've probably kept me sane, with all the geography and book talk, and all that stuff about Oxford. I feel like I've already graduated.'

'Is that all?' said Katerina, suddenly sounding a little disappointed. 'What about me and Emily?' She paused, an element of drama creeping into her voice. 'I mean, now that you have got to know us. Well, for example, would you go out with either of us?'

She blurted it out. Emily remained very still. This conversation had suddenly taken a direction which Matthew had not expected. What would he say? What could he say? He had been told about assertive behaviour in management on one of the training courses at work. It had come across in a dry academic form and he had not given it much thought. Now he was feeling some pressure of a very personal nature. It was an unusual experience for him. A woman making her presence felt, pushing herself forward, making the first move. Was that what was happening? Or was he reading too much into it? His principal experience to date was that the boy asked first and always risked rejection. That's how things worked. Now, it seemed that it was the other way round. And he suddenly realised that it was not easy. What did he want? And if he did not want, was he man enough to pass on rejection? It was doubly difficult as well because it was not even a one to one situation. He was one, but both Emily and Katerina were in this conversation. He felt he would have to deflect the question, summon up whatever his Irish heritage could provide in the form of diplomatic lightheartedness and obfuscation. At least, play for time, keep the ball in play.

'I never thought you'd ask! I'm free any time.'

Katerina had gathered herself and came back a little more controlled.

'Oh, I didn't mean to put you on the spot, old bean. It's just, you know, I think we've got to know you pretty well in the last two days. Up close and personal in the car for hours on end. I just feel I want to tell you. You are a very lovely guy.'

'Spare the poor bloke his blushes,' interrupted Emily, who herself had a reddish glow to her face.

Matthew was trying to remain cool. He had to close this off. And they needed to get moving.

'Well, I feel exactly the same about you too.' It was said with a warm avuncular smile.

He realised, as he said it, that the "too" was ambiguous. They could not be sure whether he meant "too" or "two". So much the better for the ambiguity. That kept things suitably undefined. Matthew paused for a second to let it sink in, hoping that he did not have to elaborate. Then he looked up at the clock and pointed at the time. It was just turning four o'clock.

'Another one hundred and twenty miles and we'll be in Rome!' said Matthew. 'Let's get going.'

'La Dolce Vita!' Emily said, lightening the tone in her perfect Italian accent.

July 1951

—∞—

Nora was exhausted. She had not slept properly for over twenty four hours. The journey was too much with an infant. She should have known. John grabbed hold of the cases and hurriedly placed them down on the platform. Then he went back inside the carriage to help Nora and the baby from the train. Nora felt the warm evening breeze and the pure air of Clare for the first time in nearly two years. After the stuffy compartment, she felt momentarily refreshed. Now she had the next hurdle to climb. She was going home to see her parents. Most of all, she was going to have to face her mother. John gathered the cases again. Nora held Matthew and they started off along the platform towards the station building and the exit into the town.

'Nora, Nora,' a voice was calling in the distance. Nora recognised it immediately. Her father, Hughie Gallagher, came striding towards them, a huge grin on his red face.

'You're welcome, indeed.' He was almost overcome with emotion at seeing his daughter after so long. He checked himself.

'And who do we have here?' he said, looking intently at the little baby.

'This is Matthew, your first grandchild,' beamed Nora, already at ease with herself. She knew her father loved her, and that was all that mattered.

'Come along here now and we'll get you up to the house in the car.' And turning to John, he said. 'You're very welcome, son. You'll get a surprise when you see the car I'm driving now.'

And he grabbed little Matthew out of Nora's arms without any further ceremony and marched away. 'Come on, young feller, we'll see what you make of your own country.'

Nora rushed to catch up with him. John was left to lug the cases. The car turned out to be a large black Vauxhall Velux, the size of a small bus. John was suitably impressed. The ride up to the house was less than five minutes. Nora was not looking forward to this part. Neither was John. The whole episode of their lightning engagement and wedding in England had caused a great deal of upset with both families in Ireland. None of their parents had made the journey over for the event. In truth, while they had been invited, Nora was not as bothered as John when the invitations were politely declined. The presence of her mother was one less thing to have to cope with. She was sorry that her father had not been there to give her away. That remained a huge regret. Even so, Nora had been prepared to pay the price and she had got what she wanted – she had John. For his part, John knew that he would be regarded as the interloper with no right to take Nora Gallagher off to be his wife. As the train took them closer to their destination, he would have happily traded the impending interview with his "new" in-laws for a week of night shifts. The obvious warmth in the welcome from Hughie brought an unexpected relief. He did not think it would be as simple with the mother-in-law.

All their misgivings, in fact, turned out to be unfounded. There was an obvious tension when they first landed at the house, Hughie leading the way with Nora and baby, and John taking his time to gather the cases from the boot of the car. By the time John arrived in the kitchen, he was witnessing both women in floods of tears and holding onto each other as if their lives depended on it. Hughie was cradling the infant in his big arms, the baby wide awake but fully contented. Marie was sobbing almost inconsolably.

'Nora, Nora, you're returned. You've come back. I'm so happy to see you.'

It seemed that these were tears of joy, on both sides. John could see that Nora was almost shaking with her crying, unable to let go of the mother. Hughie winked at John as if to say, 'What did you expect?' John felt at a complete loss, standing looking on. There was a little cry from Matthew, and this had the effect of tempering the emotion in the room. Nora stepped back to see what the matter was, but it was Marie who got to Matthew first.

'Come here, wee man, come to your mamo.'

Marie gathered him safely into her arms and stepped back and forth to gently soothe him. All her motherly skills were immediately revived. She made baby talk to this bright young thing in her arms, goo-goo and ba-ba-ing as if it were her native tongue. The baby's bright blue eyes never left her for a second. Nora watched. Her mother's devotion was plain. Nora could not help but admire her. That in itself was astonishing. She had long ago given up dreaming of a moment such as this. Atonement. Forgiveness. Reconciliation. Perhaps this was what a miracle looked like.

It was not all plain sailing. Nothing ever could be. Mrs Gallagher's hardness may have been softened by the arrival of her first grandchild, and the return of her prodigal daughter. However, there was still the haughtiness and the superiority and the arrogance which could rear their heads if provoked. For the most part, though, she confined these to targets outside the family. Nora thought it remarkable that there was no extended inquest over the wedding or over John's circumstances. Even with his recent success at being taken on as a skilled mechanical engineer by one of the city's most prestigious engineering firms, he could never compete with the "good doctor" in Marie Gallagher's world view. Yet nothing was said. If Marie was holding her tongue under instruction from Hughie Gallagher, that was good enough. It made for a happy two weeks. In fact, it seemed to Nora that Marie had uncharacteristically taken a shine to John after the first couple of days. She had him digging out in the vegetable plot, fixing the guttering, and sweeping the chimney. All the while doting on the baby and proudly showing him off around the town on her daily walk with Nora. John was also occupied by Hughie with a variety of jobs. It suited John fine to be kept busy. It enabled the men to build a respect for each other.

There had been little concern over the welcome they would get from the Hoolahan clan. Justifiably so. There was a genuine air of celebration when John and Nora, complete with baby, went out to the farm. John was looked over carefully, to see if and how he might have changed. Nora was looked over carefully, to see who this woman was that had captured their son. The star of the show, however, was baby Matthew. He had all the ladies enraptured. Nora quickly became close with John's sisters. Mary, her mother-in-law, made it clear that she approved of Nora and was happy to see her son married to her. All in all, it seemed that the bridges had been mended.

The really difficult part came near the end of their stay. Hughie spoke at length to Nora, trying to convince her to return home. All the arguments he put forward had merit. He could put John to work at the Store. Nora too could resume some work, and there was the prospect of them taking over the business in the future. Matthew would have the support of his grandparents and the extended families. It all sounded perfect. Except that Nora knew that it was not what she wanted. Having made the break once, she had no intention of going back. She had made a new life elsewhere. Nora agonised over whether to tell John what had been said. She hoped that he would have the same opinion as herself. And with that honesty which she could not escape from, she explained the offer her father had been pressing on her. It was such a relief when, without any prompting,

John said simply, 'I'm not for coming back. Sure, it's grand for the holidays but we have our own life now over yonder.'

If he was disappointed with Nora's non-committal response, Hughie was big enough to mask it. He asked Nora to help him go over some things at the Store during the last few days. There were some things he genuinely wanted her thoughts on. More though, he wanted to have her back in the shop just for a little while, as he remembered her, as he wanted to be able to picture her in the weeks and months to come. He wanted something of her to be present in the shop when she was gone. He was a sentimental old fool, he knew it. He longed for the easy company of his daughter, to know where she was. To know that he could look after her and, for that matter, that she could be there to look after him. He came to understand that things could not go back to how they had been. So he just clung to whatever memories he could. Marie, for her part, struggled to cope as the departure day approached. When would she see her grandson again? How would she cope second time round with her daughters gone? The emptiness of the life stretching in front of her was enough to freeze her to the core. Mrs Gallagher said her brief goodbye at the door of the house, too distraught to accompany them to the station. Then she went back inside and took to her bed. Her only hope was that time would reduce the hurt.

As they boarded the train for the journey home, Hughie slipped an envelope into John's jacket pocket. It was a very generous gift. It was the least he could do. He just prayed that it would not be too long before he would see them again.

Day Five - June 1975 - Termini

With the tank full, creaking limbs rejuvenated, and a new air of anticipation, Matthew steered them back onto the A1. He spent the greater part of the final leg of the journey in the outside lane. They mostly couldn't get much past sixty miles an hour because of the volume of traffic. Occasionally, they got a burst up to eighty but these were short-lived dashes. The miles were gradually being whittled away. By six thirty, they were getting very close. Matthew was looking for the S94 to take them towards the centre of the city. He managed to miss the turn off and had to keep on the A1 until a few miles later when they arrived at a huge intersection with another motorway. Emily could tell them from her book that this was signed GRA.

'Grande Raccordo Anulare,' Emily announced, wrapping her tongue around the impressive name. 'In other words, a big ring road!'

Matthew followed it west for a few miles and then saw the signs for the centre and they ploughed ahead. He had no idea where he was going to end up. He asked the girls if they had a preferred stopping point. Emily said that she had been given the addresses of two convents which provided cheap hostel accommodation to so-called "pilgrims". A friend from back home had "done" Rome the previous year and said it had been a hoot staying with the nuns. Emily did not need to imagine too hard what that meant. She had spent seven years under the watchful eyes of the Loreto sisters at her secondary school. She clearly did not have the makings of a nun herself but for the most part respected the sisters and was aware of how she had thrived in the community of the school. So, she had not rebelled like Baba and Kate Brady. On the contrary, she had conformed and she had won her place as an exhibitioner at her Oxford college. She could cope with the nuns, and it would probably make the visit to Rome even more special to stay in a cloistered environment. It would be a revelation to Katerina, of course! The one downside might be the early curfew, doors locked at ten o'clock each evening. The big upside would be the fact that the convent was meant to be cheap.

Unfortunately, the map in Emily's guide book was not detailed enough to pinpoint either of the addresses. In any case, the evening was getting on and Emily thought that they would now be too late. The convents would likely be filling up from early afternoon. So, based on what the guide book said and what other friends had told them, the best plan for Emily and Katerina tonight was to go to the tourist information office where it should be possible to get booked in for the night in a guest house or small hotel.

'I think the preferred option for us will be to head for the main railway station,' said Emily. 'It's called Termini, by the way. The book says that there is a tourist office at the station and they can help us find rooms. And apparently, there are loads of little hotels and pensiones around and about the station, anyway.'

'Ok,' said Matthew. 'Head to the station! That works perfectly. It's more or less where I am going anyway. My brother has booked us into a hotel which he said is no more than a five minute walk from the station. How's that map of yours? Does it give us any clues?'

Emily was navigating from the rear seat using the map that folded out of the back cover of her guide book.

'We are definitely heading in the general direction,' intoned Katerina, who had been unusually quiet for some time. 'I saw "Centro" on a sign back there and I'm pretty sure the railway station is in the centre of the city.'

'Yeah,' said Emily, 'but that was Centro Commerciale which is really just a shopping centre. You're probably right, though. I would keep driving straight down here, Matthew. If you see a name for the road we are on, tell me and I'll see if I can find it on the map.'

'Salaria,' shouted Katerina. 'Just saw it at that last corner. "Via Salaria" – there was a sign above the café.'

Progress was slow. Matthew was in second gear a lot of the time coasting at 15 to 20 miles an hour if they were lucky. It was heavily parked up, people out doing their evening shopping, vehicles trying to squeeze into or out of minimal parking spaces holding up the traffic behind them. It gave Emily time to work out the next move.

'There should be a big crossroads soon and you want to turn left down a road called Viale Regina Margherita.'

'We just passed it back there,' said Katerina. 'See where those lights are.'

Matthew was taking it all in and assessing his options. There was no chance of doing a u-turn here so he pulled right down the next side street. Another challenge as it was very narrow. He drove down to find a small intersection. There was nothing behind so he began what he hoped would be a three point turn. Half way through, with an impatient van driver appearing from nowhere behind him, clearly fond of his horn, Matthew suddenly wondered if he was in a one way street. He revved out of the turning manoeuvre with a new plan already formulated. He could simply try going round the block. A right turn at the little intersection followed by another right would potentially bring him back to the road they wanted. At the second right onto what was clearly a big wide main road, the street name said Viale Liegi. Where were they now? Amidst the confusion, Matthew could only complete the turn and hope for the best. He drove on and they crossed over the lights at a big junction just along the road. It was sharp-eyed Katerina who settled everyone's nerves.

'Look, up there, we are on Regina Margherita after all.'

Emily advised another right turn after a few minutes which took them along towards Piazzale di Porta Pia. There was a picture in her book so they couldn't miss that.

'We're in touching distance of Termini,' she declared triumphantly, and Katerina whistled enthusiastically.

'Please don't take this the wrong way, Matthew,' she said, 'but I am dying to get out of this car and the heat, and I need a long cold beer.'

You can say that again, thought Matthew. The beer first. Then a bit of time to himself would be nice for once. Driving in an unknown city was not a pleasure, especially after a long day's worth of driving beforehand.

The last mile was a test for all of them. Especially for Matthew trying to negotiate one way signs, weird traffic lights, and narrow streets with cars parked everywhere. Then the hawk-eyed Katerina announced, 'There it is, over there. At last!'

Matthew was wondering how he was going to drop them off and then find where he needed to be.

'Look, girls,' he said, 'any chance you can do me a favour and help me find my hotel? It's going to be difficult trying to drive and look at the same time. And you do have a map!'

'Sure thing!' They spoke in harmony.

'Of course,' said Katerina. 'Do you have the address of the hotel?'

Matthew had it imprinted on his brain.

'It's Hotel Aurelius, and the address is Via Marghera.'

'You don't mean that road back there that we just came down?' said Katerina.

'That was Regina Margherita,' corrected Emily.

'I am pretty sure that the road my hotel is on is called Marghera,' said Matthew and he spelled it out. 'I'd not heard of the other one – Margherita – before today.'

'Oh, you're absolutely right,' said Emily, 'I can see it on the map here. It's off to the other side of the station, but it's no distance. See if you can find the road at the front of Termini and you just have to follow round.'

After twenty minutes of tortuous stop-start, they were finally squeezed into a minuscule parking spot, half way up the pavement, and about six hundred yards from the hotel. Matthew switched off the engine and sat back, stretching his lower back muscles, eyes closed, thankful for the end of this particular chapter. He was dog-tired, eyes weary, he felt sweaty and sticky. A bit of an anticlimax for what was a mini triumph. No pun intended, he mused. And then a smile showed on his lips, and a serene joy lit up his inner being. The brief moment of despondency wrought of tiredness and stress drained away and he turned to speak to Emily and Katerina.

'Well, mes amies, we finally made it. Will you be all right getting to the station from here? I'll come along with you if you want.'

'Matthew, you don't need to do that. You've been brilliant. Thank you so much for everything.' This was Emily.

Katerina joined in with 'Here, here!'

The goodbyes were made quickly and without much emotion. Everyone was worn out. The rucksacks came out of the boot. Matthew leaned back on the side of the car and smiled as they loaded up their packs. Katerina first, followed by Emily, came up and gave him a hug and a friendly kiss on the cheek. And then they were off, trooping haphazardly down the narrow pavement, and he stood for a moment watching them go.

May 1958

—ꟺ—

'Those two need shoes. The baby's wearing old rags. And look at the state of me.'

Nora's eyes were red with sobbing. What had she become? What had they become? Scraping through week by week. They had brought four new lives into the world. What sort of life were they giving them?

'You know it's been quiet at work for the last few months.'

John remained calm, trying to defuse the row. He hated conflict. He also recognised how right Nora was.

'The gaffer reckons that it's going to pick up soon. You know I'll take all the overtime I can get.'

Nora's resentment began to dissipate. At the height of her despair, she could blame anyone and everyone – John, herself, the world. In her calmer moments, she was ashamed of the nastiness that sometimes boiled over in her.

'John, how will we ever manage? Just look at us.'

She cast a despairing hand around the small living room. It was crammed with old furniture. The small dining table by the window with four brown wooden chairs tucked around it. A worn out red sofa in front of the fireplace. A single battered armchair in the far corner. Every surface was fully laden. Clothes on chairs, washing in a pile on the floor in a corner, a few toys and books scattered around. Despite the clutter, there was one thing you could say about the house – it was clean. Nora wore her fingers to the bone every day with washing, cleaning, and trying to keep on top of the natural disorder.

'I give you everything I earn,' pleaded John. He was almost tearful himself but managed to hold onto his dignity.

'I know, John, I know.'

Nora wanted to console him now. He was by no means perfect. Nobody was. Sometimes she resented him. He was able to escape from this place every day when he went off to his work. What she knew with certainty was that there was no bad in him. That was enough to jolt her back to a more hopeful outlook. Maybe she had to go through these mood swings to reset herself for the daily battles with life.

'I've been thinking. We've still got that money from my dad. The £50 he sent when Geraldine was born. I was keeping it for an emergency. You know, if we had to go back home for any reason.'

'That's your money,' said John.

'No,' said Nora firmly. 'That's our money.'

'Well, we've no plans for a visit home. You do what you think is best. You've the brains for all of that.'

'One good thing,' Nora reminded herself, 'we haven't any debts. You know I'm not one for asking for credit for anything. We can feed ourselves and just about pay the rent with what you're earning. What's soul destroying is the constant worry and having to scrape by. It would be so nice to be able to hope for better, for a little bit more than just surviving week to week. I want to be sending the kids out decent and proper. It's getting harder all the time when they need new things.'

'I see it with my own eyes,' said John. 'I'll see what the boss has got to say on Monday about any overtime. If there's no prospect, maybe I'll have to look for something else.'

'No, John,' said Nora quickly and firmly. 'I know you're happy in the engineering. You found your feet when you got the start with Biddulph's. I can tell when a person is happy in their work. And I never want you to lose that. It's a good steady job with a big solid firm, supplying the best equipment the world over. I know you've got a pride and a genuine love of all that machinery and the heavy gear that I hear you talking to the boys about. You're able to use that brain of yours and that's a real blessing not everybody has. I'll not hear talk of changing jobs. We'll manage somehow.'

'I'll turn my hand to anything if need be,' said John. 'The money would be better on the buildings. I'm sure I could get back on with one of the crowd around Leicester. I could ask Larry Costello at the church. He's a ganger with Morrison's. I've heard they've got a big job starting soon over at New Fields.'

Nora came to a decision.

'That's enough, John. I've talked myself round. Twenty pounds will go a long way for what I'm wanting. I'll take that out of the savings. And there'll still be something left for an emergency. I'm going to kit out the children for the summer and I'll get shoes for the two. That's been my main concern all along. I can't have them looking like poor neglected wretches. I do need something for myself to wear for Matthew's communion. I'll see if Edie can get me some fabric cheap and run something up for me on the side. She's always offering.'

A few days later, it was Saturday teatime. Kathleen was tending to Geraldine. It was a thrill for her to give the baby her bottle, to hush and rock her gently. Downstairs, Nora was supervising the three boys – Matthew, Patrick, and Sean – as she gave them their tea. Tonight it was sausages and egg, filled out with plenty of bread and butter. For the few minutes that it took them to wolf down their food, a calmness descended and Nora was able to reclaim her sanity. As soon as they had finished, all three rushed out into the street for the final hour or two of play. Nora collapsed onto the sofa, the dishes left on the table. Kathleen came down the stairs, whispering to Nora as she came back into the room.

'I could take her home with me tonight! She's a wee darling.'

Nora smiled back. 'You mightn't think so when she wakens you up at three o'clock in the morning.'

'I dare say,' sighed Kathleen. 'But I'll take her anyway if you let me,' she added.

It was her customary joke. Behind the make believe lay Kathleen's longing for a child of her own that would now probably never be fulfilled. Ever down to earth, Kathleen would act out a semblance of motherhood by proxy.

She sat down beside Nora and rooted in her shopping bag at the side of the sofa. She pulled out a bag and turned to present it to Nora.

'Have a look at this. I was in Marks this morning and I couldn't resist it.'

Nora opened the bag and took out a beautiful lemon cotton smock dress. It had ruffled sleeves and fine white embroidery across the chest.

'It's beautiful,' said Nora. 'You're a devil, that's what you are. It's far too much, Kathleen. It really is.'

'Away with you,' Kathleen rebuked her. 'I'm the godmother, amn't I?'

They both laughed. Nora was delighted. It was going to be wonderful to see her little baby girl dressed up to the nines. In the scheme of things, it was completely unimportant. And yet it did such a lot to restore Nora's sense of worth and appreciation of what she had.

'Now, while I've got you on your own, I want you to have this.'

Kathleen handed a small envelope to Nora.

'What in the name of God?' asked Nora.

She opened the envelope to find five one pound notes. She started to force the bundle back into Kathleen's hand and then her handbag.

'Nora,' said Kathleen sternly. 'Put that in your purse and no more arguing.'

'I can't take that. You can't afford to be handing me money like that.'

'I'm telling you now,' said Kathleen, as firmly as she could. 'I want you to put that money in your purse. I've no need of it. Really! I've got my wages every week. Steve's got his wages. We have more than we need. It's our pleasure to help you out a bit with the kids. Just believe me, will you?'

Nora got up and put the money away safely. If it had been anyone else, Nora would have felt distraught at ending up a charity case. There was still a hint of that. However, with Kathleen, they were so close as sisters, and Kathleen was so intricately involved in the rearing of the children. The main feeling was joy and gratitude for having such a generous and caring sister – and best friend.

'I was thinking we could treat ourselves to some fish and chips when the children are settled.'

Kathleen was having all the ideas tonight.

'Steve's going to be in the Oddfellows about eight o'clock and he's expecting John to meet up with him there. So we can have a good catch up to ourselves.'

Nora's spirits were lifted. An evening with Kathleen was always entertaining. There were bound to be plenty of stories from the Gents' factory. And Kathleen could tell Nora about the holiday arrangements for when she and Steve would be taking Matthew and Patrick to the seaside in July. It would be good as well for John to go out for the evening and have a change of scene. The little things often made life just that bit more bearable.

Day Five - June 1975 - Hotel Valerius

It was nearly eight o'clock when Matthew finally found himself ringing the bell in the small reception of the Hotel Aurelius. He had left the luggage in the car until he was sure that everything was going to be ok in the hotel. He was learning to be cautious. He had had a bad experience on one of the many training courses he had been on with work. Arriving late at a hotel in Birmingham only to find that there was no booking. A long night scuttling around bed and breakfasts before he finally found one with a vacancy.

A middle aged man wearing what looked like an attempt at a uniform - black jacket, black trousers, faded white shirt, and bright green tie - appeared through a door from behind the reception counter. He smiled brightly at Matthew - it was a question asked without actually mouthing the words. It immediately struck Matthew that he should have held onto Emily for another twenty minutes while he got this sorted out. He'd been too elated, and too tired, to think that far ahead.

'Hello. Do you speak English?' He had to start somewhere.

'A little,' came the reply. 'You have reservation?'

'Yes.'

'Name?'

'It's Hoolahan. Matthew Hoolahan.'

He tried spelling it out. The man cut him short.

'One minute, please.'

He went back through the door he had entered from and was gone for a couple of minutes. When he came back, he was holding some paperwork which he laid down on the counter. Matthew could feel some explanation coming on which he was not going to enjoy.

'Un problema, signore. Hoolahan. Sorry, no room here.' He stretched out each of the vowels as he repeated the name Hoolahan.

Matthew was tongue-tied. He wanted to say a lot of things. There was a feeling of hopelessness in the situation. He might start to get very annoyed. He checked himself, realising that it was pointless. Half resigned to his own fate, he still needed to find out about his mother and father. They were meant to be staying here as well. They should have arrived the night before. He tried to think of a simple way of asking the question only to be interrupted by the clerk before he could get it out.

'Very sorry. Problema with reservation. We have no rooms.'

His wide smile and twinkling eyes were something of a surprise.

'But problema is fixed. You have room in sister hotel. Just along the street.'

'My mother and father are meant to be staying here. Mr and Mrs Hoolahan?'

'Si, signore. I know this. They also are in the other hotel.'

'What is the name of the hotel?'

'Si, it is Hotel Valerius. I show you. Very close.'

Matthew found himself walking back along the street where he had parked the car. He could see a sign sticking out from a building about another three hundred yards along. That had to be it. As he approached the entrance, he looked in through a large plate glass window. He had to peer in as there was not much light. He could see that it was a small bar. It looked like there were dining tables towards the back of the room. And there, half way back, the indisputable silhouette of his mother. He could recognise that hairdo at half a mile. A combined feeling of surprise and relief swept over him.

'Fancy meeting you here!' was his attempt at a light-hearted greeting.

Nora had been looking the other way and had not seen him come into the bar.

'Ah, love. You're here. Thank God.'

Matthew thought that it was typical of his mother not to show too much affection. But he could see that she was happy to see him.

'And where's dad?'

'Oh, he's paying a visit. Gone back to the bedroom, I think. We've got our own little bathroom. It's nice and private.'

She paused momentarily and then thought for a moment. 'And where's Kathleen?'

This was going to be tricky. That moment of contentment was probably going to be overtaken immediately by anxiety and despondency. And possibly some anger. Just then, John wandered back in and clasped Matthew around the shoulders.

'Well done, son. That must have been some drive. How's the motor?'

'Never mind about the car,' interrupted Nora. 'Where's my sister? Is she all right?'

'Well,' said Matthew, 'there's a bit of a story there.'

He proceeded to explain how things had been on the Thursday after John and Nora had left for Turin on the train. Then he had to recount how Kathleen had said that she was not feeling well enough to travel on the Friday morning but insisted that Matthew complete the journey to Rome. Nora was silent, a grimness emanating from her dark eyes. It was John who punctuated the despondency. He spoke directly to his wife.

'Nora, you know what Kathleen is like. There's no saying no to her. Matty had no choice.'

'That's all very well,' replied Nora, 'but there's no-one looking after Kathleen. She could be dying in the bed and no-one will know any better.'

'Mam,' said Matthew. 'I didn't really explain. She was definitely feeling better, on the mend. It was just that she couldn't face a day in the car. She'll be ok.'

He was not entirely convinced himself but he had to try to be positive in this situation.

'Sure she has Edith there dancing attention on her. She will be fine, if I know Kathleen.' John added this in an attempt to comfort Nora.

'It's the last thing I needed tonight,' muttered Nora.

'Still glad to see me then?' asked Matthew, trying to lighten the proceedings.

Nora softened a little, her tense shoulders relaxing a touch.

'Of course, love. It's just … Well, I keep thinking about her. But I've got you here and that is a blessing I should be grateful for.'

Taking that as his cue to move things on, Matthew asked:

'Anyway, what's the story with the hotel? What was the "problema" at the one along there, you know, the one we were booked in?'

This was a good diversion and it took Nora's mind off Kathleen for the moment.

'Oh, we had some excitement last night when we arrived. I don't know how we got out of the station alive. All these people offering us God knows what. Lucky we don't speak the Italian. Anyway, your dad reckons they were tinkers.'

'You can tell them a mile away,' said John.

'Anyways, we didn't want to start traipsing around the streets not knowing where we were going. So we got a taxi.'

'He was a robber as well,' added John.

'He didn't want to take us in the first place,' said Nora. 'Anyway, we arrived at the hotel. We couldn't make ourselves understood. We showed them our name. Then all we know is there was a problem.'

'Anyway,' said John trying to speed up the explanation, 'the long and the short of it is that we gave them the number of the English College to try to speak to Patrick. Of course, they couldn't find him but we got speaking to a lovely young priest called Edward. After a lot of to-ing and fro-ing on the phone between the hotel, the priest, and us, it eventually seemed that the hotel had overbooked. But they managed to transfer our bookings to this hotel. So, here we are.'

'Ok,' said Matthew. 'All's well … Look, I'd better get myself checked in. I need to freshen up. Have you had your dinner?'

'We went across the road earlier to that place over there, La Trattoria. There's not much in the way of food here.'

'Patrick is coming to see us for half an hour,' said Nora. 'He'll be here any minute. If you're quick, you'll get to see him.'

'We can all go over the road for a little drink,' suggested John.

Nora said, 'As long as it's not too late. We all have an early start tomorrow.'

September 1970

—∞—

It was a brilliant autumnal Saturday morning. The middle of September. A scattering of fluffy white clouds drifted across the gleaming azure sky. The hint of early mist had already evaporated. The sun was creeping slowly towards centre stage. At eight thirty in the morning, the air was still fresh and clean. Matthew made his way down Regent Road towards the station. Faded Levi jeans, denim jacket, white T-shirt, brown leather boots. He looked and felt like a West Coast rock star. He was just missing a guitar to complete the look.

He passed the park on his left hand side. Nature seemed to be at its exuberant best – luxuriant trees, richly verdant bushes, and bold coloured flowers showing off in all their finery. If anyone had asked him, Matthew would have picked exactly this sort of a day, at this time of year, as his ideal. He walked quickly, anticipation high. He was meeting Finn and Kenny. The three of them were heading off to London. City were playing away at Charlton Athletic. Finn and Matthew followed the football but rarely went to an away match. The idea of a day out in London, a change of scenery, was the real appeal for them. It was Kenny who was genuinely football daft.

'You wanna get yoursel' a bacon butty from the caff, they're ace.'

Kenny Sinclair talked as fast as he ate. The brown sauce was dribbling down his chin as he took another chunk out of the roll.

'I think I'll get another one,' he said, as he polished off the first.

They were on Platform 3 waiting for the 09:01 train to St. Pancras. Kenny had told them it was best to get an early train. They definitely wanted to avoid the football special that left at eleven. So here they were, ready for the off.

'Do you think this new bloke will be playing?' asked Finn.

'Bound to,' spluttered Kenny, now crunching through a packet of crisps. 'Ain't gonna spend all that money for nothing, are they? Stands to reason, don't it?'

They were in an old fashioned compartment with room for eight people. They had it to themselves until Kettering so the talk was free and easy. Kenny was dissecting the finer points of City's defence. Finn was keen to tell them about the girl he had met at Fusion on Thursday night. He had a date for the pictures on Sunday. This could be the one. Matthew let it all wash over him. He'd heard it all before. Next week, Finn would have a dance with someone else and he would be talking about getting engaged the next day.

Two women in their fifties came and sat in their compartment at Kettering. Well dressed, smartly spoken, and friendly to the boys. They played their part perfectly, best manners automatically on display. There was some pleasant inconsequential chatter – "off to the football", "off to the shops" – and then the conversation lulled. Matthew read the sports pages in the *Mirror*. After a while, he closed his eyes and fell into a light doze. He seemed to know exactly when to regain full consciousness. The train was slowing and the guard announced 'London St. Pancras, your next and final stop.'

'Come on,' said Kenny. 'This is us.'

Finn and Matthew carried no bag. It was just themselves and the clothes they stood up in. Kenny, the well travelled supporter, had a duffel bag slung over his shoulder. He went prepared for all weathers. And he kept a journal in which he wrote up reports of all the matches he went to. This he protected at all costs, like a personal diary. Finn and Matthew knew it existed but had learned not to press him on it. One day, they might get to read the thoughts of Chairman Sinclair.

As they walked along the platform, Matthew remembered to look up and check out the famous single span iron roof. For all the dates and names that they tried to make him learn in history, it was real things like this that had sparked his interest. Dickie Dixon could have been on the stage – flamboyant, larger than life, a comedian. His history lessons had been pure entertainment. It was just a pity that Matthew had only had the pleasure of his tutelage in the fifth form. Dickie had easily grabbed Matthew's attention. The industrial revolution, the railways, the Victorians. It all made sense when you looked at something like St. Pancras. Matthew smiled as he went through the brick arches past the ticket office. The streaky bacon brickwork was just as Dickie had described it.

'It's only quarter to eleven,' said Finn. 'How about we go and have a wander along Oxford Street?'

'Suppose,' grumbled Kenny. He was not keen but had nothing to counter with.

Finn knew a bit of London from school trips he had been on. He was consulting the map on the wall by the stairway down to the tube.

'Look. It's this blue line. Yeah, the Victoria line. It's only two, no three stops.'

Twenty minutes later, they emerged from the underground at Oxford Circus. The pavement was teeming with people at this time on a warm sunny Saturday morning. The three compatriots stood to take in their surroundings. The large buildings, the impressive shop frontages, the bumper-to-bumper traffic. They joined the heaving throng and strolled along, their eyes dancing towards the latest impressive display.

'Hey,' said Matthew, 'do you think Carnaby Street is anywhere near here?'

'I know it is,' said Kenny, 'but I'll have to look at the map to see how to find it.'

So saying, he delved into the duffel bag and pulled out a London A-Z book.

'You must have been in the Scouts,' laughed Finn.

'Yeah, well, I got lost going to Tottenham once so I bought this.'

They stood down a side street where there were less pedestrians and pored over the book. Finn cracked it.

'Look, we can go down here, and it's just along this Great Marlborough Street.'

This was exciting. Matthew drank in the whole experience. He was suddenly struck by the predominance of young people all around. They could be on a different planet to the one that they had left two and half hours earlier. The style of clothes on display was so much more extreme than he had imagined. They browsed in a couple of boutiques, amazed at some of the items and the prices. Matthew was not convinced you would get away with wearing any of this stuff at home. It did not stop Finn from buying a pure white satin shirt with fancy lace work around the top pocket. Finn had style, certainly he had pretensions. It actually suited him.

'It's quarter past twelve,' said Kenny. It was his way of saying that they would need to get moving.

'Here, Kenny, stick this in your bag, will you?' Finn did not want to be lumbered with a carrier bag in his hand for the rest of the day.

'Come on, then,' said Kenny. 'We gotta get back to the tube.'

By chance, they walked up Argyll Street right past the London Palladium.

'Oh, I can tell me mam that I've been to the Palladium,' said Kenny with a broad smile. 'We used to watch it every Sunday when I was a kid. Norman Vaughan – I liked him.'

'We know,' sighed Finn.

'Any chance we could get something to eat?' chipped in Matthew. He was suddenly starving.

'I think we better get down to Charlton first. Be there in an hour, I reckon.' This was Kenny getting anxious.

'Don't think I can wait an hour,' said Matthew.

'Me neither,' joined in Finn. 'There's a Wimpy over there. Let's just get something while the going's good.'

It was two – one for the Wimpy Bar. Kenny grumpily agreed. It did not take long for him to recover his joie de vivre though. What did the trick was the large burger – with onions – and the plate of chips, smothered with tomato sauce and squeezy yellow mustard. All washed down with strawberry milkshake. Matthew and Finn were also licking their lips, fully satisfied now and ready to rejoin the action.

The journey down to Charlton was less exciting. Matthew could see that riding the tube every day might lose its attraction quite quickly. Down into the bowels of the earth, long walks along underground tunnels just to get to the platform, sweaty bodies rocking and swaying over you all the time.

Finn mapped their route. The Central Line to Bank followed by the Northern Line to London Bridge. Kenny had already told them it was a normal train from there down to Charlton. By the time they got to Bank, they could easily have managed without a map. The Northern line train was carrying several bands of blue and white scarf bearers. It was a cheerful crowd, boisterous but not unruly. Matthew did not see anyone he knew. Kenny recognised a few faces and nodded over.

'They're in the Kop,' he explained to Finn and Matthew. 'I only see them at away matches. And I try to keep my distance,' he added quietly.

Kenny was actually a football fan. He loathed the hooligan element. He had a season ticket in the stand. Still went to home games with his dad. It was a kind of religion for them. Matthew put it down to the Scottish bloodline. You only had to think of mangers like Bill Shankly and Tommy Docherty, or uncompromising players like Dave Mackay and Billy Bremner. They lived for football. Fair play to them, thought Matthew. He did not really get it though.

Kenny was quite relaxed once they left London Bridge. It was only half past one so there was plenty of time to get to the ground and still have forty five minutes to spare. Kenny liked to soak up the pre-match atmosphere. Matthew was not sure how much of that there would be. This was the Second Division after all. It was all part of the "experience", he supposed.

The atmosphere was definitely building. There was quite a bit of singing on the train. One slightly built bloke had the gruffest, gravely voice Matthew had ever heard. He began the chants and was followed by a very bass, almost tuneless, chorus. It was clearly well rehearsed. The humour was still good. Smoke and alcohol fumes wafted through the open carriage. It smelt like they were in a pub.

It was hardly an army of fans, more a large rabble that made its way through the narrow streets to the ground. Inside, it was a revelation. It was cavernous. It was rough, though, and it was not pretty – just massive. The City fans were spoilt for choice as to where to stand. They formed a growing huddle in the middle of the wide terracing. The singing was loud when you were in the middle of it. Matthew was enjoying this bit. It was so warm that most were standing in shirt sleeves, soaking up the rays. At five to three, the players emerged. The warm up lasted all of three minutes and consisted of some cross field passing, someone taking corners to the goalkeeper, and one or two doing a few stretches. Then they lined up for the kick off.

Two hours later, it was all smiles as the City fans trooped back along the streets of Charlton to the station. There was no trouble, no confrontations. This was the Second Division and it was not Arsenal, or Chelsea, or the Hammers. The local fans could save their energies for the real enemy. Meanwhile, Matthew, Finn, and above all Kenny were buoyant with a 1– 0 away win. It made it all seem worthwhile.

'How we gonna celebrate, then?'

Finn already had an idea.

'We could go for a pint,' replied Kenny. 'There's plenty of pubs around St. Pancras and King's Cross.'

'Come on, Kenny. Don't be so boring. Let's see a bit of London. There's no rush to get the train.'

'What you thinking?' asked Matthew, keen to hear what Finn had in mind.

'Well, let's have a look round Soho. That's what I think.'

Kenny was outvoted for the second time that day. Soho it was.

At six o'clock in the evening, it was still full daylight, although the warmth was out of the sun now. Soho was only slowly getting itself ready for Saturday evening. The boys decided that a celebratory drink was needed. They liked the look of the George, standing prominently on a corner along Wardour Street. The first pint was drunk swiftly, soothing their dry throats, relaxing them and increasing the already heightened sense of elation. The second and third pints were savoured. The victory was retold, the characters they had seen were discussed. By seven o'clock, the daylight was nearly gone and Soho was beginning to light up.

'Time for a wander,' said Finn.

'Time for the train, more like,' countered Kenny.

'Ok,' said Matthew. 'We've got time for a bit of a wander. There's a train at nine, and another one at ten. Let's see how it goes.'

Everyone knew what Soho stood for. It was something else to see it in the flesh. The bright lights beckoning the punters into the shops and clubs could not mask the seedy underbelly. Bouncers propping at narrow doorways, lauding the talents of their latest act. There was a plethora of "bookshops" which did not seem to have many books in their windows. The streets were grimy and universally strewn with debris. The boys got a thrill to see the steady stream of Bohemian characters roaming the place. It was impossible to miss the outrageous clothes and to feel the drama building. When Matthew was able to tune into some of the passing conversations, the pavement patter and interchanges made him smile. It was altogether a different world. The stark flouting of convention was both a shock and a revelation. Any pre-conditioned fears of homosexuality were left unspoken momentarily. Until, that is, Kenny could contain himself no longer and let out a cry of:

'Look at that raving puffter over there! F'ing hell! We'd better watch ourselves round here.'

'What's your problem?' said Finn, adopting an unusually serious tone. 'Haven't you heard – this is the 1970's? Live and let live, that's what I say. That bloke over there won't have the slightest interest in you. None of 'em will. So you don't have anything to worry about.'

Matthew had never really thought about it like that before. Too many deep-seated prejudices, too many jokes, too many schoolboy myths. He was both surprised and impressed by Finn. There was definitely more going on there than he had imagined.

They had been wandering for twenty minutes, going nowhere in particular, when Finn broke the spell.

'Fancy one of these strip clubs?' he asked casually.

Neither Kenny nor Matthew would have taken the lead. However, they were willing to follow Finn. Curiosity was eating at all of them. Finn pointed back to a club they had just walked past. There was the mandatory red neon strip surrounding the black doorway. It was minded by a muscular bloke in his thirties, short brown hair, black jacket, no tie. The billboard promised exotic dancers in an artistic show. The pictures suggested more clearly what the boys were looking for.

'You cammin in or wot?' The doorman oozed Soho charm. 'It's a nicker each. Otherwise, piss off.'

'It was ten bob five minutes ago,' said Finn.

The doorman looked at his watch.

'Yeah, and now it's a quid.'

They conceded. It was too late to turn back now. The cash desk was just inside the doorway. A woman took their money without speaking. There were stairs down into the basement and they followed Finn into a small dark room set out as a sort of tiny cabaret bar. The décor was all done out in black. There was a minuscule stage in the far corner. Four other punters were in, all sitting separately and avoiding eye contact. The boys found three stools and parked themselves at a small table in the middle of the floor. A scantily dressed female appeared immediately and asked them what they wanted to drink. It seemed that having a drink was not optional. They settled on a bottle of beer each. At eight bob each, it was exorbitant. In for a penny, thought Matthew.

They sipped the beer and waited patiently. Kenny kept looking at his watch. They'd never get the nine o'clock train now. It was already twenty past eight. Three more punters arrived and got served. Eventually, just after half past eight, a scratchy soundtrack came over the sound system. A figure emerged from the curtain at the side of the dancing platform. A shimmer of black lace and stockings, long black gloves, high heels, short black bobbed hair, crimson lips. She was straight into the performance. A sensual twisting dance, arms expressive and enticing the meagre audience to follow her every move. Despite the dinginess of the surroundings, the dancer was living up to the "artistic" billing. The first items to be discarded were the gloves. A seductive act of removing the stockings followed. It was all done with an impressive elegance and gracious footwork. The tempo of the music increased, the heavy bass line exaggerating the thumping heartbeat in Matthew's chest. There was a long drawn out sequence leading to the removal of the brassiere. The final reveal of the breasts drew a few appreciative gasps from the audience. Matthew noticed Kenny seemed to have his mouth wide open as he gawped at the stage. The breasts were flaunted now with bends and thrusts and twists and turns. And then the performance moved inexorably to its conclusion. Eager anticipation as the G-string was tantalisingly removed. And then it was all over and she was gone.

Some dim wall lights came on and it was clear that they weren't meant to stay for a second showing. They had all seen enough to be getting on with. Kenny was very quiet on the way back to St. Pancras. Would he be writing a report on this performance? Finn openly marvelled at the sight of a naked body in all its glory.

'Worth every penny,' he conjectured.

Matthew silently found himself in two minds. He definitely felt a degree of embarrassment at having gone to the strip show in the first place. It was not something he could ever tell his mother, and he would probably not be proud to tell his friends either. On the other hand, he could not help wondering whether there was anything wrong with admiring the female form. The circumstances were obviously not the best. That was putting it mildly. And that was the problem. He would never know what sort of life the dancer had, what she had to go through, what she had to put up with. He could imagine the worst though. Paying to view – he was helping to perpetuate it. The whole thing felt grubby. Well, he'd done it now and he would just have to take the experience for what it was. You had to draw the line on feeling guilty somewhere.

All three slept on the journey home. They were exhausted physically and mentally. Luckily, Kenny heard the announcement for their stop and they emerged subdued onto London Road. Hardly pausing to say their goodbyes, they made their individual ways home. Finn forgot that his shirt was in Kenny's bag. That would have to wait for another day.

Day Five - June 1975 - La Trattoria

Matthew's hunger had caught up with him after the first bottle of cold fizzy lager brought his flagging body back to life. He ordered a simple steak and chips with a side salad under the tutelage of his brother Patrick, now a veteran of Italian ristorantes and reasonably fluent in the language as well. Patrick had a very small coffee, pitch black, with two sugar lumps.

'There's not a lot drinking in that cup,' quipped Nora. 'You could put it in your eye,' she added. This was one of her more obscure sayings.

Nora herself had a glass of lemonade. John was getting a taste for the cold fizzy beer. He supposed it made a lot of sense in warmer climes.

'So, is the hotel all right for you?' asked Patrick.

'It's grand, son,' replied Nora. She meant it. It was perfect. She also wanted to make sure that Patrick had nothing to reproach himself about since he had made the original booking. She was concerned that he might be blaming himself for the problem when they had arrived.

'Sure, we have our own bathroom all to ourselves.'

Even now, she was struggling to believe that she was enjoying this taste of luxurious living.

'I'm pleased that it has worked out well in the end,' said Patrick. 'I've no idea how the Aurelius messed up the bookings in the first place. But they seem to have come up trumps getting you into this one.'

Matthew was quiet while his attention was directed at devouring the juicy steak, savouring the taste of the meat and feeling the satisfaction and the comfort of a hearty meal. He sat back and picked up the last few chips with his fingers. Nora was starting to fuss about Patrick.

'Do you have all your clothes sorted out for the morning?' she asked.

'Yes, mam,' Patrick replied with a laugh. 'It is all in hand. I was in the laundry room yesterday getting my own stuff in order. The vestments we will be wearing in church are all done for us. Don't fret, I won't show you up.'

'I suppose it wouldn't matter,' said Matthew, 'as you'll be a holy show, anyway.'

'You're very quick on the double entendres these days – yes, very good, Matty.'

'How many is it going to be tomorrow?' asked Nora.

'There are nineteen of us,' said Patrick. 'That's plenty,' he added with a laugh.

'And do you know them all?' asked Nora.

'There are seven of us from the College. They are all good friends. The other ones are from two of the other colleges. I know some of them by sight or from lectures at the university. There are a couple of Irish lads. You'll spot them a mile off.'

'How's that?' asked John.

'That would be telling. Just have a good look at the candidates tomorrow and I bet you'll pick them out. If you don't, you'll soon hear them when you get to the reception. They both swear like troopers.'

'God forgive them!' said Nora. 'What is the world coming to?'

'It's harmless, mam,' said Patrick. 'It's just the way they speak. God doesn't mind.'

'Well, he should,' opined Nora.

'What's the deal with the reception, then?' asked Matthew. He had pricked his ears up at the sound of something more entertaining than a whole morning spent in church.

'Yes. That's a good point, Matty,' said Patrick. 'There will be a meal afterwards – and a drink, of course. And now you've reminded me ...'

He reached into the inside pocket of his tweed jacket and pulled out an envelope.

'Here are your tickets for the church in the morning. You know where you're going, don't you?'

'Haven't a clue,' said Matthew. 'I only got here an hour ago.'

John answered.

'It's ok, son, your mother and me, we went for a walk this afternoon and we found the church quite easily. It's a good fifteen minute walk, mind you, but no more than that.'

'Great,' said Patrick. 'Your seats in the church are reserved. You should try to get there by quarter to nine at the latest.'

Looking pointedly at Nora, he said:

'Remember, mam, before quarter to nine. Not nine o'clock or ten past. If you're late, you probably won't get in at all.'

Nora switched the conversation quickly.

'And are you feeling fine, son? Is everything ok? Are you all prepared?'

'I'm as ready as I'll ever be,' laughed Patrick. 'Now or never!'

'Let's have one more drink, then,' said John and he was already waving over the waiter before Nora could say anything.

They chatted sporadically for the next twenty minutes. It was the small things that were easiest to talk about in this slightly intense moment as Patrick's life was about to take a decisive course. The cost of the beer, the weather at home, the sweets that the next door neighbours had given Nora when they had left. When John had finished his glass, Nora made motions to leave and get back across the road to the hotel. Matthew said that he would follow them shortly. He had half a glass of beer left and he wanted to stay and chat with Patrick for ten minutes. And then Patrick would have to get back to his room in college. There was no curfew but he had the weight of the next day leaning heavily on his thoughts and there was still some mental preparation required. It would be good, though, for Patrick to relax for a few minutes with his older brother.

November 1961

Joe Hoolahan switched the engine off and sat back to stretch his arms. The grey and blue Wolseley 1500 which came with his job was parked outside John and Nora's house. He had driven up from London that morning. With one short stop, he had managed the journey in less than three hours. The new motorway which ran as far as Rugby was a godsend. He had other things on his mind though today and no inclination to dwell on that engineering achievement. He was on the long road home to bury his father.

The front door was open before he had stepped out of the car. Nora welcomed him in sombrely.

'What a terrible shock for you!' she said. 'It's very sad news. And your poor mother, she'll be heartbroken. I'm so sorry, Joe.'

'That's good of you, Nora. Is John bearing up?'

'You know John. He doesn't say a lot. It's hit him pretty hard, I'd say.'

'I'm just grateful that we can get over there in time. You know what they're like. Put you in the ground while the body's still warm.'

They smiled together at that. Nora ushered him through to the living room.

'And it'll be good that we can have each other's company for the journey.'

'Yes,' said Nora. 'That's a blessing.'

Nora never professed to understand the brotherly bond between Joe and John. They were very different types. They had only very intermittent communication from one year's end to the next. When John was seven, Joe had been moved away from the family to live with an aunt and uncle in Dublin. So they had not had a long childhood together. And yet they held something between them. They were comfortable in each other's company, even if they rarely craved it.

'John's just getting a bag packed. I've got a sandwich made and you'll have a cup of tea.'

'You won't need to twist my arm. Tea would be grand,' said John.

'How's Agnes and the family?' asked Nora.

'They're fine,' Joe said. 'The youngest has started with the recorder. You can imagine what the house is like with that racket!'

Nora brought the tea pot through from the kitchen. They sat and drank, sharing a moment of stillness.

'Where's the wee feller?' Joe suddenly remembered that Martin should be in evidence somewhere.

'He's upstairs having a sleep. He's a good little man, very contented.'

They heard steps descending the stairs. John appeared in the room and moved to shake his brother's hand. A mutual pat on the back was the closest to an embrace that they could manage.

'How are you doing, John?' asked Joe.

'Not bad,' returned John. 'Yourself?'

'Sure, as well as anyone can expect in the circumstances. It's been a shock, no two ways about it. I don't think he suffered, by all accounts. It was a stroke, you know, in the night.'

'We'll need to see how mother is coping,' said John.

'It won't be easy. But she's got Paul, all right, in the house. And Trish and Theresa are on the doorstep. So it's not as if she's on her own.'

Nora busied herself wrapping a few ham sandwiches for the journey.

'Are you all set?' asked Joe.

'I'm ready,' answered John.

It was only four hundred miles away but it took the best part of two days to get back to Clare.

'We'll never be done with this place.'

This was John thinking out loud. Joe nodded his agreement.

'You wouldn't want it any other way, surely?' he said.

The journey was pleasant enough. Firstly, the drive in the Wolseley up to Holyhead. Then, having parked up, a transfer onto the evening ferry to Dublin. Followed by an early morning train down the country. They were in time to go to the house and see their mother, along with Paul and the sisters. The mother seemed lost in her own thoughts most of the time. Nevertheless, it was clear that their arrival gave her a little boost.

Paul was running an old Prefect and he drove them down into Ennistymon. Nora's parents, Hughie and Marie, had insisted that the men should stay over with them. It was a kind offer and it was no slight to their mother and siblings who would struggle to accommodate them.

The whole town seemed to pass through the Hoolahan house later on at the wake. Paddy had been a hard working man who was respected and generally liked by the neighbours. He was known to rear up on the odd occasion when somebody might cross him. That only enhanced the respect, although not necessarily the affection. Paul certainly had a bit of the father in him. Maybe you needed that to survive on the land out here. Joe had a touch of the hardness, in his case refined by education and the gift of the gab. John's make-up was completely different. He had a quiet determination, it was true, but his nature was to be calm and gentle and peaceful. In any event, the evening of the wake passed by without any arguments or trouble. Everyone had a drink, nobody overdid it. The presence of the parish priest was, for once, a boon. You never knew if a row would break out at one of these dos. For the most obscure reason, or for no good reason at all.

The funeral mass and the burial took place the next morning. The church was overflowing. It was normal. It was the simplest way of honouring the dead and their family. There was a small gathering back at the house afterwards. John did not know what to say to his mother except to try to divert her with tales of the grandchildren. It seemed to perk her up a little, especially to be thinking about the baby, Martin. She had never yet seen or held him. He spent most of the day talking with his sisters. They had both followed him around when they were children. They knew him backwards despite the long distance that separated them. He slipped easily back into the closeness that they shared. They were grown women now, both married and with young ones. He admired their wisdom, their fortitude, and their insight. It gave him great comfort to be in their company again, to listen to their voices, to take their gentle jokey jibes, to remember some of the good things. It was better to have a smile on your face than to go round feeling miserable. Being with the girls was the tonic that he needed to get through the mourning.

They stopped for one extra day after the funeral. They said their goodbyes in the evening and were gone the next morning. The first part of the train journey up to Athenry was always full of sadness and regrets. There were always too many memories all coming together at once. The final few miles into Athenry were a little cheerier. John remembered his very first journey to England thirteen years earlier. There was that nice old lady who had bought him tea in the town. Bridget. He remembered the house she had pointed to when they had parted from each other at the station. Would she still be there if he were to knock on her door?

'Yer man says we've a two hour wait for the Dublin train? Would you credit it?' said Joe.

'We're in Ireland, Joe, if you hadn't noticed,' said John. 'Anyway, I've been here before. I'll show you where we can get a cup of tea.'

The tea shop had not changed. It was a different waitress, but that was about all that John could see. John recounted the tale of Bridget. Joe was interested.

'We should go up and see if she is still in the house.' He was very keen.

John was not sure. Eventually, as they still had a good hour and a bit to wait, he agreed that they could at least go and have a look at the house. The weather was dry but it was grey with a blanket cloud above them. They walked up the road, past the turn that would take them back into the station. John had already spotted smoke coming from the chimney of the house. It meant that it was occupied at least. It did not mean that Bridget was the occupier.

When they arrived in front of the house – it was actually a good sized cottage – they could see a nicely tended garden to the front. Joe was deferring to John for once.

'Here goes,' said John. And so saying he walked up to the front door and knocked twice. There was no sound from within. He was about to try again when he heard a bolt being slid back. A woman, probably approaching forty, opened the door.

'Can I help you?' she asked politely.

John stumbled with what he had thought to say. Eventually he got it out.

'I was wondering if Bridget is still living here.'

The woman looked puzzled.

'And who are you, if you don't mind me asking?' she said.

'I'm John, John Hoolahan. This is my brother, Joe.'

He continued.

'It's a long story. However, the short version is this. I once met Bridget in the town here. It's a good many years ago. She treated me to a cup of tea. And she told me that she lived up here. We happen to be passing through today and I just thought I would see if she was still here.'

The woman smiled.

'That sounds like my mother. I am Bridget's daughter. Indeed, she is still living here. Will you come in and say hello to her? She'll be thrilled.'

The woman beckoned them to follow her in.

'Come in, come in. You won't refuse a cup of tea. Mother will insist.'

Bridget was sitting by the fire in the comfortable living room. She was discomfited for a minute when the strangers came into the room. She looked the two men over slowly. She studied John. Then something clicked and the memory of their brief encounter flooded back.

'In the name of the wee man! Would you credit it? You're that young boy who was going to make his fortune over yonder. God love you. You came back to see me after all this time.'

Bridget was in her element. The daughter, Mairidh, was happy to see the spark that was kindled in her mother. John recounted the details of his life, marriage and children as fully as he could in the space of the next twenty five minutes. He found himself under severe interrogation. Bridget interrupted every so often with 'Isn't it a wonder?' and 'God love you!'

As the clock approached twenty to one, Joe started to shuffle his feet and make signs that it was time to go. Bridget pulled John over to take hold of his hands.

'Now, don't you be leaving it so long before you visit again. Away with you now and catch your train. And good luck to you.'

The journey home gave John ample time to think about the past and the future. The passing of time, the passage of life. He never dwelt on such things normally. Not even on a Sunday morning in church. The overwhelming feeling, the certainty indeed that soothed him was that his life had real purpose and meaning. It was made meaningful by Nora. It was indivisible from her and the children.

Day Five - June 1975 - Buona Notte

Patrick pulled out a packet of cigarettes. Nazionali filtered. They probably would not sell well at home with that name, thought Matthew, even if the war had ended thirty years earlier. A soft crush pack, largely white with the image of a golden sailing ship in the middle. A thick orange coloured band running down the left hand side and a thinner blue band on the right. He offered them to Matthew.

'What's this, then? Don't tell me they let you smoke?'

'I've been smoking since third year in the college. They're only Nazionali and they do have a filter tip. And it's only two or three a day. Someone gave me one of those Alfas a while ago. I couldn't stomach that. It smelt like a garden bonfire and it burnt your mouth at the temperature of an atom bomb. Probably like Capstan Full Strength and a Woodbine rolled together. Not that I have ever tried either of them back home. Anyway, yes, we are allowed. We're grown ups, remember.'

'You're still the young'un to me, pal!' said Matthew. 'I'm only kidding. I'm glad to know you have at least one vice.'

'And what would you be implying?' smiled Patrick.

'Well, it's not as if you can have a string of girl friends on the side in this chosen occupation – or should I say "calling" – of yours?'

'Oh, I see,' laughed Patrick. 'It's the usual preoccupation with the opposite sex. Maybe I shouldn't ask, but do you have such a thing as a string of girl friends?'

'Well, not at the moment. But I could have. Isn't that the difference?'

'What are you trying to say?' said Patrick in his mild-mannered fashion.

'Oh, I don't know. It's a bit late to be saying anything, I reckon. But you know me. Always ready to have it out.'

'Yes, you do pick your moments. I am going to be ordained in less than twenty-four hours. And I take it you are wanting to know if I am sure about what I am doing.'

'That's about the size of it,' said Matthew. 'You catch on quick.'

'The truth is that it's what I have been asking myself every day for the last six years. As well as what I have been asked by the tutors and the other students every day since starting out on this journey. So, it's not a surprise. I suppose the surprise is that it's taken you this long to get to it!'

'Fair do's. I could have, I suppose I should have, asked you all this years ago. But what did I know? I mean, you going off to the seminary and all that. You were only barely in your teens. I wasn't much older. For Christ's sake, I was too pre-occupied working out my own life. Hardly gave you a thought. If that's what you wanted, and it made mam happy, that's all there was to it.'

'And do you think about it much now?' asked Patrick

'Not a lot, to be fair. But I'd like to know what you really think. Do you really know what you are letting yourself in for?'

Patrick thought for a moment. For someone still only approaching his twenty fourth year, he displayed an aura of calmness mixed with a commanding seriousness of mind and purpose. In the back of Matthew's mind, he was thinking that perhaps Patrick had always been like this. That he had been born like it. Perhaps he really was just made for this.

'What is there that we can be sure of?' asked Patrick quietly. 'The love of your mother and father? Well, yes, certainly for us – though maybe not for everyone. The promise of a good life, a good job, material wealth? Can we be sure of these things? The promise of happiness? The prospect of peace and prosperity in the world?'

'What are you on about?' asked Matthew.

'As far as I can see,' said Patrick, 'the world is very imperfect. It is temporal. It is only real for a split second and then it's gone. I am putting my faith in God and the things of God. He can raise us to a higher level.'

'But you have to live in the real world. You have to eat, drink, and wear clothes. You have to live side by side with other people. Don't you want to be able to enjoy the fruits of the world that God has created? Don't you think you are going to be in a sort of prison where you can't be your natural human self?'

'I understand what you are thinking. The answer is possibly that I am different to you and many others. I'm not saying I am better, don't get me wrong. But I feel that I have been made a bit different. I am human and I agree with what you say about normal human needs. Perhaps my human needs are less than, or maybe different from, the norm. I have no desire for wealth, fame, possessions. I do crave a cigarette now and again. That is true. What I will say is that I have no intention of closing myself off from the world in a monastery. I want to play a full part in the community, whichever community I am sent to. I want to help the poor, the deprived, and the oppressed. I want to help them materially and spiritually.'

'Let's be blunt, Patrick. I would find it hell on earth – no puns intended – if I had to live within the confines of what I have seen to be the life of a priest. The rules and regulations of the church, the enforced holiness, the praying, the sermonising, the Holy Joes in the congregation. God, it makes my head hurt just to think about it.'

'You put it very succinctly,' laughed Patrick.

'I will be blunt after all,' went on Matthew. 'For Christ's sake, don't you ever think about girls, about sex? It's all right talking about a Spartan existence, that your needs may not be as great as others. But if you are a man, I just don't see how you can cut yourself off from the most fundamental needs of a grown man. There, I've said it now. Sorry, it would forever be on my conscience if I didn't.'

'Well, you are absolutely right that it is a question that needs to be asked. To be honest, I am very naïve in such matters. Perhaps I've not had enough experience of the world. However, from the little experience I have had, I've come to the conclusion that I am probably cut from the mould of the Irish bachelor type. Even if I were never to become a priest, I can't see myself falling into the arms of a wife. It's just not how I feel.'

Matthew paused for a few seconds. That last line – he was about to probe a bit further. He thought better of it.

'Ok, you seem to have got it sussed. Probably time you got going. Do you want me to walk back with you?'

'No, not at all. You get yourself back to the hotel. I'll be fine. I'll see you in the morning.'

'Well, you just remember tomorrow that we'll be cheering you on from the pews. Your supporters are in town! Minus Aunty Kathleen, unfortunately.'

'Yes, I am so sorry about that,' said Patrick. 'She'll be there tomorrow in spirit though. And I'll say a special prayer for her during the service.'

Patrick paused for a moment to draw on his cigarette.

'You know, I can't tell you how amazing it is to have you, and mam and dad, here in Rome,' said Patrick. 'For you to come all this way, to make that journey, is very humbling. But never fear, I won't start blubbing. It's just a massive boost. I feel like I'm about to score the winning goal in the FA Cup Final.'

La Trattoria was winding down for the evening. There were only a handful of customers left. Matthew paid up with Patrick's assistance as translator and local guide on the rules for tipping. The last goodnights were wished and they went their separate ways.

June 1963

Matthew was one of the two acolytes, standing alongside John Reilly. Martin Brennan, a couple of years older, was thurifer. Little Sean Payne was carrying the boat, ready for Father to spoon out the incense onto the charcoal. The priest wore the sombre black chasuble reserved for funerals. At twelve years old, Matthew had already served a dozen funeral masses. It was part and parcel of life and the church. The altar boys were professionals at this. They could usually expect a good tip from the mourning family. This, however, was no ordinary funeral, at least for Matthew. This was the funeral mass for his uncle Steve. Stephen Henry Marshall, the husband of his aunty Kathleen.

From the moment that they came out of the sacristy to begin the service on that Thursday morning, Matthew felt weak, his legs struggling to hold him up. It was the empty expression on his aunty's face, the tears in his mam's eyes next to her, and the pained expression on his dad's face as he supported Kathleen at her right hand side. Matthew had never felt anything like this before. There had been no warning for Steve. One day he was full of life, the next he was gone. Went to bed feeling a bit under the weather. Never woke up.

Kathleen could hardly breathe. She did not want to breathe. She had to endure yet another horrendous loss in her life. What had she done to deserve this? They had given her some pills to blank out the hurt. The incense swirling around the coffin, the Latin incantations, the dismal hymns – they passed her by as she prayed to be anywhere else but in that church on that June day. There were good memories. She kept telling herself that. Very good memories.

And it was true. Kathleen's eleven years with Steve had given her a new life, one that she could never have imagined after Peter. Steve had been a good bit older than Kathleen. She was twenty-five when she arrived in England and took up the job at Gents'. Steve was thirty-six and one of the shift foremen. He had joined the army in 1940 and served in North Africa and then Italy for the rest of the war. He had remained firmly a bachelor for all those years until finally being smitten by Kathleen. She had not gone out of her way to attract him. It just happened that they hit it off. They saw each other at work. They struck up a friendly banter, and then a companionship. While Nora was beginning her new life and family with John, Kathleen and Steve were taking it more slowly. Eventually, though, Steve begged Kathleen to marry him. She surprised herself and said yes.

Steve lived in a small terraced house which Kathleen transformed into a very comfortable home. She was desperate for a child, but when that did not happen, she resigned herself to enjoying all the good things that they had together. Steve had a wide circle of friends. He had played football when he was younger, was still involved with the Garendon cricket club, played darts for the Engineers club and he had a regular weekly game of billiards at the Oddfellows. Steve and Kathleen enjoyed their weekends out at one of the several working men's clubs that Steve belonged to.

And they had a week at the seaside every summer. In fact, they had taken Matthew and Patrick with them most years. It was a big help to Nora. It fulfilled something for Kathleen. Steve had frequently taken Matthew to the football on a Saturday afternoon and a bond was formed. It was also Steve who had come to watch Matthew playing for the school on a Saturday morning in his first term at the grammar school. It had made Matthew so proud to see big Steve chatting knowledgeably with some of the other dads and generally making his affable, larger than life presence felt. Matthew was a pretty good player anyway, but it always helped to have a good supporter. His own dad was usually working on a Saturday morning, and was not a natural at these sorts of things anyway. Unlike Steve. But there was no Steve now. Matthew had a lump in his throat as he thought about it.

If the church had been difficult, the scene at the grave was even more unbearable. The sheer number of people was enough to bring tears to your eyes. It seemed like the whole factory had turned out for Steve. The faces of the mourners were up close and their collective grief sounded out every emotion. Mercifully, the priest did not prolong the burial any longer than it took to get the words out. Kathleen was helped away by John and his brother Joe who had come up from London to show his respects. Matthew was fighting to hold back the tears towards the end. It was Martin Brennan who rescued the situation. He swapped his thurible for Matthew's acolyte which meant he took Matthew's place right over the grave, keeping Matthew away from danger of keeling over into the gaping hole. As soon as the ceremony was done, he ushered all the boys away and back to the car. Matthew had a booming headache. He didn't know if he would ever be able to serve a funeral again.

The days leading up to the funeral had been the bleakest that Matthew could ever remember. A silent house, a morose mother, and a distant father. In the days afterwards, the tension seemed to ease gradually. It was almost a relief to have gone through the pain of the funeral, and to get past it. Nora was doing what she could to support Kathleen, sleeping over at her house and welcoming the many visitors coming to offer their condolences. Nora was burning the candle at both ends, returning home for a few hours each day to prepare the dinner, leaving Kathleen to catch up with some quiet time and much needed rest. Nora kept the youngest, Martin, with her and he was a happy distraction for both her and Kathleen. The rest of the children were more or less left to their own devices, still going to school each day. John had taken a few days off work but would be back in from Monday. Things needed to get back to some kind of normality.

On the Sunday after the funeral, Nora reluctantly agreed when Kathleen ordered her to go back home. They both knew that it had to happen sooner or later. Kathleen wanted it sooner. She was devastated. She was bereft. But she was not giving in. If there was one thing she had learned, you had to fight. She had to get back on her own two feet, and she was determined. She would always be grieving for Steve, and Peter before him. But she was not going to let it rule her life like she had the first time round.

In July, John insisted that Nora and Kathleen take a week together at the seaside. The annual fortnight closure of the factory for the summer holidays meant that he could be at home to look after the children. Kathleen only agreed to go because she appreciated his gesture so much. And it was the start of the healing process. She and Nora spent a week laughing and crying, and getting sun burnt, and eating fish and chips. At the end of July, Kathleen gathered up all her inner strength and went back to work. It was very hard that first day. All the memories. All the kindness – it sometimes killed you. As it was, it was another turning point and Kathleen had decided she was not looking back – except perhaps in her own most private moments.

Day Six - June 1975 - Roma

The sun was already warming the city as they started along Via Marghera towards Termini, the main railway station. For once they were in good time. John had managed to get Nora moving before seven, and they were walking out of the hotel before twenty past eight, scrubbed up and in their best ever Sunday clothes. Even John had a new suit. His standard Irish 1940's couture dark blue suit was being rested on Nora's orders. That was the one with the baggy trousers that three men could fit into, and the double breasted jacket which would have been a loose fitting on Mr Universe. Nora didn't mind him wearing it to mass on a Sunday as he didn't look out of place with all the other Paddies. But not for Rome. Not for today.

Instead, she had taken him to John Collier in town at the beginning of May with the intention of getting him measured up for a new suit. As it happened, there was an off the peg beautifully cut suit in a dark charcoal pure wool which the salesman had recommended John to try on. The feel of the cloth alone gave the immediate impression of quality. It had fitted more or less perfectly – "like a glove", according to John – and the sale was made.

Nora had agonised for weeks about what she was going to wear. What would the weather be like? What was fitting for such an occasion? She needed a hat as well. Once again, she felt her prayers had been answered. After the first unsuccessful outing to the shops with Kathleen, she decided to venture out alone. At Marshall and Snelgrove, a shop she rarely used as it was one of the more upmarket and expensive shops in town, she had been met in the ladies' department by a sales assistant around her own age. Nora's expectations were low – these kinds of places normally did not hide the impression that they looked down on the likes of Nora. Far from it, however, in this instance. Nora was delighted to be put at her ease in such a skilful way after only meeting the woman for a few moments.

Her nervousness evaporated as the assistant encouraged a polite, gentle and nicely private conversation. Nora had been hesitant to say what the event was that she was going to attend. You never knew what sort of reaction you would get. Immediately feeling an unexpected warmth, Nora felt able to confide in the assistant. The reaction was one of simple kindness and understanding. The woman was not a Catholic herself, actually Church of England and belonged to the St. James the Greater Congregation. There was a mutual understanding, it seemed, a real connection.

It quickly became clear to Nora that the assistant completely appreciated the significance of the event.

The woman explained that there had been several other customers over the years in similar circumstances. She always recommended that it was best to think of the event as if it were a formal wedding. The first thing, of course, was that you would obviously want something to show you off in your best light. So the right colour choice was crucial, as well as something that was right for your age, neither too young – Nora had "mutton dressed as lamb" running through her head – and yet not old and frumpy. It should be something bright, stylish and attractive, and it would have to be something dignified for the occasion. The assistant went to work and the result had delighted Nora. She had held off making the actual purchase before getting a second opinion, the assistant promising to hold the package for a week.

Kathleen and daughter Geraldine had duly trailed back to the shop the following week to see her try the outfit on. It was awarded the thumbs up from both of them. So, here she was, dressed in her navy blue costume and sporting an elaborate white hat, looking as regal as she ever would. She did feel good in it, and that was one less thing to be concerned about. Even Matthew was impressed.

Matthew suddenly stopped.

'This is madness,' he said. 'We don't need to walk across town. I can take you in style in the car.'

'You heard what Patrick said about the traffic and the parking,' replied John.

'Look, I drive in London all the time. If I can't find a space near the church, I'll come back here. There are a few spots down this street. I can easily walk back to the church from here but it'd be better for you and mam to get a lift.'

Nora was delighted. She was already hot from the few steps they had taken. She wanted to be cool and collected for the church.

The car started on the first turn of the key. Matthew struggled a little to get out of the cramped parking spot but within a matter of minutes they were rounding Termini and driving down Via Cavour. Matthew had got a little city map in the hotel so he knew it ought to be just a few hundred yards along. As the road opened up on the left to a big square, they could see what looked like a large church on the far side of the square with steps up to it. There did not appear to be any activity though. Maybe the main entrance was somewhere else. He took a sharp left turn and they were onto a narrower street. Where the hell was this place? He kept going, a certain dread that the clock was ticking and they were not in their seats yet. It was already twenty five to nine. Then they saw the beginnings of a crowd starting at a corner on the left, and as they wound round it was a good guess that they were now looking up at the front of the Basilica di Santa Maria Maggiore.

'I'm going to let you out here. I think that's where you go in. Look, up those steps where there are people queueing. I'll get the car parked and join you inside. Save me a seat. Oh, I'd better take one of them tickets.'

With John and Nora making their way up the steps, Matthew now had a problem to deal with, the damn car. He revved up and sped on along the road he was on. It did not look like he would get a space round here. As he kept going, he saw a sign which he thought could be for a parking garage. It was signed for five hundred metres on the right.

As he approached it, he could see that it was a basement car park. He had no time to check the prices. He took his ticket from the man in the booth, drove carefully down the ramp, found a decent enough space, and locked up. All this was done on auto-pilot. His mind was already in the church. The clock was still ticking. It must have been ten to nine by the time he was exiting the car park. He started to jog back the way he had driven. He did not recognise any part of the street. He could not have gone wrong, could he? He was starting to sweat a little in the morning heat and with his exertions. Please God, just get me there, please.

As the panic was starting to boil over, it suddenly evaporated. Now he had a proper view of the Basilica. There was a big open square in front, a statue atop a tall plinth in the middle of the square. You might not take it to be a church at first glance. It was a wide building with columns in the middle. The giveaway was the tower, although that was fairly muted in the world of church towers. The building could be a museum or a gallery. Perhaps like the National Gallery looking out over Trafalgar Square, though certainly not as big and imposing. Panic over. He brushed his trousers down, tucked his shirt in, checked his tie, took a deep breath and sauntered across the square up the steps and waited behind a family who were trying to negotiate an extra seat from the ushers. Irish, of course!

February 1968

Kathleen and Nora were once again in the old house by themselves. This time there would be nobody else returning. The wake was done and the funeral service was over. The two sisters were exhausted. With the travelling. With the endless condolences. With the emotion. And there was still an amount of jobs to be completed before they could take their departure. All they wanted this evening was to sit quietly and to regain some of their strength. Kathleen invited Nora to make a pot of tea. They would not be cooking tonight. There was plenty of cold meat and they could make do with a sandwich. Neither was in much of a mood for eating. Kathleen focused on getting the fire up. It brought back a swathe of memories.

'Here we are,' said Nora, placing the pot and two cups and saucers on the kitchen table.

Kathleen suggested they pull up the two easy chairs to the fireside and take a comfortable seat to drink their tea.

They sat feeling the warmth from the peat bricks putting a glow on their cheeks. It was soothing to watch the living fire and its gradual changes. It would take time but there was that feeling of relief slowly beginning to take effect. Kathleen would always wonder why she seemed to be singled out to suffer the pain of bereavement so regularly. Here she was again, a principal mourner. Familiarity with the process did not make it any easier, possibly all the harder. All she knew was that you kept going and there would be some easing of the sorrow and the pain in time.

Nora had wept over and over again when her father had died five years before. He had gone too early. She was heartbroken for him. He loved life and lived it well. And she was heartbroken for herself. She may have declared her independence openly as a defiant young woman growing up in this house. Nora knew, though, that her father was one of the rocks that she could depend on. Now she was dealing with the death of her mother. It had hit her unexpectedly hard. She had had a long running battle with Marie Gallagher, resisting the cloying control that her mother had sought to exercise over her. The years of resentment were hard to shake off. Yet there was another layer of feelings for her mother, a deep down love and sympathy, and indeed a sadness for her. Nora had been overwhelmed at the side Marie revealed as a grandmother. Loving, doting, generous, safeguarding. It made it so hard to accept and deal with the sometime coldness that crept through in Marie's relationship with her own daughter.

Kathleen fished in her handbag for her cigarettes. She lit up and drew lightly on it, exhaling long and slowly. 'The end of an era, you might say.'

Kathleen let the words drift out with the smoke.

'You didn't have any choice,' started Nora, 'but I did.'

'Don't you start on all that! We neither of us had any choice. Not at the time. And there's no going back. Are you saying you wish you'd stayed?'

'No, I'm not saying that,' agreed Nora.

'We had our own lives to be getting on with. I had to do something different, to make changes. You needed your freedom. It's life, that's all there is to it. Don't you think it made things a bit better for you and mother? The separation and the distance? She appreciated you better. And she would never deny the glory of the grandchildren that you gave her. So, no regrets now! They wouldn't want that.'

'I suppose you're right,' said Nora.

After a pause, Kathleen moved the conversation on to more practical issues.

'There's a lot to do in the next few days. We need to sort through the house. And we have to see the solicitor on Friday morning. I suppose we'll not be able to get away before next week.'

Nora nodded, 'We have our work cut out. Let's hope we're feeling more like it when we wake up tomorrow morning.'

Two days later, on the Friday morning, they arrived a good ten minutes early for their appointment at the office of Devlin and Curran, Solicitors, in Parliament Street.

The secretary was busy on the phone and she motioned them to take a seat. They were due to see Michael Devlin at eleven o'clock. Nora knew him from the old days. He was "young" Michael Devlin in 1946 when he followed his father into the practice. Now he was the senior partner in an expanded firm. Hughie Gallagher had become one of his first clients and they had maintained the relationship down the years. When Hughie had died, Marie had continued to consult Michael when necessary. Nora and Kathleen were dressed soberly for the occasion, not quite funeral clothes but a good substitute. They sat in silence waiting. They instinctively held their tongues in a public space.

The secretary was still on the call when Michael Devlin himself came in through the front door. He was carrying a leather bag in one hand and a box in the other. He greeted the ladies warmly, immediately ushering them through to the back offices. The one with his name on the door was sparsely furnished and expensively dull. Dark wood panelling, a brown carpet, and a solid mahogany desk commanding the space in front of the grimy window. There was an office chair on castors tucked in behind the desk. There were four occasional chairs in a muddy velour fabric, two on each side of the desk backed up against the walls.

'It's good to see you, though I'm very sorry for the circumstances. My condolences once again.'

They were standing in the middle of the room. He offered to take their coats and he waved them to sit down. He pulled one of the chairs over to where Nora and Kathleen were sitting. His obvious sensitivity and straightforward manners immediately put the ladies at ease.

'How are you bearing up?' he asked. 'You've had a dreadful time.'

'We are getting through it,' said Kathleen. 'You know how it is.'

'I do, indeed,' said Michael.

He stood up and went over to his desk. He picked up a file and came back to sit informally across from Nora and Kathleen.

'Is it ok if we go over some of the paperwork?' he asked politely.

'Of course,' said Nora. 'Whatever has to be done.'

'Ok. I'll just go over the will again with you. And then we can talk about the finances and the property.'

An hour and a quarter later, Kathleen and Nora emerged from the Devlin and Curran office into a bright but cold February midday. They linked arms together and walked up the road towards the bridge. That was another burden lifted. It was another step forward. They linked arms partly for the feel of mutual support, partly for the small joy of getting through this ordeal together bit by bit.

'Will we have lunch at the Cascades?' suggested Kathleen on a whim. It had not been pre-planned. Now it seemed appropriate.

'Why ever not?' said Nora. 'It was one of father's occasional treats. I'm sure mother liked it as much as him although she would never admit it. We'll pay a little tribute to them both.'

It was later in the afternoon when they were back at the house that they were really able to talk through what Michael Devlin had told them that morning. The will, it appeared, was as straightforward as any will in Ireland could be. Hughie Gallagher had made his original will just around the time that he reached his sixtieth birthday. That was back in 1956. There was an exactly parallel will arranged for Marie Gallagher at the same time. Whoever survived inherited everything. When the survivor subsequently died, everything would go to the two daughters. In 1963, everything had passed seamlessly to Marie. Afterwards, Marie had never dared to alter her will. It was what Hughie had decreed. In truth, she never wanted to alter it. It was a relief to Kathleen when they had found a copy of the will in the locked cabinet containing the precious documents. Her fear was that Marie might secretly have been spiteful to Nora. As it was, the two sisters were going to be treated equally, just as she had hoped.

'I don't want to be talking about money at this time,' said Kathleen.

'I know what you mean,' replied Nora.

Neither of them had ever harboured ambitions for any windfall wealth from the loss of their parents. They had made it far enough in life without it. Nevertheless, it was dawning on both of them that this could make a big difference to their lives. Nora could not help think about how her children would benefit. Kathleen realised that it would be something to fall back on in older age.

As if to immediately contradict herself, Kathleen said, 'Would you ever have dreamed that they had so much tucked away like that?'

'She could have been living the life of Reilly!' laughed Nora as she pondered the update on the finances that Michael Devlin had given them.

Nora continued to muse on what had been, and what might have been.

'That would not have suited her at all. She was certainly never a spendthrift. It's a wonder she didn't give it all to the priests and the nuns, though.'

'She probably hadn't a clue how much money was there all the time,' intoned Kathleen. 'She had money from the shop rent coming in. There was father's insurance money. And the interest mounting up on all the savings he put away over the years.'

Nora was still puzzled. 'But where did she get all that cash we found in the writing bureau? We counted over £800, did we not?'

Kathleen shook her head. 'And there's not a stitch of new clothing in her wardrobe since father died.'

'That money may have been there since his time,' said Nora. 'You know how he liked to keep it from the tax man.'

Nora laughed again as she thought back to Hughie Gallagher's creative accounting. It had taken Nora a while to catch on to the way he liked to keep the books. Then she had become even smarter than him at it.

'I'm well aware,' replied Kathleen with a wry smile. 'There's a lot of things to be settled and as yer man says, it'll take time.'

'Yes,' said Nora. 'There's the shop and the house to be disposed of. And he mentioned some land up at the Point. I didn't know about that, did you?'

'Not at all,' said Kathleen. 'He didn't like to broadcast his business. Not even to us.'

'I suppose why would he, anyway?' Nora philosophised.

'What did Devlin think it would all come up to?' asked Kathleen. 'I lost the thread towards the end with all his humming and hawing.'

'He's garrulous – that's how Sister Annunciata once described George Bernard Shaw to us. That's a word I haven't thought of in twenty years!' Nora felt delighted with herself for coming up with that and Kathleen tried the word out for herself.

'Anyway,' went on Nora, 'he was reckoning that it might all add up to twenty three thousand or maybe as much as twenty four.'

'Would you credit that?' said Kathleen. 'Twenty four thousand pounds!'

'It's a fortune, all right,' said Nora. 'He said that we're not likely to see a penny of it for a good year. So don't be spending it yet!'

They both had a good laugh at that. Then the conversation returned to more pragmatic issues and decisions they needed to make.

'What are we going to do about the house?' asked Kathleen. 'We can't leave it to anyone else. We can't have strangers picking through everything. Imagine the gossip. That's something we are going to have to do ourselves. And we can't do it in England.'

'There's no time like the present. Will we stay on until it's done? We'll need to do a bit of organising like. We'll need boxes. We can sort any things we want ourselves. Pack up any valuable items for sale that we don't want to keep. And the rest can go to charity or the rag and bone.'

'All right,' said Kathleen. 'We'll give ourselves a week to get it done.'

It was a very long, hard week. At every twist and turn, there was a memory to stop them in their tracks. A lot of the early decisions were eventually reversed. They were holding on to far too much. The realisation dawned that they could not allow sentiment to rule. They had to be pragmatic. They had to be ruthless. What earthly use would either of them have for boxes of household goods, knick-knacks, even antiques from their parents' lives, from a past that they had not shared for nearly twenty years? In the end, they decided to keep only the family photographs, their mother's jewellery, and one picture each of the landscapes that Hughie had collected over the years. These few items would serve as tangible mementoes, at least.

The rest of the small contents were boxed up and taken away by Tom Duggan. They knew him and were happy that he would give a fair price for what he could sell on. They arranged for the furniture to be lifted the following week when they would already be back in England. It was going to a charitable group attached to the church. They would either find a needy home for it or sell it on and use the money for their cause.

On Wednesday and Thursday, Kathleen and Nora took a room at the Cascades Hotel. Their efforts to clear everything in the house inevitably meant that it quickly became less functional and then effectively impossible to live in. By Tuesday evening, they were confident that they could make their departure on Friday. For any emergencies, they were able to arrange for keys to the house to be held by Mrs Mulroney. It was she, along with her husband, who had taken over the running of the General Store when Hughie Gallagher had died five years before. If there was anyone that they could trust, it was her. A brief meeting was arranged with Michael Devlin for Friday morning where they could update him on progress with the house and its contents. They signed papers authorising him to proceed with realising all the assets. That meant selling the property and the land, and cashing in the shares and savings certificates. He was at pains to tell them that progress with the probate would be slow. He would keep them informed by letter. They were not to expect to hear from him any time in the near future. That was just how things were.

At midday, they boarded the bus for Ennis. The old railway had long been abandoned. It was the first leg of that familiar journey to their home in England. Nora hid the tear in her eye as she remembered that December day when she stood at the old railway station with Sean O'Callaghan. Why did that make her want to cry? After all these years? Maybe she was passing into that mysterious phase of womanhood that older women always spoke about so obliquely. Maybe it was just the emotion of the last weeks catching up with her. She thought about Sean again and this time cheered herself up as she realised how lucky she was to have found John Hoolahan.

'Come on, Missus,' said Kathleen. 'All aboard! Hold very tightly, if you please!'

Day Six - June 1975 - Santa Maria

The church was not like any church Nora had been in before. "Grand" did not even begin to describe it. Magnificent, awe-inspiring, overwhelming, beautiful. Nora's head was swimming. If there was such a place as God's house, he could probably not do better than this. Whoever had built the Basilica di Santa Maria Maggiore had managed to transcend the limited reality of man's existence on earth. They had created something which aspired to the perfection of heaven, far beyond normal human experience. Nora did not express her thoughts in anything like these words. She had no knowledge or any particular interest in architecture, nor had she any knowledge or interest in classical art for that matter. As she took in her surroundings, she simply felt humbled to see the exquisite materials, to appreciate the workmanship and the incredible detail in everything around her. And she was taken aback by the scale of this celebration of the

Virgin Mary. There was no such thing as heaven on earth. This was a pretty good attempt though.

The ushers wore pristine black suits with white shirts and black ties. There were dozens of them. They were young fit men with glowing skin and oozing calmness. John supposed that they were there for more than just showing people to their seats. They would be the security team. Nothing would be allowed to interrupt today's event. Not any wayward tourist, not any renegade madman or terrorist. The ushers each sported a sash, some bright green, some crimson, some purple. No orange. He smiled as he pondered what an Orangeman would make of this place. It was a crimson fellow that showed them to their seats. About three quarters of the way up on the right hand side. They were allotted four seats ending at the side aisle. The church was already nearly full. The noise was deafening. The usual decorum of silent prayer before mass was lost amidst the excited chatter of the many visiting family members and supporters of the nineteen men that were about to feel the power of the Holy Spirit descend on them.

Nora sat down, with John perched on the aisle seat. John always liked the possibility of a quick getaway. They were both quiet for a few moments, taking in their surroundings, looking at the crowds of people still moving around or standing and chattering away as if they were in their local pub. As the time went on, Nora started to fidget. Where was Matthew? He had better get here before they started. She asked John what the time was. Five minutes to nine. While the hustle and bustle continued, she remained hopeful that he would arrive at any second and it would all be as it should be. Well, there was no Kathleen, but she was resigned to that. The seconds ticked away in her head. She tried to say a last prayer. This was to thank God. She was not going to ask Him for anything else, not now anyway. She was thanking him mostly for Patrick and his arrival at this momentous point. She was thanking him for getting them safely here to witness and to celebrate.

Matthew had the same impression as John when he got to the top of the steps and got a better view of the ushers. More like bouncers than churchmen. He had the striking thought that they could have been drafted in from the local mafia to provide a bit of muscle for the Pope. Still, the one he showed his ticket to was very polite and gracious. He whisked Matthew through the messy throng of jostling bodies that was clogging up the area behind the main doorway. The organist somewhere unseen jolted the congregation out of their raucous cacophony as he began very loudly with an improvisation to set the tone. The usher showed Matthew along the side aisle and into his seat next to Nora. The seat on his other side remained empty, a reminder of Kathleen's absence. Nora acknowledged his arrival with a nod. Inside, she was joyous. Now she could settle and enjoy what was about to take place.

Nora nudged Matthew.

'What time is it?'

Matthew checked his watch.

'It's a few minutes after nine.'

'They're late!'

There was still a lot of movement, particularly at the back of the church.

'I don't think they're ready yet,' said Matthew.

'I may as well tell you,' whispered John, trying to make himself heard amidst the ringing organ music. 'Patrick let me know that the official start time is quarter past. It's a bit of a white lie but they have to get the congregation in and they give themselves a bit of leeway.'

Matthew thought that the Catholic Church was pretty good at white lies, but he did not dwell on that. It gave him a chance to have a look around. His first impression was how long the church was. Aside from all the obvious glitz, and the artistry, it was like a deep cavern disappearing into the far distance. It felt a lot narrower than he had expected based on his impression from the outside. The only reason that he could think of for such a deception was that there must be some extra parts beyond the main sanctuary stretching out at each side of the building. Possibly other chapels, he speculated. Within the main body of the church, a row of marble columns flanked the congregation on either side. They ran the full length of the church as far as the eye could see. It was a marvel to behold. The columns were imbued with strength, power, grace, and there was a natural beauty in their symmetry.

The inside of the church was cool. They had a lot to be grateful for as it was going to be very warm outside. The air was pleasant too. There were some nice perfumes and after shaves wafting around. He assumed that wouldn't last long once the incense was set alight. He wondered how his father would cope without being able to puff on his pipe for three hours.

Matthew's view of the altar was not great. He could

clearly see it in the distance but he would need binoculars to see any of the detail. It was raised high off the ground and seemed to be contained within a gigantic structure, like a massive four poster bed arrangement. There was a huge area around it and, he guessed, behind. What he could make out were some tall brass – or maybe gold, considering it was Rome – candlesticks. They were holding up long candles, pointing into the high heavens. He reckoned that the altar servers would have a few problems trying to get them lit. You would need a very long reach. He remembered being an altar server as a boy trying to light the candles on the high altar for the eleven o'clock sung mass. It was difficult even to hold the long-handled lighter straight let alone wiggle it about in mid air to find the wick of each candle to get it to catch light.

'Did you manage to get one of those booklets?' asked Nora. 'See, like that woman in front. They'd run out by the time we came in.'

'No, I didn't even think about it,' said Matthew. 'Maybe I could try and get one. He stood up to see if he could ask an usher. There were too many bodies milling about still at the back. He squeezed out of his seat and went back down the side aisle. A figure emerged from behind a pillar. It was a black-suited sash-wearing usher.

'So sorry, but you need to take your seat, please.'

It was perfect Home Counties English.

'Excuse me,' whispered Matthew, 'you don't have a spare booklet by any chance?'

'I'll see if I can find one, sir.'

He made a note of Matthew's seat.

‘There’ll not be one for the likes of us,’ muttered Nora as she saw Matthew return empty-handed. But before Matthew had got properly back into his seat, the usher was stretching in and handing over two copies.

‘Wonders will never cease,’ was all Nora could think to say.

Then she began to read.

July 1971

'Do you remember this place on Saturday mornings?' Richard Sewell had to shout to make himself heard. 'I still get the smell of sweaty teenagers in my head every time I look at the dance floor.'

It was already late. They had tumbled into the club after a few drinks earlier in the Shakespeare. Matthew was pressed up against the bar. There was a girl on his left and a guy to his right. He was alert, trying to catch the eye of one of the busy bar staff. In his head, the girl was before him. Matthew was before the guy. He got a nod from a barman. Matthew pointed demonstrably to his left and mouthed 'She's first.' He got a nice smile from the girl and waited for his turn.

Away from the bar now, pints propped up on a shelf at a pillar, Richard returned to his theme. 'Yeah, it makes me cringe sometimes when I think back. Spotty youths trying out all the moves. I suppose it had its purpose.'

Matthew had to raise his voice to answer.

'I played football for the school on Saturday mornings. So I never came down here. Saturday afternoons at the skating, though. I did that a few times.'

'So, how you feeling about the big move?' asked Richard.

'Yeah, like I said, I'm really looking forward,' replied Matthew. 'I think I'm ready for it. London. Big new challenge. New experiences.'

He was going to add 'New people.' He held back on that but it was true. Matthew would not have said that he was in a rut. There was just something that had been niggling at him for a while. He had slowly come to the realisation that there was more to the world than he had experienced so far. It was all very well having a laugh and a good night out. It was great to have a job he enjoyed – one that he was finding that he was pretty good at. There had to be more. Something was missing.

'You definitely handed your notice in?' asked Richard.

'Yeah, one month's notice. I'm starting at the bank at the beginning of September.'

Matthew had already picked up that Richard was either a bit envious or put out. Well, that was his problem, not Matthew's. It was not as if they were best mates. They had become friendly only as colleagues at work. He did not have any special allegiance to him. He was out with him tonight more because he felt sorry for him than anything else. A lot of people were still away on holiday and Richard had talked Matthew into a night out at El Paradiso.

Matthew was able to get on with most folk. The truth was that Richard was so different to him. He spoke differently for a start. Had a different outlook, different life, and a different way. And he was a couple of years older. He had been to a minor public school in the county. Now he drove an MG sports car and gave the impression of being a young executive. Matthew knew differently. Richard was ok in small doses. He talked a good job but was not as brilliant as he made out. He had squeezed through his A levels at school and been recruited directly into the development team while Matthew was still cutting his teeth in operations. There was money in the family and that fuelled the confidence and brashness.

'Have you seen those two over there?' Richard nodded knowingly.

Matthew looked over. From what he could make out in the dim lighting, Richard's attention was on two women that his friends would automatically dismiss as "tarts". They were standing about fifteen yards away on the edge of the dance floor, cigarettes in hand. They looked older, meaning that they were well into their twenties. Even at this distance, it was obvious that they had collected their keys to the door a good while ago. It was hard to get a proper look as they kept being obscured by the dancers on the floor who bobbed and swayed about in front of him. Matthew drank some of his beer. He managed to get another glimpse. They were looking directly at him, smiling flirtatiously.

'Come on,' said Richard. 'We're on.'

Matthew did not have time to protest. Richard gave a pull on his sleeve and they started off, walking round the carpeted area, shuffling through the drinkers, the couples talking or embracing, and the would-be dancers plucking up courage to get onto the floor.

Matthew could not hear what Richard said to the small blonde one. He just saw them disappearing into the middle of the floor as "Get It On" started up. He suddenly found himself alone with a woman who looked as if she could devour him for dinner and still have room for pudding. There was an obvious and immediate physical allure. This woman had an incredibly sexy appearance, tall, curvaceous and big breasted. She was handsome in a genuinely feminine way with beautiful smiling dark eyes. It was the overpowering make-up and the very scanty dress that rang the alarm bells. It was a pure white cotton item that tantalisingly revealed more than it covered. The ruby red lips were less than subtle. He felt that he was well out of his league. Maybe he ought not to be playing at all.

She came up close and spoke into his ear. There was an overpowering heady scent coming from her body and from the voluminous dark curly hair that flowed freely over her shoulders. Matthew breathed it in.

'Don't look so petrified,' she breathed, 'I'm only a little scary.'

Matthew was tongue-tied. He began to say something but it was lost in the ever increasing volume of the music.

'What's your name, anyway?' she asked. 'I'm Suzie.'

Matthew regained a little composure.

'Yeah, it's Matthew. Let's have a dance,' he said hopefully.

'Let me finish this fag first.'

The awkward silence was mercifully short as she stubbed out the cigarette and the next song merged seamlessly into the last one. Suzie moved off onto the floor. Matthew followed obediently behind. "Just My Imagination" was blasting out from the speaker system. Suzie gyrated slowly and sensually, Matthew tried to adapt his limited repertoire of steps to the slow rhythm of the song. He never knew if you were supposed to talk as well as dance. He did not know what to say anyway, so he just danced, mesmerised by the figure in front of him. The next number had started and Matthew was ready to continue. Suzie was walking off the floor. What was he supposed to do? He moved to follow. She turned round, gave a little smile and mouthed 'Ladies!' Oh well, he thought, that's that. He gave a little nod and a half wave of the hand, and made off towards the bar. There was no sign of Richard. He was probably in a dark corner somewhere with his new friend.

Matthew decided he needed a drink after the "experience" and waited to be served. He was still only third in the queue when a strong warm arm with a huge bangle at the wrist wrapped itself round his waist from behind and gave a friendly squeeze. The unmistakeable scent told him immediately who it was.

'Think you can get rid of me that easily? Let's have another dance.'

Matthew did not hesitate and he abandoned the bar, one hand slipped into Suzie's as she led him into the melee. The Elgins were electrifying the place with "Heaven Must Have Sent You". Suzie was alive in the dance, making wonderful shapes with her body, moving effortlessly. In contrast, Matthew felt even more awkward than usual. They stayed dancing apart for "I'm Gonna

Run Away From You". Tami Lynn was clearly a big hit with the crowd.

The tempo suddenly came to a grinding halt. It seemed like everything went silent. The opening bars of "I'm Still Waiting", warm and rich and all-consuming, reached into every corner of the room, almost sucking the oxygen out of the space. Diana Ross began to sing, her alluring voice and the slow melody held everyone spellbound. Suzie moved her body close to Matthew and clasped his upper arms before wrapping her whole body around him. He put his arms around her shoulders, hands pressed against her back. She had a slow, powerful rhythm beating through her. She transmitted it across to Matthew who responded instinctively to her movements. He was drunk with her smell, her feel and her warm body joining with his. As the song ended, she pulled his face to hers and kissed him slowly for what seemed like hours. They were still kissing, totally absorbed in the moment, as the sensitive, emotion-shredding voice of Otis Redding started in on "I've Been Loving You Too Long". Suzie held him tight and carried on the slow dance. Before the end, she pulled back from Matthew and led him tenderly off to the side. They found an empty booth and Suzie drew Matthew in close beside her.

'I made my excuses and left.' This was the recurring line reverberating in Matthew's head. It was a phrase that never failed to appear at least once a week in some undercover investigation being reported on by *The Sunday People*. The trouble was that Matthew had no idea what his excuse was. And he was not sure in any case if he actually wanted to make his excuses.

'You're a fantastic dancer,' offered Matthew. It was about all he could think of saying. He meant it, though. That was the most that he had ever enjoyed dancing by a long way. And he could not dance.

'You a student, then?' asked Suzie.

'No, what makes you say that?'

'You sound all posh. Not that you've got much to say.' She laughed at that. Matthew smiled thinking everything was relative.

'Strong quiet type,' continued Suzie. 'They're the dangerous ones. That's what they all say. What do you do, then?'

'Work in an office, that's all.' Matthew knew from experience that any mention of computers was a bad move. Nobody had a clue what they were and how they worked. It was a dangerous cul-de-sac for this type of chat. Suzie nodded acknowledgement at "office". He passed that test ok.

'Clever clogs, eh?' Suzie was weighing him up. 'I work in the hosiery,' she said. 'Mostly do undergarments. Men's and ladies'. Some lovely stuff. I get all my knickers from work. You want to see my drawers – every colour of the rainbow!'

She giggled at this. Suzie was completely unembarrassed at plain, earthy and risqué talk. She enjoyed the unsubtle innuendo. She was funny with it. Suzie was one of those rare larger than life people that you were occasionally lucky enough to meet face to face. Matthew was basking in her company. He was marvelling at how much she seemed to know herself and what she wanted. She was not so much flirting as trying him out for size.

'Where's your boyfriend tonight, then?' asked Matthew, taking a risk. There was no way that Suzie did not have a string of boys on her case. He sensed that this was dangerous territory.

'Oh, I blew him out last week,' she said quickly. 'A complete dead loss. He's in trouble with the law again. I've had enough of all that. Seen it all before.'

Matthew wanted to ask more but restrained his curiosity. He felt that he was already in fairly deep water and wondered how long he could stay afloat. There was still an hour before the club shut. He needed a drink now. Suzie asked for vodka and lemonade. The trip to the bar killed a good ten minutes. When he got back to the seat, Suzie was in a heated conversation with another girl who was standing leaning over the table. It looked like she was threatening Suzie. The other girl backed off when she saw Matthew. He just heard her spit 'Piss off!' as she went.

'Not as tough as she makes out!' joked Suzie. 'We've got a bit of history. I can handle her, all right.'

For all his normal sharp wit, Matthew was finding conversation tricky.

'You like soul?' he tried.

Suzie lit up at that.

'Can't beat it. Really gets me.'

They drank their drinks and in between sips, Suzie snuggled into Matthew and kissed him fully and intensely. It was life in the fast and slow lane all at the same time.

After an indeterminate time of passion, Suzie drew back and asked him what the time was. It was half past one. The club would shut at two.

'Time to go,' she said. 'Never get a taxi if I don't go now.'

'How do you know I've not got a motor with me?' asked Matthew, feeling bold all of a sudden.

'Because you would have made sure you told me, that's how. Anyway, you seeing me home or what?'

It was more a statement than a question.

They did not have to wait long in the taxi queue. The journey was only about four miles, up to the Southfields estate. Matthew wondered what he was doing. When they got there, he offered to pay the fare but Suzie would not let him. The house was a standard semi with a small front garden. A tall untamed privet hedge stood guard where the garden met the pavement. There was a little gate opening onto a slab path leading up to the front door. Suzie stood to one side of the gate with her back to the hedge and pulled Matthew close to her. He felt her warm strong touch, her arms clasping him tightly. The kisses were short and playful, then long and passionate. Suzie was in complete control, Matthew was simply following her lead. After a good while, Suzie broke her hold on him.

'I can't ask you in, love. I'm sorry, it's just too complicated.'

She gave him a final soft passionate kiss.

'I'm gonna have to go now. Thanks for seeing me home. I hate coming back from a night out on my own.'

It came as a huge relief to Matthew. Stepping into that house would have been one step further than he dared think about. He would have done it though, he was sure of that.

'Yeah, understood. You take care of yourself.'

They left a lot of things unsaid. There were no future arrangements made. They would probably never see each other again. They had had a good time together for a few hours. That suited them both. It was just how things were sometimes. Matthew had a long walk home. It would do him good. He would savour those moments with sexy Suzie for a very long time.

Day Six - June 1975 - Missa

The organist had continued to play a rich improvisation while the last minute arrangements on the ground were being finalised. Various people dashed around with bits of paper in their hand, numerous clerics checking items on the altar, the ushers finally managing to clear the area at the back of the basilica. It was a major effort getting the last arrivals to their rightful seats. Matthew reckoned that there were probably a few issues dealing with the odd gatecrasher and anyone whose face did not fit. He wondered if it was really ticket only or if some of the locals were allowed in "on spec". He stopped wondering when finally it looked like something was going to happen.

There was that collective sense of anticipation which falls on any type of crowd or audience just at the salient moment, not always at any obvious signal, possibly some telepathic intelligence bearing fruit. The huge central entrance doors were opened ceremoniously. They had remained shut while the congregation were checked through the doors on either side earlier. A broad shaft of sunlight shone across the threshold. It seemed entirely auspicious. There was a sparkling brightness, a dazzling brilliance that pierced the eyes of the congregation which now stood and turned to face the rear. And then began a long, long procession. It was led by a team of altar servers. They were not boys but grown men. The bearer of the cross was cosseted between two torch bearers. A priest holding aloft a large ornate bible was protected in the huddle. And the thurifer was boldly swinging the burning thurible, filling the air with the mystical smell of incense. The organist upped the tempo as he launched into an ear piercing introduction to the first hymn. This was the wake up call for everyone. There was a faint rustle of paper as the booklets were taken up. And the singing, fronted by a choir that Matthew could not see, began in earnest.

The altar servers were followed by the nineteen candidates for the priestly ordination. They wore white cassocks with a stole of glistening gold cloth across one shoulder. Then came a battalion of priests, bishops, and cardinals. It was a sea of white and gold cloth sparkling in the light streaming through the church. It was hard to tell who was who, except that the cardinal and the two accompanying bishops stood out from the throng. The cardinal carried his crook, all three of them sporting their mitre hats and their flowing vestments. There was a mini entourage surrounding the VIPs within the confines of the overall procession. There must have been upwards of ninety fully robed priests. Nora's heart was pounding. John's heart was sinking as the reality dawned on him that this was going to be one very long session. Would he ever get out of it alive?

It took three hymns and nearly twenty minutes for the procession to make its way towards the altar and for all the participants to find their places. Matthew supposed that if you were ever trying to find as large a gathering of priests as this, Rome was your best bet. There was probably another hundred doing the same thing across the street. Eventually, it was the English archbishop who stood at the ambo. He motioned for the congregation to sit. Then he made an introduction of welcome and a broad explanation of the service. Nora was pleased that she could hear every word. Another priest stood to the side and translated into Italian as each mini paragraph was completed. Patrick had told them that there were a good number of candidates today of English speaking origin – several English, Irish, and American men. There were also candidates from Italy, Germany, Holland, Argentina, and Nigeria. Bishop David Carter from England and Archbishop John Wilson from the USA were concelebrating with the Italian Cardinal Marco Rossi. The service was going to be conducted in a mix of languages. John sighed. It was going to take an age at this rate.

And so it began. The Cardinal led the proceedings, ably assisted by two efficient looking youthful priests. Everything was several times more long-winded than an ordinary mass. Everything, it seemed, was going to be sung. The thurible was recharged with incense and the first of many blessings around the altar was made. The language of the mass was Italian. It did not make a lot of difference as the many non

Italians present knew exactly what was happening at any moment. The booklet was a help as well for keeping on track when the choir went into another long piece. But the Confiteor, the Kyrie and the Gloria were obvious. It was not at all difficult for those who had spent years hearing mass in Latin. Then the readings were given in both languages. The elaborate Alleluia sung before the gospel whipped up the emotion of the occasion a further notch. Once the gospel had been read, the business of the day began in earnest.

Matthew admitted to himself that there was something special happening. His hold on any faith was at best tenuous, a long running wrestling match. He was never sure if he was clinging onto something or if there was something out there that would not let him go. In the moment, here in the beautiful magnificence of the Basilica di Santa Maria Maggiore, his skin was tingling. Maybe it was the emotion created by the crowd, a collective euphoria. Maybe it was the elegant choreography of the service. Maybe it was the music and the quality of the choir's singing. A feeling of deep joy and happiness brought a nervous smile to his lips and eyes.

He did not really know how to pray. He had not prayed in any way since he was a teenager. Since leaving home, he had only sporadically gone to church. Now, at this very instant, he was not praying but he seemed to be landed in some joyous communication with life and the world. Whether that was bound up in faith or religion, he did not know or care. Everything had come together in this perfect moment. Most of all, he was happy to have his mother beside him and for her to be able to enjoy this occasion to the full.

October 1969

Not for the first time in her life, Nora had acted decisively. The loss of her mother the previous year was something she was still coming to terms with. All the grief when she was alive, now the grief that she was no more. Nora, it seemed, was never without her own problems to attend to. She could well do without all the memories of the past being sent to try her. The good memories were sometimes even more difficult to face than the bad ones. She constantly asked herself how she and John had survived all these years. Bringing up five children in a pokey terraced house – no better than a slum – on one man's wages. The "little job" she had started a couple of years before had certainly helped. The problem was that growing families had bigger and bigger expenses.

Nora was increasingly agitated about the life she was giving to her children. In particular, she was acutely conscious of the needs of Geraldine, the one girl amongst four brothers. She was already eleven and had started at the girls' grammar school after the summer. Nora knew that before long she would be developing into a young woman. She would have needs, both material and emotional. They were just not cut out to give them to her the way things were. She went over it in her mind all the time. It was all right for the boys to invite friends round. Boys never stayed in the house. Boys were rough and ready. They would be out in the street or at the park. For a girl, it was completely different. How could Geraldine invite any of her school friends to her home? And if she could not do that, would she ever have a friend? This became Nora's benchmark for planning the next stage in their lives.

When the letter franked "Devlin and Curran" had arrived one Saturday morning earlier in May, her heart had almost stopped. Was this what she had been trying so hard to put out of her mind? If she were to think about it too much, the dream became too much to bear. It was probably just another update explaining the latest delay. Nora sat down at the kitchen table. Only Geraldine was in the house. She was upstairs finishing off some homework. Nora opened the letter carefully, trying not to rip the envelope. She was holding back the moment when she would have to read the contents. The thick creamy paper felt important. There were three sheets folded in half. Nora unfolded the bundle and started to read. It began:

'I am pleased to confirm …'

Nora's whole body was in a heightened state of alarm and tension. It was a promising start. She read on voraciously, not taking in the detail but getting the gist. She turned to the last page which was a summary of the proceeds of her mother's estate. With all expenses accounted for, the residue amount to be split equally between Kathleen and Nora was £22,496.

That was over £11,000 each. It was an incredible fortune. Nora sat motionless, trying to take it in. What would it mean? What should they do with it? It was all very well having dreams about an inheritance. It was a different matter when you were actually confronted with the reality. The spell was broken as Geraldine clattered down the stairs to announce she had finished her school work and was ready to go to the shops.

'What's that you've got?' asked Geraldine.

Nora was not ready to tell anyone yet about the inheritance.

'It's just another letter from the lawyers in Ireland about Grandma's house.'

It was not an untruth.

'Are we going out soon?' asked Geraldine, her curiosity easily satisfied.

'Yes. I said we'd meet Aunty Kathleen at one o'clock outside Boots. I'll get myself ready now and we'll head off. I was thinking we could look for a new dress for you. What do you think?'

'Are you sure?' Geraldine was slightly taken aback. Then she grinned happily and said, 'That would be fabulous.' It was one of her latest words.

Fabulous, indeed, thought Nora. And it was not merely a new dress that she had decided they would be buying. It was a new house.

Thursday 9th October was the last day Nora swept the kitchen floor of the house in Herbert Street. It was the first day of their new life in the suburbs. In terms of physical distance, they were moving almost exactly two miles away. By any other measure – comfort, space, social standing – they were moving a million miles. A transformation that she was now having a few doubts about. Had she bitten off too much? It was definitely her responsibility. John always deferred to her in these things because she had the ideas and the dreams. She had the drive and the ambition to fulfil them. He did not.

John would have been happy with the very first house that they had seen. A typical semi detached house in a nice residential area, with a back garden. It was exactly the sort of house and street that the better off families that they knew had been moving up to over the years. Nora herself would have been very happy to live there too for the rest of her life – in any other circumstance. Ecstatic would be more correct. Compared to what they had put up with for nearly twenty years, that house would be heaven. Except that the circumstances were different. Nora saw the inheritance as a gift from God – as well as, of course, from her parents. She wanted to make the best possible use of it. She plainly had a head for finance for which she thanked her father, Hughie. At the same time she had definitely inherited some of the social aspirations of her mother. Not on the same scale or with the mannered superiority often shown by Marie. But Nora wanted to be the best she could be, and she wanted that even more for her family.

The house on Highgate Road came into the reckoning

very late in the day. It was actually spotted by Geraldine who had turned to scouring the evening newspaper during this exciting period of house hunting. Nora and John were on the brink of choosing between two virtually identical three bed semis. John's focus was always the same – the roof, the windows, and the plumbing. Nora's focus was quite different. In her case, it was the street first, the amount of space, and the state of the bathroom and the kitchen. Neither put huge priority on the garden, whereas Geraldine and Martin certainly did. Geraldine could never explain why she had read the advert out in the first place. It was not in an area where they had generally been looking. It was also detached. No-one had ever mentioned detached. And it had four bedrooms.

Even before they had seen the house, just from the brief description in the paper, Nora had fallen in love with it. For days before the planned viewing, she prayed so hard. She prayed firstly that it was not falling down in a heap. She knew that John would not countenance anything that was not as solid as the Cliffs of Moher. She prayed secondly that someone else had not already snapped it up. They viewed the house on a Saturday afternoon at the end of June. Walking along Highgate Road, counting the numbers as they went, she felt John stop suddenly in his tracks. He was staring across the road at a tall double-fronted red and charcoal coloured brick house. Nora was immediately taken by the imposing front with the large bay windows top and bottom on the right hand side. John was peering up at the steeply pitched roof, and the chimney stacks on either side.

'She's sturdy looking,' he volunteered with more than a hint of approval.

This was a good start, thought Nora. The twenty minute viewing that followed was sufficient for both of them to want to make an offer. John could not find fault. It was a beautifully built house and it looked like it had been well maintained. He was mightily impressed. His only unspoken thought was that perhaps this would be a bigger move for all of them than they were prepared for. This was a very smart area with much richer and well to do neighbours than themselves. It would not just be a house move.

Nora found herself drawing in gulps of air every time she entered another room, daring to imagine, daring to hope that this could be for them. It was a youngish estate agent who showed them round. The owners were away for the weekend settling their own new arrangements. They were a retired teacher and his wife who had already bought their retirement bungalow on the east coast. The agent was businesslike and made it plain that any offer approaching the listed price would be seriously considered.

John was no haggler whereas Nora was very capable in that department. The advert had been placed with a price of £8,250. This was quite a bit more than they had originally considered. The semis they had been looking at were around the £7,000 mark. It was one of those moments where Nora felt inspired. This was her destiny. The house was more than she could ever have wished for. John approved it. Her father would have definitely seen it as a good investment. Marie, her mother, would have been proud to see her daughter in such high estate. Nora suggested a figure to the agent. The fact that he did not refuse it point blank was promising. The agony was that she would have to wait until Monday to find out whether it was going to be accepted or not. At which point, she wished that she had just offered the full price.

Whatever torture she suffered over the next forty-eight hours was instantly over when she telephoned the agent at just after eleven o'clock on the Monday morning. He was delighted to tell her that the owners were willing to accept the Hoolahan's offer of £7950 – "subject to survey" and the normal legal processes, of course. That meant that they would still have a good £3000 left over from the inheritance to put away as savings. The new house would take quite a bit of money to run, what with the rates and the heating and maintenance. However, Nora had calculated that as they would not be paying rent any more, things might just balance out if they were lucky.

Dawn on the 9th October saw an early mist quickly burnt off by the rising sun and the day was exceptionally warm and sunny for the time of year. Nora felt the sun was shining especially for them. The omens were excellent. The large removal van was filled in the morning. Matthew and John picked up the keys for the new house at twelve noon. By four o'clock, the van and the removal men had already departed. Their job was complete. The house at Highgate Road was upside down with boxes everywhere. At least the beds were in the right rooms. Once Nora had inveigled the family to help her sort out the bedding and everyone had somewhere to sleep for the night, she was able to relax and simply enjoy the moment. It was fish and chips for tea. They all sat around the makeshift living area. Nora was serenely happy though worn out. John was quietly content. Matthew was openly impressed with it all. Sean was complaining that it was a long way to the fish and chip shop. In the same breath, he was marvelling at the proximity of the golf course and the local park. Martin was a bit lost for the first evening. Were there any children his own age in the street for him to play with? Geraldine was the most animated, excited and full of ideas for décor and furniture – plus detailed plans for her own room. Only Patrick was not there to share in this moment. Nora's vow to herself was to have things in good order when he was home for half term in two weeks' time.

Day Six - June 1975 - Spirito Santo

After the gospel had been read, the congregation were signalled to sit. The Cardinal and his fellow bishops were also seated for the moment, though adding gravitas merely by their presence. The Cardinal's right hand man, one of the two efficient assisting priests, had taken charge of the gospel. Now another senior looking priest moved to the centre. From what Matthew could make out in the booklet, this was the Superior whose job was to present the candidates to the Cardinal for ordination. Each candidate was called individually by name to declare that they were present. 'Ad sum' – 'I am here' – each responded, standing up and remaining standing when their name was called. Matthew had a jolt of recollection from his two years of Latin at school. 'Sum, es, est' ran through his head.

Then the candidates were called out to the large area in front of the altar. The Cardinal was now taking charge. The formal question of whether the candidates were "worthy" was asked. Given that no-one could ever claim to be truly worthy of the promised grace, the answer was couched in terms that they were judged worthy by God's people and by those who had been preparing them over the years. Then it moved to the moment where the candidates were to make their promises. Each candidate approached individually and knelt before the Cardinal who took their hands in his. The promises of obedience and fidelity were made. Then the candidate went back to his standing position in front of the altar.

When every candidate had made their promises, everything became quiet and still. The candidates stood like mini marble columns all around the front of the sanctuary. The Cardinal rose and spoke a prayer from the book held up for him. Then, the candidates suddenly seemed to disappear. Matthew crouched up from his seat to try to see what was going on. He could just make out that they were lying flat out on their fronts on the floor. The booklet explained that this was the symbol of their humility. The cantor began to sing with the choir responding. Nora pointed the booklet at Matthew again. This was the Litany of Saints. It was the call to all the saints to pray for these men who were about to become vicars of Christ. It seemed to go on for ever. And the congregation was standing up for this. Matthew was struggling to concentrate. He found himself counting the square panels that made up the ceiling. Each panel was highly ornate, framed with gold leaf. There were five in each row stretching across the nave. He tried counting the rows but was too inhibited to take a good long look towards the back so he only had a partial number for about half the length of the church. He would try and remember to count them properly at the end.

Eventually, the litany ended and the Cardinal was back on his feet saying a prayer. Then another hymn began – "Come Holy Spirit". The Cardinal was now receiving each individual candidate and laying hands on their head. The booklet described this as "The Essential Rites". Nora was watching like a hawk. Patrick was the ninth candidate to approach the Cardinal. She held her hands to her mouth and rushed a silent prayer to the Holy Spirit through her head. It was all happening so slowly and yet years were passing by in seconds. This was her baby boy, her family, her life as a mother, her whole being.

May 1972

—~—

'How's the captain of industry today?'

Kathleen was all smiles and jokes. It was her usual Friday evening visit to Nora.

'I wish I had a gun sometimes,' grumbled Nora.

'Something must be needling you. Come on, out with it.'

'It's been a terrible week. Them damned union fellers. Trying to stop me getting to my work.'

'Well, there is a strike on. What do you expect?' countered Kathleen.

'I'm not in any union and they know it. They've never done a damn thing for us women. And those machinists shouldn't be striking, anyways.'

Nora was in her stride now.

'I told the picket feller, "You want to look out or there'll be no jobs for you to go back to." That shut him up, I can tell you.'

'I thought we were all Labour round here. Don't tell me you've become a bleddy Tory!' exclaimed Kathleen. She had her own particular way of saying "bloody" which gave it an air of respectability without diminishing its force.

'I just don't like being told what to do by anyone. Certainly not some jumped up union man with his "Clause 4" and "Subsection B" rule book. You've got to think for yourself. That's what dad always taught me. Don't be another sheep, he would say.'

'You can't do it all by yourself, though, can you? You've got to remember the battles that had to be fought in the past to get so many of the things we take for granted nowadays.'

'I know what you're saying, Kathleen,' agreed Nora. 'It's just that it breaks my heart when I see what they're doing to ruin a good business. They've got carried away with themselves. It's gone ridiculous.'

'They're only standing up for what they're entitled to,' argued Kathleen.

'Entitled to? That Ronnie Burgess, he's got plenty to say. He's never done a hand's turn in his life.'

Though they had identical views on most subjects, Kathleen's perspective on the world of work was always a bit different to Nora's. Kathleen was now into her twenty third year at Gents'. She knew the place and the people inside out. It had become part of her. Getting started there had been a massive boost when they first arrived from Ireland. It had been the life line that kept her going in the years after she had lost Steve. Kathleen loved having it in her life but she always told herself that it was a factory, simply a work place. The bosses would always be pressing the workers to make more profit. So, to Kathleen, it was simple. The workers had to remain solid otherwise they could easily be trampled on.

By way of contrast, Nora always had her streak of individualism. She had been schooled by Hughie, the entrepreneur, in running the General Store. She knew about profit and loss at the sharp end, the risks that you faced when you were in business. So she was sympathetic to a company that gave work to hundreds of people when it was trying to be successful, or in the current situation, simply to survive. Kathleen referred to Nora as the "captain of industry" partly because of the way she spoke, and partly because she now had a "position".

Nora had returned to the world of work with her part-time evening job at the fruit and vegetable warehouse. It had been a life changing release from years tied to the children and the kitchen sink. Nora revelled in the new "freedom", and the extra money was a major boost to the family's weekly spending. After the owner of the warehouse, Mr Thwaite, got her to provide emergency cover in the office for a couple of shifts, she never went back to the packing. He had accidentally discovered Nora's hidden talents. There were a few regrets initially as Nora really enjoyed the company on the bagging duty. However, she also revelled in the organisation and administration role that she was given. It all came to an end at Christmas 1970. The warehouse building was coming down as part of the re-housing plans for the area. Mr Thwaite was moving his operation to the other side of town, too far to make it practical or worthwhile for Nora. It spoiled her Christmas.

In the New Year, she resolved to find something new. And, whether through prayer or sheer good fortune, she was asked to an interview as a part-time purchase order clerk at Briggs Manufacturing Ltd. Her hopes of being taken on dropped as soon as she heard Mr William Smythe, the office manager, introduce himself. He had a sharp Belfast accent, and Nora surmised his leanings from the name. A southerner would probably not be his first choice. How wrong could she be? He was charming, friendly, and hired her after twenty minutes' chat and a brief written test. A year later, Nora's hours had increased to thirty a week. And she was dealing with orders, invoices, and the payroll. Mr Smythe obviously thought very highly of her. Nora knew it was because she was very good at her job, and she was a hard worker. Kathleen, ever the devil, liked to goad Nora with hints that maybe Mr Smythe had other reasons for promoting her. It was all intended in jest. However, Nora always flushed heavily when Kathleen started down this path. And she moved quickly to change the subject. Nora respected Mr Smythe. He was a gentleman. Surely he did not have eyes for her. She could not think about him – or any other man, for that matter – like that. And yet that feeling of embarrassment which she fought to suppress told her that somewhere deep down she was flattered to think that another man might be thinking about her. Might appreciate her. As a woman.

'Where are the two?' asked Kathleen.

She meant the two youngsters, Geraldine and Martin.

'Geraldine's upstairs doing homework. Martin will be on the park, I don't doubt. He's following in the footsteps of the Sean one. He's only in when there's food on the table.'

'What about John? I thought he'd be home by now.'

'He's away with Sean to look at a motor car. Out at Thurmaston. Next door offered to take them.'

'It'll be handy if they get something, won't it?' mused Kathleen.

'Not if it's going to sit on the driveway all the time getting fixed.'

Nora had suffered in the past. The promise of motorised transport never seemed to match the realities of owning a car. All she saw were repairs and expenses. If she had been lucky enough to get three rides in Sean's first car, that was her lot.

Kathleen decided that Nora was in one of her trickier moods. She opted for a different tack to see if she could lighten the evening.

'I'm going into the station tomorrow to book the train tickets for Mablethorpe.'

Nora warmed up at this.

'Will I come with you?' she asked.

'Of course,' replied Kathleen. 'We can do a bit of shopping at Marks. We can see if there's anything worth buying for the holiday.'

Nora smiled and nodded agreement. The talk of holidays was a tonic. Kathleen had already booked a chalet at the coast for them for the first week of July. It would be the five of them – John and Nora, Kathleen, Geraldine and Martin. It was something to look forward to. It would be a real holiday. Not like going back to Clare with all the attachments and commitments that entailed. No, a week by the seaside where nobody knew them and nobody cared.

That's what she really wanted. Especially now that they had a little extra money to be able to treat themselves at least once in a while.

Day Six - June 1975 - Miracoli

Time had been in suspense for Nora during the service. She wanted to hold onto that time for ever. She longed to remain in the bubble of hope and fulfilment that she had fallen into the moment that she had entered the church. With every hymn that had been sung, she felt herself in a special place and she did not want it to end. But she knew it had to end. She must not let the emotion get the better of her. She pulled herself back to the present, her very practical self regaining control. She watched as the new priests and all the clerical participants in the ordination service made their way gracefully down the centre aisle and out of the large central doors through which they had entered over three hours before. The organist was playing a stirring piece, loud and fast, a final triumphant flourish.

Animated conversations now broke out across the crowded basilica. Big smiles, families hugging, mothers and fathers embracing in shared relief and joy, everyone ready for a joke and a laugh and needing to let off steam. John put his arm round Nora and held her like that for a while. He leaned across and shook hands with Matthew. Lots of people remained standing and talking where they were, others started to gather their things and to make their way out. Eventually, John asked:

'What's to happen now, Nora?'

Nora was stuffing the booklet into her handbag.

'We'll go outside now and see Patrick. He told us that there is a celebration but I don't know much else.'

'Come on, then,' said Matthew. 'You've said enough prayers today. Let's go and see Father Pat.'

Nora laughed. She had not thought he might be called that.

'Father Patrick to you,' she admonished Matthew with a wry smile.

The crowd seemed even bigger outside than it did inside the church, stretching out down the steps and into the cobbled piazza. Family groups were milling around, cameras clicking away, jokes shared, hugs given, praise and compliments spoken all round. There was a buzz of excitement. It was not unlike the scene outside a graduation ceremony, everyone wearing their finest clothes, broad smiles on all the faces. John had his pipe lit as soon as he emerged into the bright midday sun. Clouds of pungent St. Bruno tobacco drifted into the Rome sky. He was making up for lost time. They made their way down the steps, peering through the crowd to try to find Patrick. Nora eventually spotted him and dragged the other two across the square with her. She did not stop until she had pulled

Patrick into her arms and given him a fond motherly kiss on the forehead. And then she stood back to have a good look at him. John shook him firmly by the hand and said quietly, 'Well done, son!'

Matthew gave him a brotherly hug. It was a little alien to both but today anything could happen. It was not so long ago that a wrestling bear hug would have been the norm.

While Nora and John silently conferred their congratulations on Patrick, Matthew was thinking about food.

'What's the deal now?' asked Matthew.

'There are photos first, and that will take a while,' said Patrick. 'Then we are going over to the Gregorian University for a celebration lunch.'

'Now you're talking,' said John.

'I think it will be nice,' said Patrick. 'You can meet my friends and you'll get to see the boss. I think it'll be a buffet but be prepared for some seriously tasty Italian food. And, of course, we'll have a good celebratory drink. I think we all need one, don't you?'

'I could eat a horse,' said Nora. She surprised herself. A few minutes before, she could not have faced a morsel.

'How do we get there?' asked Matthew, suddenly remembering his car in the car parking garage.

'It's only a few streets away,' said Patrick. 'We can walk it easily.'

There was an official photographer set up in an area that was cordoned off. A young assistant was marshalling the newly ordained priests and whisked Patrick off, leaving Nora, John and Matthew as bystanders. A group photograph with the Cardinal and the Bishops was the first. The crowd was also getting in on the act, circling behind the photographer to get their own version for posterity. A photograph of just the newly ordained followed. Then smaller groups based on their college, followed by some with other priests from their diocese or college. And then there were the individual photos including a family photograph.

It was while they were milling around in the crowd, waiting to be called for the photograph, that two miracles occurred. Or perhaps, to be more accurate, there were two quite unexpected occurrences. The first was this. Kathleen was standing right next to the photographer, camera in hand, studying the pose of the group and waiting for her moment to click.

'For the love of God,' spluttered Nora.

John looked in the direction that Nora was gazing. Unusually bemused, he mumbled, 'That's not her, is it?'

But Nora was ten yards away before he had finished the sentence.

Matthew looked across. He barely recognised her at first glance, but it was Kathleen all right. She was dressed elegantly in a lemon coloured suit. She wore a neat fitting white woven hat with a floral band. And she looked as if she owned the place.

The second unexpected occurrence was this. Matthew felt a tap on his left shoulder. He turned round and there was Emily with a big smile on her face. She grabbed him forcefully for a warm hug, holding on tight for a long three seconds and then releasing him just as suddenly.

'Hello,' she said, 'surprised to see me?'

Emily was wearing a light blue cotton summer dress that fell respectfully to knee length. She wore the brown leather sandals he had seen before. There was no hat but she had sunglasses stylishly positioned above her brow. Her long brown hair gleamed brightly in the sun. She was wearing a lovely lemony perfume. She looked cool and sophisticated. If she had had a slightly more sallow skin, she could have passed herself off nicely as one of the locals.

Matthew felt a frisson of excitement. This was completely out of the blue. He had not given any more thought to his hitchhikers once he had dropped them off outside the hotel the previous night. Now his senses were working overtime.

'Hi, Emily,' he managed to get out. Then, with a firmer voice, 'Fantastic to see you.'

Maybe that was a bit strong but it was only a greeting after all.

'After all you told me about your brother,' said Emily, 'I really thought it only right to see if I could get to the ordination. It means such a lot to you and your family. And I have to say it was a real privilege to be able to witness it. I have never been to anything like that in my life. And I've been to a lot of church services, I can tell you.'

'So you managed to get in?' asked Matthew.

'Yes, I got myself dressed up for the part.' And she laughed and did a twirl to show herself off. Matthew was seeing a more exuberant Emily, not just the practical down to earth person who was minding Katerina on a European adventure.

'I had to get up really early. When I left, Katerina was still snoring away!'

That made Matthew laugh.

'Anyway,' said Emily, 'I knew you said it was going to be at Santa Maria Maggiore. The hostel we found is really quite close, just a couple of streets down there towards the station. So, I arrived here about quarter to nine in my finest to see if they would let me in.'

'And they did?' asked Matthew.

'It was a doddle because they had a lot of unreserved seats for the locals. I managed to sweet talk one of the guards in the black suits. Actually, had a bit of a laugh – me speaking Italian, him speaking English.'

'So you got into the church?'

'I was very near the back on the left hand side. I couldn't see everything but the whole thing was magnificent. I'll never forget it. That organ and the choir, and then all the new priests. How lovely! It made me shiver at times, especially when it was communion and each new priest gave communion to their own family. I saw you and your mum and dad going up. I'm just so excited about the whole thing!'

There was a mild euphoria in the air and Matthew was enjoying the high along with everyone else.

'I'm so glad you enjoyed it. And I'm really pleased that you came.'

They were standing then looking at each other, both faces bright and smiling. A silent communication of understanding and attraction. Then Emily was distracted.

'I think that's your mum waving you over. Looks like it's your turn coming up for the photographer.'

Without hesitation, Matthew clasped her right hand in his left and said, 'Come on, you need to say hello to the old folk. And Patrick, of course. Maybe he'll give us a blessing.' He added for good measure, 'God preserve us!'

Nora was too pre-occupied with Patrick, Kathleen, and the photographer to give Emily more than a polite hello. She did place a bookmark at the back of her head to find out more about the slip of a girl that had turned up in the middle of Rome at her son's ordination. Emily did not make the official line-up. However, Kathleen made sure she got at least one snap of Emily with Matthew.

October 1974

—⁂—

Any of the self doubt that might trouble Matthew from time to time was rarely related to things concerning his work. In that area, he had an innate confidence which went along with his natural ability. It did not come for free. He worked hard. He took all the training he received seriously. He read the manuals and he practised his dark art of low level programming until he could almost speak the language of registers and processor calls. He got things wrong, of course. But he learned from his mistakes and he fixed them. He came to realise that his understanding of what he was doing was much deeper than many of his colleagues. Many of the other programmers in his department seemed to operate a "hit or miss", "suck it and see" approach. They hoped that things would work correctly. They did not know whether they would. Matthew knew. At least, most of the time.

His time in London had flown. It was already over three years since his arrival. It had been a bit of a shock to begin with. He had been more than ready for a change of scene. There was a lot to get used to all at once – the commuting, the initial bed-sit life, the new workplace. He found his feet quickly, relishing the newness of everything. Especially the project he was assigned to. And, inevitably, the new people in his office world. It was a young person's game and there was a lot of socialising. It was a great welcome for someone like Matthew arriving essentially alone in the big city.

Three years on and Matthew was still high on the oxygen of his work. The initial sparkle of the social side of life had faded. Those first few months of endless party going and after work sessions had been exciting. He had got to know a lot of people very quickly. He took part happily. All the socialising had been instrumental in finding him a room in a flat in Finsbury Park, sharing with three other boys. A step up from the dingy bed-sit he had started out in. There were a lot of laughs and he always had someone to go for a drink with. Gradually, though, the chaotic state of the flatshare wore Matthew out. Having grown up in a family of seven in a pokey little terraced house, he did not crave company. Increasingly, he relished precisely the opposite. After a hard day at work, he simply wanted a bit of peace and quiet. The rent for his one bed flat in Wood Green was high. He thought it was worth it. The privacy was priceless. And while there had not been any flings in a while, at least it gave him the possibility of an uninterrupted tête-à-tête if a romantic attachment arose. Matthew was not giving up on a social life. Far from it, he just wanted a better balance. He was focused on his work, and he had ambitions. He wanted a decent car, first and foremost. And he wanted to be able buy a flat sooner than later.

Matthew had an appointment with Nick Lee at eleven o'clock. Nick was one of the senior managers. He was still only in his early thirties. Unlike other parts of the bank, the data processing group was less bound up in hierarchy. Nick mixed freely with his staff every day. It was the way that projects ran. Matthew had worked closely with Nick on several developments, and they could quite easily have chatted over a coffee or even perhaps a pint. However, Matthew had asked to see him in the office. This was business.

'What is it, then, Matt? What can I do for you?' asked Nick. He was relaxed, sitting back from his light coloured Scandinavian style desk. Matthew could see a folder of design documents and a notepad full of jottings. Nick was hands-on, that was clear.

'Look, thanks for seeing me,' Matthew began. He had no qualms about what he was going to say. He did not think he had anything to lose. He had no desire to cause Nick a problem. On the other hand, as he had read somewhere, he did not come to work to make friends. He had to look after himself. In these situations, he felt emboldened. The frequent run-ins he had experienced at school had inured him to the stress that he might otherwise have felt.

'I wanted to tell you. I have been approached by Chris Hughes. He's made me an offer.'

'Interesting,' smiled Nick. 'I can understand why they would be sniffing around. Not exactly cricket. Or subtle. I suppose it's the way these companies get the talent.'

Nick was musing things over, half talking to himself. Matthew held his tongue. The ball was firmly in Nick's court.

'You clearly saved their bacon,' Nick went on. 'How many times did they crash the system with that TP monitor they delivered?'

It was a rhetorical question. Matthew decided to spell the answer out.

'Well, it never stayed up for longer than ten minutes,' he said.

'And it was never going to perform at the throughput we need in production,' added Nick. 'The recoding you did – well, let's not beat about the bush, we all know you basically redesigned and rewrote their core modules.'

Nick was always the first to recognise good work.

'So, what's the offer?' he asked, getting to the nitty gritty.

Matthew wondered if he should bump up the figure that he had actually been offered. He thought better of it. It was already probably a stretch too far for Nick to be able to make it up – even if he wanted to, and that was no certainty.

'£8K, plus benefits.'

'Mmm. £8K. Plus benefits.' Nick mulled this over. Then he said, 'What are we paying you now?'

'£4,400.'

'That's a big leap,' said Nick.

Matthew got the feeling that he had not yet dismissed it totally out of hand. However, he would be amazed if Nick did not have some comeback on the figure. He felt like saying 'You get what you pay for.' But he held back for the moment.

Nick continued. 'Are you saying that you want to take them up on their offer?'

This was the ball heading back to Matthew temporarily.

'What I'm saying is that, as things stand, I would be stupid to turn it down. It's a pure product development role. They've got some very interesting projects lined up. And I've got a reasonable idea of what they are like to work for. That's always a good start.'

'I would be loathe to let you go,' Nick volunteered.

Matthew was quick to take him up on this.

'I hope that does not mean that you might think of putting pressure on them to take the offer back.'

Matthew was not prepared to leave things unsaid. He knew how the nudges worked and he was not going to let himself get caught in the middle.

'I would have to seriously consider my position if that happened,' he said.

'I have no intention of doing that,' said Nick, a little defensively. 'I was simply trying to say how much I value you.'

'I suppose that's about the size of it,' said Matthew with a firm smile. 'Value.'

'Look,' said Nick, 'can you give me a couple of days to work on this?'

'Ok,' replied Matthew.

The following Tuesday, Matthew was working late. He was the only person left at his end of the large open plan office. Nick Lee breezed in through the double doors and pulled a seat up beside Matthew.

'Problem?' he asked.

'This rollback routine keeps causing an index corruption. I'm just coding up some diagnostics to see if I can identify exactly what's going on.'

Nick double checked that they were alone.

'I've got some news for you.'

Then he had second thoughts about the open office and invited Matthew along to his room.

'I've spoken to our director. It wasn't easy, I can tell you. The offer is £7K per annum.'

Matthew was staggered that they were prepared to offer so much, and at the same time disappointed that it was still a long way from the £8K already on the table. He was about to say something when Nick continued:

'Plus a one time bonus of £1000 for your work on the transaction processor.'

And he added, 'Starting on the first of next month with the bonus paid in next month's salary.'

Matthew knew instantly what he thought but he remained inscrutable. They agreed that he should sleep on it.

There was no sign of Nick the next morning. Matthew was finding it hard to concentrate. He found an excuse to walk past Nick's room every hour or so to check if he could see him through the glass panel. By quarter to twelve, he was starving and went out to his favourite sandwich bar a few streets away from the office building. Matthew ordered coffee and a sandwich to take out. Rich milky Italian coffee – in a Styrofoam cup. The sandwich production line of three staff in white aprons produced the sandwiches to order. In half an hour, the queue would be snaking round the counter and out of the doorway. Before twelve, the rush had not yet started and Matthew only had to wait a couple of minutes to be served. His customary order was wrapped neatly in white paper – ham and cheese on brown bread, some lettuce, tomato and onion, with a slather of mayo spread over one side of the bread. As he paid up at the till, there was a tap on his shoulder.

'Are you going over to the park to eat your lunch?' It was Nick Lee.

'Yeah!'

'Ok if I join you?'

'Perfect,' said Matthew.

The weather was good for October. It was dry, certainly not cold. Matthew sat out in the park for lunch in most weathers. He had eaten lots of subsidised canteen meals when he first arrived in London. Eventually, he got fed up with the food and the company. It was good to get out of the office and get some fresh air even if it was just for twenty or thirty minutes. Only the pouring rain would deter him. He sat down on one of the nearest benches and waited for Nick to join him.

'I was looking out for you this morning,' said Matthew.

'Had to go to Watford. Presentation to a DP conference. They were very interested in what we are doing. Anyway, have you made your mind up?'

'I would like it in writing,' said Matthew, trying to keep this bit strictly businesslike. 'And I would be very happy to accept the offer you have made.'

'Right,' said Nick. 'Excellent. You do realise you're going to have to earn it.'

‘Suits me fine,’ said Matthew.

The truth is that he did have second thoughts about turning down the Chris Hughes job. Obviously, there was the money involved. £8K was a lot more than £7K to start with. Then there was the actual work. It was likely that working for a mainstream commercial development company – rather than an in house development team – would be much more leading edge. And good experience to fall back on in the future. Against that, he knew the bank and he enjoyed working there. It was leading edge in terms of the sheer scale that it demanded from its computing. He had made a name for himself already and was likely to be picked up for the key projects. There was the intangible element of job security as well. You never knew whether the commercial developers were going to be in business next year. The thing that really made up his mind, however, was the very handsome bonus that was being offered. He would start looking for a car straightaway.

Day Six - June 1975 - Festa

—∾—

They were standing in the central atrium of the Pontifical Gregorian University. This could be another vision of heaven on earth. The scale of the architecture was immense and powerful, surpassing mere mortal imagination. In design and dimension, it spoke of perfection to the human eye. A huge rectangular space, a double height ceiling that seemed to float high above, soaring heavenward. The floor of white marble elegantly zoned in a series of large rectangles marked off by black marble tiles. A delightful openness – a salute to the infinite – expressed through the creamy white colonnade of wide arches stretching along each side, giving off to a further space. The roundness of the arches appealing directly to the senses of proportion and balance. The open balconies on the upper floor looking down into the main hall that added to the feeling of space and possibility. The sunlight piercing through the monumental central skylight. There was more daylight streaming in through the fellow skylights positioned congruently in the four corners. The overriding colour palette was of gleaming whites and creams, giving off an enticing brightness. It was like the vestments worn earlier. Celebratory, triumphal. It was a nod to the transfiguration, that vision of Christ so dazzling and bright.

Matthew could imagine himself in a film. One of the epics set in an opulent palace where dynasties were fighting amongst themselves. The smell of power and treasures, the glint of marble and gold, the enormous scale of the architecture reflecting the grandiose ambition and style. It could be a spy movie where the clipped heels of an upper class Bond like character step noisily across the gleaming white marble tiles to deliver the message that the game is up. He shook himself out of his reverie. This was not a film set. It was the real deal. He was drinking it all in. The company of suited and booted folk was animated, leaving behind now their earlier reflection and piety. They were chatting noisily, laughing raucously, strangers becoming friends in a shared experience and endeavour. They were all holding onto the magic of the moment.

To make matters even better, the drink was flowing. Cold beer in the bottle, ice-cold white wine, heart-warming red. There was food being laid out on long trestle tables at one end of the atrium. Nibbles were already being circulated, half of which they struggled to identify but were very happy to eat just the same. There were no sausage rolls or cheese and pickled onion cocktail sticks. Before the celebration was properly underway, there was a speech from the Rector of the University. He was mercifully brief in his welcome to all and in his congratulations to the newly ordained. Then there were similar speeches of praise and thanks from the Rectors of the Beda College and the Venerable English College.

After that, it was time to eat. The buffet was simple and delicious. Patrick explained that the main dish was called chicken milanese – otherwise known as chicken fried in breadcrumbs. There were huge dishes of pasta in a rich tomato sauce as well. John kept saying to Nora how marvellous it was and that she would have to look for pasta when they got back home. Everyone was ravenous. There were tables where they could sit to eat and the party gathered around a couple of tables that they pulled together. Patrick introduced some of his fellow priests and students, a few tales were told of the exploits of the seminarians. It was all music to Nora's ears.

Kathleen had said she would explain everything once they had got the photographs over and done and when they were all together and able to relax a bit. Now she was centre stage, some tomato sauce clinging to her lower left lip which Nora casually pointed to, simultaneously handing her a napkin. Nora had already squeezed the edited highlights out of her. She had not been able to wait.

'So, you want to know about the miracle of me being here?' Kathleen commanded the attention of everyone.

'I was not worth a light on the Thursday. I've never been as bad in a long while. By the way, that doctor was good, wasn't he, especially for a Frenchman?'

'What have you got against the French, Aunty Kathleen?' said Matthew, hoping to provoke some amusing prejudice.

'I'll just say that he was a gentleman and leave it at that,' said Kathleen. 'And he knew what he was talking about.'

She went on.

'I had a better night on the Thursday but I was not up to travelling on the Friday morning. I told Matty that. I wouldn't have got into that car for a hundred pounds, ordination or not.'

'When did the miracle take place?' asked John to try to move her on. Kathleen was good at spinning out a yarn.

'So Matty went off and I had a lovely little sleep. I can't remember when I woke up but I was feeling different. Hungry. Desperate for something to eat. I got myself up and went downstairs. Pascal sat me down and brought me soup, and bread and water. I felt like a new woman after that.'

She broke off to sip her water. She was being careful today. No wine and only small quantities of food, just in case.

'I got speaking to Edith. Well, you know, hardly speaking on account of the language. But we managed somehow. She had a dictionary and that was very handy. To cut a long story short, I was letting her know that I felt well enough now to continue the journey if there was any way I could get to Rome in time.'

'I don't see how you could,' said Matthew.

'Ah, well, that's where Roberto comes in. Roberto is one of the regulars at the Relais Lamartine. He's a lorry driver from Genoa and he drives up and down to Paris every couple of weeks. What a lovely feller! I'd have him as a son. You want to see his lorry. It's the length of a football pitch. And the inside, you know the cab, well it's like a little caravan.'

Kathleen was warming to it and her audience was riveted.

'Edith fixed it with him to take me to Genoa. We didn't leave until the Saturday morning. I was up at four. Had to make sure I was still A1 at Lloyds. I hardly slept with the excitement. I'd been in bed for nearly a day so I wasn't minding getting up, anyways. We were on the road for six. You should have seen me, up there in that big cab looking down on all the cars. Mind you, Roberto had to give me a bit of leg up to get in.'

'What time did you get to Genoa?' asked Matthew.

'Will you hold yer whisht?' exclaimed Kathleen. 'I'm just about to tell you. We had a few hold ups along the way and I think it was about two o'clock when we got to Genoa. You'll never believe it. The next thing is I'm in his flat – I should say "apartment" – meeting his wife and their little baby, a wee girl. You should see the morsel! Anyway, then they have me eating a full dinner. Oh, God love them!'

'Then what, aunty?' asked Matthew.

'Edith had me booked on the six o'clock train to Rome. Roberto drives me to the station. He takes me right inside to the platform. Waits for the train to come and gets me seated in the right place.'

'And all that without a word of Italian,' said John in amazement.

'I had a good sleep on the train and the next thing I know someone is waking me up and we are getting into

Rome. I looked for the first taxi and he took me to the hotel that Edith had arranged. What a great girl she is!'

'But how did we not see you this morning in the church?' wondered Nora.

'Oh, well I was a bit late getting there. The taxi went to Dublin and back on the way to the church. It was already starting and they weren't going to let me in. I played bleddy hell with them. I said, "Do you think I'm coming to Rome to see my nephew be ordained and miss the service?" I showed them the passport and that did the trick. The luck of the Irish! I only got a seat at the back and I had to get out sharpish at the end, you know, for a call of nature. Anyway, as they say, there's no show without Punch.'

While the plates were cleared away, Matthew went and found another couple of bottles of beer for him and his father. Nora and Kathleen were desperate for a cup of tea. He hoped that they had some. In the meantime, the spotlight fell on Emily. Matthew had spontaneously invited her when they were outside the church to come and join them at the celebratory lunch. She had been excusing herself until John stepped in. With his quiet engaging Irish manner, he made her feel like a special guest which indeed she was. The element of superstition and omens continually dwelt in the Irish psyche and Emily was clearly a sign of good luck. She gave a good account of herself by just being herself. There was some connection found quickly between the college in Rome and a priest she knew in her parish back home. When she mentioned that she often went to Sunday morning mass in Oxford at St. Benet's Hall, Patrick could recount a weekend that he had spent there with the Benedictine community a few years before.

Nora was conscious of not wanting to be like her own mother. Although she did not want to be, in her own words, "an interfering bitch", she knew that she did not always have the strength to resist. She was stronger today and kept her questions mostly to herself, letting everyone else do the asking. In spite of herself, she was taking to the girl. She was indeed very pretty, clearly very smart, well mannered, and well spoken. Nor did she appear to be putting on airs and graces. She was just so natural. She was very posh, of course. Was she too young? Did it matter? She seemed like a very sensible girl.

'Oh, what am I thinking?' Nora thought to herself. 'They've only known each other for a couple of days. They haven't even been on any kind of a date. What are you getting so bothered about?'

She knew why though. Because her instinct told her that this was more than just a passing acquaintance. Emily was a beautiful, intelligent girl. Moreover, she was clearly attracted to her son. In all probability, just the type of girl that she would wish for Matthew. In thinking all this, she realised that not only had Patrick now been launched on his own path in life but also very soon her oldest son would be doing something similar. Moving on and taking a wife. In fact, she wanted and hoped for that in many ways. Just like she was so happy watching the children developing day by day when they were young, playing, learning, and prospering. Nora also knew that she felt threatened by it because it felt like it would be a loss of something in her.

That was what it was. She was being selfish and she needed to be more generous of spirit. That was life. Growing up, standing on your own two feet. She had done it herself, in much less harmonious circumstances. Could she be a good mother now and let things take their natural course?

Before the celebration lunch came to its natural conclusion, Matthew managed to spend a bit of time with Emily away from the rest of the family. They wandered down towards the great statue of Jesus set back within the massive archway at the far end, losing themselves amongst the crowd. Matthew was asking banal questions about what plans Emily and Katerina had for the rest of their trip. She was responding with her usual zest and enthusiasm, talking about the various museums and sites that she wanted to visit in Rome. About Florence in another week. And maybe a few days on a beach somewhere before they went home. They stopped walking and Matthew turned directly to her.

'You know, after I dropped you off last night, I never imagined that I would ever see you again. And now that I have, I think I would really miss not seeing you a lot more.'

Emily blushed a little and looked straight back into Matthew's eyes, a serious expression formed on her face.

'That's the nicest thing that anyone has ever said to me.'

She fiddled with the paper napkin that she still held in her left hand. Then she broke into a broad smile.

'I never thought,' said Emily, 'you know, when I asked you for a lift at that petrol station … I never thought that I would find myself wanting to meet up again in real life. Yet here I am. And this is so real. What an amazing day!'

Spontaneously, Emily pulled Matthew close to her. Stretching up on her tiptoes, she leaned slowly into him and kissed him softly on the lips. She whispered almost breathlessly, 'You are lovely, Matthew. So lovely.'

She cradled her head on his chest for a few more seconds. Then she pulled back gently, still firmly clutching his left hand, radiant, joyful, brimming with excitement.

'A little decorum, Emily,' she admonished herself, with a broad smile. 'The Pontifical Gregorian University might never recover! I might not recover!'

She looked around the atrium, at all the people enjoying this moment. They were all oblivious of the intense and special moment that Matthew and Emily were sharing. Then the serious expression returned and she looked intently into Matthew's eyes.

'What would you think …? I mean, could we …? This is special, isn't it?'

Matthew put his finger gently to her lips.

'Yes. The answer is yes. I think this is very special. You are really special.'

It was a little quieter now and there were the tell tale signs that the proceedings were beginning to wind down. It was certainly not a case of time being called. There were just some gentle hints that the very worthy and joyous celebrations had run their proper course and it was time for the Gregorian University to return to its more prosaic business self. The waiters and serving staff were quietly and efficiently going about their tasks of clearing the tables. More to the point, the two barmen were in the process of closing down their serving area. Maybe just time for one more celebratory drink – especially if you had spent five days driving over twelve hundred miles to get here. Family groups had been drifting away for the last half an hour. John was starting to look at his watch.

Matthew and Emily were deep in conversation. Addresses had already been exchanged. They would not be able to see each other for another two weeks. However, a date had been set. The Triumph was going to get a run down to Hampshire in the very near future.

As the Hoolahan party came back together, Patrick took command and said:

'I just want to say a big thank you to all of you for being here with me to celebrate today. I couldn't have done it without you. I still can't believe the journeys you've had. Let's hope that the return leg is just as exciting.'

'Less of the excitement, I think,' said Nora. 'Anyway, we have another day here with you. You're celebrating mass in the morning, aren't you?'

'Yes, it's ten o'clock at the college. I'll show Matty where it is. And after that, I can show you around Rome.'

'Christ,' said Matthew.

'Sorry,' he managed to get in before Nora was able to say anything.

'I've just remembered about the car. I can't drive it now I've had a drink.'

Matthew was lost in thought for a few seconds.

'Actually, I've worked it out,' he said. 'I'll just leave it in the car park. Forget it today. We'll need to give it a check over and fill up with petrol before we head off on Tuesday. But we can do all that tomorrow.'

He looked round to take in the sumptuous atrium once more. He turned back to look over their little group. Patrick, Kathleen, his mother and father. And, of course, Emily. He had such a good feeling running through him.

They had really made it. He had really made it.

Acknowledgements

Publishing is a journey in its own right and I have been helped greatly by a number of people along the way. In particular, I would like to thank Jon Carr for his early encouragement and generous guidance. I am deeply indebted to John Kelly for his editorial direction and gentle mentoring. I wish to thank Paul Carroll for his kind and insightful advice. Special thanks to Anne Hare for her unstinting support and assistance at each stage of the process. Finally, it is hard to overstate how important and invaluable the feedback from my early readers has been – my grateful thanks to all of them.

Acknowledgements

[illegible]

About the Author

Born to first generation Irish immigrant parents, James Hare was brought up in a close-knit working class Catholic community in the English East Midlands. James enjoyed a rich and eclectic childhood as the fifth child in a family of six children, all of whom have pursued a range of academic and artistic endeavours. A philosophy graduate, James has worked for many years in software development and education. He is particularly interested in the importance of popular culture and its nuanced influence on everyday lives. He now lives and writes in Edinburgh.

This book is printed on paper from sustainable sources managed under the Forest Stewardship Council (FSC) scheme.

It has been printed in the UK to reduce transportation miles and their impact upon the environment.

For every new title that Matador publishes, we plant a tree to offset CO_2, partnering with the More Trees scheme.

For more about how Matador offsets its environmental impact, see www.troubador.co.uk/about/